ATHENE

Image and Energy

ANN SHEARER

VIKING ARKANA

VIKING ARKANA

Published by the Penguin Group
Penguin Books Ltd, 27 Wrights Lane, London w8 5tz, England
Penguin Books USA Inc., 375 Hudson Street, New York, New York 10014, USA
Penguin Books Australia Ltd, Ringwood, Victoria, Australia
Penguin Books Canada Ltd, 10 Alcorn Avenue, Toronto, Ontario, Canada m4v 3b2
Penguin Books (NZ) Ltd, 182–190 Wairau Road, Auckland 10, New Zealand

Penguin Books Ltd, Registered Offices: Harmondsworth, Middlesex, England

First published 1996
1 3 5 7 9 10 8 6 4 2

Set in 11.5/14.75pt Monotype Bembo
Typeset by RefineCatch Limited, Bungay, Suffolk
Printed and bound in England by Clays Ltd, St Ives plc

A CIP catalogue record for this book is available from the British Library

ISBN 0–670–857971

Contents

List of Illustrations

Author's Acknowledgements

Many people have contributed to the making of this book. Among friends and colleagues I should particularly like to thank the following for a generosity of assistance and expertise: Ean Begg, Nicolas Coldstream, Gunnar Dybwad, Petrina Morris, Anne Redmon, George Schöpflin, Alistair Shearer, Molly Tuby, and Therese Vanier. I'm grateful for the help and encouragement of Janice Brent, Annie Lee, Lily Richards and Robin Waterfield at Penguin Books. People from the Athenaeum Club, Bank of England, Canadian High Commission, London Library, National Army Museum, Natural History Museum, Royal Mint, St Thomas's Hospital and United States Information Service have not only answered my queries but often followed them up with kindness and enthusiasm. Thanks to them all, and especially to Jane Bircher of the Bath Museums and Erica Davies of the Freud Museum, London. As the Notes and Bibliography show, I owe a great deal to those who have gone before; I should like particularly to acknowledge the work of Marina Warner, and of Anne Baring and Jules Cashford, whose detailed, loving and imaginative evocation of *The Myth of the Goddess* has been an indispensable source of both information and ideas.

Neither they nor anyone else I have cited or consulted, of course, bears any responsibility for what I have made of their material. But they have all enriched and enabled the making, and I thank them for that.

————————————————

Be ever watchful, wanderer,
For the eyes that gaze into yours at the bend of the road
May be those of the goddess herself.

(*Oracle at Delphi*)

August Lady

City Preserver
City Destroyer
Daughter of the Aegis-bearing Zeus

Goddess of Spoil
Driver of Booty
Marshaller of the Host

Athene of Strength
Athene the Warrior
Goddess of Vengeance Deserved

Athene of Eyes
Of the Flashing Eyes
Unsleeping
Farseeing
Bright-eyed
Sharp-eyed
Owl-eyed
Hard-eyed

Golden-haired
Of the Cheeks
Of the Wind

Market Athene
Workwoman
Contriver
Deceitful

Many-Skilled Athene
Of Crafts
Of the Trumpet
Of the Girdle
Of Horses
Of the Bridle
Of Abundance

Athene of Health
Healer
Healer by Touch

Maiden
Virgin
Mother

Athene of the Road
Of Counsel
Guardian of the Anchorage

Prologue: Birth of a Goddess

So there was Zeus, father of gods and men, pacing beside Lake Triton in Libya. Every step he took reverberated with the crashing headache that hammered inside his skull. He thought his head would burst. He roared. It took Hermes to see what had to be done. He called up Hephaestus the smith-god, or maybe Prometheus the Titan, or maybe both of them, so great was that headache. And between them, they swung the axe and split Zeus's head right open.

And then
out sprang Athene!
full-grown, and fully-armoured too, shaking that golden spear of hers, a bellow of a war-cry on her lips, in a great shower of golden rain.

It was aweful, that birth.
The earth itself groaned and shuddered.
The ocean foamed up hugely and then stopped, just there.
The very sun halted his course across the skies
Time stood still, waiting.
It was as if all creation held its breath.

And then,
Athene moved.
Her spangled gold armour glinted and her bright grey-green eyes flashed. And she danced. Her very first steps on this earth were a war-dance.

And then – enough.

The goddess took off that golden armour, put down her spear, shook her bright golden hair free from her helmet, eased her shoulders a little.

Ah! The earth gave a great sigh and settled back into shape. The ocean refound its rhythm and the sun moved on his accustomed course.

'O Lor',' said Ares, 'this one's going to be trouble.'
Zeus just laughed.[1]

When Athene sprang so impatient and fully formed from her father's head, it was as a new goddess for a new age. The waves of invaders from the north had brought with them to Greece a race of sky-gods to overwhelm the timelessly ancient reign of the mother-goddess. Or, to put it another way, it was already the Age of Iron, in which we still live. The Golden Age of Cronus, when humans lived like gods, free from worry and fatigue, was long past; now his son Zeus reigned, having vanquished his father as Cronus had himself overcome his father Uranus, the starry sky, son and consort of Mother Earth herself.

So now the gods lived high and far away on Mount Olympus, their golden apartments shrouded by clouds from human gaze, dividing up between the twelve of them the tasks of deity that Mother Earth had once encompassed alone. Yet father Zeus still had his work well cut out. As Joseph Campbell puts it, 'wherever the Greeks came, in every valley, every isle and every cove, there was a local manifestation of the mother-goddess of the world whom he, as the great god of the patriarchal order, had to master in a patriarchal way'. And so he set out on his 'long career of theological assault by marriage'.[2] It was from this policy that his daughter Athene was born, yet with her he had gone one better. No need for that dazzling array of disguises to cajole, overwhelm or force the woman into submission this time, no need for showers of gold or transformations into animal or bird to give expression to the inexpressible coming of a god. This time he did it all by himself: this brain-child was his own idea!

And not, to many modern sensibilities, an attractive one at all. The circumstances of Athene's birth have defined her as the very image of the father's girl. 'To the end she remains manufactured, unreal, and never convinces us. We cannot love a goddess who on principle forgets the earth from which she sprung.' Thus the classicist Jane Harrison passionately sees Athene as 'a sexless thing, neither man nor woman', and her birth from her father's head as 'a desperate theological expedient to rid an earth-born Kore of her matriarchal conditions', 'a dark, desperate effort to make thought the basis of being and reality'.[3] At a time when the long Western struggle with the relationship between mind and body, and patriarchal consciousness itself, are being so soberly, intemperately, sadly and angrily assessed, her words ring as clear as they did over ninety years ago.

Yet we are all still children of the patriarchy, our ideas and minds formed by the particular consciousness of our era: that is the way it is. And not least of the conundrums with which Athene presents us is why on earth (and in the heavens) the deity of war, of civil defence, the inventor of juries and inspirer of heavy metal workers as well as of the gentler crafts, should be feminine. They say that Hesiod's own account of the forming of the world in his *Theogony* ended with Athene's birth and that all the rest is later addition: it is as if with this birth the world came to a decisive pause of which we must still take account.[4] So the stories and images of the goddess, as patriarchy's particular child, can speak particularly to us of what has happened to one aspect of the power we dub 'feminine' in the era of the sky-gods, under whose aegis we still live. And they can do so in a particular way.

Those stories, those images, are not primarily to do with the sociology of religion, or of gender politics either – though both may and have roped them into service. They are not allegories, because allegory has to do with moulding the image and the tale to express something we already know; here they work on us as

3

symbols, to bring us to something as yet unknown but which one day we may recognize. When we talk of the mythic world, we are not talking of fibs told to placate the children, or even of ways in which peoples have attempted to explain the phenomenal world to themselves; we're talking rather of the layer of psychic reality that informs our perception of that world. 'Myth,' says Jung, 'is the natural and indispensable intermediate stage between unconscious and conscious cognition.'[5] And maybe more than that. 'It would not be too much to say that myth is the secret opening through which the inexhaustible energies of the cosmos pour into human cultural manifestation,' says Campbell.[6]

Once that secret opening is ajar, we may glimpse a wholly different perspective on our mundane realities. When Pausanias, that delightful guide to the monuments that give a local habitation and a name to the mythic realm, visited Greece in the second century AD, he decided quite early on to give up trying to reconcile the many and various versions of the stories of the gods and humans; he concluded that it was simply in the nature of Greeks to disagree with each other. By the time he neared the end of his journey, he had reached a different conclusion: that the famous wise men of Greece had told their stories in riddles, and not out of stupidity.[7] The experience had worked on him: he had entered that paradoxical world where, for instance, it is not simply possible but natural that the goddess of war and destruction should be, at one and the same time, goddess of healing and of all the peaceful arts.

'Only when we become aware of a sudden consistency between incompatibles,' says Calasso, 'can we say that we have crossed the threshold of myth.'[8] And when we cross that threshold we are in the world of the energies that Jung defined as archetypal, those 'forms or riverbeds along which the current of psychic life has always flowed', 'the fundamental elements of the conscious mind . . . systems of readiness for action and at the same time images and emotions'.[9] The Roman historian Sallust had much the same perception some 2,000 years ago when he wrote *Concerning the Gods and the Universe*: 'These things never happened, but they always are.'

We can never know the archetype as such: it is the archetype which forms our perceptions, not our perceptions which create it, and just as the ancient deities punished those who saw them too closely by blinding them, at the least, so we cannot get too close. 'The most we can do is to dream the myth onwards and give it a modern dress.'[10] So what we can do, in tracing the manifestations of the archetypal energy that we know in images of Athene, is to muse on the nature of a 'feminine' energy that is intrinsically battling, scrapping and fierce, as well as intrinsically skilful and wise. And in tracing the way those images and the perceptions of them have changed, we can learn something of what has happened to that energy in the era of the sky-gods.

When Athene first appeared, they say, it was fully armed and battle-ready. But what we're also told is that it was when she had gained some distance from her father Zeus's head that she was able to take her armour off. And it was then that the natural state of creation was restored, the fundamental elements returned to their accustomed ways. In that first image of the goddess armed we can glimpse perhaps not just how a particular feminine energy has defended itself in the era of the sky-gods, but how prevailing consciousness has protected itself against that energy by making sure that the armour is well in place to contain it. If Athene were able to disarm herself today, who knows what natural state of things would be revealed?

CHAPTER I

Under the Aegis

Sailors making their way from Cape Sunium up to Athens knew when they were approaching home: they could see from far off the sun glinting on the spear-tip and helmet-crest of the great thirty-foot-high statue of Athene on the Acropolis. And this is still our accustomed first sight of the goddess: Athene Promachus, Athene the Champion. The statue itself, erected as a trophy and sign of Athenian valour in the Persian war, was as impregnable in its armed virginity as the rocky fortress was to be against any invader. The image redounds from other rocky heights: the goddess was protector of the acropolis in Argos, in Sparta, in Epidaurus, in Mycenae; on the citadel of Troy she was honoured as the Warrior, at Troezen as Athene of Strength, Guardian of the Anchorage.

Yet it was the building on the Acropolis of Athens which housed another image of the goddess that was to become one of the most famous in the Western world. In the Parthenon, the maiden's chamber, loomed Pheidias's colossal Athene Parthenos, forty feet high this time, they say, clad all in gold and ivory. The statue itself is long since gone, but we have Pausanias's word for it and a later small copy by Varvakion by way of souvenir [Pl. 1]. The goddess stands erect in an ankle-length tunic, staring fixedly ahead, her huge helmet ornately spiky with griffins and sphinx and set four square across her brow. Round her shoulders is a neat little snake-trimmed tippet, which we know to be her father's goatskin aegis, and as neatly on her bosom sits the Gorgon's head.

Perched on her right hand is a Nike, goddess of victory and itself no less than eight feet high. Her left hand holds her huge shield, against which, as it rests on the ground, coils a large serpent. Here is the very image of the virgin protectress of the city, shielding its dynastic succession (for the serpent, they say, was Erichthonius, from whom the ancient royal family of Athens claimed descent). From the fixity of the stare, the tension in the shoulders, the goddess appears quite corseted, almost unable to breathe. The Gorgon's head on her breast must in any case avert the gaze which would discern what lies behind this majestic, unyielding exterior. And there are other precautions, too, against those who would come closer to this solid and impregnable image: according to Aristotle, the original had a hidden mechanism that would cause it to fall apart if any attempt were made to remove so much as one of its parts.[1]

Yet there is nothing corseted about Athene as she speeds down from the heights of Olympus like a meteor blazing through the sky and throwing off a galaxy of sparks, on her way to spur on her favourites in that terrible tug of war between Greek and Trojan. There is nothing stolid about the goddess as she girds herself for battle and leaps into Hera's flaming chariot to flash through the skies, their horses covering with one bound the distance a man can see as he gazes from a watchtower over the wine-dark sea. Strutting like a pigeon in her keenness to get to the action, turning up in disguise as a warrior herself, sliding through the ranks to beef up a favourite, deceive a Trojan – this goddess is all movement and fiery energy.[2] This is Athene of the Flashing Eyes, Unsleeping Child of Zeus, Destroyer of Cities, Driver of Booty, Goddess of Spoil, Marshaller of the Host. This is Hesiod's

> Grey-eyed Athene, fearsome queen who brings
> The noise of war and, tireless, leads the host,
> She who loves shouts and battling and fights.[3]

This is the goddess who can urge Achilles to an orgy of appalling destruction and vindictiveness against all that is honourable in his treatment of Hector's body, and in another mood turn an enemy spear away from a favourite as gently as a mother swats a fly from a sleeping child, or deflect a blow with the merest soft exhalation of her breath.[4] She may be as distant as the heavens when she girds for battle and as close as the voice in your ear in the field.

All this action because she's miffed that Prince Priam of Troy was overwhelmed by Aphrodite and her promises and gave her the golden apple as the fairest of all? Was it this that lined up the gods of Olympus to pull tauter and tauter the rope and still allow neither Greek nor Trojan to break it or undo the knot to end that desperate and even tug of war?[5] Surely not: the truth of the matter is that to many of the Olympians, this is sport. Now backing one side, now another (and even Athene was choosy among the Greeks when it came to granting them a passage home after the war), it is all part of their game. As Achilles tells Priam, when he finally relents to allow the old man to take Hector's body home: 'We men are wretched things, and the gods, who have no cares themselves, have woven sorrow into the pattern of our lives.'[6] And in this battle-game, Athene the Warrior can be counted among the first in the field.

> War is what she likes
> and the work of Ares; fights and battles
> are what she likes.[7]

No wonder she threw away her own invention of the flute, when Hera and Aphrodite laughed at her puffed-out cheeks as she tried to play it. Her war-trumpet sounds more like her altogether: even her voice has its brazen note.[8]

Yet this is also the goddess who brought to her people of Athens the great gift of the olive tree, whose branch is still our sign of reconciliation and peace. When the Chorus of elders of Colonus hymn their land to poor wandering, blind King Oedipus, its great glory is that here

> Our sweet grey foster-nurse, the olive, grows
> Self-born, immortal, unafraid of foes;

and they are speaking of the goddess herself.[9]

This is how the olive came to be the glory of Athens. One day in the reign of Cecrops, the first of its kings, an olive tree, never before seen, sprang up, fully grown, from the rocky soil of the Acropolis. And at exactly the same moment, up gushed a spring of salt sea-water! The Delphic oracle was, of course, immediately consulted. And word came back: both Athene and her uncle Poseidon, Lord of the Seas, were laying claim to the city, and the people must choose between them. There must have been some trembling then: who could envy such a choice? But they set to and organized a referendum of all the voters, women and men both in those good old days. The women wanted peace and plenty, flowing with generous oil: their vote was unanimous. The men wanted safe passage for their ships, mastery of the sea and security for the state: so was theirs. But it happened that in Athens in those days, there was just one more woman than there were men. So the vote went to Athene.

There were certainly some reverberations after that decision, old Earth-Shaker saw to that. Poseidon was so furious that clearly something substantial had to be done. So to appease him, it was decreed that from now on women would no longer be allowed to vote, pass their name on to their children or enjoy the status of citizens.[10] The men of Athens built Poseidon a large and beautiful temple of his own at Cape Sunium, which commanded his own realm of the sea from its high clifftop. That placated him, and the olive worked its reconciliations, too. Athene got her own small temple at Sunium. The salt-water spring was enshrined in a well in the temple on the Acropolis called the Erechtheum, and the extraordinary thing about it is that when the wind blows from the south, you can hear the sound of waves booming up from the well.[11]

The women still hold up the porch, near to the olive tree, those statuesque young maidens we call the Caryatids, though the women of classical Athens never did get their citizen status back. But what they and their menfolk did get was access to a huge range of skills. For the fierce goddess of war is also patron of all the peaceful and useful arts. Of all the Olympians, it is Athene who is most closely involved in human affairs. It is only in her role as Defender of the City that she lives in the high rocky fortresses. While the other two virgin goddesses keep well away from the rough and tumble of the streets – Hestia private at home, tending the hearth, Artemis roaming the wild mountain places – Athene is to be found in the market-place, down in the transactions of every-day. She is the Ever-Near. *The Homeric Hymns* make many petitions to the different gods, and most of these have to do with a deity's particular attributes. To the Ares, the prayer is for an end to cowardice and courage to keep the peace; to Poseidon, for the protection of sailors; to Aphrodite, for the song that seduces. Only to the Sun and Demeter are the petitions more general: 'for a life my heart desires' is the prayer, which perhaps only the deity knows in its fullness. But to Athene, the approach is simple and direct: 'Bring me good luck and happiness.'[12]

In Arcadia, Athene is worshipped as the Contriver because, says Pausanias, this goddess invented all kinds of ideas and devices.[13] That huge fierce energy is also harnessed for all manner of material transformations by Athene Ergane, the Workwoman. The skill which invented the wooden horse that smuggled the Greeks into Troy also inspires joiners to build wagons, and shipwrights to shape timbers. Gold- and silversmiths are her disciples, the smiths who construct ploughshares her servants, and the potters call out to her, 'Come to us, Athene, and hold your hand over our oven!' There is delicacy in such skills as well as useful function: the craftsman trained by Athene takes care to put a graceful finish to his work when he overlays silverware with gold.[14]

Nous kai dianoia, mind and thought, was a later description of this crafty goddess's quality. But essentially, in her multitude of transformative capacities, she is Polymetis – *metis* signifying always a practical understanding and counsel and wit, the *nous*, perhaps, of today's street-shrewdness. Polymetis is also applied to Odysseus, and it is with his guile that Athene is so well pleased. 'What a cunning knave it would take to beat you at your tricks!' she cries. 'Even a god would be hard put to it! We are both adepts in chance. For in the world of men you have no rival as a statesman and orator, while I am pre-eminent among the gods for invention and resource.'[15]

Ah, that Odysseus! Is there nothing she won't do for that man? 'Dammit,' shouts Ajax as he spits out mouthfuls of dung after she has sent him sprawling and sliding so that Odysseus can win the foot-race at Patroclus's funeral games. 'Dammit! It's that goddess again, the one who dances attendance on Odysseus like a mother!' And everyone just roars with laughter, because, dammit, they know it to be true.[16]

If in the *Iliad* it is to feats of honour and daring that Athene urges her favourites, in the *Odyssey* her gifts to her most particular favourite are very different. As his companion on that long road home, through all his extraordinary adventures and encounters, it is the skills to live with peace, not war, that he must learn. When the hero becomes Odysseus, as Calasso so well has it, 'then to his first vocation of slaying everything he can add a new one: understanding everything'.[17]

In his first adventure on that long road home he was still the brutal plunderer: but when he had sacked Ismarus, slain its men and plundered its wives and goods, Zeus sent a tempest which blew his ships beyond the boundaries of his known world. Already his fate was cast: he could not stay with those Lotus Eaters whose desire to act had been sapped by their magic food. And so began his adventures in understanding. His first trial was to overcome the Cyclops Polyphemus, and he did it in two stages. The first was to put out the drunken giant's single eye – for understanding demands more than the single vision, it needs a multiplicity of viewpoints. The second was to reply, when the giant asked his name, that he was called Nobody. So when the other Cyclopes came running to the giant's yells, he could explain only that it was Nobody's treachery, Nobody's violence, that was doing him to death – and in that case, they concluded, he must be sick and could do no more than pray to father Zeus for aid. At one level, a clever trick; at another, Odysseus had already learned that in this new world he was indeed nobody, his feats of war as nothing to him.

And so, through many and difficult passages, to the first of his encounters with the feminine, the enchantress Circe, who sent him to where no man had yet journeyed and returned: the underworld, the land of the dead. And once returned from there, past the Sirens, past Scylla and Charybdis, symbols of the enticing, dangerous, engulfing feminine, to the isle of the beautiful goddess Calypso, where he remained in thrall for eight long years.

It is at this point in his story that Athene intervenes on his behalf with her father Zeus, and Odysseus is finally set free for the reclaiming of his kingdom Ithaca, with the constant help of the goddess. But really, we suspect, the goddess has been at his side all along, for the love affair that underlies the entire journey is that between the hero and the goddess herself. When he is at last reunited with his faithful Penelope, in that new reconciliation of feminine and masculine brought about by Athene, it is his description of their bed, built of and round the great living olive which is the goddess's own tree, that convinces Penelope that this is indeed her husband. And then the goddess grants them the most loving of boons:

Dawn with her roses would have caught them at their tears, had not Athene of the flashing eyes bestirred herself on their behalf. She held the long night lingering in the West, and in the East at Ocean's Stream she kept Dawn waiting by her golden throne, and would not let her yoke the nimble steeds who bring us light, Lampus and Phaethon, the colts that draw the chariot of Day . . . Not until she was satisfied that he had had his fill of love and sleep in his wife's arms did she arouse the lazy Dawn to leave her golden throne by Ocean Stream and to bring daylight to the world.[18]

When Athene goes to war, it is under her father's aegis and literally, for what she throws over her shoulders as both protection and emblem of authority is that great goat skin which some say Hephaestus had given Zeus, embellished with all the smith-god's skill. It was formidably beautiful: from it fluttered 100 golden tassels, each exquisitely fashioned and each worth 100 head of cattle. When the light changed, it could also be formidably terrifying, beset at every point with Fear, carrying Strife and Force and the cold nightmare of Pursuit within it, and bearing too the ghastly image of the Gorgon's head.[19]

Yet what Athene more normally wears is the softest of embroidered robes, made by her own incomparably skilful hands. And even Pheidias, sculptor to the state, was known to have clothed her sometimes quite differently, 'infusing a blush into the cheek, that instead of the helmet a blush might serve as covering for her beauty'.[20] The further the goddess is from her father's head, the freer she is to pursue her own idea, the richer the variety of her manifestations. For this goddess is a shape-shifter as well as a sturdy icon of state, appearing to Odysseus now as man, now as tall, graceful woman, now as sea-eagle, now as swallow perched high on the smoky main beam of his palace hall. Now you see her, decked out like a visiting chieftain, now you don't, as she zooms up and away like a bird through a hole in the roof.[21]

Yet Zeus is still father of the gods as well as of humankind. That is not to say that he has the last word. That belongs to Destiny or Fate, to which even he must finally bow. It is not on his whim that the fates of the Greeks and the Trojans are decided, for instance; he simply puts them in his golden scales, and when that of the Greeks falls to the bountiful earth while the Trojans' soars up to the sky, then Zeus no less than the other gods must bow to the decision.[22] But within that overriding imperative, it is Zeus whom the Olympians must heed. Athene, favourite child that she is, has special privileges: she alone knows where he keeps the key to his thunder-bolt storeroom and has permission to use that mighty arsenal as well. Yet just because she can get away with more than the other gods, just because her words have a special way of reaching her father's ear, there's an especially delicate balance to be kept. When she and Hera decide to go to the aid of the Greeks, to stop Zeus undoing all their efforts by favouring the Trojans, then he makes the limits of his tolerance roaringly clear. If they don't pull up that instant, he will hamstring their horses, hurl them both from their chariot and unleash such damage from his thunderbolt that they will still be feeling the effects ten years on. And it is not against Hera that his wrath is mainly directed, for in the stormy course of their long marriage those two have come to understand and re-spect each other's powers pretty well; it is his daughter's defiance that has hurt and enraged him. Hera knows where the limits lie. 'Daughter of aegis-bearing Zeus,' she says, 'I have changed my mind.' And back they go to Olympus and sit very quietly, just till the storm blows over, in their golden chairs.[23]

So when Athene goes into action, whether for peace or for war, it is very often under her father's aegis. It is with his permission that she sets in train Odysseus's homecoming; it is for fear of enraging him that the final act of this drama is the end she brings to civil strife in the hero's kingdom. For Zeus she speeds to the front to incite the Trojans to break the truce, with his permission she shrieks through the air like a bird of prey to feed Achilles. Sometimes this service to her father can seem pretty one-sided: as she complains to Hera, he never thinks of her endless bailing-out of his favourite Heracles, who only had to whimper to have her sent off yet again to get him through another labour.[24] But what to do? In the end, this is father's show.

The regime is not an easy one to live with; even the Olympians are broken-hearted to see the sufferings of their favourites on the battlefield, and Zeus's reprisals against the older powers he has con-quered can be fierce. As Hephaestus tells the Titan Prometheus, chained in agony on that rock, his ever-regenerating liver

destroyed each day by that ravenous vulture in punishment for
his championship of the human race against the new sky-god,

> the heart of Zeus is hard to appease.
> Power newly won is always harsh.[25]

Yet within the constraints of the new patriarchy, it is Athene
who works constantly to redress the balance of power between
Olympus and the human race, who champions human skill and
understanding against the inexplicable ways of the gods, bringing
new consciousness to illuminate what would otherwise appear all-
powerful in its archetypal force. When Hephaestus and Prometheus
himself release her from her father's head it is not simply to relieve
Zeus of that almighty headache. It is the start of a lasting alliance
between these two male midwives and herself. And it's an alliance
that taps into older powers than her father's, for the smith-god, in
his workings with all manner of metals, claims a privileged relationship with their source, Mother Earth herself, and Prometheus is
representative of an older order than Zeus's.

When Prometheus in his agony enumerates his gifts to human
beings — the very ones for which Zeus is now exacting such a
terrible reprisal — they are the very ones, too, which Athene safeguards for the benefit of humankind.

> What I did
> For mortals in their misery, hear now. At first
> Mindless, I gave them mind and reason . . .
> In those days they had eyes, but sight was meaningless;
> Heard sounds, but could not listen; all their length of life
> They passed in shapes like dreams, confused and purposeless.
> Of brick-built, sun-warmed houses, or of carpentry,
> They had no notion; lived in holes, like swarms of ants,
> Or deep in sunless caverns; knew no certain way
> To mark off winter, or flowery spring, or fruitful summer;
> Their every act was without knowledge, till I came.

The ability to determine the rising and setting of stars, number,

writing itself – 'the all-remembering skill, mother of many arts' –
were given by Prometheus, he says; so were the capacity to harness
beasts for human use, to build ships, to work the metals of the
earth, and the healing arts as well.[26] These are the powers that
Zeus was jealous of, and that Athene safeguards.

Who knows where they came from first? All of human knowledge, if we can take off our historical, linear spectacles, can be
understood as a remembering of what was once known and is bit
by bit reclaimed from a place so deep that there's no fathoming it.
What is sure is that it is Athene's energy which guides in that
remembering, harnessing knowledge for the work of civilization,
just as she taught the hero Bellerophon to harness instinctive
energy when she helped him to throw the first bridle round the
neck of the great winged horse Pegasus. That she was there with
Prometheus from the first we know: when he fashioned the first
human beings from Mother Earth's own clay, it was Athene, they
say, who breathed soul into them; when Zeus would withhold
from humankind the essential gift of fire, it was she who sneaked
the Titan up the back stairs of Olympus to steal it and bring it to
earth.[27]

It wasn't easy, this wresting of human consciousness from the
realm of the gods. Some say that the vulture which so horribly and
endlessly pecked at Prometheus's liver was the goddess herself, as
punished for her defiance by her father as was the Titan. When
she tried to give Asclepius the healer the power over life and death
itself, she had definitely gone too far in this business of redressing
the balance between gods and humans. Zeus was besieged by com-
plaints from his brother Hades that his own underworld realm
would be seriously depopulated if this was allowed; Zeus thunderbolted both physician and patient (though he did later relent to set
Asclepius among the stars, holding his healing serpent).[28]

Yet uneasy though Athene's task could be, she continued in it.
She invented the jury, for instance – so giving human beings both
the power and the responsibility to make discernments until now
hidden in the realm of the gods. (And if a jury vote was tied, her

own casting voice was always given for acquittal.) In her patronage and encouragement of heroes, she fostered the ordering of the state. Certainly this was often not just with her father's approval but at his command; would she have put so much energy into Perseus, for instance, if he hadn't been one of Zeus's offspring and in need of a dynasty to found to his father's greater glory? Would she have helped Cadmus found Thebes by showing him how to sow the serpent's teeth that grew up to be his people if Zeus hadn't been so taken by his sister Europa? Yet even in her implication in the spread of Zeus's power in the kingdoms of men, Athene can bring more than simply dynastic considerations. When the goddess has visited one of her favourites, he can feel her energy. She leaves young Telemachus, Odysseus's son, 'full of spirit and daring' when she has visited him in disguise to urge him to join battle with his mother's unwanted suitors; 'he felt the change and was overcome with awe, for he realized a god had been with him'. She adds strength and stature to Laertes, the hero's father, so that Odysseus himself is amazed to see the old man looking 'like an immortal god'. In this sort of transformation, Athene brings human beings that much closer to their own spark of divinity.[29]

Athene of Eyes, of the flashing eyes, unsleeping, far-seeing, bright-eyed, sharp-eyed, owl-eyed, hard-eyed: of all the epithets with which humans try to convey the particular energy that the goddess represents, those which have to do with sight are the most numerous and varied. Her bird is the owl – the classical equivalent of 'taking coals to Newcastle' was 'taking owls to Athens' – and what's special about the owl is its ability to see all around and in the dark. Bright-eyed Athene Glaucopis has this quality, as well as the attunement with the elements that gives the leaves of the olive tree their beautiful grey-green sheen when the wind moves through them, and the focus of the lion-about-to-spring.

These are the qualities which the goddess brings to her works of transformation, both of matter, as patron of the useful arts, and of human consciousness. This is 'seeing' in the sense of understanding and it's a dynamic force. '*Now* I see,' we cry as a prelude to action, '*now* I see what that is all about, where it's going, what I'm going to do.' And this seeing can have a reflective, sideways quality as well, a taking-in from all angles which is also a necessary defence. Athene's gift to Perseus when he sets out to decapitate the Medusa is a shield, which he can use as a mirror to reflect her too-terrible image: if he had looked at her directly, he would have been paralysed, turned to stone. The mirror unites time and place: it offers us a composite image of ourself as we are now against what is behind us, so we can reflect on the 'me' which is also ahead. We must make sense of what we see if we are to act; we must assess and measure the evidence of our eyes if we are to act wisely. And when we do, it is Athene who is at work through us.

Reflection, assessment, making sense of what we see: the second of the goddess's great civilizing gifts is precisely that ability to think before we act, to bring our human consciousness to bear on the matter-at-hand rather than simply plunging blindly ahead, at the mercy of whatever may drive us. Athene may exult in the valour and daring of her heroes in the battlefield, but her very first action in the *Iliad* is to restrain her favourite Achilles from his enraged determination to slaughter Agamemnon for stealing the girl he reckons to be his.

This goddess above all knows the crucial difference between necessary and unnecessary aggression, between what is fated and what is simply the untutored arrogance of the human desire to win at all costs. And that distinction she tackles at its archetypal roots. Through all the bewildering alliances of the Olympians in the war between the Greeks and the Trojans, one of the constants is the enmity between the goddess and Ares, that mad, indiscriminating force of simple aggression, hated by father Zeus himself because he can think of nothing except the next battle. His sister Strife shares his nature, helping him in his bloody work. 'Once she begins, she cannot stop. At first she seems a little thing, but before long, though her feet are still on the ground, she has struck high heaven with her head . . . It was the groans of dying men she wished to hear.'[30]

Athene's way is very different. It is she who lays a restraining hand on Ares's arm and persuades him out of the battle; it is she who knows when persuasion isn't enough at all, and simply knocks his helmet off his head and his spear out of his hand and bawls at him to stop. He hates it: he complains to Zeus himself about that crazy daughter of his, about the way he favours her, lets her get away with things that no other Olympian would dare. But Ares can't win against her, as he discovers when he strikes her and she lobs a huge boundary stone at him, bringing him down to measure his length, all nine roods of it, in the dust. What a fool, to think that he could ever be the stronger![31]

And what fools the mortals who think that they can act without the goddess's help. In the stories of her wrath we can discern what happens when Athene's energy turns negative, and it brings the very opposite of her gifts. When Bellerophon thought he could fly Pegasus, bridled by the goddess herself, to the very peaks of Olympus, he was thrown clean out of the air to land on earth and spend the rest of his life wandering lame and blind, unseeing and lonely. When Arachne refused to acknowledge that it was from the goddess that she had learned her skill in weaving, Athene's wrath was such that, finally brought to her senses, all the girl could think to do was hang herself. The goddess relented to restore her life; but in turning her into a spider she ensured that the very skill which Arachne had so prized now kept her from any further growth in understanding, caught in the web of her own devising. When Ajax thought he could fight without the gods' help (and set himself particularly against Athene's favourite Odysseus), the goddess's rage was terrible. In the madness she sent, he became unable to distinguish men from beasts, slaughtering the animals in a bloody and terrible frenzy because he thought they were the sons of Atreus. 'My eyes deceived me, and my brain/ Wheeled wide of my intention,' he says when he comes round, and he knows that this has been the work of the goddess. His eyes, his focused intent, his hand – the whole sequence that takes us from perception to intended action has been fatally destroyed, and in his inability to distinguish men from beasts, Ajax has lost the very heart of his humanity. His suicide is inevitable; this time, Athene does not intervene. And at his burial, the Chorus laments:

> Many are the things that man
> Seeing must understand.
> Not seeing, how shall he know
> What lies in the hand
> Of time to come?[32]

It is that seeing, that understanding, which is the goddess's greatest gift. Foresight, discrimination, a harnessed power that understands precisely the fitness of every action: these are what Athene brings to her works of transformation, this is how she moves things on, in the world of matter, in individual lives and in the progress of human civilization itself. It is Athene's energy which is at the heart of the myth of progress which has defined what we call Western civilization. And at a time when humans have achieved so much by way of technical skill, can use the art of numbers to cast a communications girdle round the earth, have so exploited the material world to the advantage of the few and the suffering of the many, we might perhaps remember that the goddess's gifts include also, and crucially, that capacity to bridle the instincts, to under-stand the fitness of actions to the matter-at-hand, and to use our capacity for seeing to look ahead to the probable consequences of our actions.

All this from father Zeus's head, all his own idea?

There is another temple of Athene on the Acropolis of Athens, set between the Erechtheum in which she is worshipped together with Poseidon and her own maiden chamber of the Parthenon. For the goddess's own people, this temple held far more of her *numen* than did the Parthenon itself, certainly at first. (It was only later, it seems, that that great edifice housed a cult at all: it was built originally as a proud statement of civic strength rather than a place of worship.)[33] Now only a jumble of stones remains of that other, more ancient place. But from its eastern pediment, which portrayed the battle between the Olympians and the giants, we still have an image of the goddess, and it is very different from those stern icons of state [Pl. 2].

Athene looms hugely. Heavily restored, she lacks both spear and shield; the helmet which is supposed to have covered her head is missing too. But rather than rendering her image partial, this actually offers us a glimpse of who the goddess might be behind the protective armour. She has thrown her weight on to her left foot; her knee is slightly bent and her right leg is extended behind her under the folds of her robe; she is all readiness for movement. She holds out her huge serpent-fringed cloak by the snake she grasps in her left hand. Seen from behind, the cloak billows like a great bird's wing, both protecting and brooding; you can still see the snake-scale patterns traced across it. Freed of the helmet's constraint, the goddess's long crimped hair snakes forward across her left shoulder and backward over her right; the curls across her forehead are banded by a close-fitting cap that itself looks as if it is made of coiled serpents. What does Athene see of us below her? The guidebooks tell us that she is looking down at a vanquished giant she is about to dispatch. But because that giant is now hardly there, her slight smile of utter assurance is the more mysterious.

Officially, the statue is incomplete. Yet this image of balanced power, remote attentiveness and flowing energy could hardly be said to be that. And it guides us to aspects of the goddess which lie behind the armour: to a feminine heritage that goes back very far indeed.

CHAPTER 2

The Maternal Measure

When Athene sprang so fiercely from her father Zeus's head, she wasn't simply his brainchild, his headache and his idea. Of course she had a mother as well, even though the poets of Zeus's time didn't always mention it. What had happened was this: when Zeus embarked on that career of marriages, that prolifically inventive sowing of his seed that secured his pre-eminence over the old order, his very first wife was something of a coup for him. This was Metis. She was a Titaness, and so of the older order, the order of 'kings', of Zeus's father Cronus's generation, in fact. Metis was one of the very many daughters of Tethys, the goddess of the moon, and Oceanus, that vast water that encircles the entire earth. Some say that these two bore all living creatures and the gods as well, that this couple was the source of all life. Others say that they were among the children of Eurynome, the primal goddess and the great serpent Ophion that she herself brought into existence by dancing up a great wind and rubbing it between her hands; that she gave them, as she gave the other Titans, a planet to take care of, and that theirs was Venus.

How can we ever finally know where it all began? What we can say is that Metis was a powerful queen indeed. She had rule over the fourth day, presiding over the planet Mercury, and she governed all wisdom and knowledge as well. Some say her real and first name was Ge-Metis: the earth herself as source of all wisdom. Others call her Wise Counsel. Not a bad catch for an upcoming god – and a matter of catch it was too, they say, she not being that keen by any means on this alliance, and not surprisingly considering that Zeus had usurped her brother Cronus and banished most of her relatives to a British island in the farthest west. So Zeus had to pursue her quite hard, while she twisted and turned and shifted shape as such divinities will. But eventually he caught up with her, and she conceived.

The old order would not yield place as easily as that, however. An oracle of Mother Earth herself told Zeus that this child would be a girl (and so presumably no final threat in these new patriarchal times, even though she would be his equal) but that if Metis conceived again, she would bear a son and he would overcome his father. Well, Zeus knew all about that sort of thing; it was the stuff of his family history that first his own father Cronus had usurped grandfather Uranus, then Zeus had usurped Cronus. Now it seemed that the whole cycle of father–son hostility was about to start again, that push-pull between the forces of conservatism and the forces of change which characterizes the way we inch towards greater social understanding to this very day.

Zeus thought that, forewarned, he could cut short the old pattern and safeguard his own rule. So when Metis, pregnant with their first child, was one day sitting thinking about not much of anything at all, he came and sat down beside her in a most affectionate and husbandly way. Perhaps she was preoccupied with thoughts of the coming child; perhaps she welcomed him gladly, with his amazing repertoire of glorious guises and his voice like honey scented with sun-warmed thyme. In any event, lulled or distracted, she gave Zeus his chance. He just opened his great mouth and gulped her down. And so Wise Counsel is lodged in his belly, seat of right thinking, to this day, to counsel him for both good and ill.[1]

But listen, she was pregnant at the time! And if we can say that each of Zeus's children, whoever their mother, would from now on partake of some of Metis's quality, we can most certainly reckon that her own child would inherit a great deal more. So *this* is where Athene gets that practical wisdom, that unerring sense of the fitness of things in their moment and space, that earthy connection between thought and action! And it is Metis's own connection with the planet Mercury, perhaps, which makes Athene so at home in the market-place, ever-near in her communication with the world of human affairs.

From Metis to Polymetis – skills multiplying from mother to daughter. The root *me-* gives us *metron*, measure, rule, standard, and this is a most ancient feminine quality. Athene's grandmother Tethys gets her name from *tithenai*, which means to dispose, to order: it is when Tethys contains and gives form to the vast semen of Oceanus that Metis is conceived. (Some have a different tale: they say that Athene's grandmother was in fact one Daedale, whom we know better through her masculine form in Daedalus, the master-craftsman who gave us the Cretan labyrinth and the lost-wax method of casting metal and much else besides. Which is why, of course, Athene is such a pre-eminent technician.)[2]

Invention and resource, ideas and devices – in that practical wisdom which is particularly Athene's and which, we now learn, is in her maternal inheritance, can we discern a specifically *feminine* consciousness? Certainly it is very different from the bright clear light of Athene's half-brother Apollo. He who shoots from afar, they call this god, and that is exactly the way we experience this aspect of his energy. That idea that suddenly strikes out of nowhere, that jolting flash of clarity that illuminates and energizes, that sharp 'Aha!' that is like a rush of adrenalin: *these* are the arrows of the Archer, striking us out of his high blue sky before our eyes can see them, unerringly to the point. This is the power of abstract thought, pure reason. Its beauty is precisely that it is uncontaminated by the ambiguities and complexities of the material world, that it takes us beyond to participate in Apollo's own uncluttered clarity. And that, of course, as our poor battered earth now groans out, is also its danger.

Athene's action, as we have seen, is quite different. Apollo shoots from afar; she is the Ever-Near, right here in the rough and tumble of life's market-place. His energy is hot and solar; her grandmother Tethys was the moon and she also is known by that title.[3] Apollo's arrows are pure thought and may be loved for themselves; Athene's seeing relates thought to the matter-at-hand and leads to action. 'It would be all over with Athene if she lost her hands,' says an Orphic verse.[4] Her wisdom is grounded in that relation between mind, material and action which brings her particular transformations.

Transformations, transitions – as in matter itself so in the relationships of the material world, and of the world of the gods as well. That work of changing, developing, moving things on which is so much Athene's she also got in her maternal inheritance. Great-grandmother Gaia, Earth herself, was first distraught and finally enraged when her son-lover Uranus the starry sky kept stuffing their offspring back into her womb because he was so terrified that one would displace him. At last she drew from her own flesh a hunk of metal and fashioned it into a sharp sickle. Of all her many children, only Cronus dared what she asked of them; he cut off his father's genitals and threw them into the sea. So he came to power in his turn. And so, in time, the pattern started again. Earth's suffering was lived once more by her daughter Rhea, sister-wife to Cronus, who had to endure his swallowing each of their newborn children. Finally Gaia spirited Rhea away to safety in Crete to be delivered of Zeus and old Cronus asked no questions when they gave him the latest swaddled bundle, but simply gulped it down, not realizing that he was smacking his lips, this time, over a stone. Well, we know that Zeus overcame father Cronus in his turn, but let's remember too that it was Metis who mixed up a special emetic for him to give the old man so that he sicked up each of those earlier bundles – Hera, Demeter, Hestia, Hades, Poseidon, all blinking and stretching into the light. So the Olympian order wouldn't have got started if it hadn't been for Metis's willingness to lend it her skill. It wouldn't have continued, either, if Athene in her turn hadn't shown Zeus where to find the herb of immortality without which the new gods could not have defended themselves against the giants.

How we keep coming back to these stories of beginnings! And no wonder, either, when that tension between old and new, the inertia of the known and the adventure of discovery, is so fundamental to us. Here let's just note one aspect of the stories. Each time it is the feminine force and energy that moves us on, that brings new levels of consciousness, while it is the masculine that takes the part of caution. It is in Earth's plan that we should so evolve. Who else produced the narcissus that enchanted young Persephone for just long enough to allow Hades to snatch her down into his underworld kingdom? The seasons of a woman's life and all our years are part of Gaia's scheme. The pattern is woven across times and cultures. It was not Adam who was the first to eat from the tree of knowledge and so set in train that long human journey to consciousness from the unconscious bliss of Eden. He would have lived that bliss for ever, we suspect, had not his wife, Mother-of-all-the-living, moved him on.

We have seen how Athene, in her place and her turn, also shifts knowledge from her father to humankind, just as she moves on her heroes in the work of civilization itself. As in these great transitions, so in those of everyday life which are no less heroic for those who pass through them. The goddess presides over the ancient male societies which had characterized the transition between the reign of the goddess and that of the new sky-gods and which later, as brotherhoods or *phratries*, had charge of the maturational ceremonies for young boys, and eventually girls, in the festival of the Apaturia, leading them to marriage.[5]

For young women, the goddess has a special care. Parents would take their daughters to the Athenian Acropolis before their marriage to offer to Athene; she protected the wedding itself and ensured the conception of a child. Her priestess, herself a married woman, visited newly married wives wearing the aegis, and so representing the goddess. This concern for motherhood is not just for individuals. On Holy Island, near Troezen, girls would sacrifice a girdle to Deceitful Athene before their marriage, and this was because the goddess had deceived Aethra by a dream into coming to offer there; Poseidon was waiting, as Athene well knew – and that is how Theseus was conceived, the hero who would save Athens from Crete. At Vathy in Elis, there is a shrine to Athene as Mother and this is why: once the local women, their country brutally stripped of its youth in war, prayed to the goddess that they might conceive the very next time they lay with their men, and she granted their prayer. (So delicious was the experience that they called the place Sweet and its river Sweetwater.)[6]

From birth to death: at all the great transitions of life, Athene is there. At the Itonian sanctuary in Boeotia, she is worshipped together with her uncle Hades, Lord of the Underworld. Her own bird, the owl, is a death-bird, a creature of night and of darkness. There is an Athene of Victory who carries in her left hand a helmet and in her right a pomegranate – the fruit, in its many seeds, of fertile womanhood, and also of the myriad of souls in the underworld, of which Persephone became queen when she had tasted the fruit itself at the hand of her husband Hades.[7]

Some say that Athene's presence at and care over the great transitions of individual lives is above all a care for the well-being of the state, part of her function as protectress of the civic order. And of a civic order at that which is anything but honouring of women, their status being, as we have seen, rather less than that of slaves. And furthermore, as we have also seen, that women only started being treated thus as a punishment for voting in the goddess as patron of the city in the first place! So what sort of a deity is it that rewards her own sex like this? Follow this line and the answer seems irresistible: not to put too fine a point on it, a patriarchal stooge.

It's a tricky one. But so is any relation between an archetypal force and the actuality of its expression here on middle earth, and looking at these interactions through sociological spectacles seldom seems to take us far in understanding what's going on. The goddess, inescapably and of her nature, is the daughter of patriarchy. But she is a crafty one too, and what she very importantly shows us is how the feminine can protect itself and operate within the constraints of that order. Penelope knew that, as she used the goddess's gift to weave and unpick, weave and unpick, and so keep her unwanted suitors at bay through all those years until Odysseus came home. And it was not just her skill in weaving, or the guile so to make use of it that she owed to Athene, but 'the genius she has in getting her own way'.[8]

The Acropolis of Athens, the very sign and statement of civic order, was a sacred place for women as well as men. The priestesses of the temple of Athene Nike, Athene of Victory, were, uniquely, elected from among all the women of the city. And the very ground of the Acropolis bloomed for them: here grew a flower called the *parthenion*, which was said to be unique to this place. Hard now to tell exactly what it was, but *parthenium* is a member of the chrysanthemum family, and that is said to be the ancient name for a plant allied to *matricaria*, so called because it was known to be helpful in relieving inflammations of the uterus. It seems to be very close to what we call feverfew, which later ages knew to be governed by Venus, and used as a strengthener of wombs, cleanser and regulator of menstruation, as well as a specific against melancholy, heaviness of spirits and the headaches that these days we call migraine. (Go to the Acropolis in the springtime and you will see it blooming profusely still among the ruins of Athene's most ancient temple. And while we're on these botanical subjects: on the very summit of the great fortress of Mycenae, at the site of another of Athene's temples, there was growing, until recently at least and in its own season, a tiny pink cyclamen – a plant which among its other properties eases earache and the pain of labour.)[9]

So at the height of the masculine world of civic power we can find flowering in symbolic synthesis an energy which aids both the ancient feminine mystery of birth, the primal transformation, and the understanding that comes through the unblocked ear and the clear head. And if Athene is showing us what she is up to through the produce of Gaia, she is doing the same through the great edifice that we know as one of the greatest expressions of Western civilization.

Within the Parthenon itself, it is the rites of women, not men, which are most honoured. The story is something of a hidden one. Lord Elgin first and the British Museum since have accustomed us to seeing the Parthenon frieze, which tells it conveniently displayed if we happen to be in London and even more conveniently reproduced if we don't. But when the frieze was in place, it was not simply at a neck-cricking height (as we can still see) but was visible only in chunks through the columns of the outer porch; amazingly, that keen-eyed traveller Pausanias doesn't even mention it. So to arrive at the central theme of the Parthenon, the one nearest the image of the goddess herself, we have to penetrate behind the triumphalist civic story which the building first presents; we have to get beyond the historical fact that it was designed to commemorate the great victory over the Persians, to make a proud display of Athenian valour.

First then, the civic statement. The metopes of the outer colonnade represent, on the west side, a battle between the Greeks and the Amazons and on the north, scenes from the Trojan war; on the south, it is the centaurs who are getting the battering, and on the east − under which is the main approach to the temple itself − it is the giants, this time at the hands of the Olympians. Above these scenes of triumph for the Greeks and their gods were the pediments on the short ends, and these depicted important moments in the life of Athene herself: on the west, the contest between herself and Poseidon for the sovereignty of the city, and on the east − above the temple's entrance − her birth from the head of Zeus.

But move behind this outer colonnade, and the scene is very different. Scholars still debate the meaning of that great procession and what exactly it is that the Olympians sit waiting for. But as they are so evidently relaxed about it, so domestic in their casual clothes as they pass the time together, perhaps we too may be allowed to enjoy the scene without getting too het up by rival interpretations of what is going on.[10]

The essential moment in the whole story is at the centre of the east frieze and so both behind and under the depiction of Athene's birth. Framed by two columns of the outer porch, Zeus and Hera sit together on the left and Athene and Hephaestus on the right. Two couples, then, and between them three children, a priest and a priestess; the boy hands the priest a folded cloth, each of the girls carries a stool and one a footstool as well [Pl. 3]. It is a marvellous moment of anticipation. Something is about to happen.

And that, they say, is the presentation of the *peplos*, the sacred garment woven for Athene and presented to the goddess on her birthday, which fell in the first month of the Athenian calendar, bridging our July and August. Some say the ceremony happened each year, others that it was held every four years, at the cul-mination of the festival called the Great Panathenaea. This huge celebration, as its name suggests, was open to all – women and men, citizens and foreign workers processed to the Acropolis accompanying the ship-cart on which the *peplos* itself billowed like a great sail.

Now this procession, this ceremony, had nothing to do with the huge cult figure that loomed so stern and corseted within the Parthenon itself. As Jane Harrison points out, she would scarcely have known what to do with a new *peplos*, decked out as she already was all in gold, armoured with shield, spear and helmet. It is a very different Athene who sits with Hephaestus waiting for the presentation in flowing dress, her spear long gone, the aegis slung casually across her knees. The image of the goddess for whom the new robe was made was the one which really mattered and lived in her more ancient temple – an image made of olive wood and so ancient and revered that it was said to have fallen from the sky at a time beyond recording to become 'the Madonna of the People', here renewed by redressing.[11]

What pleases this aspect of the goddess is not gold, nor a portion of plunder nor even the most excellent work of her craftsmen: it is something woven, the traditional work of women's hands. In this art, as we know, and Arachne learned to remember, the goddess herself is pre-eminent. Just how much she valued this skill could be seen in her great statue in Troy, the Palladium, which held a raised spear in the right hand and a distaff and spindle in the left. At Erythrae in Achaea the great wooden Athene of the City carried the same message, seated on her throne with a distaff in her hand and 'the universe round her head'.[12] And here in Athens itself, at the summit of its power, the work of women has pride of place. Maybe the ceremony of the *peplos* has to do with a rite of passage for young girls of marriageable age; certainly it brings right to the centre of the public domain the private craft of women.

The weaving of the *peplos* started nine months before Athene's birthday, at the festival of the Chalceia; it was initiated by the *arrephoroi*, girls between the ages of seven and eleven, dedicated to serve the goddess for part of one year, and completed by the priestess of Athene, girls of marriageable age and women from noble families in the city. The Chalceia was originally a festival of Hephaestus, and given their shared interest in technology perhaps it is not surprising that he and Athene should share elements of celebration as well. But the Chalceia carries a secret too, and that seems to have to do with another sort of relationship between god and virgin goddess.

The public version is well enough known. Hephaestus once made a new armour for Athene and it was so beautifully and skilfully wrought (as indeed his work always was) that she probably really meant it when she said she didn't know how to repay him. Slyly, and perhaps shyly too – crippled as he was, with something about him that makes you burst out laughing, though not unkindly, just to look at him – he told her that he'd take payment in love. Would she, impervious always to Aphrodite's charms, even have heard what he said, imagined what he might mean? Some say that the whole unlikely situation was Poseidon's joke, a bit of rib-digging between the lads to get the old girl going a bit. Maybe

Hephaestus really believed him ('G'wan, you know she's longing for it!') Maybe the very blankness of the goddess's response made him the more determined. Well, whatever, he tried to extract payment, clumsy fellow that he was, got her against the workshop wall and just kept at it and finally couldn't contain himself any longer, ejaculated against her thigh.

Was she surprised? Disgusted? She picked up a piece of wool and wiped away his semen and threw it to the ground. Did she know that Mother Earth herself, ever-fruitful, would conceive? Is that what she'd intended all along? (It wouldn't be the first time that Gaia and one of her female line had got together to move things on a bit.) Anyway, nine months later – and yes, they made that sort of count then too and it was just at the time of the goddess's own birthday – that child was born. Erichthonius, he was called – young Wool-Earth (*erion cthon*). Athene simply swept him up – a birthday present! – and wrapped him in her great aegis, and carried him about with her, this magic child, and he grew up to become king of Athens.

Athene would not be the last goddess, as she was not the first, whose mysteries included the bearing of a child while remaining perpetually virgin. But this story is not over yet. The night before her birthday, the three young daughters of Cecrops, first king of Athens and the one Erichthonius was to succeed, were entrusted with a very special task. They were, and by night, to take a closed basket down a secret staircase on the north side of the Acropolis to the Temple of Aphrodite in the Garden, and they were to bring another one up. And above all, most particularly above all, they were not, not on any account, to open either basket. No prizes for guessing what couldn't but happen. Pandrosus took her responsibilities seriously; Aglaurus and Herse, safety in numbers perhaps, giggling a little maybe, couldn't resist just the smallest, the quickest of peeks inside that basket before they set off down those stairs.

Was it terror at what they saw that made them fling themselves to their deaths off the rock? Was it a greater terror still, of the wrath of the goddess whose injunction they had disobeyed? She was on her way back to her fortress when news reached her of the girls' betrayal, carrying a huge boulder that would make a useful bulwark, and she was so enraged that she simply dropped it. (And that is how Athens got Lycabettus, the highest of its hills.)

It doesn't do to pry into the secrets of the gods. But what we can say is that Aphrodite is after all somehow implicated in this tale. We can surmise too that the very names of the daughters of Cecrops have their significance. All of them have to do with dew, that magical substance which was thought to fall from the moon and to bring richness, fertility and renewal; later it was known as 'daughter of Zeus' and so invokes Athene herself.[13] We also know that when Pausanias visited Athens, so very much later in the scale of human time, that annual mystery was still important enough to be enacted:

There was one thing that amazed me which not everyone knows; I shall describe what happens. Two virgin girls live not far from the temple of Athene of the City; the Athenians call them the Bearers. For a certain time they have their living from the goddess; and when the festival comes round they have to perform certain ceremonies during the night. They carry on their heads what Athene's priestess gives them to carry, *and neither she who gives it nor they who carry it know what it is she gives them* [my italics]. In the city not far from Aphrodite-in-the-Gardens is an enclosed place with a natural entrance to an underground descent; this is where the virgin girls go down. They leave down there what they were carrying, and take another thing and bring it back covered up. They are then sent away, and other virgin girls are brought to the akropolis instead of them.[14]

There was another commemoration in the Parthenon which is scarcely less mysterious, this time within the maiden's chamber itself. On the base supporting the huge statue of the armed Athene you might expect to see more scenes of the triumphs she inspired. But not at all. Once more, just as on the eastern pediment above the entrance to the chamber, the gods are gathered to witness a birth; the scene is framed by Helios the Sun and Selene the

Moon. The birth above is that of the goddess herself; the one below is of the first of mortal women.

By Hesiod's sour reckoning – and that is the one that has lasted – Pandora was sent into the world by Zeus as punishment for the theft of fire. This 'lovely evil', this 'ruin of mankind', he calls her, and from her comes all the 'deadly female race and tribe of wives/Who live with mortal men and bring them harm'. What to do? If you take a wife, says Hesiod glumly, she'll bleed you dry; if you don't, you'll have a miserable old age with no one to look after you and your property will go to distant relatives when you die.[15] And that, of course, is only the start of it. Another of these women who can't resist opening the casket! This time, though, we know only too well what was inside it:

> Before this time men lived upon the earth
> Apart from sorrow and from painful work,
> Free from disease, which brings the death-gods in.
> But now the woman opened up the cask,
> And scattered pains and evil among men.
> Inside the cask's hard walls remained one thing,
> Hope, only, which did not fly through the door.
> The lid stopped her, but all the others flew,
> Thousands of troubles, wandering the earth.
> The earth is full of evils, and the sea.
> Diseases come to visit men by day
> And, uninvited, come again at night
> Bringing their pains in silence, for they were
> Deprived of speech by Zeus the Wise. And so
> There is no way to flee the mind of Zeus.[16]

Not even, it seems, in the Parthenon itself. But what is Pandora doing here? Is she a sobering reminder to mortal folk of the distance between themselves and the gods? Is Athene crushing this evil beneath her monumental sandal, as Christian saints were later to stand on vanquished dragons and serpents? But listen, Athene was implicated from the start – from the moment, in fact, that she helped Prometheus steal the fire. In Hesiod's account in *Work and Days*, Zeus ropes in several of the Olympians to create his revenge: Hephaestus to form the girl from clay and water and give her voice and movement, Aphrodite to give her charm and desire and 'body-shattering cares', Hermes to put in 'sly manners and the morals of a bitch' and Athene to clothe her and teach her to weave. But in the *Theogony*, thought to be the earlier version of the tale, it is Hephaestus and Athene alone who create Pandora, she crowning their achievement with a wreath of spring blossoms and a golden crown he's made.

Pandora, the All-Giving: this is one of the titles of Rhea, Zeus's own mother, daughter of Gaia herself. Pandora's other name, Anesidora, means 'she who bestows gifts from below'. Whatever else is going on, once more the ancient feminine is brought into the very citadel of masculine pride. Once again the parents are Athene and Hephaestus. And just as Pandora is at the base, the foundation even, of Athene's image in the Parthenon, so was the birth of Erichthonius commemorated on the base of the statues of both god and goddess in Hephaestus's own temple that overlooks the market-place at the foot of the Acropolis hill.[17]

Four children 'unnatural' in their birth: Pandora, Erichthonius, Athene and Hephaestus (for Hera had him in the old parthenogenic way in retaliation for Zeus's brainchild). Two created from Earth herself: Erichthonius, the product of passion, from her womb, Pandora, the product of technical skill, from her substance. Two created from the heavens, yet with their own earth natures, too: Athene through her mother Metis, Hephaestus through his foster-mother Thetis, who reared him under the sea and taught him his trade when Hera, in disgust at his lameness, threw him out of Olympus. Four is the number of completion, and something has come together here in these multiple relations of masculine and feminine at patriarchy's centre.

So when at the great climax of Aeschylus's *Eumenides* Athene forswears all that is maternal in her judgement of Orestes, we may perhaps be permitted to wonder what she is up to, she of many counsels, so adept in guile. It is a decisive moment: the ancient feminine order and that of the new sky-gods face each other with claim and counter-claim. The Furies, those ancient children of Night that some know as the Grudges, some as the Curses, have pursued Orestes to Athens itself and they demand his blood in payment for his matricide, just as blood has always had blood under their ancient law, in a never-ending and terrible cycle of revenge and counter-revenge. Orestes has been driven more than half-mad by their hounding, and by his deed itself: he needs no reminding that to kill a mother is a terrible crime indeed. Yet it was Apollo who insisted on it when Orestes consulted his oracle; the god stands by that, your Honour, as you will hear, and so by Orestes himself. How could the man have done other than he did?

Yet if anyone can plead extenuating circumstances in this dreadful bloodsoaked business, surely it is the still unavenged shade of Clytemnestra, the murdered mother, whose cause the Furies plead. There was no hint, your Honour, that she had been other than an exemplary wife and mother, dutiful and loyal, until her husband Agamemnon demanded that impossible, that appalling sacrifice, the offering of their young daughter Iphigeneia – and all so that he could persuade the gods to give him a wind to take his ships to Troy, to pursue that mad war that no one needed to fight in the first place. Even then, let us emphasize, she was loyal to her husband and to the demands of the gods. But it would not be an exaggeration to say that it drove her mad, mad with grief, your Honour – the condition is well documented. Her taking of a lover in her husband's lengthy absence, the obsessional thoughts of re-venge – all followed from that death. When she finally saw her husband again, after all those years, he added insult to her suffering by bringing the captive Cassandra into their house and bed. How could the woman have done other than she did?

So Athene, and the jury she has called together, the first ever of its kind, face multiple dilemmas. Can there be such a concept as extenuating circumstance in this tragically imperfect world of human endeavour or must the old law of blood for blood rule for ever? If it must, then what hope is there of human advancement in responsibility and mercy? If not, then is judgement to fall for the wronged woman or the man obedient to the demands of the new sky-gods? And if the second, then again what hope for humankind, for the Furies are starving, they have pursued Orestes to the point of exhaustion and if they are not fed they will blast the land and its children, the canker of their rage rendering all infertile, all diseased.

This is what Athene must resolve, and she calls on all her patience and guile to do it. In one sense, perhaps, there is no choice, for she is daughter of the new order and in casting her deciding vote she declares her inevitable allegiance:

> It is now my office to give final judgement;
> and I shall give my vote to Orestes.
> For there is no mother who bore me;
> And I approve the male in all things, short of accepting marriage,
> With all my heart, and I belong altogether to my father.
> Therefore I shall not give greater weight to the death of a woman,
> One who slew her husband, the watcher of the house;
> Orestes is the winner, even should the votes be equal.

So the votes were, and so he was. In coming to her own judgement, Athene has accepted Apollo's argument that the mother has no importance. As he puts it:

> She who is called the child's mother is not
> its begetter, but the nurse of the newly sown conception.
> The begetter is the male, and she as a stranger for a stranger
> preserves the offspring if no god blights its birth;
> and I shall offer you a proof of what I say.
> There can be a father without a mother; near at hand
> is the witness, the child of Olympian Zeus . . .[18]

At one level Apollo is voicing contemporary biological belief: it was thought that the father's semen did indeed contain the new human being in miniature entirety and that the mother provided the environment in which this already fully formed creature could grow. Many-Counselled Athene, we can imagine, knows better than that. But in giving the ostensible judgement for the masculine order over the ancient feminine way, she breaks for ever the old cycle of blood vengeance and secures Apollo's allegiance for her city as well. If she had found for the Furies, and so for Clytemnestra, nothing would have changed. Her own nature, which is to move us continually from being blindly driven to greater consciousness, would have been betrayed.

Now the goddess must complete the task. Somehow she must reconcile the Furies to the new order, find them new food to appease their ravening hunger for blood, stave off that terrible threat of deathly blight. Never once does she fail to respect the ancient power which she now woos for her land, and in that marvellously patient and skilful weaving and interweaving of complaint, persuasion, offer and counter-offer the goddess works one of the greatest of her transformations: that of the Furies into the Eumenides, the Solemn Ones, the Aweful Ones, those who are, finally, Kindly.

The Eumenides have their new place of honour; the land has the beautiful generosity of their blessing. And something else has happened as well. In placing the shrine of the Kindly Ones under the Areopagus, the Hill of Ares, just opposite the Acropolis, Athene has worked another of her transformations. This hill was once the camp of the war-god's daughters by Aphrodite, the Amazons; now it will be the meeting place of the new citizen's court the goddess has established. At one level, she has replaced the independent, warring feminine with a new bastion of masculine civic order. And yet, just as behind the civic statements of the Parthenon there is an honouring of something much older and deeper, so below the civic reforms on the Areopagus the goddess has established for ever an underpinning and foundation of ancient energy. In the shrine of the Kindly Ones, too, there is a further reconciliation of masculine and feminine at a deeper level yet: they are worshipped together with Hades and Hermes, lord of and guide to the underworld, and with Mother Earth herself.

Could any energy except Athene's, with her father's authority and her mother's deep and ancient wisdom, have pulled it off?

CHAPTER 3

The Feminine Heritage

One of Athene's paradoxes is that we know both precisely where she came from and not at all. Even the precision of that birth from her father's head is contested. The Libyans swear that she is water-born — the daughter not of Zeus but of Poseidon and the Trito-nian Lake, as anyone can see from those grey-green eyes, the very colour of her father's. They say she was found there, on the lake shore (it wasn't just Moses who had that sort of beginning!) by the three nymphs of Libya, who nurtured her and brought her up. Herodotus the historian backs up this tale. If you want proof, he says, just take a look at that aegis she wears: it is exactly like the working gear of any Libyan woman, 'except that their leather garments are fringed with thongs, not serpents'.[1]

So it was her *father* from whom she won the rule of Athens — a new twist to that old tale of parent–child hostility after all! Or was it? Some say that aegis of hers means something quite dif-ferent: that her father was actually a hairy winged giant called Pallas, and that after he tried to rape her — the old goat! — she didn't just kill him but skinned him too, and wore his hairy goat-skin for ever after. Well, certainly the goddess is also and often known as Pallas Athene, or even simply Pallas. But would she have wanted to carry for ever the sign of such a horror, such intrusive violence? Others claim that Pallas was actually the name of her dearest playmate in those youthful Libyan days, and that the name attests to that, meaning no more — and no less — than 'maiden' and maybe 'tough maiden' at that. And that one day as they were horsing around, these tough young girls, things got a bit too rough, a bit out of hand, and that by a dreadful accident she killed the girl. And that for ever after, heartbroken, she bore the name herself, and even put up that great temple of hers, the Palladium of Troy, as a memorial to the person she'd loved best in the world.[2] (And for ever devoted herself, we might add, such are the effects of childhood trauma, to trying to repair that first and terrible damage she'd inflicted, by working to moderate the use of force, to conquer undisciplined violence – as Ares could angrily attest.)

So wherever did Athene come from? Plato opted for the Libyan claim: he thought she was originally their goddess, but that there, as later in Egypt, she was called Neith. Others have since agreed. His version, they reckon, clears up the fundamental puzzle of her name – which certainly isn't Greek, but may, as the city name Athens itself, derive from the Egyptian Ht Nt, meaning the temple, or house, of Neith. Or did she come first from Minoan Crete, where an inscription in Linear B script from the palace at Knossos makes reference to *Atana Potinija*, meaning 'Mistress of At(h)ana'? Or maybe she first appeared in Mycenae, as warrior and defender of the citadel, later bringing the olive tree which figures on so many Mycenaean seals as her particular gift to Athens. Or maybe again this is all too literal, too fixed to time and place, and she was in her origins a personification of one of the great elemental forces of air, earth, water or thunder, given a form and a name which means simply 'the goddess' – *A Thea*.[3]

We are talking about an archetypal energy here, and there can be no final knowing of where archetypes have their beginnings. 'It seems to me,' as Jung says, 'that their origin can only be explained by assuming them to be deposits of the constantly repeated experience of humanity' – and each age and each culture will give its own image to what is finally unknowable.[4] What we can say is that in those differing stories of Athene's origins there is a thread which has to do with a tension between the feminine and the masculine powers, and that the goddess – in her battling against the rape by her maybe-father Pallas, in her return to the feminine

society by that Libyan lake, in her honouring of the girl Pallas –
has an allegiance to feminine ways which the later story of her
birth from her father Zeus's head directly challenges. And we can
say too that in this bewilderment of theogenies there is a strong
energy to which somehow Athene is heir, an elemental energy of
air, earth, water or thunder. The image in that Trojan temple was a
great sacred stone, its origin so mysterious that it was said it had
been hurled from the heavens. The very name Palladium, it's said,
means 'sky-fallen' – and we remember that even under the reign
of the sky-god Zeus, Athene alone had access to her now-father's
thunderbolts. And maybe too that energy can be found in a place
far more intimate: some say that what Pallas really means is 'throbbing', 'pulsating' – and that Athene takes the epithet from her
rescuing of Dionysus's still-throbbing, still-living heart after his
dismemberment by the Titans, so that father Zeus could sew this
vital organ together with the other bits into his thigh and render
the new god twice-born to bring his energy to the world.[5]

So where does *that* energy come from, that throbbing, pulsating,
thunderbolting, earthy, watery, airy energy that is also Athene's
own? The fact that the question can't ever have a final answer
doesn't stop us from trying to find it. 'But where do I *really* come
from?' small children ask after the conscientious parental explanations of ova and sperm, daddy's seed and mummy's tummy. Parents
know that the child will grow up to understand these realities in
time, while the child grows up to continue to seek the answer.

To begin, then, somewhere nearer the beginning, when human
beings were already giving their own answer to that archetypal
question, already giving form to that primary force which encompasses life and death and all the experiences in between. Some
20,000 years ago and more, forged from earth's own substances,
'the image of a goddess appeared across a vast expanse of land
stretching from the Pyrenees to Lake Baikal in Siberia. Statues in
stone, bone and ivory, tiny figures with long bodies and falling
breasts, rounded motherly figures pregnant with birth, figures with
signs scratched upon them – lines, triangles, zigzags, circles, nets,

leaves, spirals, holes – graceful figures rising out of rock and painted with red ochre . . .' By the time we know as the Neolithic era, between 10,000 and 3500 BC, the urge to discriminate, so fundamental to human consciousness, had already separated the realm of this original Mother Goddess into the three regions of Sky, or the Upper Waters, Earth, and the Lower Waters, or the Waters Beneath the Earth, and each realm had its differentiated images of deity. As above, so below: what characterized the Neolithic era was that human beings discovered the arts of agriculture and formed settled communities. So developed a coherent culture, illuminated by the pioneering work of Marija Gimbutas as 'Old Europe', which reached its height between about 7000 and 3500 BC and stretched from Malta in the south to Kiev in the north, Belgrade in the west to Bucharest in the east, taking in Hungary, the south and centre of what used to be called Yugoslavia, Bulgaria, Romania and eastern Austria, southern Czechoslovakia and southern Poland, parts of the Ukraine, southern Italy and Sicily, Malta, Greece, Crete and the Ionian and Aegean islands and the west coast of Turkey.[6]

So developed a new relationship between human beings and the creation of which they were a part. Instead of having simply to accept what the natural world sent them and what they could wrest from it day by day, they learned to interact with it and to transform its gifts to their own use. In these interactions and transformations, this new relationship between mind, hand and matter, we are in the realm of energy which became, as we have seen, so distinctively Athene's own. In those days, the arts of agriculture were indeed very much those of women. As below, so above. Marija Gimbutas called the first edition of her work on the mythical imagery of this era *The Gods and Goddesses of Old Europe*. Ten years and many discoveries on, the emphasis had changed, and she called the new edition *The Goddesses and Gods of Old Europe* to reflect this. The male element represented for these people, she now felt, powers that were spontaneous and life-stimulating, but not life-generating; 'the culture called Old Europe was characterized by a domination of woman in society and worship of a goddess incarnating the creative principle as Source and Giver of All'.[7]

This energy took many forms, from abstract patterns that hint at her nature, to animals, to amalgams of animal and human forms – for human consciousness was not in those days differentiated to the point where human beings saw themselves as apart from (and superior to) the rest of sentient creation. So she appears as dog and doe, toad and turtle, butterfly, bee and bear. And at the height of the Old Europe civilization, around 5000 BC, she manifests in two particular and sophisticated images as Mistress of the Waters that encompass known creation: 'Lady Bird' and 'Lady Snake'.[8]

Sometimes the energy is single-imaged. This is how it manifests, for instance, in the extraordinarily potent statuettes of the Cretan snake-goddesses who are wreathed in that chthonic energy, bringing it forth and holding it high in their hands – and themselves the inheritrixes of more ancient imagery still [Pls. 5, 6]. Sometimes the goddess manifests as both snake and bird. In either guise, the image expresses a unifying creative power. The snake, with its water-like undulations, brings energy from the mysterious places below to earth itself to unite the dimensions; in many cultures the image of the snake with its tail in its mouth – the *uroboros* – signifies the waters that encircle the whole of creation. The energy that comes from below encompasses the reality of death as well as life in that great round; in the snake's ability to shed its dead, outworn skin is a potent symbol of the continually regenerative force of nature itself. Snakes have been both symbols of healing and used in its rites from ancient times and to this day they entwine around the *caduceus*, or physician's staff, on the letterheads of medical societies. That staff unites the energies that come both from above and below: it once belonged to Hermes, messenger of the sky-gods, who was also conductor of souls to the underworld.

If a snake licks your ears, they say, you can understand the language of birds.[9] Those no less mysterious messengers from the unimaginably distant ends of the Waters Above are also adept at moving between and so uniting the dimensions, as they alight on earth, and dive into water and bring up its treasures. If you can understand their language and the patterns of their flights, they can signify what the gods have in mind; when we humans are seized by flights of fancy, when it is a little bird that has told us, then we too experience the imaginal soaring that goes beyond mundane thinking.

In her own uniting of the dimensions – the bringing together of mind and thought and the material world in creative transformation – Athene's energy comes directly from this symbolic heritage. We have already seen just how snaky this goddess is – and even in her own days in Greece the identity between deity and serpent has not yet entirely been superseded by a consciousness that discriminates the human from the creature. The historian Herodotus reports that in Athens they have a great snake which guards the Acropolis and to which each month offerings of honey cake are made, and graciously received. But at the time of the Persian invasion, the snake refused to eat the offering. 'And when the priestess announced this, the Athenians deserted the city the more readily *because the goddess herself had deserted the acropolis*' (my italics).[10] And even when Athene's own snaky nature is less explicitly stated, her association with the serpent remains for all to see. As stern guardian of the Acropolis, the goddess is accompanied by that great snake which encircles her shield, thought to be Erichthonius himself – that very babe born in such mysterious and not-to-be-pried-into circumstances, and nurtured next to the goddess's own breast, wrapped in her great goatskin. In that image of the human goddess nursing a snake there is an exact mirror-image too – of the very many figurines of snake goddesses from Old Europe who are suckling human babies, nourishing them with their own regenerative energy.

If that energy comes from the earth and the places below it, then the capacity to work on earth's yield comes from above, from the realm of thought and discernment and understanding. We have already glimpsed Athene as 'Lady Bird', perching like a swallow on the smoky main beam of Odysseus's hall to watch the battle with the suitors that she has inspired, flying up and away as birds will through a hole in the roof when only an instant before she had been wise Mentes, the visiting chieftain who became mentor to young Telemachus. She is sea-bird too, as were so many epiphanies of the Old European bird goddess. When she turns once more from her guise as Mentes into, this time, a sea-eagle, everyone is confounded – everyone, that is, except wise old Nestor, who recognizes that this is Athene straight away.[11]

Athene has other bird-guises. In Megara, she is worshipped as storm-bird, or diver-bird – another common manifestation for the Old European goddess, in its capacity to move through the three great Waters which comprise creation, its long neck symbolizing perhaps the union of her bird and snake natures. In Elis there is a cock on Athene's helmet – maybe, says Pausanias, because cocks are known to be always extremely ready for a fight, or maybe (rather hastily?) because this is the sacred bird of Athene the Worker.[12] But of all the birds associated with the goddess, the one which is most particularly her own is the owl. In her own day, its image appears on the obverse of hers on Athenian coins [Pl. 7]. In times since, the two have become inseparable: whenever we see an image of an otherwise unidentified woman who has an owl perched on her or near by, we can be pretty sure that it is the goddess we are looking at. (And she still lends her name to a genus, whose member species range from the well-known Little Owl (*Athene noctua*) to the Burrowing Owl of the Americas (*Athene cunicularia*), whose underground habits put it in touch with not just the Waters Above but the Waters Below.)

Some say it was not always so, that Athene's bird was originally the crow, who was in turn a metamorphosis of a beautiful princess called Coronis, rescued thus by the goddess from the unwanted attentions of Poseidon. The grateful girl, in her new downy plumage, soared into the air to become Athene's faithful attendant. But alas, she was not quick enough in her new element to understand when messages need to be delivered with discretion. When the daughters of Cecrops looked into that mysterious basket, the crow flew straight to the goddess with the news and suffered the traditional messenger's fate: her lovely plumage, until now white as her own purity, was turned as black as Athene's rage and she was forbidden ever to return to the Acropolis. Instead, Athene chose the owl as her own bird. That's an odd tale too. The owl had originally been one Nyctimene and, so they say on Lesbos anyway, she was transformed as the result of a foul crime, a violation of her father's bed; her guilty conscience keeps her for ever from the light of day, driven off by all other birds as she tries to hide her shame in darkness.[13]

Well, what are we to make of that? Just what was that crime so foul and shameful? And what was Athene doing condoning it? Given that we have the story from Ovid, so from well into the era of the sky-gods' consciousness, we may perhaps be allowed to ask whether there hasn't been a little inversion of the truth going on here, whether it wasn't, perhaps, the father who attempted the violation of a more ancient order. Or are we supposed to understand the tale to be a sly reference to the community of women poets who gathered on Lesbos, celebrating life and the ancient feminine ways, and a not-so-sly insinuation about what they got up to there, made to undermine their authority? The second may be possible, for the identity between Athene and the owl underlines just how ancient the goddess's heritage is [Pl. 8].

The very earliest image of a bird of a recognizable species known to Marija Gimbutas was a snowy owl, engraved in an Upper Paleolithic cave at Les Trois Frères in southern France, and dating from around 13,000 BC. For her, the owl image of the goddess represents profound wisdom and oracular power, and an ability to avert evil as well. This is the deeply transformative aspect of the goddess, the ruler of death and regeneration. Images of owls have been found in ancient burial urns; the bird was also a symbol of the maternal uterus not just in Europe but in Asia and Africa as well. More specifically, it expresses some of Athene's particular qualities: here in ancient Greece on a terracotta plaque, it uses its human arms to spin wool; there in Sardinia, Corsica, Liguria, southern France and Spain it wields a sword or dagger; everywhere it expresses in the extraordinary acuity of its vision the goddess's particular gift of seeing.[14]

Elsewhere, the gifts and qualities of the owl are carried by the vulture, another epiphany of the goddess of death and resurrection. This bringing of life from death is startlingly portrayed in one Old European image, where the deity's breasts are sculpted over the skulls of vultures, their beaks protruding from the nipples. The vulture which is the Egyptian hieroglyph of death also means 'mother' and 'the compassionate', its ancient power attested by the fact that it is parthenogenic, fertilizing itself and giving birth to its own creation. Athene has her own vulture-nature, too. She perches in its guise with Apollo on her father's sacred oak to enjoy the sight of the massed ranks of Greeks and Trojans; she swoops from heaven 'like a shrieking, long-winged bird of prey' to bring nourishment to her favourite Achilles. She is also the vulture in its terrible aspect when she pecks so horribly at Prometheus's liver, as punished as he is, perhaps, for challenging the power of the immortals by bringing their gifts to human beings. One of those was Athene's own gift of foresight, and this is most especially the bird of prophecy; one of the many things that Prometheus had taught human beings was to discern the meaning in 'the various flights of crook-clawed vultures'.[15]

In her snaky, bird–like nature, then, Athene partakes of the most ancient of powers and wisdoms. And through their undulations and flights, she is linked to many other goddesses whose attributes she shares. All over Old Europe, from the Basque country to the Baltic and across the Slavic lands, images appear of goddesses who are patrons of craft, their symbols of snaky meander and bird–eye whorl etched on to the loom-weights of the weavers and the metal-workers' artefacts. Celtic Brigit, whose very name denotes power (Irish 'Brig') and renown (Welsh 'Bri') was patron of weaving, bringer of knowledge and civilization itself; her two sisters were Brigit of Healing and Brigit of Smithcraft. The web spins far in time and space. In cultures as geographically far apart as native North America and Borneo, the feminine creative power that spins the world into existence takes the form of a spider. The Keres Indians of New Mexico venerate the creative power as Thought Woman, who is ever-far yet, like Athene, ever-near; her earthly counterpart is Spider-Woman.[16]

These weavings and interweavings unite the powers of life and death. The Greeks knew it in the image of the Fates, their triple nature a reflection of that of the ancient moon-goddess; and the Greeks knew too that even Zeus must bow when Clotho spun a human life on her spindle, Lachesis measured its span on her rod and Atropos cut it off with her shears. The Egyptians knew it in the image of Neith, with whom Athene, as we have seen, was so closely identified.

Neith was called 'the oldest one'. The depth of her power is attested in the inscription of her temple at Sais: 'I am all that has been, that is, and that will be. No mortal has yet been able to lift the veil which covers me.' This goddess of creation often appeared as serpent, and as parthenogenic vulture too. She it was who first brought forth the sun-god Ra and then took up her shuttle, strung the sky on her loom and wove into existence the world itself. In her association with Khnum, who made the gods on his potter's wheel, there is another image of creation, which recalls the cooperation of Athene and Prometheus in the creation of the first human beings. Like Athene, Neith is patroness of war: her emblem is a shield surmounted by crossed arrows. But like Athene, she also presides over the useful arts and a school of medicine called 'The House of Life' is attached to her sanctuary. In her governance of life and death, she teaches human beings to weave both bandages and shrouds; she guards coffins and canopic jars and is patroness of marriage as well.

How these images of the goddess of life and death reflect and reappear! Athene has been identified, for instance, with the Near-Eastern Anath, defender of cities, caparisoned in helmet and shield. But in older representations, Anath carries snakes as well, and her work is to preserve the fertility of the earth. Both virgin and mother, she is intimately bound to the sowing of seed and the sprouting of grain, descending, in the Canaanite myth, into the underworld to rescue her brother-consort Baal, the bringer of rain, from his dark brother Mot, who personifies the scorching drought her land knows and dreads. Sometimes she is shown standing on a lion, or even lion-headed, so closely is she identified with that fierce, proud energy. This is a quality she shares with lion-headed Egyptian Sekhmet, who of all the warrior goddesses of Europe and the Near East is perhaps the most blood-thirsty. Everywhere she goes, she spreads terror; she accompanies the king into battle, and is often known as his mother. 'When I slay men,' she cries, 'my heart rejoices!' Her name means 'the mighty one' and her weapons are not just the arrows with which she pierces hearts, but the fiery glow which emanates from her body; the hot desert winds are her breath. Yet even this goddess has her dual nature: she is also known as 'the one great of magic', her knowledge devoted to healing; she could bring pestilence, but she could also stay it.[17]

As in the Near East, so in the Celtic kingdoms. Brigit, bringer of civilization and its arts, has her darker sisters in the warrior goddesses of Ireland. Yet the Morrigan was originally a triple goddess of life and death, as was Macha. They presided over war and destruction. But they were mothers too, territorial guardians of the land itself. Macha is also mare, and as such goddess of agricultural prosperity. The very mountains were the paps of the Morrigan. This goddess will shape-shift at will: she is snake, bird, mare and nurturing cow. She may be maiden, she may be hag, for she is the changing of the seasons. She may be crow or raven, which is also a transformation of Badb, gloating over the blood of battle (and we recall Coronis, the crow, who was once Athene's own bird). Yet Badb was also a serpent goddess, and so unites the ostensible world and the world below. She is represented with a huge vulva, and is associated with the rites of childbirth. And as crow or raven she carries the dead to the underworld, clutched in her claws.[18]

The discriminations of Western consciousness find it hard, perhaps, to hold such dual images; the thrust is always and continually to divide the light from the dark, so that we may know which is the good. Yet perhaps too we can still intimate the older way through a civilization where the gods still live and inform the life of everyday.

At the very creation of the world, so Indian mythology tells us, there was Brahma, the Unbounded, embodiment of creative energy, and his consort Sarasvati, 'the flowing one', one of the three sacred rivers of India. She is the goddess who brings together power and intelligence to give creation its shape and form, playing the very universe into incarnation as she plays her *vina*. She is patroness of learning, eloquence, music and the arts; this civilizing work has echoes of Athene's own [Pl. 9]. These days, Sarasvati has little public cult, for like Brahma's, her main work of creation has been done. Yet she is still beloved by students, artists and intellectuals. At her annual festival, her image is still crafted from clay and straw in multiple representations and impeccably decorated to move through the reality of today's world and remind her people of that world's beginnings. On that day, none of her devotees is allowed to read books or to play an instrument. Instead, these are cleaned, placed on the family altar and worshipped in a recognition from whence they came.[19]

If the image of Sarasvati carries the grace and light of the civilized arts, there from the beginning of time, then she is only one of the myriad images of that Supreme Being which is Devi, the Goddess, and Sakti, the feminine principle itself. The gods themselves know how utterly essential this energy is in the preservation of cosmic order. Once, their power was usurped by the buffalo demon Mahisa and they were quite unable to reclaim it. They assembled, they debated, they stoked their great and terrible wrath – and from it emanated a huge brilliance, which fused together like a flaming mountain that pervaded the whole sky. The flames took form, they became a beautiful woman and to her each of the gods gave his own best gift. This is Durga, and, her own eyes ablaze, she sets to. First she demolishes the demon's armies and then she grapples with him in his many guises – as buffalo, lion, man, elephant and finally buffalo again. She takes a swig of wine, she gives a great shrieking laugh and finally cuts off the demon's head. The gods praise her as supreme protector and boon-giver. Before she disappears, she grants their request that she will return whenever they remember her. And to this day she is remembered by her people across North India too, her slaying of the buffalo-demon of ignorance commemorated in countless popular prints, her beauty and energy blazing from page and shrine as she rides her lion-tiger, given to her at her creation by the Himalaya, her sword of discrimination in her hand. The very name Durga means 'difficult of approach': this is an energy so terrible in its fierceness, so bright in its flaming hugeness (for is it not made up of the best of all the gods?), that human understanding can only begin to intimate its power. But as today's shrines and images bear witness, it is an energy fundamental to the cosmic order. It brings supreme blessing as well as destruction – just as the energy of that other lion-goddess, Egyptian Sekhmet, brought both battle and healing, just as did the energy of Neith and of Athene herself.[20] [Pl. 11].

To try to understand that dual nature of the feminine is inescapably part of our era's task, for in the great cycle of creation we now live in Kali Yuga, an age as dark as the age of iron which was lamented by Hesiod and is the current incarnation of Western consciousness. *Kali* means the worst of anything; it is the losing throw in dice, it has to do with strife and quarrel, battle and war. And for us small humans, that is the way it is, for this age, which began on Friday, 18 February 3102 BC has a life-span of 432,000 years.[21]

Durga's energy is also that of Kali, the Dark One, as we can see, for instance, in the great festival of Durga-puja in Calcutta, one of today's main centres of the Kali cult. Kali is one of the consorts of Shiva, the Lord of the Cosmic Dance. He presides over the constant change, the cycle of forming, dissolution, reforming and dissolution again which is the reality of existence; she is Time itself. How can we not experience her as terrible, in her inexorable unfolding, against which the best of our human endeavours are so tiny, within which they must be enfolded, consumed, suffocated, devoured, disappeared?

Kali is black, the supreme night. She is naked, like truth itself, clad only in space. She is destroyer: she stands on a corpse and wears a necklace of skulls, she dwells near the funeral pyres. She is devourer: her long tongue thrusts out to lick up the blood of sacrifice, her fearsome laughter shows her dreadful teeth, her maw receives all that is created. In her great strength, she is four-armed: in one of her hands she wields a sword and in another she carries a severed head. She is always young, bursting with blood, and always ancient, an emaciated hag whose hunger will never be satiated. She stamps on the body of Lord Shiva: she is before consciousness itself [Pl. 12].

Yet what many images of Kali also tell us, in the gesture of her third hand, is 'Fear Not.' And in her fourth hand, she will carry the bowl of abundance, from which she feeds all the children on her earth with sweet milk rice. 'Both the shade of death and the elixir of immortality are thy grace, Oh Mother!' says one of her devotees in the ninth century. 'Oh, she plays in different ways!' Shri Ramakrishna, her greatest devotee of recent times, tells us about 1,000 years later: she is protectress in times of epidemic, famine, earthquake, drought and flood just as much as she embodies the power of destruction. 'Is Kali, my Divine Mother, of a black complexion? She appears black because she is viewed from a distance; but when intimately known she is no longer so . . . Bondage and liberation are both of her making. She is called the Saviour, and the Remover of the bondage that binds one to the world . . . She is self-willed and must always have her own way. She is full of bliss.'[22]

Kali, the Divine Mother, was there, says Shri Ramakrishna, 'when there were neither the creation, nor the sun, the moon, the planets, and the earth, and when darkness was enveloped in dark-

1. Athene of Varvakion: second–century copy of Pheidias's famous statue in the Parthenon (National Archaeological Museum, Athens).

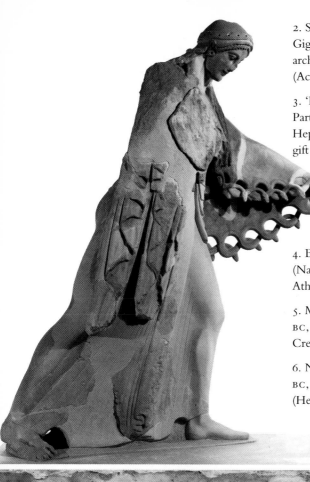

2. Statue of Athene from the Gigantomachy pediment on the archaic temple on the Acropolis (Acropolis Museum, Athens).

3. 'Peplos scene' from the Parthenon frieze: Athene sits with Hephaestus awaiting her birthday gift (British Museum).

4. Bronze statue of Athene (National Archaeological Museum, Athens).

5. Minoan snake goddess, c.1600 BC, from the Palace of Knossos, Crete (Heraklion Museum).

6. Neolithic snake goddess, c.4500 BC, from Kato Ierapetra, Crete (Heraklion Museum).

7. Head of Athene on a four-drachma coin with her owl on the reverse (British Museum).

8. Bird goddess in the form of a vessel, first half of the fifth millennium BC (Mid-Vinca, Macedonia).

9. Sarasvati, Hindu goddess of learning, plays the universe into creation (author's collection).

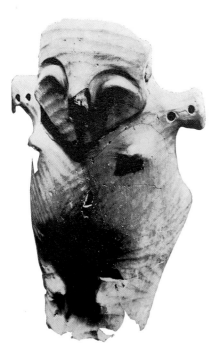

10. Etruscan Minrva, goddess of the thunderbolt (British Museum).

11 and 12. Hindu images of feminine power: Durga, who embodies aspects of all the gods, and Kali, Time herself (contemporary Indian prints).

13 and 14. The Gorgon
Medusa: in marble relief at the
temple of Athene (Corfu) and
in bronze (British Museum).

15 and 16. The enduring image of the snake
goddess: in Roman Atargatis (Museo
Nazionale, Rome), and in a contemporary
Hindu painting from Bihar (author's
collection).

17 and 18. Goddess and Gorgon: from the Temple of Sulis Minerva (Roman Museum, Bath).

ness'. She will be there at the end of the great cycle: 'She is like the elderly mistress of the house, who has a hotchpotch-pot in which she keeps different articles for household use . . . After the destruction of the universe, my Divine Mother, the embodiment of Brahman, gathers together the seeds for the next creation.' On one bank of the river Hoogly in Calcutta today, devotees gather to worship in the peace of the temple where Ramakrishna spent his life in service of this great power. On the opposite bank, they jostle at her shrine to offer garlands of blood-red flowers and the sacrifice of animals to her terrible image – and to receive her blessing for their marriages and their new motor cars, their own driving energy, as well.

And in Kali's own perspective, the perspective of Time itself, all this is finally as unreal as it is real. It is the stuff of *maya*, the illusion which is also existence, the spontaneous self-transformation of the original, all-generating divine Substance which produces the universe and the deities themselves. The noun *maya* is related etymologically to 'measure', formed from the root *ma*, which means to measure or lay out – the plan of a building, for instance, or the outline of a figure – to produce or to shape, to create or display.[23] We have met this concept before, in Athene's own mother Metis, where the root *me-* gives *metron*, measure, rule, standard. Yet the developments and discriminations of Western consciousness have brought a very different concept of that original divine measure. It has proved very hard to hold the dual images of the primal feminine power in the way that the Indian mind still can; the West has constantly sought to resolve paradox, to replace 'both–and' with the discriminations of 'either–or'. So the image of the goddess who rules both life and death became fragmented and with that fragmentation came a dethroning of the feminine itself. In the Indian cosmology, masculine and feminine energy still unite, often in images of great beauty and tenderness, in partnerships which are essentially equal. Importantly, Sarasvati, Durga and Kali are honoured independently. But they are consorts as well, and in her regenerative power, even Black Time reanimates Lord Shiva as he lies at her feet, to join with him finally in an image of their total union, the deity who is half male, half female.[24]

In the West, even by the time of Athene's birth, the archetypal union of masculine and feminine had little of this final bliss: 300 years of ecstatic honeymoon had long given way, for Hera and Zeus, to a constant power-play which you'd have to be a deity to endure. This tension between masculine and feminine was already set up as the warp on the loom that was weaving the pattern of Western consciousness. And the woof was already in place as well, in the growing tensions between the different aspects of a once-unified feminine.

It fell to the unfortunate Paris, son of King Priam of Troy, to weave these tensions on, and by his notorious judgement between the already differentiated energies of Hera, Athene and Aphrodite to start a weaving too of bloodshed and suffering for humankind. Yet maybe the judgement was not finally his at all, maybe he was as much judged as anyone in what was already fated, already set up in the pattern preordained for the consciousness of the West.

It all seemed to start innocently enough. Thetis the Nereid was marrying Peleus, and Zeus was pleased, because he had fixed the match. He'd have claimed Thetis himself, if not for one of those by now familiar prophecies that any son of hers would be greater than his father, so he'd made assurance doubly sure by ensuring that she married a mere mortal. That was his story. Hera's version was that Thetis had actually, whatever Zeus said, rejected him, out of loyalty to the goddess, who was her foster-mother; so Hera had rewarded her by choosing this noblest of mortals for her and summoning all the Olympians to honour the wedding. Either way, there they all were, complete with their golden thrones, and all seemed to be going with great rejoicing. But, as so often, there was one who had not been invited to the feast, and as we know from countless fairy-tales, that was bound to mean trouble. No one wanted Eris at the party, nobody wanted Strife. But of course she came and, when no one was looking, just gently bowled that golden apple so that it landed at the feet of Hera, Athene and

Aphrodite. They were chatting amicably enough, until they saw that little ticket which said 'For the Fairest'. Maybe it seemed a bit of a joke at first; maybe Zeus could have found a way to keep it light when the goddesses asked him who should claim the fruit. But he refused to choose – would he be so foolish? And from then on the whole business escalated until it became a full-scale Judgement.

Paris, living at that time as a simple cattle-herder, was not keen at all to learn from Hermes, Zeus's messenger, that he had been given the job of arbiter; just because he had given the prize for best bull to the one who was really Ares in disguise, that certainly didn't mean that he had any expertise at all in the judging of goddesses. But Zeus, said Hermes, insisted. The goddesses duly presented themselves, even disrobed, so that the trembling Paris could better judge their charms. In turn they paraded and in turn they offered him payola for the prize. Hera offered to make him lord of all Asia and the richest man alive, Athene offered to make him victorious in all his battles and the wisest man in the world. But Paris was not an ambitious man. So when Aphrodite offered him Helen, as beautiful, as irresistible, as the goddess herself, there was really no contest. And when he judged Aphrodite the fairest, as everyone knows, the Trojan War was already as good as started. So was set in train that whole wretched episode which pitted not just Greek against Trojan but Olympian against Olympian, Athene and Hera literally coming to blows with Artemis and Aphrodite on the battlefield itself. (Ah, these females, hysterics all!)[25]

Yet what is this story really about? To look on a deity naked, to come as close as that to an archetypal energy, is impossible for any mortal who wishes to keep their senses, their understanding or even their life; we have examples enough of the blinding or de-struction of men who accidentally glimpse a goddess bathing, let alone tell her to take her clothes off, to attest to that. So can we really imagine that these three great goddesses would disrobe and reveal themselves? Even a decade after the event, some people found the whole story decidedly fishy. Hecabe, King Priam's widow and Paris's mother, bitterly accused Helen of simply inventing it to cover her own guilt.

> Why should they indulge such frivolity
> As travelling to Mount Ida for a beauty-match?
> What reason could the goddess Hera have for being
> So anxious about beauty? Did she want to get
> A husband of higher rank than Zeus? Or was Athene,
> Who begged her father for perpetual maidenhood,
> Disdaining love – now husband-hunting among the gods?
> To cloak your own guilt, you dress up the gods as fools;
> But only fools would listen to you. And Aphrodite,
> You say – what could be more absurd? – went with my son
> To Menelaus' palace! Could she not have brought
> You, and your town of Amyclae, from Peloponnese
> To Ilion, without stirring from her seat in heaven?
> No; Paris was an extremely handsome man – one look,
> And your appetite became your Aphrodite.[26]

Hecabe had her own stake in the matter, of course. But others since have echoed her feelings. 'The myth in its present form,' declared Jane Harrison, 'is sufficiently patriarchal to please the taste of Olympian Zeus himself, trivial and even vulgar enough to make material for an ancient satyr-play or modern *opéra-bouffe* . . . The kernel of the myth is, according to this version, a beauty-contest . . . a beauty-contest vulgar in itself and complicated by bribery still more vulgar.' She points out that in the great majority of vase-paintings of 'the judgement', Paris doesn't even figure: the scene is simply of Hermes leading the three goddesses. For her, these are representations of the three Gift-Bringers, bringing royalty and grandeur, wisdom and prowess in war, and love. 'They are their own gifts . . . And Hermes has led them long since, in varying forms, before the eyes of each and all of mankind. They might be conceived as undifferentiated, as mere Givers-of-Blessing in general. But it needs only a little reflection to see that gift often wars against gift, and that if one be chosen, others must be rejected.'[27]

The story of the judgement of Paris has woven its way into the development of what we know as Western consciousness. In setting a mere mortal in judgement over the goddesses, it shows the ancient feminine energy as depotentiated; in setting those goddesses at odds, it shows a growing fragmentation of a once-unified force. In this unfolding tale of feminine energy in the time of the sky-gods, Athene plays a central part. We have already seen how she ensures that the ancient feminine is honoured in the very seat of patriarchal power, how she works to safeguard the old wisdoms for humankind's use. Now we turn to not just the goddess's deeds but her very person, for an image of how she holds together the paradoxes of the ancient feminine in a consciousness which would increasingly fragment them, judging some good and to be used and even venerated, others bad and to be rejected and even destroyed.

CHAPTER 4

Remembering Medusa

When Perseus told King Polydectes that he would bring him any wedding present he cared to name, up to and including the Gorgon's head, it was perhaps a bit of bravura. For as everyone well knew, that last was pretty much of an impossible task. The stories were part of folklore. If you went on going west, people told each other, until you reached the very end of the world, and then went to the edge of the underworld, there was a cave so deep that no one had ever seen the bottom of it and lived to tell the tale. But nevertheless and somehow, everyone knew that at the bottom there was a terrible she-monster, with snakes for hair which hissed horribly if anyone approached her, and so woke her up from her usual deep sleep. And if she looked at you! Well, that was it. You were turned to stone, just like that. Those statues that the cave was full of, that seemed to catch so eloquently the very image of terror – well, no wonder they looked so lifelike, they'd been real animals, real men, until the monster looked at them!

So when young Perseus told Polydectes that he'd bring him the Gorgon's head, he maybe had a moment of panic when the King immediately took him up on the offer. But it was challenge and counter-challenge, the young man squaring up to the older, the older calling his bluff to jostle back into first place. The usual generational tensions were heightened here. The King had been forcing himself on Perseus's mother Danaë and the boy was determined to save her from this dreaded match: the present he so rashly offered was his way of trying to make Polydectes honour his pretended promise to marry Hippodameia instead. The situation was particularly tricky for Danaë and Perseus. Everyone knew how Polydectes had taken in mother and infant when they had been washed up on the shore of Seriphos, his island kingdom, and brought Perseus up in his own house with not too many questions asked about how they'd come to be afloat in the first place in that wooden casket, banished by Danaë's father after she'd given him that story about finding herself pregnant by Zeus himself in a shower of gold. So Polydectes had plenty to remind her about and the boy as well. But there's nothing like the attempt to force a debt of gratitude for turning gratitude itself to stone. Besides, it was time Perseus left home; he was of an age to set out to be a hero, old enough to seek the threshold to manhood, young enough to want still to be his mother's champion. And from the story of his birth and beginnings he knew that a very great hero was what he was destined to become.

As soon as he'd thrown out that challenge and promise to Polydectes, Perseus got the sort of confirmation of his destiny that heroes pray for. Athene had overheard the whole angry exchange and straightway appeared to promise her help. With that bright discrimination of focused energy working for him, it took Perseus no time at all to get organized. Athene herself gave him a brightly polished shield and taught him the tricky business of working from a mirror-image, so that he would never have to look directly at the Gorgon. She drew up a list of necessary supplies – helmet of invisibility, sickle for decapitation, winged sandals for getaway, magic wallet for containing the power of the head itself – checked out with Hades and Hermes that they would supply the first two and gave Perseus his itinerary. First he must go to the Graeae, those three fateful sisters from whom he'd learn where to find the Stygian Nymphs. From them in turn he would collect his gear. Then he would be ready to fly off and slay the Gorgon. And so he was and so he did. And that was just the beginning.

Some see the story of Perseus as the very type of the myth of the saviour-hero. The mysterious birth, from god and virgin human mother, the rejection by the earthly father(s), the early hazardous journey: the very familiarity of these beginnings alerts us to their archetypal nature. Perseus's unfolding adventures have the same numinous glow. In the typical cycle, the hero sets out on a life-journey that will take him through trial and ordeal into the very darkness of the underworld, from which he will return to claim a reward which may be his sacred marriage to the goddess-mother, his recognition by the father-creator, or his own divinization. If he is so blessed, he will return, bearing a gift that restores the world. The variations on this central theme are of course endless, but in the story of Perseus we can see a hero indeed. He set out on a dragon-quest which takes him, through the test of wresting their secret from the Graeae, to the limits of the known world and the underworld itself. He slays the dragon and releases new soaring energy: from the Gorgon's severed neck spring the hero Chrysaor and the great winged horse Pegasus. He returns to find his reward and establish his kingdom. First, for he has now crossed the threshold into manhood, he claims his bride, by rescuing Andromeda from the rock to which she is chained, threatened by her own monster. Then he returns to Seriphos to find his mother has taken refuge from Polydectes in a temple; he uses the power of the Gorgon's head to turn the King and his companions to stone (and you can still see the circle of boulders they became). Finally, after many further trials, he becomes the founder of Mycenae as well as ruler of Tiryns, the first head of the House of Perseus which would number the hero Heracles among its descendants.[1]

None of this would have been possible if Athene hadn't been at Perseus's side, from the moment she heard him roar that he was going to get the Gorgon's head, that very moment which was the start of his adventures. At first sight, this is just the sort of thing that would appeal to the goddess: a hero to urge to greater feats of daring and prowess, a dynasty to be founded – and not just any dynasty, after all, for this boy was her own half-brother, child also of her father Zeus. But the direct, straightforward view of things is not always, as Athene herself taught Perseus, the most revealing. The start of the story, for her, was when she overheard Perseus say he was going to get the head; the end of it, in one sense, is when he brought it back to her as she commanded. So the goddess has her own agenda. She wants the Gorgon's head for herself, and when she gets it, she will wear it on her breast for the rest of time.

What is going on here? They go back a long way, Athene and the Gorgon. That hideous, paralysing creature was once, they say, a most beautiful young princess by name Medusa, the only mortal sister of another trio. So lovely was she that she caught the fancy of Lord Poseidon, old Earth-Shaker himself. Did she take refuge in Athene's temple, praying to the virgin goddess to protect her virginity as did so many others? Did she go there willingly, even lead the way? Or was she simply so overwhelmed by that gigantic, earth-shaking, oceanic force that she neither knew nor cared where she was? For Athene, the answer mattered not at all. She was enraged and affronted by the desecration of her temple. Maybe she also had her own story with Poseidon, with whom, as we know, relations were always somewhat stormy; it is the fate of mortals sometimes to get caught up in archetypal energies over which they can have no control. For Medusa, however, the workings of the goddess's mind hardly mattered: all she knew was that she'd woken up that day young and lithe and able to run into the sunlight and that now she was chained in darkness, immobilized but for those snakes that weaved and hissed in place of her once-lovely hair. How long was it before she found she had suffered that other terrible change? Did she hear the approaching beasts, even a human step and just for a moment rejoice that her exile and isolation might be over? Did she writhe to greet them, only to be faced by that look of total, annihilating horror that was instantly frozen into immobility? To have been so beautiful, and to have to look for ever at the reflection of how terrible you have become in those unblinking eyes! Did there come a point when the only way to endure was to embrace that horror, even rejoice in that paralysing power?

This terrible power is the one Athene gave her; this is the power that the goddess reclaimed. And if we can dare to look more closely at Medusa, we can see that in its origins that power is very ancient. The princess, they say, was the granddaughter of Gaia, Mother Earth herself, who married her son Pontos, the deep ocean, and by him gave birth to both Phorcys, the wise old man of the sea and one Ceto, 'the monstrous'. They in turn bore the three Gorgon sisters. The very number gives the hint: they are a manifestation of the ancient moon goddess (as the Orphics knew when they called the moon 'the Gorgon's head'). The sisters' names honour their power – Stheino means 'strength', Euryale 'the leaping one', and Medusa herself is 'Mistress', 'Queen', 'Ruler' and 'the Cunning One'. Their appearance gives shape to their qualities: they have great brazen wings, staring owl-like eyes, serpents for hair and sometimes for girdles as well, tusks like boars and long lolling tongues.[2]

We have seen these attributes before. In her snaky, bird-winged nature, Medusa is a manifestation of the ancient Mistress of the Waters, ruler of life and regeneration. Her image re-echoes in a snake-haired, bird-faced goddess from the fifth millennium BC; we see it again in a Celtic goddess with bee-wings, serpent legs and staring, owl-like eyes. The Gorgon's lolling tongue reminds us of Kali's; but it is also to be found on an image from Rhodes of the sixth century BC, where, they say, farmers venerated it because it sought out the moisture that would make the crops grow.[3]

This then is the power which Athene reclaims – a power, as we know, to which she herself can trace her beginnings. Her association with Medusa may be closer yet. Some say this Mistress ruled the people of Lake Tritonis in Libya – the very place where the goddess was born and maybe grew up. Medusa was of an older generation than Athene: can we even imagine that the goddess was reared in the ways of her court? There is more to this story, too. It's said that this princess, this ruler, was a noble warrior (of course!) and that when Prince Perseus invaded she led her troops boldly into battle against him. He won the day, but was so struck

by the beauty of even her dead body that he took her head back
to Greece with him.[4]

So maybe we can look again at that tale of Perseus and the
Gorgon's head and see in it a story of what happens to the ancient
feminine power in the era of dawning heroic consciousness. In
images of Medusa, what we most often see is either that the power
is on the run – pursuing, pursued? – or unable to run at all,
because it is only a head, disembodied, carried by Athene. When
Medusa can stand straight and proud on her own bird feet, we can
still glimpse her original strength [Pls. 13, 14]. But the essential
image of the Perseus tale is the very opposite: of the once-great
energy in banishment at the ends of the earth, unconscious and
immobilized.

And immobilizing. Heroic consciousness, it seems, must reject
the paradoxical nature of the ancient energy. The goddess of life
and death, decay and regeneration, has become either all-helpful,
as Athene, or all-terrible. In that second aspect, there can be
nothing enlivening about her. Her very dwelling place, on the
edge of the underworld, is a place of terror now rather than of
regenerative resource. She has joined the many other manifestations of the ancient energy turned bad. She is like the stinking,
winged and vulture-legged Harpies, who bring nothing but
storms and pollution to everything they touch. She is like the
bird-clawed Sirens who lure men to their death. She comes from
the same country as the Lamia, whose very name means lechery
and gluttony and who with her gang of Empusae devours lovers
and young children. There is no end to the multiplicity of forms
that this malign feminine force can assume, no end to the dangers
it can bring: did not the Lamia herself transform and multiply into
a whole species of creatures that seduced with their apparent
beauty, while too late it became apparent that they were snakes
from the waist down?[5]

And yet it is with this terrible power that Athene wants to
connect. This is what she sent Perseus to fetch for her, this is what
she wants to wear next to her heart. Should we see this as a gesture

of contrition for the suffering she has inflicted – as some see her adoption of the name Pallas in honour of that accidentally murdered companion? Or should we rather wonder whether it was Fate herself who nudged Poseidon to notice Medusa and so set the whole business in train? Athene too is caught up in the great movement of consciousness, just as she is inescapably her father's daughter as well as her mother's. That said, we may also wonder what she is up to this time within these inevitable confines. Medusa was not the only Cunning One; as we know, Athene Polymetis, Many-Skilled, was renowned for all manner of ideas and devices, inventions and resources.

At first sight, again, there could hardly be a greater opposition than that between Athene and Medusa. The goddess, for a start, is inspiration to her heroes; her energizing strength is the very opposite of Medusa's paralysing inertia. Athene is bringer of consciousness; Medusa's natural state, unless those snakes alert her, is deepest unconsciousness. Athene has the focus of the lion-about-to-spring; Medusa's snakes writhe and turn, caught for ever without the possibility of using their energy for transformation. In the split between Athene and Medusa which comes, it seems, with heroic consciousness, there is both illustration and warning of what happens when intelligence and matter, mind and the material world, become estranged.

It is particularly Athene's genius, as we have seen, to keep the two in harmonious relation: it is by her gift that we see and understand the fitness of things. Once that connectedness is lost, all we can be left with is matter that is inert and intelligence that has lost its moorings. So the material world becomes the enemy of the soaring intellect; it holds it back, confines its ambitions, just as the inert and paralysing Medusa confined the glorious flight of the winged horse Pegasus. It is when Medusa is finally dead that that now-spiritualized instinct can escape. The denigration of the material sphere is complete; the way is open for all manner of despoliations of what was once the venerated body of Gaia herself and is now only dead matter. This is very far from the vital connection between mind and understanding, hand and material to be worked, which is Athene's *techne*, her supreme skill. She knew that what the Orphics said was true, that it would be all over with her if she lost her hands. It has taken us a long while to realize that our intellect-driven technologies, unrelated as they are to the reality of the matter to be worked, have created a state where it can sometimes seem perilously near to being all over with us.

In Athene's reclaiming of Medusa's head, in that reuniting of the aspects of the ancient power that have become separated into positive and negative poles, there is a constant reminder of the wiser way. It isn't easy, it seems, for heroic consciousness to hold to that image; we have only to look again at the tiny tippet round the neck of the Varvakion copy of the great statue of Athene as protectress of civic order to see how readily Medusa's head becomes an embarrassment. Yet some say that the goddess's great aegis itself is made from Medusa's skin, that far from wanting just a token of that ancient power, Athene wants to envelop herself in it, to assume it.[6] What she wants above all, it seems, is that we should somehow hold to that dual image, so that when we see one aspect of the power, we should also see the other. And not just see it, either, for the Medusa, once reclaimed, brings her own gifts.

It wasn't only Medusa's head – the essence of her power, as the ancients thought – that Perseus brought back to the goddess in that magic sack. There were also two phials of blood, one drawn from the veins of her right arm, one from the veins of her left. And just as Kali carries both destruction and abundance, terror and a release from its paralysing effects, so Medusa's blood brings both life and death. We have already seen how Athene wanted to give this gift to Asclepius and how Hades complained until Zeus thunderbolted the physician for his presumption. They say that the goddess reclaimed the phials, and tied them round the wrist of her foster-child Erichthonius, who in turn passed them on to his son, who passed them to his daughter Creusa who got caught up in one of those lost-heir-recognized-in-the nick-of-time dramas and tried to kill her own son Ion with Medusa's deathly drop.

Fortunately, Athene and the boy's secret father Apollo intervened to restore both family happiness and the good governance of Athens. (Interestingly, Medusa had her part in the drama too. It was the boy's baby shawl, decorated with a Gorgon's head and fringed with snakes, together with the ornament of golden snakes first given by Athene to Erichthonius and the imperishable olive-wreath from the goddess's own tree, that identified Ion indisputably as child of the royal house of Athens.) And what happened to Medusa's blood? The fatal drop destined for Ion got poured to the ground and killed only a dove. But for all we know, the two phials may have been passed on and passed on for ever, so that each human being can work for either life or death in their own way and for all time.[7]

Nor is even this the end of Medusa's gifts. Some hint that in that sack were also the letters of the alphabet – which may not be as far-fetched as it might appear (or rather, may be fetched from just as far as it takes to find the Gorgon). This fundamental expression of human consciousness, it seems, may come from a very ancient place. Some say that when Sarasvati first played the universe itself into manifestation on her *vina*, she also played the sounds of the Sanskrit alphabet; others say that that garland of skulls Kali so terrifyingly wears has the exact number and note of those very sounds.[8]

So the head of Medusa is a reminder of the seat of the original power that governs life, death and regeneration, and of the origin too of our ability to record what we know and pass it on to those who live after us. The head still carries the power of destruction, as Perseus found out to his advantage. Its terrible strength lives on, and not only from the breast of the goddess; Agamemnon is just one of many warriors to evoke it by carrying a grim Gorgon's head on the centre of his shield.[9] Yet the terrible face turned to the outside world also protects what is inside. Householders, for instance, would protect their property by putting a Gorgon's head on their outside wall; bakers would put one on their oven doors to deter would-be thieves. To those who honour her, Medusa may bring protection. We may even imagine that her power protected Athene herself, keeping inviolate from the new heroic consciousness something essential to the goddess's own nature.

Athene's insistent reuniting with the older feminine forces is not hers alone, and through other such tales we can discern a movement as urgent as the development of heroic consciousness itself. When that consciousness seeks to separate and discriminate and even to fragment the once unified round of life and death, decay and regeneration, then an equal and opposite force, it seems, seeks to bring together again what has been separated. In Athene's own day, it is the story of Persephone which carries the force of this movement; in her descent into Hades's dark kingdom, she does in person what Athene does only by proxy. Yet the two are not unrelated. It is not by accident, perhaps, that Athene was playing with the young girl when the earth opened up and she was snatched away on Hades's chariot with its great black horses. Athene too, as we have seen, had her connections with the underworld and the transition to death; in the story of the birth of Erichthonius, of that mysterious descent by the side of the Acropolis and the coming up with new life, there is an echo too of other mysteries of death and rebirth. Athene was known to carry the pomegranate whose seeds Persephone tasted at her dark husband's hand, making her forever Queen in his kingdom. Sometimes she is even greeted by Persephone's own titles.[10]

Persephone did not go willingly to claim her own underworld realm, snatched as she was from the bright light of day and her mother's care. The abduction of her daughter was no easier to bear for Demeter; the *Homeric Hymn*'s description of her terrible grief as she searches unceasingly for nine days, unable to eat or even to bathe herself, and her no less terrible anger when she discovers what has happened, must surely rank among the most poignant descriptions of the effects of loss ever recorded. But there is an inevitability in the tale. It was Gaia herself, after all, who set the scene by planting that fascinating flower to distract the girl's attention, just where the chariot of Hades would burst through to claim her. And in the final restoration of the seasons, Demeter's summer fruitfulness balanced by the annual death of vegetation while Persephone rules in her underworld kingdom, the old unity of the realms is once more restored.[11]

The insistent urge towards maintaining that connection is extraordinarily ancient. Some time in the third millennium BC, there was another descent, this time more willing. At this time and for all of 3,000 years, the goddess the Sumerians called Inanna (Ishtar to the Semites) unites two of the three great realms of creation as Queen of Heaven and Earth. She is 'clothed with the heavens and crowned with the stars'; the rainbow is her necklace and the zodiac her girdle. She is also known as 'The Green One', 'She of the Springing Verdure'; she pours forth grain from her womb; she is the virgin lunar goddess who both gives life as the waxing of the moon and withdraws it as its waning. She is the goddess of sexual love: her breastplate is called 'Come, man, come' and 'Plough my vulva, man of my heart,' she cries in one of her beautiful hymns to her lover Dumuzi, her 'honey-man'. And she is as passionate a warrior as she is a lover: 'all-devouring in . . . power . . . attacking like the attacking storm', with awesome face and angry heart, she hymns herself as falcon among gods who are sparrows, as a splendid wild cow among gods who can only trundle along.[12]

Yet even this great and glorious, joyfully confident goddess, who unites in her power and passion so many of the qualities that are later dispersed in small parcels among the different Greek deities, is subject to changing times. It is from her father, Enki, the god of wisdom, not of right, that she has the *me*, the holy tablets of the law, handed over in an extraordinary drinking bout. The two of them drink beer, and more beer and yet more beer together, each toast a challenge between them. With every toast Enki makes an offer ('The setting up of lamentations! The rejoicing of the heart! The giving of judgements! The making of decisions!'). With every toast, Inanna cries, 'I take them!' Fourteen times he offers, fourteen times she accepts. When he wakes up and realizes what he has done, Enki sends to recover his power; six times he tries, six times he fails and finally he gives up and concedes to his daughter (and her harder head?). But for how long? Even with this great power, Inanna's rule is not to remain secure. 'In the first days, in the very first days' she had planted her *huluppu* tree in her holy garden of Uruk and waited to receive her shining throne, her shining bed. She waited for five years and then for ten and she wept. Finally, her brother Gilgamesh cut down the tree and from it fashioned both throne and bed. But later, he turns against her and claims her authority, and she is dispossessed:

> The bird has its nesting place, but I – my young are dispersed
> The fish lies in calm waters, but I – my resting place exists not
> The dog kneels at the threshold, but I – I have no threshold.[13]

The feminine power has been depotentiated, exiled; the era of the sky-gods has truly arrived. Was it at this time that Inanna 'opened her ear', and so her understanding, to the third great realm, the underworld? The hymn that tells of her descent into this hitherto unknown kingdom is dated at about 1750 BC, which makes it relatively late, as these mind-stretching timescales go, but the recording may be of a much older tale. What is sure is that at some time this great goddess found that she needed, just as so much later did Persephone and Athene herself, to unite with the dark wisdom of the third, underworld realm.

It was a wisdom that until now Inanna had rejected. Even in those first days, those very first days, she had wept to share her tree with 'a serpent who could not be charmed' and 'the dark maid Lilith', both of whom had moved in uninvited and would not be budged. Even in those very first days, then, there was a fragmentation in the ancient feminine power, and its underworld aspect was a cause of grief to the Queen of Heaven. Time was, it seems, when Inanna herself was also known as Nin-ninna, 'Divine Lady Owl'. But already here that dark side is carried by Lilith, who 'smashed her home and fled to the wild, uninhabited places' when Gilgamesh cut down the tree and killed the serpent.[14]

Yet at some point Inanna must make contact with that dark

force, make that terrible descent to the underworld. Why has she come? she is asked at the threshold. 'Because . . . of my older sister, Erishkigal,' she replies. And though she adds that she has come, and properly, to the funeral of her sister's husband, we feel that that first, direct reply is the one which really matters: Inanna knows she has something to learn from her elder sister, from a power that is more ancient than her own. The learning is a terrible ordeal. One by one she must give up the trappings of her authority, until she is stripped naked. Each time she asks why; each time she is told that the ways of the underworld are perfect and may not be questioned. Finally naked, stripped to her own truth, she is judged by her terrible sister who, like the Gorgon herself, fixes her with death-dealing eyes. She is hung like a piece of meat from a hook on the wall. For three days and three nights, Inanna hangs there, rotting. Her faithful servant desperately asks the sky-gods to rescue her; two refuse in identical fashion:

> My daughter craved the Great Above
> Inanna craved the Great Below.
> She who receives the *me* of the underworld does not return
> She who goes to the Dark City stays there.

The sky-gods cannot tolerate that Inanna should succeed in uniting the realms, that she should hold the *me* of both the Great Above and the Great Below. Finally, however, Father Enki is approached and immediately sets out to rescue his favourite daughter, his hard-headed drinking companion. From the dirt under his fingernails he produces two little creatures who sneak into the underworld like flies. They find Erishkigal moaning and sighing like a woman about to give birth. She moans for her inside, she moans for her outside, for her belly, for her liver, for her heart – and each time she moans these little creatures, instructed by Father Enki, faithfully moan with her. It is in a sense a horrible scene: perhaps no one before has ever entered into Erishkigal's suffering enough to empathize with it, and here when it looks like empathy it is only a sky-god's trick. But it achieves what it sets out to do.

Erishkigal offers to reward the little creatures for their under-standing and when they say, as instructed by Enki, that all they want is that bit of rotten meat hanging on the wall, she gives it to them.[15]

So Inanna returns to the Great Above. Yet there is a price: no one can return from the underworld without leaving someone in their place. When the goddess sees how her consort Dumuzi has been enjoying himself during her absence, sitting in his shining garments on his magnificent throne, enjoying her *me*, when he doesn't so much as stand up when she arrives, then her own 'eye of death' fixes on him. In Dumuzi's journey into the underworld, in the eventual agreement that he should spend half the year with Erishkigal and half with Inanna, there is a resolution more com-plete than that achieved in the Persephone cycle. Here, masculine is united with both aspects of the ancient feminine power. By the time that other descent is made, the sky-gods can avoid relating to the underworld aspects of the feminine altogether – unless it is to send their heroes to destroy them.

And yet Athene, favoured daughter of Zeus, still and insistently wears Medusa's head next to her heart as sign and reminder of another, more ancient way. Just what has become of the goddess's attempt to hold to her maternal heritage in the era of the sky-gods is what the rest of this tale tries to trace.

CHAPTER 5

The Mind of Minerva

When Aeneas, son of the goddess Aphrodite and King Anchises of Dardanus, escaped from the ruins of Troy, he took with him, they say, not just his crippled father but also, and most importantly, the image of the Palladium from the city's great temple to Athene. The old man died before his son could found his kingdom. But the Palladium made it to Italy and later to Rome itself, where it became known as 'the luck of the city', faithfully guarded by the college of Vestal virgins.[1]

So in one of those reverses of the heavens so bewildering to earthly perspectives, Athene turns her wrath from the Trojans to support their descendants. How can you ever know where you are with these deities? No wonder the rumour persisted that it wasn't Aeneas at all who brought the Palladium to Italy, but the goddess's greatest favourite, Odysseus. At least that would have been consistent with Athene's known feelings, and if it had been Odysseus who carried the sacred stone, then no wonder Rome prospered! Some say the honours should be equal, that it was he together with Aeneas who brought Rome's luck. A bit of a politician's tale, perhaps, that one: ancient alliances, two great peoples, hands across water, shared values, working together for good of Europe, that sort of thing. (But then maybe nothing should surprise us about Odysseus.)

In any event, it seems that the goddess blessed the Italian project. And her presence later hovers over the founding of Rome itself. When Remus and Romulus took up their rivalrous stances

– he on the Aventine Hill, he on the Palatine – and asked for a sign from the gods, what they got was a vision of vultures. First six for Remus, then twelve for Romulus; Remus claimed precedence through priority, but even then more meant better. The wings of the vulture still beat over such matters countless generations later. When young Octavian seized the consulship in 43 BC, he asserted that he too, as heir to the divine Caesar and so to Romulus himself, had seen the twelve vultures in the sky; thus Octavian became Augustus.[2]

So the goddess in one of her bird epiphanies hovers over Rome. But such echoes of her ancient beginnings have been getting fainter for a long while now. Perhaps her essence was brought from Troy in the mysterious image of the Palladium. But by the time she arrived in Rome and for long before, she was already Minerva. The very name denotes a shift in what humans perceived of this archetypal force. Athene may, as we have seen, be a version of Ht Nt, of House of Neith, or it may mean simply *A Thea* – the Goddess. Minerva derives from *mens*, mind: already one aspect of that rich and complex energy that was imaged as Athene has become emphasized at the expense of others.

Yet Minerva too has her ancient powers. They say the name belonged first to Etruscan Menrva, Menrfa, Meneruva, Menarva, who in some of her manifestations appears as a winged goddess carrying an owl. In others, like Athene herself, she is a proud and beautiful warrior, goddess of the thunderbolt [Pl. 10]. Somehow, the two images met. (For the historically minded, some say that this was in 241 BC and at the town of Falerii, from where the Romans carried the image of Menrfa home.)[3] Sparks would fly, you'd have thought, at such a meeting. What an alliance that could be! So whatever happened to that fierce and focused energy?

By the time Aeneas, half-mortal, half-divine, sets out from the ruins of Troy on his own odyssey, his own heroic quest to wrest the treasure from the underworld and found his line and his kingdom, Minerva has already taken something of a back seat. The great alliance between Athene and Hera against the Trojans which is hymned in the *Iliad* has not surprisingly been selected out of the memory of the Trojan who seeks now to carry Minerva's aid to Italy, and out of the *Aeneid* itself. The antagonism to Troy is now all Hera's: it is she, now Juno, who is 'perpetually nursing her heart's deep wound', her corrosive rancour against Aeneas – for the betrayal of her beloved Carthage which is to come as well as for the 'judgement' by that other Trojan, Paris, which is past. The first time we hear of Minerva in the *Aeneid* is through Juno's envy: how can the Fates forbid her to destroy the Trojan travellers, how can she be so dishonoured, when Minerva is allowed to wreak whatever revenge she wants and borrow Jupiter's thunderbolts to do it with? The second time we hear of Minerva is when Aeneas is recounting the tale of the wooden horse whose Greek warrior contents spilled out to destroy his city, and acknowledges the goddess's divine inspiration for this treacherous gift.

So the first references to Minerva are to her power, her special place in the pantheon as the father's favoured daughter, and to her technical skill. These are familiar attributes of the goddess. But as the story unfolds, we hear little of either: the real protagonists are the ever-wrathful Juno and Venus, Aeneas's mother, the irresistibly attractive numinosity of her incarnation as Aphrodite now domesticated into clucking concern for a favourite son. The references to Minerva are tangential. She is the grudging goddess of the housewife 'whose burden it is to endure life in dependence on her distaff and Minerva's slight aid'. The woman warrior Camilla can claim neither inspiration nor protection from the goddess. Indeed, her very nature explicitly estranges her from Minerva's own energy: 'She was a warrior; her girl's hands had never been trained to Minerva's distaff and her baskets of wool.'

There are some echoes of the goddess's other aspect. The Cyclopes Thunderer, Lightener and Fire-Anvil still work the iron in their vast workshop under the roar of Mount Etna to hammer her out a horror-inspiring aegis; they still vie with each other to polish the sparkle on its golden serpent-scales, twist the snakes into shape on either side, place the Gorgon's head, its eyes yet rolling, at just the right angle. But this is for Pallas, the fierce aspect of the goddess's energy, 'when her serenity is disturbed', and it is hard to see much use for it in these *Aeneid* days. In fact, it's not even a priority job. When word comes down from Vulcan — once Athene's companion Hephaestus — that there's a rush order on for arms for Venus's lad, work on the aegis stops immediately, along with the polishing of a thunderbolt and the making of one of those chariots with flying wheels which Mars uses to inflame both warriors and whole cities. In those vivid scenes of his people's future glory which decorate Aeneas's new shield, there's a hint too of Minerva's place in the order to come. She is certainly there when the monstrous gods of Egypt attack the Romans on behalf of Antony and (the shame of it!) his Egyptian wife. But, like Neptune and Venus, she is more attacked than attacking. It is Mars who rages in the midst of battle, while from the sky the scowling Furies let loose their savagery, Strife strides joyfully in her torn robe and Bellona follows with her blood-stained scourge. And it is Apollo who ensures the victory of Augustus.[4]

So when it comes to the battles which were once Athene's joy, Minerva is at best an onlooker, even under attack. In the *Aeneid*, the ancient feminine force that used to hold together the paradoxical energies of peace and war has become further divided. When Hera wanted to stir up trouble, she either called up that fiery chariot and zoomed into the fray with her ally Athene or worked out a plot to seduce Zeus's attention to her own considerable charms and away from the action that she'd planned. When Juno wants to make things tough for Aeneas, she does it by proxy. She sends for Allecto the Fury, creatrix of grief, daughter of the Dark, of Pluto himself, 'who dearly loves war's horrors, outbursting wrath, treachery and recriminations with all their horrors'.

With those countless black serpents sprouting from her head and her great wings whirring with the hiss of snakes, we can recognize Allecto's image straight away. But now that ancient energy imaged as snake and bird has become nothing but negative, creatrix of 'a thousand types of mischief, a thousand artful ways of doing harm'; the power that Athene transformed from Furies to Kindly Ones, protectresses of Athens, has now become nothing but Fury once more. Allecto drives Queen Amata mad by sending a great poisoned snake to wrap her in its coils. She incites the women to the madness of a Bacchic orgy, forsaking their duties for 'the wilderness where only the beasts had their homes': the feminine turned bad and dangerous upsets the orderly ways that the 'good woman' must observe. Images of this powerful and destructive feminine force recur through the *Aeneid*. At the entrance to the underworld, Aeneas must endure the sight of 'Strife the insane with a bloody ribbon binding her snaky hair' and Harpies and Gorgons as well. When poor deserted Dido wanders crazed with grief, her own death is presaged in the lamentations of the lonely owl on the rooftop, 'drawing out her notes into a long wail'. In such images the snakes and owls which were the ancient forms of the goddess now bring nothing but suffering.[5]

It is to Minerva's care that the peaceful aspects of that once paradoxical energy now fall. When Aeneas comes within sight of founding his kingdom, he sends his hundred ambassadors into negotiation armed with her olive branch.[6] The seal of her patronage is set on Rome itself by the dedication of the great temple on the Capitol to the trinity of Jupiter, Juno and Minerva in, so they say, the very first year of the republic. She is a truly useful goddess – protectress of commerce and industry, artisans, doctors and schoolteachers, who were paid their annual stipend on the day of her festival. In these concerns, we can see how she is identified with Athene the workwoman and healer. In other aspects, although Rome had its own Great Mother in Cybele, brought on her lion-drawn chariot from Asia Minor, she carries at least a reminder of the ancient agricultural powers. She is honoured together with Mars, originally himself a local agricultural deity, and their five-day festival of Quinquatrus falls during the spring equinoxes.[7]

But both are far more deities of the state than they are of the natural order. Mars, after all, was the father of Rome's own founding father, Romulus himself. And Rome had a far more potent image of fertility than the essentially civic Minerva. There is all the energy of the ancient Lady Snake in Atargatis as she emerges from the serpent's very maw [Pl. 15]. Some say this Dea Syria was once Inanna herself. But she finally went the way of so many of the ancient images of the goddess and her energy was turned bad: she became the type of the mermaid, that dangerously sexual creature, half woman half fish, which lures sailors to their deaths.[8] We have to look to contemporary Hindu images to see again this aspect of the goddess's coiled power emerging in honour just as it did in Atargatis 2,000 years ago [Pl. 16].

Stately Minerva has none of this energic charge. Never-wed though she is, she carries all the *gravitas* of the matron; there is nothing fishy at all in her steadfast gaze. Nor, as we've seen, is she much of a battler, despite her inheritance from both Athene and Etruscan Menrfa. When Mars becomes warrior, he goes into battle neither with her nor even against her, as Ares and Athene used to engage. His companion is Bellona, whether as wife, sister or daughter, and hers is a fierce energy indeed. They say she came from Cappadocia, where she was known as Ma, brought by soldiers in the train of Great Mother Cybele herself. Like Cybele's and like Atargatis's too, her cult is orgiastic and ecstatic, bringing its adherents to self-flagellation and, in the rites of Cybele at least, to self-castration. Bellona's *bellonarii* would brandish the double-axe, ancient accoutrement of the goddess, as they danced and pranced in the streets to the whirl of that wild music, and would wound themselves until they streamed with blood. So strange were the ways of these foreign goddesses, so awesome their demands, that it was only under the Empire that they were incorporated into the Roman state religion. Until then, no Roman was allowed to serve in their temples or take part in their rites at all. Instead, it seems, the citizens simply stood and watched those wild demonstrations that took place under police supervision, separated and protected from such fierce energy by that *cordon sanitaire*, yet knowing too that it must be honoured. Later, Bellona becomes more of a Roman and importantly so: her priests are now gladiators and when Rome goes to war it is the 'war column' in front of her temple that is struck to signal it.[9]

Minerva has the warrior's gear, she carries helmet and spear and shield. But somehow it isn't convincing as any more than a bit of panoply proper to the patron of a soldierly state; you don't expect her actually to use it any more than you expect the Queen of England to bivouac on the battleground just because she is Colonel-in-Chief of all those regiments. When Athene invented the flute, she chucked it away immediately when Hera and Aphrodite laughed at her puffing cheeks as she tried to play it. She invented the brazen war trumpet instead and that echoed the very tone of her voice. Minerva has a special care for flute-players; every year they hold a concert to honour this most civilized of goddesses.

Minerva wasn't simply one of the main patrons of Rome. She also *was* Rome, a goddess of place in the ancient tradition of the goddess of the earth herself, just as Athene in that sense was Athens. It is in the guise of Roma that Minerva would appear on coins, emblem of the very energy of the state and of the way its power could be spread and used throughout so much of the known world. Athene had long travelled in this way too. Her image, with her owl on the reverse, had first appeared on Athenian coinage in the sixth century BC, when the coins were known as *korai* or 'maidens', an ancient title of the goddess herself. The great Alexander put her head on the gold coinage of his empire and his successors in those far-flung places did the same. So Athene's image and qualities informed and energized the transactions of Macedonia, Thrace, Pergamum, Cappadocia, Syria, Egypt, Syracuse and the New India.[10]

Now it was Rome's turn. When Zeus had brought his own conquests to the lands of the goddess, as we've seen, he enforced the rule of Olympus by an explosively energetic policy of marriage and propagation, his seed spilling, it sometimes seemed, into every grove, cave and stream of Greece. For the Romans, it was similarities to be annexed rather than othernesses to be overcome that were the basis of conquest. When Julius Caesar arrived among the Gauls, he found that he could tick off a satisfyingly neat list of correspondences: 'Among the gods they most worship Mercury . . . After him they set Apollo, Mars, Jupiter and Minerva. Of these deities they have almost the same idea as all other nations: Apollo drives away diseases, Minerva supplies the first principles of arts and crafts, Jupiter holds the empire of heaven, Mars controls wars.'[11]

So Minerva came to the Gallic kingdoms. In the one the Romans called Britannia, she met with another great goddess of the civilizing arts, Brigid of Ireland, patroness of poetry and knowledge itself, her very name meaning 'power' and 'renown'. In Northumberland, this energy was known as Brigantia; a Romano-British image of her shows her with Minerva's shield, spear and Gorgon's head.[12] Elsewhere in the province, the identification of the ancient local energy with the Roman perception of it went further yet. Just as Athene *was* Athens and Minerva herself was Rome, so Minerva became also Britannia, goddess of the land. And that is how we got the image of Britannia that we still know so many centuries later. If she took her lion from Mother Cybele, her helmet, shield, spear and olive branch are all Minerva's.

The image was carried through the land. Among the coins recovered from the Sacred Spring at Minerva's major sanctuary in Britain, for instance, is a bronze one of the emperor Hadrian, from the second century AD, showing Britannia seated, just as she was to be on British coinage in so many other centuries. That coin, of course, was only one of cascades thrown into those awesomely steaming, endlessly flowing, opaquely greenish waters. By this time Aquae Calidae – the Hot Waters – was already the kind of place to which people were drawn from far as well as near. Roman soldiers who had been stationed there returned in their retirement. Others came to take a cure in those famously healing waters from the

European mainland as well as different parts of Britannia. And so, in an unbroken tradition, have people come to bathe ever since at what became Bath.

As time went on, Aquae Calidae became more widely known as Aquae Sulis – the Waters of Sulis – thus honouring their presiding deity. Sulis, they say, was above all a goddess of healing, uniting the power of those deep and mysteriously appearing underground waters with the energy of the sun in that work. Already by the time the Romans arrived at her sanctuary, the place was well known. Back in the ninth century BC, Bladud had returned from his studies in Athens, together with four philosophers, to succeed his father Ludhudibras as ninth King of the Britons. Some say that it is thanks to his magical powers that the hot water first sprang forth from the ground. Certainly he brought quite some skills back from Greece, founding a university at what is now Stamford in Lincolnshire. (Later he overreached himself. He learned to fly on feathered wings, but crashlanded on the temple of Apollo at New Troy and died, leaving the succession to his son Lear.) Others say it was not like this at all, that Bladud contracted leprosy when he was in Athens and on his return to Britain was locked up, eventually escaping to get employment as a swineherd. Being of an observant mind, he noticed that his pigs liked to wallow in the warm mud of a particular patch, especially in cold weather; he noticed furthermore that they were free of the scurfs and scabs that were so common in those days among both humans and beasts. Figuring that what worked for pigs might also work for humans, he too bathed in the mud, and his leprosy was cured. So he returned to court to reclaim his kingdom and founded the baths of Sulis at Caer Badum from that miraculous mud, so that his people too might benefit from the goddess's curative genius.[13]

Either way, by the time the Romans brought Minerva to the site of those springs, the cult of Sulis was already important enough for the incomers to respect its precedence: the sanctuary became known as that of Sulis Minerva, the goddess's name always in that order. And the site became vastly more important yet.

Works extended from the enclosing of the main spring and building of baths and temple in about 60–70 AD to the massive rebuilding of the temple and construction of a vaulted chamber to cover the entire bathing establishment more than 200 years later. The sheer scale of even the original work suggests that this was an official project, undertaken perhaps to counter the lasting bitterness left in the wake of the Romans' brutal suppression of Queen Boudicca's rebellion in the year 60.[14]

This would certainly be consistent with Minerva's own patronage of the gentler, civilizing arts. As we know, she was not herself a fighter; that she should support the power of the state which honoured her even against a woman and a warrior has its own irony but is just the kind of behaviour that we would expect from this steadfast deity. Yet the new sanctuary, as we know too, also enclosed and contained energies drawn from a wider and deeper source than Minerva's mind. Sulis herself, it seems, was worshipped in triple form, and so was epiphany of the completed power of the ancient goddess. The fire that Bladud lit in the new sanctuary was never extinguished, burning as perpetually as Brigid's own. And Bladud's pigs lead us to the ancient feminine powers of fertility as well as knowledge and healing, for in his day there was nothing loathsome, unclean or gross about this animal of the goddess herself. Just as Demeter and Persephone in Greece were not in the least dishonoured by the sacrifices of pigs in their own rites of fertility's renewal, so Bladud's occupation as a swineherd would be more likely to indicate to the Celtic mind his service to the goddess and closeness to the powers that governed prophecy, abundance and good fortune than disgrace in the eyes of men. Even in the early Christian times, it was not unknown for pigs to lead their masters to the site for a new monastery – as happened, for instance, to St Dyfrig or Dubricius near Hereford. Some say that he was Merlin himself, the very representative of the Celtic spirit; certainly Merlin had a little pig as one of his familiar beasts, lively and lustful, as any manifestation of the ancient feminine power must be.[15]

That power, as we already know, has a paradoxical quality which is very far from Minerva's own steadfast consistency. The beneficial energies of the sanctuary of Sulis Minerva are known to this day, and in invoking them we can imagine a healing that is not simply to do with cure of physical ills. In both Celtic and Roman times, the sanctuary seemed to specialize particularly in problems of sight. This links it with many other Celtic healing waters. It has led some to evoke Sulis as the 'eye goddess', a title whose resonances go back as far as a temple in Eastern Syria dating from about 3000 BC that honours this special aspect of Inanna–Ishtar. With the eye's power to ward off evil as well as to deal death, we are back in the realm of the ancient goddess as bringer of both life and destruction. We are also in the realm of Athene's particular healing, which brings to that fundamental process the 'seeing' that means 'understanding'.[16]

So it should come as no surprise, perhaps, that among the many artefacts and offerings dredged up from Sulis Minerva's awesome waters there are none of the representations we might expect of limbs and other body parts for whose healing the goddess's power is sought. Instead there are curses – over 100 of them, written on lead and carefully folded so that none of their venomous energy can escape. There is nothing healing in these prayers to the goddess. What they seek from her is that she turns her wrath on to the one who has wronged the supplicant, taking back the very gifts for which she is most revered: mind, sight and even lifesblood itself. There is nothing haphazard about the prayers either. They were written to a formula that seems to have held good for 200 years or more: 'May the goddess make he who [did the deed] whether he be male or female, boy or girl, freedman or slave, pagan or Christian [suffer the retribution].' And they ended with the helpful addition of a list of suspects – on whom the effect of fearing they were named can be imagined.[17]

Thus Sulis Minerva was evoked as bringer of both healing and destruction in the context of a justice greater than humans could manage for themselves. In that work she was unquestionably the most powerful deity of that site: the altar before her temple, carved with images of Jupiter and Hercules, Apollo and Bacchus, Mercury and his Celtic spouse Rosmerta, bears witness to both their support and her supremacy. And the images we have from the temple itself bring their own story of a union of energies that is powerful indeed.

In the very centre of the temple pediment, so looming over every worshipper as they approached the lifesize bronze image of Minerva herself, is a great face carved on a roundel which probably represents a shield, supported by a winged victory on either side, each standing on a globe. This is the 'Gorgon's head' [Pl. 18]. Certainly the position is familiar. Athene wore the Gorgon's head on her aegis, as her heroes wore it on their shields and buildings on their walls, to both protect what was inside and project a powerful force – and this is just what you might expect from a temple pediment. Certainly too this image has, so craftily integrated into its flaming aureole of hair that at first you hardly discern them, Medusa's wings and snakes as well. The association with Minerva is plain for all to see: below the victories and next to the globes are two helmets, both recognizably her own, the plume on the left one denoting her military aspect, the owl on the right denoting, by now, her 'wisdom'.

Yet this is a Gorgon's head like none we have seen before, unquestionably Celtic and, as unquestionably, radiantly masculine with its lavishly flowing moustaches. Are we looking at the union of Medusa and Oceanus, the sea-god supported by those Tritons, half men, half fish, who sit at either side of the pediment, themselves the sons of Poseidon? Is it the union of Medusa as the power of the spring and the god of the river that flows from it? Perhaps the figure, with its flaming locks, represents the energy of the sun, perhaps it unites the energy that beams down on the earth and the energy of the waters that flow below it. The images on the pediments on either side of the altar of Sulis Minerva herself echo and reinforce these images of union: Luna rides her chariot across the dark night sky, Sol commands the heat of the springs, and the power of the goddess is between them to hold them both.[18]

Feminine and masculine, moon and sun, sun and water, sky god and earth goddess and Celt and Roman too: the more you look, the more the imagination is brought to unions of the energies, whether in nature's own forces or on the plane of human politics. And Sulis Minerva, who herself unites different aspects of the goddess's power, is both the catalyst and the force that holds together. In those multiple images of union we can glimpse a glorious moment of balance between masculine and feminine powers. The ancient energy that was once encompassed entirely by the goddess has been clearly differentiated, but without, it seems, either a striving for dominance or a denigration of any of the energic parts.

Could that state of affairs possibly last?

Towards the beginning of the fourth century, the sanctuary of Sulis Minerva was despoiled, presumably by Christians. There was a brief revival. As a dedicatory inscription records: 'This holy spot, wrecked by insolent hands and cleansed afresh, Gaius Severius Emeritus, centurion in charge of the region has restored to the Virtue and Deity of the Emperor.' But soon the province of Britannia fell apart into warring factions. After the Romans left in 410, baths, temple and all gradually collapsed and silted up until they were reclaimed by that mud which had delighted Bladud's pigs so very long ago. By the time sacred buildings once more appeared in the area, they were dedicated to a very different order. In 675, King Osric of the Hwicce granted estates to the Abbess Berta to endow a convent of the Holy Virgins at Bath; about 100 years later, land was made over to brothers of the monastic church of St Peter. By the time Edgar was crowned King of England here at the end of the tenth century, the church at Bath was said to be of 'wondrous workmanship'. When the Norman monastery replaced it and the new King's Bath was created, the site officially re-established its earlier purpose.[19]

As for the lifesize statue of Minerva herself, it was entirely lost for something like 1,400 years. Then one day early in the eighteenth century, workmen digging a sewer turned up her gilded bronze head in the south-west corner of the baths. As the jagged edges round the neck bore witness, the head had been violently hacked from its body. Some say that this had been done to destroy the very essence of the goddess's power, others that that same essence had been preserved by careful burying, to protect it from those who would destroy it. Either way, we are left with an image of Minerva which has become all head [Pl. 17]. Her very name derives from *mens*, from mind – and now we see her as nothing but that. The image of the goddess which once stood between and held together the energies of masculine and feminine, above and below, is now all head-stuff, nothing but an idea. That one jagged severance of mind from body, idea from matter, above from below, can stand symbol for very many others at this time, in other minds and other places. In the same way, that one burying of the essence of Minerva's inherited energy for so many hundreds of years is also countless others. As we shall see, the effect on perceptions of feminine power and of its place in the scheme of things could hardly have been more profound.

CHAPTER 6

Fallen Angels and the Daughters of Men

How on earth was Clement of Alexandria to impress upon the inhabitants of his own Greek homeland the utter folly and impiety of their continued worship of the ancient gods? Even the birds of the air knew better than to revere their images! 'Swallows also and most other birds settle on these very statues and defile them, paying no heed to Olympian Zeus or Epidaurian Asclepius, no, nor yet to Athene Polias or Egyptian Serapis; and even their ex-ample does not bring home to you how destitute of feeling these statues are!' At other times and in other places, those swallows might have been recognized as an epiphany of Athene herself, for as we know, it was as swallow that this shape-shifting goddess once perched on the beam of Odysseus's great hall to oversee his battle with the suitors. But that was all long ago and far away, and Clem-ent, writing in the second century, had a new faith to expound with his impassioned urgings.[1]

Once more, just as when Athene herself had sprung fully armed from the head of Zeus, the universe had halted in its tracks to mark a miraculous birth. 'Now I Joseph was walking, and I walked not,' the author of the second-century *Book of James* or *Protevange-lum* tells us in an extraordinarily vivid evocation of that world-changing moment.

And I looked up to the air and saw the air in amazement. And I looked up unto the pole of the heaven and saw it standing still, and the fowls of the heaven without motion. And I looked upon the earth and saw a dish set, and workmen lying by it, and their hands were in the dish, and they that were chewing chewed not, and they that were lifting the food lifted it not, and they that put it to their mouth put it not thereto, but the faces of all of them were looking upward. And behold there were sheep being driven, and they went not forward but stood still; and the shepherd lifted his hand to smite them with his staff and his hand remained up. And I looked upon the stream of the river and saw the mouths of the kids upon the water and they drank not. And of a sudden all things moved onward in their course.[2]

As human faith and understanding moved onward in their own course, they found their accommodations with the ancient deities. The very sounds of their names could be incorporated. Inanna, Anath, gave the 'an' which generally signifies nourishment and abundance to St Anne, mother of the Virgin and so grandmother of Jesus himself; Nanna, that grandmotherly title, was also the Greek word for aunt, an epithet for Cybele; the vulgar Latin 'nonna', or old woman, gave those women who devoted their lives to Christ their title of 'nun'. The ancient goddesses could become Christians too. So Celtic Brigid became St Brigit of Ireland, midwife to the Virgin Mary, foster-mother to Christ, even, some believed, Mary herself returned to earth. St Brigit's feast day, 1 February, the day that the serpents came forth from their holes, had also been Celtic Imbolc, the celebration of new life as the ewes started their lactation; the very next day became Candlemas, the day of Mary's purification after her own bringing forth of the life that promised renewal to the world itself, the birth of her son.[3]

In these transformations, Athene too had her part. We glimpse her in the flickering light of the magical beliefs that lasted well into the first centuries of the Christian era (and well beyond there, too), and in these the virgin goddess could undergo some startling changes of character. Simon the Magician, for example, claimed that his companion Helen, rescued from a brothel in Tyre, was the reincarnation of many, including the Mother of All, Helen of Troy and Athene herself; his followers displayed images of Zeus and

Athene to represent Simon and Helen. A love charm, to be said seven times to the cup which is to be offered to the object of desire, gives another tantalizing example of Athene's powers. 'You are wine; you are not wine but the head of Athene,' it begins. 'You are wine; you are not wine but the entrails of Osiris, the entrails of Iao Pakerbeth, Eternal Sun . . .'[4]

Not all the new appearances of the goddess were as obscure as that, although the compelling inner need to establish a continuity of belief, as well as more obvious political considerations, could lead to some strange enough twists and turns. Athene was widely identified, for instance, with St Katherine of Alexandria, that city which bubbled as the melting pot of old and new. Katherine, broken on the wheel and finally beheaded for her refusal to marry the Emperor because she was dedicated as a bride of Christ, understandably became patroness of virgins through a virginity that was as defining to her essence as Athene's own. Her patronage of philosophers – and hence all students, clergy and apologists – she owes to her successful rebuttal of the arguments of the fifty sent to convince her of the errors of Christianity; her care for nurses stems from the miraculous fact that milk rather than blood flowed from her severed head; her concern for all who work with the wheel – hence potters, wheelwrights and especially spinners or spinsters – entirely befits one who, although broken on the wheel herself, yet broke the wheel of what appeared to be her fate. The correspondences with Athene's own special gifts and cares can become clear to all who would seek them, and so bring to St Katherine herself a heritage that can only strengthen her power.[5]

In such transformations, Athene could draw on ancient alliances for company. In the distant and unimaginable future of the fourteenth century, St Katherine was to become one of the Fourteen Holy Helpers who enjoyed a collective cult in the Rhineland, united especially by the efficacy of their intercession against various diseases. Another of the fourteen was St George, soldier, martyr and one day to become patron of England. And he had once been Perseus, with whom Athene had had such important dealings in the matter of Medusa. Now as St George he had another monster to slay, another king's daughter to rescue from being sacrificed to its insatiable appetite – just as in his ancient incarnation as Perseus he had rescued Andromeda from being devoured by the sea monster to save *her* parents' kingdom. The later evocation of St George as patron of military chivalry is of a piece with Perseus's own heroic founding of kingdom and dynasty and with Athene's concerns of state as well. The alliance has proved a lasting one: to this day the little chapel on the top of Lycabettus, that hill in Athens the goddess let fall when she heard of the betrayal of her trust by the daughters of Cecrops, is dedicated to St George. They go back a long way, too, he and the goddess: very many centuries earlier, the Athenian temple of the goddess's closest companion Hephaestus had been transformed in its turn into a church of St George. Soaring over that new dedication, the Parthenon itself was consecrated in the sixth century to the Virgin as Mother of God, and became the Metropolitan Church of Athens. From reverence for the daughter of the father-god to reverence for the mother of god-the-father's son: a certain process might seem to have been completed.[6]

Of the wealth of relationship between Athene and the Blessed Virgin Mary, more later. Back in the second century, all these correspondences and transformations were maybe the vaguest of intimations, but hardly more formed than that. To those early fathers, the struggle was to establish a church against a galaxy of different deities and across a distance that stretched from Lyons in the west to Dura Europo, overlooking the Euphrates, in the east. To travel from one to the other would have taken all of eighty days.[7] And who can guess at the number of versions of the new and precious truth the traveller might meet along the way?

Clement himself had travelled in search of his truth. Certainly Greek and perhaps Athenian, he ended up in Alexandria where he became a presbyter of the church and taught for more than twenty years. He was prodigiously well-read, citing in his different writings no fewer than 300 authors whose works have not survived, let alone the major ones we still know. He admired the great philosophers as preparing the way for Christ and knew so much about the mystery cults that it's probable he had been initiated into at least some of them. So he knew whereof he spoke when in his first book he made his passionate *Exhortation to the Greeks* to give up the follies of their religion.

Who were these gods the people still revered? Their very number was proof of their unreality. Take all those different Apollos, for instance – and one of them the son of Athene and Hephaestus, too, 'which puts an end to Athene's virginity'! As for her, who was she? He can list five different versions of this same goddess: the daughter of Hephaestus, called 'the Athenian'; the daughter of Neilus who is 'the Egyptian' of Sais; the daughter of Cronus, who is 'the discoverer of war'; the daughter of Zeus; and the child of Pallas 'who impiously slaughtered her father and is arrayed in the paternal skin, as though it were a fleece'. In these slips and confusions of identity we can still discern the goddess. What is new, of course, is the use Clement makes of them. And that is only the start of his indictment.

Next then: what sort of god is it that acts like a slave? Poseidon and Apollo, so we're told, worked as navvies to build the walls of Ilium; 'Homer is not ashamed to speak of Athena lighting the way for Odysseus, holding a golden lamp in her hand.' The complete unsuitability of such menial tasks, however, is of less importance than what they lead to. 'As a natural consequence, these amorous and passionate gods of yours are brought before us as subject to every sort of human emotion.' They can get wounded; they can bleed; even more disgustingly, their wounds can putrefy. So they need attendance and nourishment and so they are subject to all manner of human immoralities – for which Plato himself had condemned them as long as 500 years ago. 'So they have feasts, carousings, bursts of laughter and acts of sexual intercourse, whereas if they are immortal, and in need of nothing, and un-touched by age, they would not partake of the pleasures of human love, nor beget children, nor even go to sleep.'

And being mortal, these gods are already dead. The buildings that are called their temples are in fact their tombs; Erichthonius, for instance, is buried in the temple of Athene Polias on the Acropolis of Athens. And their statues are as dead as they are. Everyone knows that the Athene at Athens, for instance, was made by Pheidias. But even the one called 'heaven-sent' at Troy, the Palladium, was actually made out of the old bones of Pelops (presumably a reference to his ivory shoulder), just as the one of Olympian Zeus was made out of the bones of 'an Indian beast'.

In these stories of the deaths of gods, is it possible to detect a slight nostalgia for the bad old days? 'What a fine Zeus he is,' says Clement ironically,

the diviner, the protector of guests, the hearer of suppliants, the gracious, the author of all oracles, the avenger of crime! Rather he ought to be called the unjust, the unrestrained, the lawless, the unholy, the inhuman, the violent, the seducer, the adulterer, the wanton lover. Still, there was life about him in those days, when he was all this, when he was a man; but by this time, even your legends appear to me to have grown old. Zeus is no longer a snake, nor a swan, nor an eagle, nor an amorous man . . . He has grown old, wings and all. For you may be sure he is not repentant because of his love affairs, nor is he training himself to lead a sober life. See the legend is laid bare. Leda is dead; the swan is dead; the eagle is dead. Search for your Zeus. Scour not heaven, but earth . . . Yes, Zeus is dead (take it not to heart), like Leda, like the swan, like the eagle, like the amorous man, like the snake.[8]

Nostalgia or not, these dead gods are for Clement now mere shadows, daemons or ghosts. The people, of course, would take some persuading of that, and his is far from the only contemporary voice inveighing against their adherence to the old ways. Here is Tatian the Syrian, for instance, abhorring the festivals of religious drama (a favourite target) in his own *Address to the Greeks*: 'Your sons and daughters see [the gods] giving lessons in adultery on stage!' Here he is giving his own version of the tale of those two phials of Medusa's blood: Athene and Asclepius divided those drops of blood between them, he says, 'and while he saved lives by means of them, she by the same blood became a murderess and instigator of wars'.[9]

But who were these gods and where had they come from? Were they mere mortals, now dead, no more than ghostly presences, as Clement claimed? Then how had they become so powerful in the first place and how was it that their spirits so lingered? Clearly these sorts of questions were extremely important to those trying to establish a new order which raised its own questions about the nature of the deity. Justin the Philosopher, who had come from Samaria to Rome in the second century to study philosophy, and there converted to Christianity, had a very particular explanation of the origins and nature of the gods he had once worshipped and now reviled: they were the fallen angels, cast out of heaven at the very beginning of time.

According to Genesis, the mighty men of ancient times, the men of renown, commonly called giants, were the result of the union between God's angels and the 'daughters of men'. As Justin explained it, some of the angels to whom God had entrusted the administration of the earth had betrayed that trust by seducing women and corrupting boys (the story of Zeus and Ganymede was a great favourite with Christian writers). They then 'begot children, who are called demons'. When God discovered this, he expelled them from heaven. They, however, tried to recapture their lost power by working with their demonic offspring to enslave the human race. They 'showed such terrifying visions to people that those who did not use their reason . . . were struck by terror, and being carried away by fear, and not knowing that these were demons, they called them gods'. The power of these demons was enormous. Only a few, like Socrates and Jesus and present-day Christians, could challenge their brainwashing, and they, as the demons made sure, were destroyed.[10]

This explanation of the origins and nature of the gods was certainly of a piece with what was known of them from their legends and could still be observed in their rites. It also accorded with a general view of the time that it was the fall of the angels (not of Adam and Eve) which seemed to account for the wretchedness of the world.[11] And if Justin could have looked ahead he would have found confirmation enough of the terrible tenacity of the demons' hold over humankind, for at the beginning of the fifth century Augustine was still writing about it in much the same terms as his second-century forebears.

The first book of *City of God*, that 'great and arduous work', was started in 413 and the twenty-second and last was completed thirteen years later, when Augustine was seventy-two years old. It was begun in the wake of the sack of Rome by the Goths, the terrifying destruction of the very symbol of civilization, which had withstood attack for nearly 1,000 years. (As Jerome had cried, 'If Rome can perish, what can be safe?') But it was not just that the old gods of all the nations gathered in Rome had so dismally failed to protect it; it was not a simple matter of using the city's fall to prove the impotence of these deities. Christians believed that no lesser leaders of their own faith than Peter and Paul had laid their own bones to rest there and clearly they hadn't warded off the Goths either. By now, too, there was a swell of feeling against the ancient deities which was independent of Rome's fate. Augustine himself would preach to great crowds in Carthage amid shouts and cheers of 'Down with the pagan gods!' and Christians knew all about using violence in their enthusiasm to 'cleanse' the old shrines. According to Peter Brown, the danger to St Augustine seemed less from popular dismay at the sack of Rome than from the aristocratic paganism that still dominated the intellectual life of his age. When it comes to *City of God*, then, Brown says, 'it seems as if Augustine were demolishing a paganism that existed only in libraries. In fact Augustine believed quite rightly, that he could best reach the last pagans through their libraries.' So he deliberately builds his arguments to show that he too could 'move among cumulus clouds of erudition'.[12]

Yet among the cumulus clouds are some familiar arguments. For a start, there is that absurd multiplicity of deities, whose very number denotes both their unreality and their impotence. 'Is it not more like a scene of scurrility than a lecture of divinity?' demands Augustine. 'If a man should set two nurses to his child, one for the meat and another for the drink as they do two goddesses, Educa and Potina, he should be taken for an ass.' And again:

Durst they trust one god with their lands, think you? No, Rusina must look to the country, Jugatuus to the hill tops, Collatina to the whole hills besides and Vallonius to the valleys. Nor could Segetia alone be sufficient to protect the corn; but while it was in the ground Seia must look to it, when it was up and ready to mow, Segetia; when it was mown and laid up, then Tutilina took charge of it, who did not like that Segetia alone should have charge of it all the while before it came dried unto her hand. Nor was it sufficient for those wretches, that their poor seduced sons, that scorned to embrace one true God, should become prostitute unto this meaner multitude of devils. They must have more: so they made Proserpina goddess of the corn's first leaves and buds; the knots Nodotus looked unto, Volutina to the blades and when the ear began to look out, it was Patelana's charge; when the ear began to be even bearded . . . Hostilina's work came in; when the flowers bloomed, Flora was called forth; when they grew whiter, Lacturcia; being ripe Matuta, being cut down Runcina. Oh, let them pass; that which shames not them I loathe.[13]

The contrast between the power and majesty of 'the one true god' and this gang tripping over each other in the fields as they squabble their way through endless demarcation disputes could hardly of course be more marked. Even when the division of influences between the gods seems clear, their very numbers make it impossible that it should be so. Minerva, for instance, is said by the pagan doctors to have charge of 'men's wits', of the memory in children and of knowledge. Yet where is her place in the scheme of things? If Jove is said to be the greatest god, why does he need to divide his power over sea, earth and air with Neptune, Pluto and Juno? And as the world is complete in these four, where is Minerva's share? 'If she dwell in the highest part of the sky and therefore the poets feigned her to be the birth of Jove's own brain, why is she not then made the absolute empress of heaven, seeing that she sits above Jove? Because it is not meet to make the child lord over the parent? Why then was not that equity kept between Saturn and Jupiter?' And so on. Augustine underlines the point – or rather the pointlessness and unreliability of these powers – yet again by his lengthy listings of the pestilences they did not cure, the allies of Rome they did not support, the civil wars they did not prevent.

The very great difficulty with these gods, of course, is that while they can be shown to be absurdly limited in their powers and indeed often impotent, their influence is at the same time still enormous. Where does it come from? Augustine describes them as 'devils' and 'unclean spirits'. He also, however, goes into some complicated datings which suggest a far more time-bound quality. So, for instance, Mercury and Heracles were more or less con-temporaries of Moses. Minerva was born far earlier, at about the time of a great deluge said to be contemporaneous with the founda-tion of Rome – 'a woman indeed of many good inventions, and the likelier to be held a goddess because her origin is unknown, for the story that she sprang from Jove's brain is absolutely poetic and in no way real history'.

Whatever their origins, however, and whatever good inventions might have come with them, there can be no doubt at all about the fundamental nature of these devils. They are gluttonous, treach-erous, wasteful, cheating, dancing, luxurious, filthy, shameless, malevolent – and corrupting. It was they, not men, who first commanded the stage plays – 'those spectacles of uncleanness, those licentious vanities'. And it was they who kept their worship-pers in a state of what to the new eye could only appear as sin. This enslavement of the people was one of Augustine's major indictments of the devils. 'What might one think (I pray ye),' he demands, 'of those gods that would abide with the people that worshipped them, and yet would never teach them any means to leave their vices and follow what is good?'[14]

By now, the definition of what was vicious and what virtuous was irrevocably, tortuously and obsessionally entwined with sexuality. In the long battle between the church fathers and the ancient gods, it was their sexual exploits and licentiousness that increasingly became the focus of condemnation. And that narrowing of focus was itself the outcome of an equally lengthy and tortuous exploration of the relations between mind and matter, body and soul, with whose effects Western women and men still live.

The struggle in which the church fathers engaged was hardly a new one. Some 500 years before the birth of Christianity, Plato had understood the soul as by its nature perfect, but tainted by the body which contained it. At the start of the Christian era, St Paul had expressed his own anguished sense of not simply the gulf between the two, but their continuing warring. 'We know that the law is spiritual, but I am carnal, sold under sin. I do not understand my own actions. For I do not do what I want, but I do the very thing I hate . . . For I know that nothing good dwells within me, that is, in my flesh. I can will what is right, but I cannot do it . . . I see in my members another law at war with the law of my mind and making me captive to the law of sin which dwells in my members. Wretched man that I am! Who will deliver me from this body of death?'[15]

The way in which this perception of a painful and unending battle between will and action, spirit and body, life and death, became lived out around issues of human sexuality is a large part of the story of the development of the early church and the defining of its nature.[16] By no means all the early fathers saw the subduing of the flesh as synonymous with a rejection of sexuality or the world itself. Clement of Alexandria, for instance, writing more than 100 years after Paul, was at pains to emphasize how Paul's teachings endorsed both marriage and celibacy. And he specifically denounced celibates and beggars 'who say that they are "imitating the Lord" who never married, nor had any possessions in the world, and who boast that they understand the gospel better than anyone else'; he found such extremists arrogant, foolish and plain wrong. Tertullian, rather later, brought body and soul together in his consideration of the nature of orgasm. 'The whole human frame is shaken,' he writes, 'and foams with semen, as the damp humour of the body is joined to the hot substance of the spirit. And then something of our soul goes out in that last breaking wave of delight.' For him, this proves that neither body nor soul is intrinsically superior: both are created at the same moment. What is essential is that the power of (masculine) sexuality is carefully used, lest the heat of the spirit be reduced. In this view, Tertullian was doing no more than echoing the biological understanding of the time. But as the debate continued, that understanding came increasingly to underpin the promotion of celibacy as a superior expression of Christian life, difficult though that was for a movement that many of its adherents at least wished to see spread rather than brought just yet to its final days. (Marriages that became chaste after the production of children were often seen as a worthy compromise.) By the start of the fifth century, the debate still continued. Augustine himself wrote defences of both marriage and virginity as having a place within the church – though the first has been called conscientious, and the second quite lyrical.[17]

It is Augustine, however, who supplies a context for all this questioning whose implications go far beyond those of the sexual mores of what was after all a minority of adherents of a still-growing faith. In *City of God*, he takes to task those who hold God to be the soul and the world the body, with its corollary that there is 'nothing on earth that is not part of God'. If this were true, he says, 'a man . . . should not tread, without treading part of God under his feet; and in every creature that he killed, he should kill a part of the Deity'. He finds this notion appalling: 'I will not relate what others may think of it. I cannot speak it without exceeding shame.'[18]

How far perceptions of the universe have moved! Once the ancient understanding had held that every manifestation of nature was enclosed in the web of the goddess and so inextricably interrelated. Mother Earth, Great Gaia, who as we have seen continued to play her respected part even in the days of father Zeus's rule, is indeed now nothing but dead matter. The continuity between the Olympians and the natural world, between spirit and nature, manifested in the ease with which they shifted shape between god and creature, is now irrevocably broken. Even the echoes of the ancient power which led the Romans to reverence the goddesses of the land are silenced – as we have seen in Augustine's ridiculing of the Roman deities of grain and harvest.

What we are seeing here is the triumph of another tradition, born with the Babylonian creation myth, the *Enuma Elish*, which is the first we know in which a creator god rather than a goddess brings the universe into being. And Marduk does it by slaying the goddess herself, the great she-dragon Tiamat. It is a bloody business, this slaying:

> The lord spread out his net to enfold her,
> The Evil Wind, which followed behind, he let loose in her face.
> When Tiamat opened her mouth to consume him,
> He drove in the Evil Wind that she close not her lips.
> As the fierce winds charged her belly,
> Her body was distended and her mouth was wide open.
> He released the arrow, it tore her belly,
> It cut through her insides, splitting the heart.
> Having thus subdued her, he extinguished her life.
> He cast down her carcass to stand upon it.
>
> The lord trod on the legs of Tiamat,
> With his unsparing mace he crushed her skull.
> When the arteries of her blood he had severed,
> The North Wind bore it to places undisclosed.
> On seeing this, his fathers were joyful and jubilant,
> They brought gifts of homage to him.
> Then the lord paused to view her dead body,
> That he might divide the monster and do artful works.[19]

Out of one half of Tiamat's lifeless body, Marduk creates the sky, out of the other, the earth. It is the first recorded instance of creation being forged from dead matter, and it was a story whose time had come. From about 1700 BC, for about 1,000 years, it was recited in Babylon at the time of the spring equinox. It strongly influenced the Hebrew creation myth, to which Augustine and dominant Western consciousness ever since have inevitably been heir.[20]

(Some 1,400 years later, Chief Seattle brought his own questions to that dominant view. 'Will you teach your children what we have taught our children?' he asked the incomers to his people's North American lands. 'That the earth is our mother? What befalls the earth, befalls all the sons of the earth. This we know: the earth does not belong to man, man belongs to the earth. All things are connected like the blood which unites us all. Man did not weave the web of life, he is merely a strand in it. Whatever he does to the web, he does to himself.'[21] Well, we know what the answer has been to that.)

Western consciousness has its own story of how the manifest world came into being and how humans acquired their privileged place in it. God's word alone had done it, the Logos of discrimination and differentiation. It had created heaven and earth and the light which he separated from the darkness, and heaven which he separated from the waters below, and the earth which he separated from the seas, and the vegetation that covered the earth, and the lights that ruled night and day, and the living creatures of air and sea and earth. And God saw that all this was good. Then God said (and it was now the sixth day of his creation):

'Let us make man in our image, after our likeness; and let them have dominion over the fish of the seas, and over the birds of the air, and over the cattle, and over all the earth, and over every creeping thing that creeps upon the earth.'

So God created man in his own image, in the image of God he created him; male and female he created them. And God blessed them and God said to them, 'Be fruitful and multiply, and fill the earth and subdue it; and have dominion over the fish of the sea and over the birds of the air and over every living thing that moves upon the earth.' And God said, 'Behold, I have given you every plant yielding seed which is upon the face of all the earth, and every tree with seed in its fruit; you shall have them for food. And to every beast of the earth, and to every bird of the air, and to everything that creeps on the earth, everything that has the breath of life, I have given every green plant for food.' And God saw everything that he had made, and behold, it was very good.[22]

All that abundance, all that gift, all that effortless supremacy! How can they possibly have gone wrong? How could we have lost such bliss? The question is as archetypal as the notion of a lost paradise itself, the search for an answer as compelling as the search for the map that will take us back to somewhere which at least borders that dear lost land.

Some say the creation didn't happen quite like that, that God had the idea of bringing in a man quite early on, back on the day when he made earth and heavens, but before the earth was yet planted. He made this man, they say, out of the dust of the ground (which had once been the body of Mother Earth herself but was now simply that, the dust of the ground) and he breathed his own spirit into the nostrils of the man, so that he became a living being. And then he created for this man a garden in Eden, in the east, out of which grew every tree that is pleasant to the sight and good for food. And again, God formed every beast of the field and bird of the air so that the man should not be alone, and gave the man the chance to name them and so establish his own view of things over theirs. And finally, they say, God caused a deep sleep to fall upon the man, and while he was thus unconscious, took a rib from his side and closed up the place again and out of the rib made a woman and brought her to the man to be his helpmeet. When the man woke up, what did he see? Did he puzzle over the unlikeness of this unnamed animal to the ones he already knew? Did he recognize her instantly? How long did he study her before the realization dawned and he exclaimed, 'This at last is bone of my bones and flesh of my flesh!' He named her Woman because she was taken out of Man. And though both were naked, they had nothing to be ashamed about. So how could they possibly have gone wrong?

Well, some say that from the moment Woman arrived in that paradisial garden, there was bound to be trouble. Certainly it doesn't seem to have been as simple to get her there in the first place as it had been to install Man. According to the two accounts in Genesis itself, God seems to have tried at least once before to make for Man an acceptable mate. Some say that the first version was made from filth and sediment rather than the pure earth used for Man, and so wouldn't do. Others say that Man woke during the assembly of Woman and was so repelled by the sight of all those limbs and glands and organs being stitched into place that he could not bring himself to accept the finished product. So next time God ensured that he slept soundly until all the messy bits were finished with, so that when he awoke he could just see that beautiful creature, like nothing so much as an image of himself, and cry delightedly, 'This one *at last* is flesh of my flesh!'

But how delighted was he? Philo of Alexandria, Jewish philosopher and contemporary of Jesus's, thought that Man lacked nothing for his delight in that garden; it was God's notion that he should have other human companionship. 'Woman becomes for [Man] the beginning of a blameworthy life. For as long as he was by himself, as accorded with such solitude, he went on growing like to the world and like God.' For Philo, the Essenes had the right idea, when they abjured marriage, 'because a wife is a selfish creature, excessively jealous and an adept in beguiling the morals of her husband and seducing him by her continued impostures . . . [H]e who is either fast-bound in the love-lures of his wife, or under the stress of nature makes his children his first care, ceases to be the same to others and unconsciously has become a different man and has passed from freedom to slavery.'[23]

Was this inevitable? For Philo, the very nature of woman made it so. While Man represents *nous*, or mind, the nobler, rational element, Woman represents the body, or sensation, *aisthesis*, the lower element, source of all passion. Certainly and as anyone could see, she was Other to that template, that original, the first and therefore the true version of what a human being should be – the one, indeed, 'made in the image of God'. And as so often happens, Other is defined as inferior (especially when they come second).

Take, for a highly pertinent instance, the understanding of the respective parts played by male and female in procreation and how that was developed to explain the very nature of men and women. Apollo had used the classical biological view in his defence of Orestes's slaying of his mother Clytemnestra, as we have seen: the mother finally, when it came right back to basics, didn't matter, for it was the semen which contained the embryonic new human being and the womb simply nourished its growth. 'She who is called the child's mother is not/its begetter,' as he put it, 'but the nurse of the newly sown conception,/The begetter is the male and she as a stranger for a stranger/preserves the offspring . . .' Craftily, Apollo used this understanding to argue that there could be a father without a mother – and who was Athene, Orestes's judge, to disagree with that?

Aristotle, in his *On the Generation of Animals*, put it this way: '[I]f the male is the active partner, the one which originates the move-ment, and the female *qua* female is the passive one, surely what the female contributes to the semen of the male will be not semen but material . . . the natural substance of the menstrual fluid is to be classed as "prime matter".' No inherent superiority, then: semen needs its material to work on, the embryo needs a container in which to grow. Yet this balance of respect between active and passive cannot, it seems, be held. The Other must become inferior.

So by the thirteenth century, Aristotle's view is still held, but has also become explanation of why woman is not up to the standard of man. '[T]he active power in the seed of the male tends to produce something like itself, perfect in masculinity,' says Aqui-nas; 'but the procreation of a female is the result either of the debility of the active power, of some unsuitability of the material, or of some change effected by external influences, like the south wind, for example, which is damp.' For Aquinas, woman is *igno-bilior et vilior*, and as her natural superior, man 'makes use of his subjects for their own benefit and good . . . For good order would have been found wanting in the human family if some were not governed by others wiser than themselves. So by a kind of subjection woman is naturally subject to man, because in man the discretion of reason predominates.'[24] So woman by her very nature is debility, second-rate material, a falling away from the 'true' human being, who is created in God's image as she is not. She represents the lower part, matter and the senses, rather than the higher masculine powers of reason and of mind. With this sort of element introduced into that paradise garden so early, no wonder there was so soon to be, and despite man's superior wisdom in governance, not simply the taint of imperfection but disaster.

How did that serpent get in? Some say that of course he was there from the start, or at least from the sixth day, when God put the animals and the birds and the creeping things into the garden and man himself as well. (Did the man hesitate as he named him, look him in that glittering hooded eye, knowing somewhere even then that dubbing would not, in this one case, bring dominion?) Others say that it was only later that the serpent managed to slip his way in, after he had so thoroughly softened the woman with his beguilements and promises to pluck that luscious fruit for her that she simply melted, no longer even wanting to resist him, and opened that gate to paradise's delights.[25] One way or another, anyway, the serpent started his seduction, slipping into the conversation, casually perhaps, as if it hardly mattered, his soon-to-be-essential question. Knowing perfectly well, of course, what the woman's answer would be, for he had overheard God's stern injunction against eating of the fruit of the tree of the knowledge of good and evil, and the man's careful and maybe even rather repetitive explanations to the woman, in the interests of good governance, of why she shouldn't even think about it.

When the serpent told the woman that if she ate the fruit she would not die at all, but know good and evil, and be wise like God himself, she can't even have known what he was talking about, for what 'good' meant, or 'evil' or 'wise', was still enclosed within the glowing, unbroken skin of that forbidden fruit. But how could she have not wanted to find out? And can her disappointment be imagined when, after all that lead-up, all her hard work to per-suade the man to share the fruit, the very first education in that promised thing called 'knowledge' was that it was 'evil' to be naked and 'good' to get sewing fig-leaves into aprons as fast as possible?

The second education, of course, was the most terrible that there could be: it was the definitive education in what it meant to have transgressed the laws of God and in the implacable consequences.

> To the woman he said,
> 'I will greatly multiply your pain in childbearing;
> in pain you shall bring forth children,
> yet your desire shall be for your husband,
> and he shall rule over you.'
> And to Adam he said,
> 'Because you have listened to the voice of your wife,
> and have eaten of the tree of which I commanded you
> "You shall not eat of it,"
> cursed is the ground because of you;
> in toil you shall eat of it all the days of your life;
> thorns and thistles it shall bring forth to you;
> and you shall eat the plants of the field.
> In the sweat of your face
> you shall eat bread
> till you return to the ground,
> for out of it you were taken;
> you are dust,
> and to dust you shall return.'

And to make doubly sure of that, God sent them out of that beautiful garden for ever, and set the cherubim to guard that other tree, the tree of life, so that never again would humankind have the opportunity to snatch the prerogative of the gods, and make themselves immortal as well as discriminating. They left with the skins God gave them to cover their nakedness. And they left with their names. It is when God curses the man that he is first called Adam. He in turn calls his wife Eve 'because she is the mother of all living' – the act by which he establishes dominion over her as he has over the rest of creation.[26]

So Adam and Eve leave the garden for ever, and very many hundreds of years later, their wanderings bring them into the anguished debates of the new faith which is trying to establish itself and to understand the nature of the fallen world that Christ has redeemed. At first, there was by no means universal agreement about just what that all-defining primal sin had been. Tatian the Syrian, for instance (he who taught that Athene had kept Medusa's death-dealing blood to become 'murderess and instigator of wars'), was convinced from the start that the knowledge brought with that first forbidden bite had been carnal. God, he taught, had expelled Adam from Eden (together of course with his all-too-willing wife) for inventing marriage. Yet in the early centuries of the church, other views were also jostling in the debate. Tatian's contemporary Clement was far from alone in insisting that the first sin was not sexual, because sexuality was not a sin but part of nature: to engage in procreation was to assist God in his own work of creation. As late as the fourth century, the rigorous asceticism of the desert fathers was a living witness to their belief that the first sin of all had been greed.

For Clement and others too, that first sin was disobedience. But even they saw that the disobedience was a sexual one. Clement explains that Adam and Eve rushed into sex like impatient adolescents, instead of waiting for their father's blessing; he blames Adam, who 'desired the fruit of marriage before the proper time, and so fell into sin . . . they were impelled to do it more quickly than was proper because they were still young, and had been seduced by deceit'. Irenaeus points out that in fact, 'having been created just a

short time before', these two were still under age. Adam knew
very well, he reckons, that sexual desire had incited him to sin, for
the fig-leaves with which he covered what came to be called the
'shameful parts' of himself and Eve were scratchy, 'while there
were many other leaves which would have irritated his body
much less'.[27]

But even the scratchiest of fig-leaves could not subdue those
disobedient members in the minds and imaginations (at the least)
of the framers of church policy. For Augustine, the appalling
thing about that first and all-defining sin was the way in which
the body had detached itself from the control of the soul and the
rational will. Until then, the sexual organs had gone about their
lawful business of procreation by a deliberate act of will, 'like a
handshake'. But after their act of defiance, both Adam and Eve
'felt for the first time a movement of disobedience in their flesh,
as punishment in kind for their own disobedience to God . . . The
soul, which had taken a perverse delight in its own liberty and
disdained to serve God, was now deprived of its original mastery
over the body.' And in this was the original sin of humankind, to
be passed for ever from generation to generation by the act
which now represented sin itself. For had the first couple, once
they had eaten the forbidden fruit, not immediately covered
those shameful parts? 'Ecce unde!' cried Augustine in one of his
passionate sermons. 'That's the place! That's the place from which
the first sin is passed on!' And there was nothing whatsoever to
be done about it. For now on, the sons of men would be
racked by the war between their god-given, conscious and
rational mind and the one 'great force' which would forever
escape its control.[28]

From now on, too, the daughters of men would also be racked
and in a very particular way. As that first great and enduring sin
was teased out, the image of Eve, 'mother of all living', itself under-
went some extraordinary changes. At first, as we have seen, some
at least of the church fathers blamed Adam particularly for his hot-
blooded impatience – for they too had once been adolescent

males and known what Augustine himself had known from his headlong, eager rush into the painful bonds of love through the bodies of those who loved him. Eve, as we first meet her – composed as she is of secondary, imperfect stuff, lacking in will, passive, a bit damp – is just the sort to be easily seduced. As more than one early commentator pointed out, the serpent knew what he was doing to slither in there rather than approach the man. ('And I too,' said Luther so many centuries later, 'believe that if he had attempted Adam first, the victory would have been Adam's. He would have crushed the serpent with his foot and would have said, "Shut up! The Lord's command was different!"')[29]

But as the years go by, each time the story is told, each time Eve opens the gate to paradise, and each time the sinuous serpent entwines more closely round those delicate young limbs, the story of forbidden fruit becomes more and more a tale of 'stealing apples'. And so gradually and then indisputably the terrible, shameful equation emerges. For is not 'apple' *malus* in Latin, which is also 'evil', and is not 'stealing apples' one of those euphemisms for, you know it, sex itself? Sex, forbidden, serpent, theft, sex, evil, sex – Eve!

A century and more before Augustine put his grim and dreadful seal on the inherited inevitability of the original and all-defining sin, Tertullian (repenting now perhaps of his delight in orgasm) excoriated each and every woman born of woman in God-ordained pain:

By every garb of penitence woman might the more fully expiate that which she derives from Eve – the ignominy, I mean, of the first sin and the odium of human perdition . . . Do you not know that you are each an Eve? . . . You are the devil's gateway; you are the unsealer of the forbidden tree; you are the first deserter of the divine law; you are she who persuaded him whom the devil was not valiant enough to attack. You destroyed so easily God's image, man. On account of your desert – that is, death – even the Son of God had to die.[30]

This is an extraordinary transformation. The woman, albeit inferior to Adam, is now seen as finding it entirely easy to destroy man, who is also God's image, and as bringing a death that not even the Son of God can escape. Who on earth and in the heavens can this power be? Adam himself gives the clue – though it is only when he is on the verge of expulsion from Eden that he can recognize and name this awesome force: it was Eve who did it! And it is Eve who is the Mother of All Living.

Now we can begin to see the force which the new order was up against – and how it dealt with it. The Mother of All Living was an ancient title and honour of the goddess. As time goes on, the identity of Eve with this power is emphasized by her ever closer intertwining with the serpent. At first, as we have seen, they say the serpent is male. But even then, some say, 'Look again!' Do you not see that Eve has, from the start, been created from the feet of the serpent (which is both why women are so false and serpents have no feet)? Others say 'Listen!' for what they hear in the sounds of *hawwah* is not 'Mother of All Living' but the Aramaic *hiwya*, which means 'serpent'. Clement of Alexandria, that moderate man, is shocked by the rites of the 'raving Dionysus', the orgies of the Bacchantes, their feasts of raw flesh. 'Wreathed with snakes, they perform the distribution of portions of their victims, shouting the name of Eva (Evia), that Eva through whom error entered the world; and a consecrated snake is the emblem of the Bacchic orgies. At any rate, according to the correct Hebrew speech, the word *hevia*, with an aspirate, means the female snake.'[31] And as time goes on, portrayals of Eve and the serpent either give them identical features, or entwine them so closely that they effectively become one – just as in the ancient images of Lady Snake and her descendant in the Dea Syria of Rome [Pls. 22, 15].

The image evokes the ancient power but the story tells us something completely different. Eve is no longer revered as mistress of life, death and regeneration. Instead, she is both feared for the power of her sexuality and denigrated for what has become her sole responsibility for the fall from God's grace and love. Feared and denigrated – the fate of the feminine turned bad.

And in giving that once great title to Eve, in calling her Mother of All Living, man underlines it. For Eve is now seen as bringing a separation from God, which means death itself, rather than as commanding the great and natural cycle of life, death and regeneration which had once been her charge. The Living she mothers are no longer the whole of the created world, for that has a new master. The Living to whom Eve is Mother now are the human creatures who will forever carry the taint of her own sin.

As she herself carries the taint of another's. For although she is the first version of woman whom Adam can accept, she is not the first version. That woman whom God had made, some say, out of filth and sediment rather than the pure earth he used for man hadn't just crumbled back to dirt when he rejected his handiwork. Her name was Lilith, that dark maid, and we have met her already as tenant to the unwilling Inanna in her *huluppu* tree. When the hero Gilgamesh had cut down the tree to make his sister Inanna a throne and a bed, Lilith had 'smashed her home and fled to the wild, uninhabited places' − one more flight, one more exile, for aspects of the feminine that heroic consciousness cannot accept in the days of the sky-gods.

This has become the story of Lilith's life. Created of filth and sediment she may have been (and may not, but the later tellers of her tale had to account for her somehow). Essentially, however, she was made of the very same substance as Adam, and so she insisted he remember, claiming in all their relations the equality that was rightfully hers. That was not so easy for him, particularly when she seemed to attack the very essence of his manhood by insisting that she too liked sometimes to be on top when they had sex. All became bitterness and recrimination. There seemed no repairing of this marriage, so in despair Lilith evoked the ineffable name of God and was granted the wings that enabled her to fly off from the paradise that had become her prison. Things must certainly have been more peaceful in the garden then; maybe Adam thought that Philo of Alexandria was right when he said that life without women was just what men needed. But something was missing. And, wait a minute, did Lilith have the right, after all, to take such independent action? Adam appealed to God and three angels were dispatched to bring the errant wife back home. She said 'No!'; she refused to capitulate. So, in a foretaste of the punishment of Eve, she too was condemned to bring forth children in sorrow and pain. For her, the travail would be unending and the children innumerable – and each day she would have to watch 100 of them die. It was intolerable. Lilith threw herself into the Red Sea rather than endure such a fate. The angels took pity on her, and tried to balance this terrible score by giving her power over all newborn babies – for eight days in the case of boys, twenty in the case of girls, and for the lifetime of children born out of wedlock.

So Lilith flies into the ranks of the dangerous feminine powers, potentially death-dealing, from whom human children must be protected by amulets. Her own home becomes that terrible desert place of brimstone and burning pitch called No Kingdom There, which God creates for his day of vengeance. But of the threat of her malign power there can be no end, for in that place she makes her nest and hatches her brood and gathers them in her shadow, and each one of those innumerable offspring of hers is a demon. Well, not entirely all, perhaps. Some say that after the death of Abel, Adam and Eve abstained from sex for 130 years, and that during this time, Lilith would secretly entertain him. One of their offspring was a wise frog, which taught the languages of humans, animals and birds, as well as the healing properties of herbs and precious stones.

We can immediately recognize that that frog has inherited at least some of the attributes of the ancient goddess, just as we can as immediately recognize Lilith when we glimpse her in her night-flight. She is screech-owl, she is night-hag, she is Lamia, who was once the goddess Neith but is now, in her lechery and gluttony, devourer of lovers and of young children too. She is the ancient power which was once imaged as Divine Lady Owl, whom the Sumerians had known as Nin-ninna, and countless generations in earlier times and distant places had revered as an epiphany of the bird goddess[32] [Pl. 20].

But now any assertion of that once-great power has become intolerable. Its expression, as we have seen, has become less and less possible in the era of the sky-gods, until we can sometimes intimate only its faintest echoes. Even where the goddess is still honoured, we know how her power has been diluted. The little owl which crouches so squashed and cross at the feet of one Romano-British image of Minerva can tell us all we need to know about a moment of transition from the ancient world to the new era. Just as Minerva herself is half-way towards rejecting the power of the owl which was once another expression of her own, so are the Christian saints going to tread underfoot the feminine dragon which was once another epiphany of the goddess [Pl. 19].

And in this new era, the ancient power becomes intolerable in a very particular way. It becomes a sin, and not just any sin, but the first and essential one: the sin of disobedience. In Lilith's disobedience first of all to the command of God and then to the will of Adam is the taint which is to be inherited by Eve. However God changes the method of creation, whatever the substance of which he makes that second wife for man, there is no getting away from disobedience, it seems, as part of woman's nature. Woman's 'No!' is encoded in her very essence and in that is her sin.

Did they tell Pandora, that other first woman, that above all and whatever else she was not, repeat not, to open that jar? And did she, like Eve, just have to disobey, to do that one forbidden thing, and so let fly into the world every grief, pain and sickness known to humankind? As we know, Pandora, the All-Giving, is one of the titles of Rhea, daughter of Gaia, Mother Earth herself; her other name, Anesidora, means 'she who brings gifts from below'. Some say that what she contained in her great *pithos*, her great jar, was nothing less than the power of the goddess, the cycle of life and death itself. But for some of the early church fathers, the parallel was irresistible between their own struggles with Eve and Hesiod's glum characterization of Woman as that 'beautiful evil' who is source of all the sorrows of men. Tertullian, for instance, recalls Pandora for his own purposes when he's preaching to women against the wearing of chaplets, or garlands of flowers:

If ever there was a certain Pandora, whom Hesiod cites as the first woman, hers was the first head to be crowned by the graces with a diadem; for she received gifts from all and was hence called 'Pandora'; to us, however, Moses . . . describes the first woman, Eve, as being more conveniently encircled with leaves about the middle than with flowers about the temple.

And as Eve, so all her daughters. For what else is woman, asks John Chrysostom more than a hundred years later, but 'a foe to friendship, an inescapable punishment, a necessary evil, a natural temptation, a desirable calamity, a domestic danger, a delectable detriment, an evil nature, painted with fair colours?'[33]

Well, what indeed? With the breaking of the seal of Pandora's jar, another seal is set, on a misogyny whose effects will last for every century that is yet known to lie ahead. Pandora, bringer of all gifts, who became bringer of all ills, has become Eve, who was given all gifts and betrayed both the divine giver and her children for ever. The lovely chaplet of blossoms of spring grasses that Athene so delicately wove into the golden crown of Pandora – her own creation! – has become the leafy apron which cannot ever adequately cover women's shame.

Ah, Athene! It is some time since we have glimpsed the goddess, not since Augustine sought to show that there was no rational room for her in even the domestic economy of the ancient gods, let alone the new order. He seems to have succeeded. But can we be surprised at her absence now? There is indeed and absolutely no room in this story of Eve and her daughters for the bright, fierce, inquiring and creative energy that is Athene's. Augustine and those who shared his passion excoriated the ancient gods for the shocking example they set their followers, the shamefully im-moral lessons they taught them. But there are stories enough from those ancient days of the appalling fates that befell mortals who would imitate the gods to underline that example, and education was not what those ancient deities ever had in mind, or their followers either. What the old goddesses and gods had offered, through their amazing adventures, the variety of their guises and the complexity of their moods, was a landscape of imaginal possibility. In a sense, nothing was impossible, everything might one day happen, for men and women both, because the image for it already existed, because the deities had already done it.

But now there is no place for Athene's gift of soul to human beings. The Lord God is the maker who breathes life into the one made in his image, and leaves his secondary creation to perplex later schoolmen with that tricky question '*Habet mulier animum?*' – can woman be said to have a soul at all? There can be no place either for the essential understanding of the interplay of mind and matter, hand and eye, which makes Athene so uniquely skilled in craft. Now the creation of the material world and all that is in it stems from the mind of the creator god and the word which is its expression. The burden which Adam and Eve must bear as they go sorrowfully from that garden is that mind and matter, spirit and the material world, are now separated and at odds, and that they must live that separation in their very natures. From now on, as we have seen, it is to be the masculine which carries the 'nobler' powers of the mind, of rationality, of thought, while the feminine has become the 'lower', material element, source of the baser passions which are nothing but destructive to man's higher purpose.

The shift in understanding of the nature of masculine and feminine – and so, inevitably, of man and woman – could not have been more profound. Athene as *nous kai dianoia*, Minerva as *mens*: these essential qualities of mind, thought and understanding which were once intrinsic to the feminine spirit are now entirely matters for the masculine. There is now no place in the concept of the feminine for the bright, inquiring energy that Athene brings to her transformations of matter, for any one of her ideas and devices, inventions and resources. There's no place either for that 'seeing' which is the flash of understanding – of the way things fit, how they work, where it's all going. When Pandora and Eve exercise that very energy, when they want to explore, to find out, to move humankind on a bit, just as the goddess so often did herself, it is not their courage or their adventurousness which is praised but their disobedience which is condemned. The very curiosity which is the motor of the human urge to understanding, the very refusal to accept the given ways without question, become part of woman's sin. All those openings through the ages – of jar, of gateway, of forbidden locked room – are supposed now to lead to nowhere but a crudely sexual metaphor for woman's insatiable and dangerous lust. So the very act by which human beings were wrenched from the primal bliss of Eden to conscious-ness, from an undifferentiated lack of awareness to the capacity to discriminate and learn the difference between good and evil, is condemned as woman's inability, when it comes to it, to keep her legs together.

And yet, *O felix culpa!* Oh happy fault, the church would sing, oh necessary sin of Adam! As the fifteenth-century carol would put it:

> Ne had the apple taken been, the apple taken been,
> Ne had our Lady abeen heavene queen.
> Blessed be the time that apple taken was . . .
> Therefore we moun singen *Deo gracias!*[34]

For Tertullian, back in the church's early days, there was a beautiful symmetry to be discerned:

For unto Eve, as yet a virgin, had crept the devil's word, the framer of death. Equally, unto a virgin was introduced God's word, the builder of life: so that what had been lost through one sex might by the same sex be restored and saved. Eve had believed the serpent, Mary believed Gabriel. The fault which the one committed by believing, by believing the other amended.[35]

As the medieval schoolmen were to enjoy pointing out, Eva

reversed gives us *Ave!* Hail. Mary! In the very perfection of the symmetry, in the all-inclusive reversal of Eve's sin by Mary's re-deeming grace, how can there be room for any other image of the feminine than these two?

CHAPTER 7

The Seat of Wisdom

By the time the Parthenon of Athens was dedicated to Mary as Mother of God in the sixth century, she had taken on many of the images and honours of the ancient goddesses as well as moving into many of their temples. Portraits of her from the end of the fourth century often show her seated with Jesus as Isis used to be with Horus, the crown of Cybele or Diana on her head and the Gorgon of Athene painted on her breast. Mother of God, *Theotokos*, is the greatest of her titles, and with it comes official recognition of her cult. The title was bestowed in 431 at the Council of Ephesus, where worship of the many-breasted, multiply-maternal Diana had recently been smashed by the local Christians with the same enthusiasm as they now poured into the veneration of Mary. 'Mother of the Gods' had once been a title of Isis, as Mater Dei had been a title of Cybele, and soon Cybele's temple on the Capitol of Rome will be replaced by Sancta Maria Maggiore, with its huge, triumphal mosaic of the Virgin enthroned and glorified. Like Inanna before her, she will be hailed as the Queen of Heaven; she will inherit Anat's honour as Morning and Evening Star; she will be known, like Isis, as Star of the Sea. And people will pray to her exactly as they used to pray to Athene herself – as Virgin, Terrible, Hearkening to Prayer.[1]

Already in the early years of the fifth century, Mary is recognized in the sermon preached in Constantinople on her December feast day not simply as 'servant and mother', but as 'the only bridge between God and men, the awesome loom ... on which the garment of union was woven'. There is an echo here of another loom, another weaver – Athene's Egyptian counterpart, Neith, who as creating mother wove the loom of the sky, 'the first to create the seed of gods and men'. The shift in the imagery is instructive: the feminine is no longer the active, creative weaver, but rather the passive loom, that upon which a greater power is at work.[2]

Yet many of the evocations in the first major Marian hymn composed to be sung in churches, at the start of the sixth century, are anything but passive. The Akathistos ('not sitting' – you have to stand for it) salutes Mary as, among other titles, vanquisher of demons, strength of martyrs, opener of paradise, fortress of all who have recourse to her, citadel of the church, healer of bodies and rescuer of imperilled souls. The hymn was adopted immediately in the Eastern church and certainly by the ninth century in the West. When Constantinople was threatened by barbarians in 626 and the danger was repelled, it was enlarged to become a song of thanksgiving for deliverance. When the same happened in 717, the Patriarch Germanus declared in his celebratory sermon that 'No one, Lady All-Holy, is saved except through you!' So strongly did he hold this that he added two radically new ideas about Mary's nature and status: she has authority over Christ in heaven, and she can intercede for mercy against God's justice. By 754, an imperial edict condemned anyone who did *not* worship Mary as Mother of God (for the title had had its fierce detractors) and seek her intercession.[3]

So Mary came to occupy a uniquely powerful place – not herself a goddess, yet the Mother of God himself, mortal woman, yet able to intercede with God for humankind. All this, the reward for her exemplary obedience to God's word, her reversal of Eve's sin of disobedience? Between the image of that simple, trusting girl, who confides herself so absolutely to the fate announced by God's messenger and the extraordinary majesty of the mother of compassion who stretches her protecting, brooding wing over tiny, huddled humanity, is all the implacable majesty of the goddess

[Pl. 21]. We have felt just that brooding presence before in the image of Athene as slayer of the giants – and so protector too of humankind, in her own time, against the forces which would overwhelm it [Pl. 2]. The link between the two is in the Parthenon – not just because it has in turn been dedicated to first one and then the other, but because of another dedication that bridges them both. When the Christians first came to the Parthenon, they worshipped there not Mary at all, but another, more ancient power. The story of that power, of Hagia Sophia, Holy Wisdom herself, can tell us more about what is happening to the concept of the feminine – and particularly that aspect of it once carried by the Parthenon's own goddess, which now in some measure at least passes to Mary.

The Lord created me at the
beginning of his work,
the first of his acts of old.
Ages ago I was set up,
at the first, before the beginning of the earth.
When there were no depths I was brought forth,
when there were no springs abounding with water.
Before the mountains had been shaped,
before the hills, I was brought forth;
before he had made the earth with its fields,
or the first of the dust of the world.
When he established the heavens, I was there,
when he drew a circle on the face of the deep,
when he made firm the skies above,
when he established the fountains of the deep,
when he assigned to the sea its limit,
so that the waters might not transgress his command.
When he marked out the foundations of the earth,
then I was beside him, like a master workman;
and I was daily his delight,
rejoicing before him always,

rejoicing in his inhabited world
and delighting in the sons of men.[4]

This is Wisdom, God's companion and joyful overseer of works at the very creation of the world. She is essential to God's project: it is by her that he founded the earth itself. She is 'the fashioner of all things' and she 'effects all things'. She is 'a breath of the power of God', this awesome power, 'a pure emanation of the glory of the Almighty', 'a reflection of the eternal light'. She is more beautiful than the sun, more excellent than any constellation of stars.[5]

She reaches mightily from one end of the earth to the other, and she orders all things well . . .
She knows the things of old, and infers the things to come;
she understands turns of speech and the solutions of riddles;
she has foreknowledge of signs and wonders
and of the outcome of seasons and times.[6]

Those who seek Wisdom know that she is more precious than jewels, that nothing they can desire compares with her. She holds long life, wealth and honour in her hands, her ways are the ways of pleasantness, and all her paths are peace. To those who find her, she is a tree of life, and those who hold her fast are called happy. No wonder that 'Jesus, son of Sirach', writing about 180 years before the birth of Christ, urges his readers to 'Pursue Wisdom like a hunter, and lie in wait on her paths.' She dwells in the high places, and alone makes the circuit of the vault of heaven as well as walking in the depths of the abyss.[7] Yet for those who can recognize her, she is not so distant – and she longs to be discovered.

Wisdom cries aloud in the street;
in the markets she raises her voice;
on the top of the walls she cries out;
at the entrance of the city gates she speaks:
'How long . . .?'[8]

So the image of the feminine as Eve was by no means the only one which came to the early church fathers through the Jewish scriptures. The beautiful and powerful attempts to express the inexpressible Wisdom of God start with the earliest of the 'Wisdom' books, the Proverbs of King Solomon – compiled, as its opening words tell us, 'that men may know wisdom', and written down from earlier texts, they say, in a semitic language and in Palestine, in the fourth century BC. Sirach (or Ecclesiasticus) was composed in about 180 BC, in the same sort of language and place. The Wisdom of Solomon was probably written in Greek and in Egypt, in the first half of the first century after the birth of Christ. In all these works, Wisdom is the first creation of God the father, poured forth from his own mouth, his breath; she is his emanation. But the texts all draw too on a much more ancient tradition, for they look back to an era when the creative power was the goddess herself, encompassing the very universe, from the vault of heaven to the depth of the abyss, just as does Wisdom in her turn. Like these more ancient epiphanies of the primordial feminine power, Wisdom is parthenogenic, giving birth of herself, forever fertile, forever virgin, entire to herself. 'Though she is but one,' as the Book of Wisdom says, 'she can do all things, and while remaining in herself, she renews all things.' It is she, too, who maintains the essential order of the universe, who knows the past and foresees the future. In this essential task, she is both transcendent and immanent: she both dwells in high places, her throne a pillar of cloud, and is poured out by the Lord into all his works, dwelling in all flesh according to his gift. And her ordering, her knowing, is essentially related to the material with which she works. She is fashioner, artificer, mistress of works and forewoman to God's great project – the one who makes sure that the idea actually works on the ground.[9]

For in her there is a spirit that is intelligent, holy,
unique, manifold, subtle,
mobile, clear, unpolluted,
distinct, invulnerable, loving the good, keen,
irresistible, benificent, humane,

steadfast, sure, free from anxiety,
all-powerful, overseeing all . . .'[10]

This essential quality, this relatedness of hers, is what the Greeks used to call *sophia*. It is a word which means 'wisdom', but of a very particular sort; Homer would speak, for instance, of the *sophia* of the shipbuilder, of his supreme craft and skill. It is the wisdom that sees the relationships between idea and understanding, understanding and hand, hand and material in a sequential chain which leads to action fitting to time and place. It is a wisdom, in short, which depends on an intimate connection between mind and matter, spirit and the body which is the material world. It is a wisdom which we by now know well as very particularly that of Athene. We know it in her multiplicity of ideas and devices, inventions and resources, in her essential craftiness – and in that moment when we cry, 'Now I see! Now I understand how this fits with that, how to translate the idea into something I can see and touch and smell!' No less than Wisdom does Athene play an essential part in creation: when she breathes soul into the human beings whom Prometheus has fashioned, she too dwells, as does Wisdom, in all flesh. And in the evocations of Wisdom, we hear again and again the qualities of mind and thought which are also Athene's own. Wisdom is intelligence; she is knowing. Her qualities unite what is above with what is below: she is both 'overseeing', and 'under-standing'.

These qualities transcend time and space: Wisdom is Foreknowledge, which is very precisely Athene worshipped as Pronoia. Knowing in our turn what came next, the most striking and extraordinary aspect of these comings-together of traditions and these hymnings must surely be that the qualities of creativity and of mind are neither those of the masculine god alone, nor those of the male of the species whom he creates in his own likeness. The power which is also essential to the work of creation, which is the power of mind and the energy of intelligence, knowledge and wisdom itself, is supremely and specifically feminine.

Yet gradually and in the development of both Jewish and Christian thinking this older knowing became intolerable. 'Apocrypha' used to mean 'hidden'; the Wisdom literature was from early on 'apocryphal' because it spoke of hidden things. But by the fourth century of the Christian era, 'apocrypha' had come to mean that which was discarded from the scriptural canon as heretical. The disputes over what was 'true' and what 'false' in the received writings by now went so deep that they were to inform both the development of and the divisions in Christian understanding for centuries to come – and deep in these disputes was the understanding of the nature and power of the divine feminine itself. Early manuscripts of the first Greek translation of the Hebrew bible, the Septuagint – begun in the third century before the birth of Christ and completed some time before 130 BC – certainly included Proverbs in the canon, but sometimes did and sometimes didn't include the Wisdom of Solomon and the 'Wisdom of Jesus, the Son of Sirach' as well. By the fourth century after Christ's birth, the church fathers were fiercely divided. Jerome thought these Wisdom texts, though edifying enough, were not authoritative scripture; he didn't translate them into Latin. Augustine was devoted to them. In a flash of Wisdom's own foresight we can see that well over 1,000 years ahead, in 1546, the Roman Catholic church will finally decide at the Council of Trent for Augustine's way: ever after, it will consider these two books to be 'deuterocanonical', of a second canon, and revere them as inspired, as will most of the Eastern Christians. Protestants, for their part, will go with Jerome: Luther will set the tone by deciding that although these texts are an edifying read, they are not equal in value to the scriptures. The Church of England will deny their doctrinal value in its Thirty-nine Articles of 1503; and although the King James Bible of 1611 will include them (grouped together and apart from the main scriptures), the British and Foreign Bible Society will decide to throw them out altogether some 200 years after that.

The founding fathers of the new faith, however, have their own immediate concerns with the nature of creation and of the creative power itself. Even before the first of the Wisdom literature has been recorded, there is already an alternative understanding of Wisdom's quality. For the philosopher Pythagoras, active around 530 BC, *sophia* is no longer about that supreme skilfulness, adroitness or practical expertise, but instead has to do with looking on at the world. Life is like the festival games, he said (or at least someone who shared his views): 'Some come . . . to compete, some to ply their trade, but the best people come as spectators.' Aristotle was later to agree: the life of God, he thought, is a life of pure contemplation.[11]

This view could hardly be more opposite to the understanding of Wisdom's essence as sheer delight in the bringing together of mind and matter, of the creative force and the material which is to be worked and so transformed. Instead of that essential unity, there is as essential a divorce between spirit and matter. As the Olympians might have seen it, it is the shift from Athene, the ever-near, the mistress of crafts, to Apollo, who shoots from afar his arrows of pure, bright and abstract thought. In the terms of this book's hypotheses, it is a decisive shift in the understanding of the nature of consciousness. There is no room in this scheme of things for a creative feminine consciousness. Already the creative power of mind is being sexed as wholly masculine.

How could this understanding not catch on? It could not but be attractive, in a time that was grappling hard and long with not just the nature of creation but the anguish of the human fall from God's grace, which was not just trying to articulate a concept of Wisdom but reckoned to know, and bitterly, all about Eve as well. The depth of the emerging split in the image of the feminine is starkly emphasized in the writings of Jesus the son of Sirach to his fellow Jews of the second century BC. His hymning of Wisdom is ecstatic; whoever loves her loves life itself, he cries, those who seek her early will be filled with joy, he who pursues her will dwell in the midst of her glory. Yet this same author is as fervent against the potential for evil of mortal women as he is devoted to the spiritual expression of feminine power; the very exaltation of the ideal is bound to bring bitter disillusionment with the actual. So there is, for him, no wickedness greater than that of a wife; any other iniquity is insignificant by comparison (may a sinner's lot befall her!). A wicked wife even begins to look like a bear; her husband is driven to take his meals with his neighbours. For a quiet man, living with a garrulous wife is like struggling up a steep hillside of sand. Woman's beauty is a snare, and her possessions can only bring disgrace if she is the one who supports the household.[12]

A dejected mind, a gloomy face,
and a wounded heart are caused by an evil wife.
Drooping hands and weak knees
are caused by the wife who does not make her husband happy.
From a woman sin had its beginning,
and because of her we all die.[13]

So just as Wisdom, the divine feminine power, brings life itself, so does mortal woman bring death. The old understanding of the feminine force, the goddess, as holding the great cycle of life and death, creation, destruction and regeneration, in her care, is shattered into the polarization of the divine good and the human evil. And from there it is not so large a step to demotion of the creative power of the feminine altogether. So the attributes of mind, of intelligence, of understanding, which have been specifically Wisdom's own, become masculine. And so, as we have seen, mortal man will carry through Adam these higher and nobler attributes, while woman, through Eve, incarnates the grosser, material realm. And then what is 'progress' for humankind? Nothing else, as Philo put it, than 'the giving up of the female gender by changing into the male, since the female gender is material, passive, corporeal and sense-perceptible, while the male is active, incorporeal and more akin to mind and thought'.

Mind and Thought! *Nous kai dianoia* – the very evocation, for an earlier generation, of Athene's own qualities! Yet Philo's understanding of the nature of male and female demands that these superior qualities become masculine. So he starts by challenging the essential equality of Wisdom as consort of the creator God: she is rather, he says, his daughter. But then he goes further, to posit that although Wisdom's name may be feminine, her nature is in fact masculine.

[T]hat which comes after God, even though it were the chiefest of all other things, occupies a second place, and therefore was termed feminine to express its contrast with the Maker of the Universe who is masculine, and its affinity to every thing else. For pre-eminence always pertains to the masculine, and the feminine always come short of it and is lesser than it. Let us then pay no heed to the discrepancy in the gender of the words, and say that the daughter of God, even Wisdom, is not only masculine but father, sowing and begetting in souls aptness to learn, discipline, knowledge, sound sense and laudable actions.[14]

So Wisdom becomes masculine, her gender attribution simply a discrepancy that conceals his true nature. It is not long either before Wisdom becomes identified not just with the god who is father-creator, but with his divine son, who brings a new understanding to the very concept. Has not God made foolish the wisdom of the world? demands St Paul.

For since, in the wisdom of God, the world did not know God through wisdom, it pleased God through the folly of what we preach to save those who believe. For Jews demand signs and Greeks seek wisdom, but we preach Christ crucified, a stumbling block to Jews and folly to Gentiles, but to those who are called, both Jews and Greeks, Christ the power of God and the wisdom of God.[15]

So Christ becomes the Wisdom of God, and the identification is enshrined not just in doctrine but in bricks and mortar. The dedication of the great church of Hagia Sophia in Constantinople is to Holy Wisdom as the wisdom of Christ.[16]

Yet for some at least, that identification does not mean that Wisdom has passed entirely to the masculine. 'I desire that you understand,' the risen Christ tells his disciples, that First Man is called 'Begetter, Mind who is complete in himself'. He reflected with the great Sophia, his consort, and revealed his first-begotten, androgynous son. His male name is called 'First Begetter Son of God'; his female name is 'First-Begettress Sophia, Mother of the Universe'. Some call her 'Love'. Now the First-Begotten is called 'Christ'. Since he has authority from his Father, he created for himself a multitude of angels without number for retinue, from the spirit and the light.[17]

That comes from a text called *The Sophia of Jesus Christ*, one of the Gnostic gospels which date from the earliest centuries of Christianity, before the scriptural canon was fixed in the form we know it today. In these times, a proliferation of Christian groups clustered around their own teachers or spiritual guides, each seeking in their own way that *gnosis* which is the knowing or understanding that comes not through a set of defined teachings or the mouth of an appointed preacher, but through a movement of recognition by the individual heart. To a church whose own priorities were to establish a homogeneity of belief and structure outside of whose boundaries there could be no salvation, such seekings soon became a source less of energy than of threat. As Bishop Irenaeus, who supervised the church in Lyons towards the end of the second century, cried in warning: 'They imagine that by means of their obscure interpretations, each of them has discovered a god of his own!' To the mainstream church, such *gnosis* soon became heresy. Irenaeus himself devoted five volumes to *The Destruction and Overthrow of Falsely So-Called Knowledge*, so that his readers might urge all those with whom they were connected 'to avoid such an abyss of madness and blasphemy against Christ'. By the time that Constantine made Christianity the official religion of his empire there was no room for divergences in what that might mean and by the middle of the fourth century the Gnostics were officially suppressed, their meetings prohibited and their books ordered to be burned. Yet enough has survived – most amazingly in the texts discovered at Nag Hammadi in Upper Egypt some 1,500 years after they were first concealed – to remind us of an older and different Wisdom.[18]

'Every one of them generates something new every day!' stormed Irenaeus, and there is certainly nothing simple in the Gnostics' arcane cosmologies. But interweaving among the different texts there is also a common understanding, and two of its tenets are these: that creation was the work of a primal feminine force just as much as of the masculine, and that this force encompassed precisely those attributes of mind and intelligence which orthodoxy, as we have seen, was to attribute entirely to the masculine.

According to Valentinus, one of the greatest Gnostic guides, who came from Rome to Alexandria and taught there in the middle years of the second century, God is essentially indescribable. But, he suggests, we can envisage the divine as consisting in the one part of the Ineffable, the Depth, the Primal Father, and in the other, of Grace, Silence, the Womb and 'Mother of the All', who receives the seed of the Ineffable Source, and from this brings forth all the emanations of divine being. Some Gnostic writings see the feminine and masculine forces as coming to creation at the same time. From the power of Silence, says the *Great Announcement* in its own explanation of the origins of the universe, appeared 'a great power, the Mind of the Universe, which manages all things and is a male . . . the other . . . a great Intelligence . . . is a female which produces all things'. Other writings envisage, as do the Wisdom books, that the feminine force is the first creation of the original power. 'This is the first power which was before all of them,' says *The Apocryphon of John*, 'and which came forth from his mind, that is the Pronoia of the All . . . This is the first thought, his image; she became the womb of everything, for she is prior to them all . . .'

Sometimes, again, there can be no distinction of masculine and feminine, male and female in that great creative force. The Pronoia of the All, the text above continues, is 'Mother–Father'. The figure of light which has earlier appeared to John – first as youth, then as old man, then in the form of a servant – urges him not to be afraid. 'You are not unfamiliar with this likeness, are you? That is to say, be not timid! I am the one who is with you for ever. I am the Father, I am the Mother.' Elsewhere, Jesus speaks of 'my Mother, the Spirit'. And in the text *Trimorphic Protennoia* (literally, 'Triple-Formed Primal Thought), this force announces herself in terms that recall the ancient parthenogenic goddesses:

I am androgynous. I am both Mother and Father since I copulate with myself, I copulate with myself and with those who love me, and it is through me alone that the All stands firm. I am the Womb that gives shape to the All by giving birth to the Light that shines in splendour.[19]

What is this primal feminine force? It is Intelligence, it is Thought, it is Foresight, Perception and Knowledge. For some writers, it is also Wisdom, Sophia herself, and it is around her image that the story grew which would explain the terrible and anguished discrepancy between the divine work and the sufferings of humankind. Some say it was Sophia, some her daughter of the same name, who overreached herself by wanting to create something on her own, without her consort. She had done this, after all, in the most ancient days, but now things were different, and in her unilateral action she threw the divine harmony of opposites out of kilter. So what she produced was abortive and defective – and that is how, according to Valentinus at least, suffering came into human existence. Some say that to shape and manage this defective creation, Wisdom produced the Demiurge, the creator-God of Israel. Others say that what she produced was an arrogant beast that resembled a lion, and that it opened its eyes, looked around and simply declared: 'It is I who am God, and there is none other apart from me!' So Sophia and her daughter Zoë (life) must embark on a battle against this 'god of the blind' which cannot be resolved until the True Man reveals the existence of the Truth of existence. Others again say that Wisdom herself is banished, fallen into the gross world of matter, from which she must struggle to liberate herself and reunite with the divine.[20]

So for all the Gnostic pursuit of the individual quest against the demands of institutionalized dogmas, for all that some groups seem actually to have held women and men in equal respect, there are also some familiar enough themes. For the Gnostics as for mainstream Christians, the world of matter is a sorry place, the struggle must be to escape it, and the reason that it is so and that we suffer is that the feminine overreached herself. The negative connotation of the feminine and the gross, material world, in opposition to the positive, masculine realm of spirit, simply cannot, it seems, be escaped.

Or can it? For some Gnostic writers, the story of Eve is the story of the soul suffering in separation from her spiritual self; her marriage with Adam represents the longed-for union with this higher aspect. But others see it differently. For them, it is Adam who represents 'psyche' or ordinary consciousness, while it is Eve who represents the higher principle. According to *The Hypostasis of the Archons*, for instance, the Rulers, who are in charge of creation in its fallen state, put Adam into the deep sleep of Ignorance, and are horrified when Eve awakens him. But Adam cries: 'It is you who have given me life; you will be called "Mother of the Living". For it is she who is my mother. It is she who is the Physician, and the Woman, and She Who Has Given Birth.' And then the Female Spiritual Principle comes to them in the form of the Snake, the Instructor, and tells them that is is only through the arrogant Ruler's jealousy that he has told them not to eat of the tree . . .

And when they did, says the text called *On the Origins of the World*,

their mind opened. For when they ate, the light of knowledge shone for them. When they put on shame, they knew that they were naked with regard to knowledge. When they sobered up, they saw that they were naked and they became enamoured of each other. When they saw their makers [the seven Rulers] they loathed them since they were beastly forms. They understood very much.

If for the orthodox teachers the human desire for knowledge is the root of all sin, for the Gnostics it is knowledge itself which is the route to redemption. As the author of *The Testimony of Truth* demands, a little later on in the story of Adam and Eve, 'Of what sort is this God? First he envied Adam that he should eat from the Tree of knowledge. And secondly he said, "Adam, where are you?" And God does not have foreknowledge, that is, since he did not know this from the beginning. And afterwards he said, "Let us cast him out of this place, lest he eat of the tree of life and live forever." Surely he has shown himself to be a malicious envier.'[21]

In all the twists and turns of the Gnostic accounts of the beginnings of the world and its fall from grace, what can still be discerned is a thread that stretches from more ancient beliefs. Well into the Christian era, it is possible to hold an image of a creative force which is feminine, whose powers are those of mind and intelligence and whose *sophia* has to do with incarnation in the material world. From one tradition the thread is spun from the literature of Wisdom; from another, from the attributes of a feminine consciousness which was imaged as Athene.

Well, as we know, that thread could not be held. Athene becomes a demon, many Wisdom texts become secondary, the Gnostic teachings are buried or burned and the serpent, the wisest beast of all, becomes the very devil. Yet can such a thread, once spun, be lost? The archetypal image exists; it will go on seeking for expression. As time goes on, Sophia becomes more hidden from the general view. She has her lovers, appearing to the scholar Boethius, for instance, at the beginning of the sixth century as he awaits death on the orders of the barbarian emperor Theodoric.

Her eyes sparkled with fire, and her look was far more piercing than that of any mortal. Her complexion was comely and healthful and she seemed to possess all the vigour of youth; nevertheless, her appearance was such as denoted her to have lived many years, and that her existence began long before the present age. The height of her stature could not be determined, as she varied it at pleasure; now, she seemed to contract herself to the ordinary size of men; anon, she appeared to reach the skies with her head, nay, she would at times elevate herself still higher, and penetrate so far into the heavens, as to surmount the reach of the most acute and discerning eye. The stuff of which her robe was composed was indissoluble; it was of the finest thread, woven with wonderful art . . .

Later, she told Boethius that she made her clothes herself. Of course! Her teachings were the greatest comfort to him as he struggled to understand life's apparent injustice, and as *The Consolation of Philosophy* would influence generations of scholars.[22] But in general, in those days, Sophia would walk in hidden paths.

Yet as this image of the feminine fades, so another becomes ever stronger. By the sixth century, many significant moments in the life of Mary, Mother of God, have their own formal commemorations: the Annunciation, the Purification, her own Conception, her Nativity. What people have known for generations, that she was on her death assumed into heaven, will eventually be formally recognized too: in the celebration of the Assumption, which dates from the ninth century, Mary becomes, if not goddess, at least a dweller with the god. As her image is amplified, she also becomes more powerful on earth: as was Athene before her, she is an icon of state, protector of her people. Already in the fourth century, Ephraem of Syria is begging her to be a 'tower of strength' to the faithful. He is the first, they say, to cry as so many will afterwards in their evocations of her blazing power:

> Who is this that looks forth like the dawn,
> fair as the moon, bright as the sun,
> terrible as an army with banners?[23]

And her power could be mighty indeed. In 438, the Empress Eudoxia sent to her sister-in-law an ikon of the Virgin said to have been painted by St Luke himself – the oldest portrayal known, with the possible exception of a second-century mural from the catacomb of St Priscilla in Rome. This image became known as the Nicopoeion, Creator of Victory – and under this sign, the Empire was to hold fast for another 1,000 years. In the sixth and seventh centuries, the image of Nike, ancient goddess of Victory, was struck from the imperial seals and replaced with that of the Virgin and Child. At the turn of the seventh century, the emperor turned against his enemy Phocas, 'that gorgon's head', another terrible head – 'the awe-inspiring image of the pure Virgin'. In the seventh and eighth centuries, the paintings of the Virgin and Child which were displayed on the gates of Constantinople and carried around its walls repelled besiegers. As in the East, so in the West: King Arthur, they say, carried her image on his shield, just as so many other heroes had carried the image of the Gorgon's head, 'and the heathen were put to flight'.[24]

Yet if this is Mary as daughter of the fathers, protector of their civic and military order, she carries also, of course, the ancient feminine tradition, as her very early hymning as Mother of God attests. From about 600 in the East and a couple of hundred years later in the West, the cult grows up of the Grand Mother of Jesus, the Great Mother herself – St Anne, mother of the virgin. In the paintings, she often stands behind and above mother and child, or contains them on her own lap, both protector and reminder from whence they take their life. When she sits more intimately with her daughter, she is portrayed as teaching her from the Book of Wisdom.[25]

As Mary acquired feast days of her own, the Wisdom texts from the Old Testament were woven into the scriptures appointed to be read on them. As Geoffrey Ashe observes, this was 'under a compulsion that was never discussed';[26] yet it became general in both Eastern and Western churches to link the ancient Sophia with her contemporary daughter. So at her Nativity (and what was much later to become the feast of the Immaculate Conception): 'The Lord created me at the beginning of his work, the first of his acts of old . . .' So at the feast of the Assumption and the later one of the Queen of Heaven: 'From eternity, in the beginning he created me, and for eternity I shall not cease to exist.' (Rome tried to exclude this portion of the scripture, but it found its way into the Carmelite rite; other verses from this chapter were also, from the seventh century, included in the liturgy which celebrated those women who had consecrated themselves to God and withdrawn from the world.)[27]

In early times, the link between Mary and Wisdom was obscured; as we have seen, the dedication of Hagia Sophia in Constantinople under Justinian was to the Wisdom of Christ. It was only in the Russian church that the identification of Wisdom and Mary became explicit; it was to institute a special mass which combined the Holy Wisdom with the Assumption. Yet the impulse to assure a continuity in the image of the divine feminine cannot be suppressed. By the eleventh century, St Peter Damian, one of Mary's early Western devotees, is taking as his text on the feast of her Nativity the biblical description of the Seat of Wisdom, King Solomon's throne. He draws parallels between this description and her own qualities: its ivory is the whiteness of her virginity, the twelve lions – one on each side of the six steps that lead up to it – are the twelve apostles who gaze up to the Mother of God and cry, 'Who is this arising like the dawn . . .?'[28]

Solomon built that great throne of his, they say, after the visit of the Queen of Sheba, who had heard of his wisdom and came to try him with hard questions. Some say she conceded his superior learning and heaped on him great mounds of gold and precious stones and quantities of spices the like of which have never been seen before or since. But others remind us that she too was an incarnation of Wisdom. King Solomon gave her all that she desired, and the Song of Songs which celebrates their union must be among the most ecstatic love poetry ever written. In the twelfth century, Bernard of Clairvaux was to preach no fewer than eighty-six sermons on it, in his turn celebrating the ecstatic love of Christ for his bride – who was sometimes the church, sometimes the individual soul, the monks of Clairvaux or the Virgin herself. In his sermons for the Assumption, St Bernard takes as his text the verse which asks, 'Who is that coming up from the wilderness like a column of smoke, perfumed with myrrh and frankincense, with all the fragrant powders of the merchant?'[29] There is an echo here of Wisdom's glorying in her own beginnings:

I came forth from the mouth of the Most High,
and covered the earth like a mist.
I dwelt in high places,
and my throne was a pillar of cloud.[30]

By the twelfth century, Mary has become identified with that
throne, hymned as Sedes Sapientiae – herself the Seat of Wisdom.
She is pictured on her throne which like Solomon's own has a lion
at each arm. In this image, we can see an equal honouring of the
wisdom of feminine and masculine, just as there was between
Solomon and the Queen of Sheba. And we can see too a return to
an image of the goddess, flanked once more by her beasts, which is
of even more ancient provenance.

'I was sent forth from the power,' says the feminine force which
speaks in *The Thunder, Perfect Mind,* the most extraordinary of the
Nag Hammadi texts, 'and I have come to those who reflect upon
me,/and I have been found among those who seek after me . . .

> Do not be ignorant of me.
> For I am the first and the last.
> I am the honoured one and the scorned one.
> I am the whore and the holy one.
> I am the wife and the virgin.
> I am the mother and the daughter.
> I am the members of my mother.
> I am the barren one
>   and many are her sons . . .
> I am the silence that is incomprehensible
>   and the idea whose remembrance is frequent.
> I am the voice whose sound is manifold
>   and the word whose appearance is multiple.
> I am the utterance of my name . . .
> You who tell the truth about me, lie about me,
>   and you who have lied about me, tell the truth about me.

You who know me, be ignorant of me,
    and those who have not known me, let them know me.
For I am knowledge and ignorance.
I am shame and boldness.
I am shameless, I am ashamed.
I am strength and I am fear.
I am war and peace.
Give heed to me.
I am the one who is disgraced and the great one . . .

There is nothing in this awesome litany to identify it with particular Jewish, Christian or Gnostic themes; it does not presuppose, either, a particular Gnostic myth. In her paradoxical proclamations, this power transcends them all, to evoke a unity of Sophia and Eve, Eve and Mary, and all the images of the goddesses which have gone before. From the Perfect Mind comes an idea of unfathomable entirety. It is one to which succeeding generations are going to find it increasingly hard to hold.[31]

CHAPTER 8

The Armour of Allegory

Anyone who wished to learn about the preparations and conduct necessary to war, thought Francis Bacon, could usefully consider the story of Perseus. For it offered three valuable pieces of advice, laid down 'as if they were the precepts of Pallas'. The first is that it is well not to fight with the neighbours, but, like Perseus, to go as far from home as possible. The second is that the cause of war should be just and honourable, 'for this adds alacrity both to the soldiers and the people who find the supplies; procures aids, alliances and numerous other conveniences'. (And what could be more just and laudable than 'the suppressing of tyranny, by which people are dispirited, benumbed or left without life and vigour, as at the sight of the Medusa'?) And the third is that, just as Perseus singled out the one mortal Gorgon, you should choose such wars 'as may be brought to a conclusion, without pursuing vast and infinite hopes'.

And further, Bacon continues: to pursue his purposes, Perseus needs foresight (which he gets from Pallas), secrecy (from Pluto) and dispatch (from Mercury). He must also consult the Graeae, who are 'treasons', the degenerate sisters of war; he needs their eye to give him indications of what's going on and their tooth for 'sowing rumours, raising envy and stirring up the minds of the people'. Just how well this strategy works can be seen in the effects of his conquest. His fame flies abroad (Pegasus) and he achieves the greatest possible defence and safeguard (by putting Medusa's head into Pallas's shield). 'For one grand and memorable enterprise, happily accomplished, bridles all the motives and attempts of the enemy, stupifies disaffection and quells commotions.'

So the old tale still had its lessons for the seventeenth-century *realpolitik* in which Bacon was embroiled. He called his interpretation *The Wisdom of the Ancients* and for him there was no doubt that wise they had been. For he belonged to a generation which still held the time-honoured belief that progress in human understanding is not linear but cyclical, that the human enterprise is not to invent the new but to re-cognize what, somewhere, we already know. Just as the ancients had longed for the return of the Golden Age, just as Renaissance philosophers had held that Christianity itself had been known to Hermes, Orpheus and Plato, Copernicanism to the Egyptians and Paracelsian chemistry to Hermes again, just as some were to believe that Newton's system of the world had first been revealed to the initiates of an ancient mystery – so did Bacon and his philosophical contemporaries hope for a return to the state of Adam before the Fall, when they could recover that pure and sinless contact with Nature which would enable them finally to gain knowledge of her powers.[1]

So for Bacon, it was impossible that the ancient fables should *not* have their lessons for those who could discern their 'concealed instruction'. That this was their purpose rather than anything more historical is evident, for him, from the story of Pallas's birth from the head of Jupiter. Taken literally, it is 'monstrously absurd'. Understood allegorically, however, the whole sequence, from Jupiter's swallowing of Metis onwards, seems to contain a state secret about princes and their councils. It shows

with what art kings usually carry themselves towards their council, in order to preserve their own authority and majesty not only inviolate, but so as to have it magnified and heightened among the people. Kings commonly join as it were in nuptial bond to their council, while making sure decree seems to come from themselves. And as this decree or execution proceeds with prudence and power, so as to imply necessity, it is elegantly wrapped up under the figure of Pallas armed.

So Bacon the politician perceives Athene once more at her father's right hand, hard at work in the citadel to ensure that the business of government rolls smoothly, using her *nous* in the service of his political ends. But to Bacon the scientist, she imparts a very different sort of wisdom, when in the story of the birth of Erichthonius, that mysterious snake-child, he finds explained 'the improper use of force in natural philosophy'. Erichthonius, he says, being the product of Vulcan's rape of Minerva, was thus while comely and well-proportioned enough from the middle upwards, shrunken and deformed like an eel in his thighs and legs. 'Conscious of this defect, he became the inventor of chariots, so as to show the graceful, but conceal the deformed part of his body.' Vulcan, explains Bacon, represents Art and Minerva, Nature – 'by reason of the industry employed in her works'.

Art, therefore, whenever it offers violence to nature, in order to conquer, subdue and bend her to its purpose, by tortures and force of all kinds, seldom obtains the ends proposed; yet upon great struggle and application, there proceed certain imperfect births, or lame abortive works, specious in appearance, but weak and unstable in use, which are, nevertheless, with great pomp and deceitful appearances, triumphantly carried about and shown by imposters. A procedure very familiar, and remarkable in chemical productions and new mechanical inventions, especially when the inventors rather hug their errors than improve upon them, and go on struggling with nature, not courting her.

So here is Athene teaching once more that sense of the fitness of things, of the essential relationship between the inventive mind and the natural law which governs the material to be worked. (A very great pity, too, that Bacon did not always heed her lesson! Elsewhere, and notoriously, he wrote that Nature should be 'made a slave', and 'put in constraint', while the scientist tortured her secrets from her. In his conviction that the human animal was the centre of the created world – 'in so much that if man were taken away from the world, the rest would seem to be all astray, without aim or purpose' – he was very much a man of his time.)[2]

Not all his contemporaries, however, would agree with his approach to mythology. For some, the characters who peopled these ancient tales were indeed historical: they were women and men of reknown who had, because of their outstanding qualities, been taken for deities. The forging of this exemplary link between the human and the divine was itself of ancient pedigree. The first to do it was the philosopher Euhemerus, who worked in the third century BC – and whose name still describes his approach. His idea immediately caught on and his writings were among the first to be translated from Greek into Latin.

At first, as we have seen, the Christian philosophers enlisted the euhemeristic approach to strengthen their attack on the ancient deities. 'Those to whom you bow were once men like yourselves!' cried Clement of Alexandria. Augustine made some complex calculations in his own attempt to time-date these demons and so demote them to a place that was historical rather than heavenly. But as time went on, the historical question spun its own fascinations: when *did* these extraordinary people live, what *were* they like? And what, importantly, can we learn from their lives and attributes, formed as they were from the same clay as ourselves, infused with the same spirit? Genealogies and cross-connections proliferate in the attempts to place them among the known and valued hierarchies of patriarchs, judges and prophets. The great mythic figures are honoured for their civilizing gifts to humankind, remembered as later generations will remember Galileo and Harvey, Faraday and Stevenson. So Heracles can be set side-by-side with Moses and Solon as the legislators who saved humanity from the consequences of its own frailty; the letters of the alphabet were said to have first come to us from an Egyptian woman called Isis; it was an Italian woman called Minerva who had introduced the skills of weaving and other useful arts. By the fifteenth century, the old deities had secured an honoured historical place. And for some, they could once more have their place in a gloriously inclusive heaven as well. 'Shouldst thou follow in the footsteps of David,' wrote Zwingli to Francis I of France, 'thou wilt one day see God himself, and near to Him thou mayst hope to see Adam, Abel, Enoch, Paul, Hercules, Theseus, Socrates, the Catos, the Scipios . . .'[3]

So these heroic figures forged a chain that stretched not just back through time but between heaven and earth as well. In their historical reality they offered something that we humans, assailed with the knowledge of our impermanence, do not cease to seek: a sense that we belong to what went before and will have a place in whatever may come after. In the Middle Ages and beyond, this could be important to whole peoples: nations would look to a mythic ancestor who was also a protector. As we have heard, it was Aeneas who founded Italy, and France too could look back through the Franks to their Trojan origins, this time through Hector. The English had known ever since the historian Geoffrey of Monmouth had recorded it in the twelfth century that they too, as Britons, had Trojan blood: it was Aeneas's grandson Brutus who had claimed their land from Gogmagog and the other giants, and founded London as Troynavant, or New Troy, to celebrate his triumph.[4]

This mythic ancestry could be no less important to the identity of individuals than to that of whole peoples. In the imagination and writing of one of the most enchanting euhemerists, we can glimpse just how enlivening to the sense of self the connection with the reality of the ancients could be.

One day at the very start of the fifteenth century, Christine de Pizan was sitting at her desk reflecting on the very many things male authors through the centuries had said about women. And very depressing this became – as well it might to a highly educated woman who had been widowed at the age of twenty-five, left with three small children, and became the first woman in Western letters to support herself and her family by her prolific pen. Finally, Christine was brought in her depressing musings to wondering how it was that God had come to make such an abominable work as woman at all, when we have the word of so many learned men for it that she is 'the vessel as well as the refuge and abode of every evil and vice'. And as she sat there with a great unhappiness welling up in her heart (and a tongue very firmly in her cheek), there appeared to her three crowned ladies, the brightness of whose faces illuminated Christine herself and the whole room. So begins her mission, directed by Dame Reason, Dame Rectitude and Dame Justice, to build a new city, beautiful without equal and of perpetual duration, whose sovereign is to be Mary Queen of Heaven herself. This is to be the City of Ladies, built on the Field of Letters, on a flat and fertile plain where the earth abounds in good things, and it is to be a refuge and defence for all the ladies of fame and women worthy of praise whom jealous men have wrong-fully attacked for so long.[5]

It is these women whom the Dames introduce to Christine, demonstrating to her (and of course her readers) through their characters and exploits that women too have held government and made discoveries in the world of learning and science; that it is very far from true that women are invariably unfaithful in love and create problems in marriage; that they may be as constant too in their love for and devotion to God. The polemic doesn't take much seeking, but so delightful is Christine's passion and learning that there isn't a sour brick in the edifice she constructs. Some-times her comments can ring as startlingly contemporary, but overall her purpose is a modest one to a modern ear. Even when the new City is completed as the refuge and defence of all virtuous women, it is the qualities of patience, simplicity, piety and prudence, charity and above all humility, as exemplified by the City's Queen herself, that Christine especially urges on its future inhabitants. Yet as she herself has made crystal clear, the women whose magnificent presence these future inhabitants will join have a lot more about them than that.

And what a parade of them there is! Saint and sibyl, contempor-ary noblewoman and mythic queen – all are given equal status, all presented as equally real. So here, among the throng, is Medea, who was 'very beautiful, with a noble and upright heart and a pleasant face', and who surpassed all women in her knowledge of herbs and spells. Here is Queen Circe, who knew so much about the arts of enchantment 'that there was nothing which she might want to do that she could not accomplish'. Here is Queen Ceres of Sicily, the first to discover cultivation and invent the necessary tools for it, including the yoke for oxen and the plough. Isis, who moved from Greece with her brother, taught the Egyptians short-hand and how to set up vegetable gardens and make plant grafts, as well as instituting some good and upright laws. Arachne invented the art of dyeing woollens and the 'fine thread' technique of weaving pictures into tapestries, as well as the cultivation of flax and hemp and the arts of snaring and trapping birds, fishes and cruel and strong wild animals as well. Medusa was one of those famous for her extraordinary beauty – that long curly blonde hair of hers spun like gold and her beautiful face and body so attracting every mortal creature on whom she looked that they seemed im-mobilized. All of these, and many more, from the first of them onwards, are to be valued. For, as Dame Reason explains, God created Eve from Adam's rib precisely to signify 'that she should stand at his side as a companion and never lie at his feet like a slave, and also that he should love her as his own flesh'.[6]

Dame Reason and her two companions are of course allegorical figures, their purpose pinned earnestly to their sleeve for all to see in the fashion of the day. Yet they also have more ancient and mys-terious identities, for they are also none other than the three Fates. 'And of the three noble ladies whom you see here,' Dame Justice tells Christine, 'we are as one and the same, we could not exist with-out one another; and what the first disposes, the second orders and initiates, and then I, the third, finish and terminate it.' Dame Reason herself, 'the disposer', shares many of the attributes of Athene. It is she who speaks first to Christine, and she seems to her 'the most wise lady who . . . knew in her mind what I was thinking, as one who has insight into everything'. Dame Reason's emblem is a mirror – as Rectitude's is a ruler and Justice's a measure – so that she can show to each man and woman their special qualities and faults and so pursue her duty, which is to straighten people out when they go astray and to put them back on to the right path. 'I would thus have you know truly,' she tells Christine,

that no one can look into this mirror, no matter what kind of creature, without achieving clear self-knowledge. My mirror has such great dignity that not without reason is it surrounded by rich and precious gems, so that you see, thanks to this mirror, the essences, qualities, proportions, and measures of all things are known, nor can anything be done well without it.

The seeing which is understanding, and the understanding of right measure: this is truly Athene's realm, as it was also that of her mother Metis before her.[7]

The goddess appears to Christine in other guises too. Were there ever any women, she asks Reason disingenuously, who 'through the strength of emotion and the subtlety of mind and comprehension, have themselves discovered any new arts and sciences which are necessary, good and profitable, and which had hitherto not been discovered or known'? Why, yes indeed, replies Dame Reason — and goes on to give her many examples, including Queen Ceres, the Egyptian woman Isis and the Asian maiden Arachne, whom we have already met. The first of these skilled and subtle women to be introduced, however, is the noble Nicostrata, whom the Italians call Carmentis, the daughter of a king of Arcadia named Pallas. This woman had a marvellous mind, and was so well versed in Greek literature and so eloquent that her contemporaries said she was beloved of Mercury himself, and that her child was not by her husband at all but by the god. When this lady had to leave her native land for Italy, a great many people followed her. Having disembarked from the river Tiber, she climbed a high hill which she called the Palatine, after her father — and this was where the city of Rome was later founded. Meanwhile, she and her son built a fortress and set about bringing civilized laws to the local people, who until then had been simply savages — and that is how Roman Law, the inspiration of all other legal systems, got its start. Exceptionally gifted as she also was with the spirit of prophecy, Carmentis could foresee that one day the Roman Empire would rule the whole world, and it did not seem right to her that it should do so while using the strange and inferior letters of another country. So she invented the Latin alphabet and syntax, and a complete introduction to the science of grammar as well. The Italians quite rightly recognized this skill, with all the utility and profit it brought with it, as the most worthy yet invented. So they elevated her not just above any man but above men themselves by making her a goddess and building a temple in her honour, and by naming many things according to her 'science of Latin', even calling themselves 'Latins' to ensure her eternal remembrance.

How news travels! This is mythology become divine gossip, the tale that grows and shifts in shape and colour as it weaves its way through changes in consciousness. In Carmentis's story, of course, we can see how the Palladium, sacred emblem of the goddess, came with Aeneas to Rome to become the luck of the city; we can see how persistently the goddess is linked with those alphabet letters which she once shook, together with Medusa's head, out of the bag that Perseus brought back from his adventures.

Minerva, that maiden of Greece by surname Pallas, was also good with signs and symbols: Dame Reason recounts how she invented a most useful Greek shorthand, as well as numbers and a means of quickly counting and adding sums. So enlightened was her mind with general knowledge, however, that this was only the start of her inventions. She it was who first understood the making of woollen cloth, right through from her new idea of shearing the sheep to all the techniques of carding and spinning, to weaving itself. She also discovered how to extract oil and juices from olives and other fruits, and invented flutes and fifes, trumpets and wind instruments and the use of wagons and carts for ease of transport. Most remarkably, 'because it is far from a woman's nature to conceive of such things', she invented the art and technique of making harnesses and armour from iron and steel and she taught the Athenians how to deploy an army and fight in organized ranks.

They held this maiden in such high esteem that they made her a goddess, erecting a temple to her after her death in which they placed a statue portraying her as representing wisdom and chivalry.

This statue had terrible and cruel eyes because chivalry has been instituted to carry out rigorous justice; they also signified that one seldom knows toward what end the meditation of the wise man tends. She wore a helmet on her head which signified that a knight must have strength, endurance and constant courage in the deeds of arms, and further signified that the counsels of the wise are concealed, secret and hidden. She was dressed in a coat of mail which stood for the power of the estate of chivalry and also taught that the wise man is always armed against the whims of Fortune, whether good or bad. She held some kind of spear or very long lance, which meant that the knight must be the rod of justice and also signified that the wise man casts his spear from great distances. A buckler or shield of crystal hung at her neck, which meant that the knight must always be alert and oversee everywhere the defence of his country and people and further signified that things are open and evident to the wise man. She had portrayed in the middle of this shield the head of a serpent called Gorgon, which teaches that the knight must always be wary and watchful over his enemies like the serpent, and furthermore, that the wise man is aware of all the malice which can hurt him. Next to this image they also placed a bird that flies by night, named the owl, as if to watch over her, which signified that the knight must be ready by night as well as by day for civil defence, when necessary, and also that the wise man should take care at all times to do what is profitable and fitting for him.[8]

Christine's pedagogical purpose is fairly immobilizing here; her painstaking portrayal of the goddess's allegorical attributes renders her as stolid and unyielding as was that great statue of state on the Acropolis itself. But maybe too Christine needed to armour herself against the image's archetypal energic force. Throughout the book, she is careful to distance herself from those foolish people of bygone times who mistakenly took her notable women for goddesses; to make assurance doubly sure, she here takes the goddess as role model for the chivalric knight rather than his lady, for the masculine world rather than the feminine one which she herself is constructing. Elsewhere, though, she is less careful. For *The Book of Feats of Arms and Chivalry*, written some six years later, she evokes the aid not just of an acknowledged human expert, but of the goddess herself.

O Minerva, goddess of arms and chivalry . . . Adored lady and high goddess, do not be displeased that I, a simple little woman, who am as nothing compared to the greatness of your famed learning, should under-take now to speak of such a magnificent enterprise as that of arms . . . Please look on me kindly, for I can share in some little way the land where you were born, which was formerly called Magna Graecia, that country beyond the Alps now called Apulia and Calabria, where you were born, and so like you I am an Italian woman.[9]

So Minerva is both a mortal woman, as geographically anchored as Christine herself – and goddess after all. She is both natural and a supernatural force, and in that she can take her place among the cloud of saints whose protective presence could be evoked through time and place to shield believers in a harsh and arbitrary world.

The Book of the City of Ladies had its first (and until 1981 its last!) translation into English in 1521. Sixty years later than that, the Kentish squire Reginald Scot was mockingly recalling a galaxy of popular devotions:

Our painters had Luke, our weavers had Steven, our millers had Arnold, our tailors had Goodman, our sowters [cobblers] had Crispin, our potters had S. Gore with a devil on his shoulder and a pot in his hand. Was there a better horseleech . . . than S. Loy? Or a better sowgelder than S. Anthony? Or a better toothdrawer than S. Apolline? . . . S. Roch was good at the plague, S. Petronill at the ague. As for S. Margaret she passed Lucina for a midwife . . . in which respect S. Marpurge is joined with her in commission. For madmen and such as are possessed with devils, S.

Romane was excellent, and friar Ruffine was also prettily skilful in that art. For botches and biles, Cosmus and Damian; S. Clare for the eyes, S. Apolline for teeth, S. Job for the pox. And for sore breasts S. Agatha.

The Reformation had supposedly put an end to all that – and in fact the worship of saints seems already to have fallen off during the previous century. But the very indignation of Scot's indictment – couched in precisely the same terms as St Augustine's inveighing against the proliferation of pagan demons all those centuries before – bears witness to how real these personified energies continued to be as messengers and intercessors between earth and the manifold mysteries of that other, supernatural world. Who can ever know their nature and extent? Half a century later, we can even catch a glimpse of the goddess herself in the complaint of a pious observer that people thought it so unlucky to kill a swallow that even robbing their nests was held by 'some old beldames . . . a more fearful sacrilege than to steal a chalice out of a church'.[10]

But by then such free-wheeling, shape-shifting sightings of the goddess are rare, to be snatched out of the corner of the eye if at all. She has her occult, hidden life, appearing for instance as Minerva in *The Torch of the Thirty Statues*, the last of the extraordinarily complex treatises on the art of memory of Giordano Bruno, the renegade Dominican and hermeticist. Here, says his interpreter Frances Yates, 'she is the *mens*, the divine in man reflecting the divine universe. She is memory and reminiscence, recalling the art of memory which was the discipline of Bruno's religion. She is the continuity of human reason with divine and demonic intelligences, representing Bruno's belief in the possibility of establishing such communications through mental images. By THE LADDER OF MINERVA we rise from the first to the last, collect the external species in the internal sense, order intellectual operations into a whole by art, as in Bruno's extraordinary arts of memory.'[11] But by the end of the sixteenth century, Bruno has been burned as a heretic. And the image of the goddess has been annexed by an orthodoxy which knows precisely where it wants her ladder to lead.

The rungs of that ladder have been carefully constructed over many centuries, for in a world which believed that all contemporary understandings are recognitions of a divine truth which has always been, the ancient mythologies must also contain that original. By the twelfth century, the finding of edifying meaning in these ancient tales and the allegorical use of their characters to personify abstract virtues is already well-established and set to multiply. So Ovid's *Metamorphoses*, for instance, becomes a 'mine of sacred truth'. The anonymous early-fourteenth-century *Ovide Moralisé* sees the whole of Christian morality and even the Bible itself in Ovid's tales of transformation: Threefold Diana becomes the Trinity, Acteon is Christ, Ceres anguishedly seeking Prosperpina is the church seeking to recover the souls of the faithful who have strayed from the fold. The approach had its critics. Rabelais was one of those who was to ask his readers whether they honestly believed that Ovid was thinking of the Sacraments when he wrote his *Metamorphoses*, any more than Homer had this sort of thing in mind when he wrote the *Iliad* and the *Odyssey*. But Boccaccio's *Genealogy of the Gods* continued to be the best-seller that it had been ever since its first fourteenth-century edition, translated through many more for moralizers to draw on even 200 years later.[12]

In this allegorization of the ancients, the goddess too was assigned her important part. Prudence assumed the features of Minerva, Fortitude and Justice those of Athene herself. In the Tarrochi, the fifteenth-century set of fifty engravings which some say were the prototype of the Tarot and all the playing cards we know today, Philosophy stands solid with her spear in her right hand, shield emblazoned with the Gorgon's head in her left. Sometimes by now the goddess's qualities are subsumed altogether by a higher, masculine power: in the Franciscan John Ridewall's version of these truths, Benevolencia, who is Jupiter, subsumes Prudentia, Intelligencia and Sapientia – Lady Wisdom herself. So is Athene swallowed up once more into the head of Zeus from which once and so gloriously and energetically she had burst forth.[13]

19. Minerva stamps her owl underfoot: Romano-Celtic bronze found at Charlton Down, Wiltshire (Devizes Museum).

20. The Burney Relief: terracotta plaque of Inanna–Ishtar, *c.*2300–2000 BC (whereabouts unknown).

21. *Madonna della Misericordia* by Piero della Francesca
(Museo del Sepolcro, Borgo Sansepolcro, Italy).

22. *Adam, Eve and the Serpent*
by Hugo van der Goes
(Kunsthistorisches Museum,
Vienna).

23. Notre Dame des Neiges:
the Black Virgin of Aurillac
(Cantal, France).

24 and 25. Athene's owl becomes malevolent: in Hieronymus Bosch's *Garden of Earthly Delights* (detail), and when *The Sleep of Reason Produces Monsters* for Francisco Goya (Museo del Prado, Madrid).

26 and 27. Athene as moral guardian: taming the centaur (Sandro Botticelli, Uffizi, Florence) and expelling the Vices from the garden (Andrea Mantegna, Louvre, Paris).

28 and 29. Athene assessed: by Paris (Peter Paul Rubens, National Gallery, London) and by Queen Elizabeth I (Hampton Court).

30 and 31. Athene in alchemy: as Lady Alchemia in an anonymous fifteenth-century manuscript (Biblioteca Apostolica Vaticana), and born in a shower of gold in Michael Maier's seventeenth-century *Atalanta Fugiens* (Glasgow University Library, Department of Special Collections).

Aurum pluit, dum nascitur Pallas Rhodi, & Sol concumbit Veneri.

EPIGRAMMA XXIII.

R Es est mira, fidem fecit sed Græcia nobis
    Ejus, apud Rhodios quæ celebrata fuit.
Nubibus Aureolus, referunt, quòd decidit imber,
    Solubi erat Cypriæ junctus amore Dea:
Tum quoque, cùm Pallas cerebro Jovis excidit, aurum
    Vase suo pluvia sic cadat instar aquæ.

N 3   AURUM

32. *Eve Tempted by the Serpent* by William Blake (Victoria and Albert Museum, London).

33. 'The dragon kills the woman and she him and together they are soaked in blood': Emblem 50 of Michael Maier's *Atalanta Fugiens* (Glasgow University Library, Department of Special Collections).

EMBLEMA L. *De secretis Naturæ.* 209.

Draco mulierem, & hæc illum interimit, simulque sanguine perfunduntur.

EPIGRAMMA L.

ALta venenoso fodiatur tumba Draconi,
    Cui mulier nexu sit bene vincta suo:
Ille maritalæ dum carpit gaudia lecti,
    Hæc moritur, cum qua sit Draco tectus humo.
Illius hinc corpus morti datur, atque cruore
    Tingitur: Hæc operis semita vera tui est.
        Dd   DRACO-

Sometimes again, the goddess still makes her own appearances – if her own they can be called when, for instance, she is seen simpering for Rubens in full-frontal soft-porn pose, the Gorgon looking on aghast, as well she might. The ancients knew that even to glimpse a goddess naked was punishable by death, so powerful was her *numen*; the many painters who made *The Judgement of Paris* a favourite subject knew rather that there was plenty of potential for portraying naked female flesh if only you clothed it in a suitably classical theme [Pl. 28].

In many more of her other appearances, however, the goddess is not only clad but armoured – though these guises are hardly more her own either, when their allegorical purpose is made so ponderously plain. Here she is, for instance, in Botticelli's *Pallas and the Centaur*, where her flowing curves and playful tousling of that hairy head should deceive no one into imagining that she intends anything other than a demonstration of Wisdom's Taming of Brute Force – unless it is also a celebration of Lorenzo de Medici's return to Florence after the conspiracy of the Pazzi [Pl. 26]. Here she is again in Tintoretto's *Minerva and Mars*, repulsing the war-god as surely as the Venetian senate, in its own Wisdom, kept the horrors of war at a distance. The goddess may also step from the canvas into living personification. The Magnificences of 1581 with which the court of Henri III of France celebrated the marriage of the King's favourite the Duc de Joyeuse to the Queen's half-sister, Marie de Lorraine, offered a different and lavish entertainment every day for about two weeks, and the most famous of these was the *Ballet Comique de la Reine*, whose theme was the transfer of power from the enchantress Circe to the French royal family. In this, the elemental world of nature over which Circe held sway, represented by sirens and satyrs, was defeated by an alliance of the Virtues and Minerva with the celestial powers, the whole given dazzling shape by the ballets danced by the Queen, the bride and other ladies of the court.[14]

In such appearances, Minerva sternly represents the triumph of civilization over the lower world of the instincts and the senses;

she is as surely the daughter of the fathers as she was so long ago when she was closest to Zeus's head on the Acropolis of Athens, carrying out his idea in defence of the priorities of the ruling order. In this task, she assumes the duties of a one-woman vice squad — depicted in such favourite pictorial themes as the battle between Pallas and Ares, in which Reason triumphs over Passion, or the Choice of Hercules, in which the fully-armoured Pallas firmly disentangles the hero from the blandishments of naked, luxuriant Pleasure to embrace the Virtue which is her own stern reward. In Mantegna's *The Expulsion of the Vices from the Garden of the Virtues*, the goddess's mission of purity extends to the entire environment: nothing less than a clean sweep through the litter-louts and layabouts will do for her [Pl. 27].

Along the way, it is her chastity which has become her protection — and which she in turn protects. In Alcrati's *Emblematum Liber*, first published in 1531 and the prototype of the many and popular books of 'emblems', or pictures with a hidden moral meaning, Pallas appears with a dragon at her side, and what that signifies is the virgin's need for strict guardianship and protection against the snares of love. 'Why is that animal a companion to the goddess?' the readers are quizzed. 'Because it has the custody of things; thus it protects the sacred woods and the temples. Un-married girls should be guarded with ever-watchful care. Love lays her snares everywhere.' So is Athene's ancient snaky nature turned to new account! A hundred years later, her protective power is still being evoked against the baser forces of instinct. When the Lady in Milton's *Comus* is lost in the forest, her brothers are deeply concerned — as well they might be, she having been kidnapped by the eponymous villain, who is the son of Circe and Bacchus. Yet they can comfort themselves with the thought that their sister has the very special strength of chastity, which means that she is 'clad in complete steel' and so can go through all perils and places and withstand any manner of goblins, ghosts and hags. For,

> What was that snaky-headed Gorgon shield
> That wise Minerva wore, unconquered virgin,
> Wherewith she freezed her foes to congealed stone,
> But rigid looks of chaste austerity,
> And noble grace that dashed brute violence
> With sudden adoration and bland awe?[15]

Their confidence was not, of course, misplaced. And how, in a sense, could it have been, when for hundreds of years by now there has been a steady converging of three streams to carry the tradition which, however unconsciously, they are evoking?

> Wisdom has built her house,
> she has set up her seven pillars.
> She has slaughtered her beasts,
> she has mixed her wine
> she has also set her table.
> She has sent out her maids to call
> from the highest places in the town,
> 'Whoever is simple, let him turn in here!'
> To him who is without sense she says,
> 'Come, eat of my bread
> and drink of the wine I have mixed.
> Leave simpleness, and live,
> and walk in the way of insight.'[16]

Back in the eighth century, Wisdom's house had been identified as the house of learning and the pillars as the Seven Liberal Arts: the threefold way to eloquence (Rhetoric, Dialectic and Grammar) and the fourfold way to philosophy (Music, Arithmetic, Astronomy and Geometry). Five centuries later, Albert the Great applied the same text to the Virgin Mary, asserting that 'she possessed the seven liberal arts . . . perfect mastery of science'. As time goes on, as we have seen, Philosophia begins to assume the characteristics of Minerva; so, increasingly, does Sapientia, Wisdom herself, the leader of all the liberal arts. The goddess begins to accumulate at least three of the Four Cardinal Virtues to herself: Prudence appears as Minerva, Justice and Fortitude as Athene. The leadership of the Muses, in ancient times Apollo's, passes to the goddess as well, and so she becomes patron of the arts as well as learning. ('Oceans as yet undared my vessel dares,' says Dante of his own great enterprise. 'Apollo steers, Minerva lends the breeze/And the nine Muses point me to the Bears.')[17]

There are glimpses of the ancient figure of Wisdom. On the ceiling of the Sistine chapel, dedicated to the Assumption of the Blessed Virgin Mary at the start of the sixteenth century, a beautiful and mysterious young woman nestles in the crook of God's left arm, watching intently as his right extends in that huge gesture of the creation of Adam. Is this Wisdom, 'beside him like a master workman . . . rejoicing in his inhabited world and delighting in the sons of men'? Is it 'the idea of Eve', or the Virgin herself, or the human soul? That all these interpretations have been offered, and into our own century as well, is itself testimony to the enduring mystery of the Wisdom tradition.[18]

Yet by the sixteenth century, Wisdom has lost her biblical depths and is almost always represented by the figure of the once-classical goddess. And in the allegorizing of Athene, she has been depotentiated too. The ancients knew that no mortal could look directly at a goddess and live. In today's language, they knew that human consciousness could never approach the archetype directly, never comprehend the vast depths of the unconscious on which it rests. So the many and mysterious epiphanies of their deities can be only the images of archetypal powers, symbols of something whose essential nature is – to us as well as them – unknowable. To see the epiphanies of the goddess symbolically is to recognize, at the very least, that there is a lot more here than the rational mind can grasp. To see them allegorically is to train on them the very opposite vision. Allegory can only present what consciousness already knows. It translates 'this' into 'that' with a more or less deadening or enlivening precision, and it *manages* its material to its own didactic or moral purpose. Symbolic images work on us to bring us nearer to something we somewhere 'know' but have not yet consciously understood. Allegorical images are worked on by us to convey a previously encoded message.

And where do you go when you've got it? A symbolic approach encourages imaginal expansions, a constant enriching of that first image. But the boundaries of allegory are already set. Once you understand, with Christine de Pizan, that Athene's helmet means that a knight must have courage and endurance, her spear that he must be the rod of justice, the Gorgon's head that he must always be watchful and careful, and so on, there is not much more you can do – except to admire and to note the lesson so elegantly and economically portrayed. And then, perhaps, to add on. An allegorical image cannot, by definition, take its charge from what it imaginally evokes, because its meaning is fixed from the start. What it can do is to become more powerful by becoming bigger, by making lists. So the allegorical figure of Wisdom continually expands to encompass the *three*fold path to eloquence, the *four*fold path to philosophy, the *four* cardinal virtues, the *seven* liberal arts, the *nine* muses. And then? Well, very much further ahead, in America, that New Found Land, the Library of Congress's Great Hall will be able to offer a list of its own. Minerva will hold up a scroll on which are inscribed Agriculture, Education, Mechanics, Commerce, Government, Astronomy, Geography, Statistics, Economics, Geology – all these and more, gifts from Wisdom's store.[19] In a sense, everything will have changed, for these are the useful knowledges that make up what we call 'progress', and we can go on adding to that list again and again. Nuclear Sciences, Astronautics, Quantum Mechanics, Genetic Engineering . . . there is room on Minerva's scroll for all that human ingenuity can devise. And in another sense, nothing will have changed at all, for by adding to Wisdom's weight, we add nothing to our understanding of her essence.

And how could that essence be understood with the rational mind to which allegory must make its appeal? Allegory deals in concepts – Justice, Prudence, Faith, Hope, Charity. Athene's essential gift, the understanding of the relation of mind and matter, is discarded for an amassing of abstractions. And there can be no room for ambiguities here either, no place for the play of opposites in Dame Reason's lesson-book. So, as we have seen, the image of the goddess, whose energy once flowed and flashed precisely from its many-layered and paradoxical complexity, becomes an ever-more stolid figure of Virtue. And there can be nothing paradoxical here. Athene's owl, creature of night and symbol of the goddess's dark and underworld power and 'seeing', is now banished to the realm of Vice – the realm of body, of instinct, of sexuality, of forbidden knowings. Here it squats over the copulating, apple-bedecked lovers in Hieronymus Bosch's *Garden of Earthly Delights* [Pl. 24]. There it broods malevolently beside the Witch of Endor, sign of her nature and her evil, in van Oostsanen's depiction of Saul's consultation. The owl's knowledge of the other side, its very ability to see all around and in the dark, is taken and used against it: now it stands for heresy, for 'the Jewish church' – and so all that would destroy the one true faith. By the eighteenth century, it still carries this force on its wings. *The Sleep of Reason*, Goya terrifyingly shows us, *Produces Monsters* – and it is owls and bats that fly out of the darkness of the mind to destroy that age's true faith in its turn [Pl. 25]. A century on again, Poe's raven will perch horribly on the 'pallid bust of Pallas, just above [his] chamber door', its implacably reiterated 'Nevermore' a knell to his soul's yearning, its presence casting an immovable black shadow of despair over all the goddess's domain of reason and the consolations of learning; and we remember that the crow, or raven, was also once Athene's own creature.[20]

So Athene's own depth of understanding has been shattered and split into the Reasonable and the Monstrous, just as she has become the embodiment of Virtue and the scourge of Vice. Yet as the different virtues have been accrued to her safe and reasonable keeping, each one has become too another plate of armour welded into place to encompass and mould her form. The allegorical armouring of Athene was intended to protect her honour. But what it did was to contain and manage that once-fierce energy of hers and annex it to didactic purpose.

In that armouring, the old honouring of the virginity which is so much part of the goddess's essence becomes a concern for chastity, and that is not the same thing at all. The ancient goddesses were 'virgin' because their essence could not be violated. 'I am the whore and the holy one,' said the Gnostic Thunder, Perfect Mind: however many the sexual engagements of this great force, however many the children she bore, she remained whole, herself, undiminished. Virginity in this sense is ever-new, ever-renewed and ever-renewing, too. Chastity is a literalization: there is something which *can* be lost and lost for ever, and must therefore be protected. Virginity allows for openness to experience and can withstand whatever the consequences may be; chastity is fearful, closed, and has to do with the fixity of maintaining what is, unchanged. The allegorizers in their armourings certainly protected Athene's chastity. But in their fixings of her image, they took away her virginity.

CHAPTER 9

Virgins, Witches and Uncommon Gold

At some time back in the third century, the prefect of a cohort stationed at the eleventh fort on Hadrian's wall in Northumberland raised an inscription to the goddess Virgo. For him, she was 'inventress of justice, foundress of the city'; she incarnated those solid imperial qualities of Virtus and Pax. Here is an epiphany of Athene as protectress of the state and its order, and with it an incarnation of other ancient goddesses whose relation to her we have already glimpsed. One is the middle-eastern Queen of Heaven – for is not Virgo to be seen in the heavenly constellation that bears her name? Another is the Mother of the Gods, Cybele herself. Another again is the Syrian Atargatis, the Dea Syria who, as we have seen, carries and is carried by the ancient power of Lady Snake.

The return of this great force to protect the city is momentous indeed. For with the advent of the age of iron, as Ovid tells us and as we mortals know to our bitter cost, she had finally left this blood-soaked earth of ours, the last of the immortals to give up the struggle to remain. Before she fled to the heavens, she had been the maiden Astraea or Justice, and she left behind a world which sorely needed her care. For with the age of iron, all manner of crime had been born. Modesty, truth and loyalty fled and treachery, deceit and violence took their place. Friend was no longer safe from friend, wife from husband, husband from wife or either from their children's plots. The very land, once common to all like the sunlight and the breezes, was now divided and defended by war; even its bowels were invaded, and the iron and gold they yielded became a further incitement to wickedness.

Yet one saving grace was left: the longing for the return of that first, golden age long before iron's rule, when Justice, the maiden Astraea, would descend once more to earth. And Virgil thought to see it dawn.

> Now the last age of Cumae's prophecy has come;
> The great succession of centuries is born afresh.
> Now too returns the Virgin; Saturn's rule returns;
> A new beginning now descends from heaven's height.
> O chaste Lucina, look with blessing on the boy
> Whose birth will end the iron age at last and raise
> A golden through the world . . .

Some say the child foretold in Virgil's fourth Eclogue was the one to be born to Antony and Octavia, the sister of Octavian, the great Augustus, with whom he had so recently been at odds and with whom, by the treaty of Brundisium of 40 BC, he was now reconciled. But for Constantine, the first Christian emperor, it is not the coming of the golden Augustinian age which is foretold, but the birth of Christ himself. When Constantine asks 'Who is that virgin who returns?' he is thinking not of Justice, but of Christ's Virgin Mother. Augustine also took the prophecy as messianic; the tradition became woven into medieval belief.[1]

And then, to those whose eyes were properly trained, Astraea indeed walked the earth again, to strengthen and dignify another kingdom altogether. As Frances Yates has shown, Elizabeth I of England was clothed in the symbolism of the goddess from the very start of her reign. Her Justice, her Virginity, her Peace in uniting the houses of York and Lancaster (itself symbolized by her fair pink and white complexion, the very epitome of the English Rose) – all drawn from that heavenly source, all hymned in an untiring explosion of pageant and poetry, pomp and portraiture. 'But whereto shall we bend our lays?' asks Sir John Davies of Hereford in his *Hymns of Astraea*, and gives his own answer:

Even up to Heaven, again to raise
The Maid, which thence descended;
Hath brought again the golden days,
And all the world amended.

There are twenty-six of these *Hymns*, the initial letters of each
line of each spelling out ELISABETHA REGINA, so giving the
reader twenty-six opportunities to relate the Queen to Magnanim-
ity, to Will, to Wit, and to all the other qualities that Davies so
tirelessly praises. This is indeed Athene come back to walk among
us! 'Excellent jewels would you see?' the poet inquires when he
writes 'Of her Memory'. Then, 'Lovely ladies! Come with me!'

Read this fair book, as you shall learn
Exquisite skill, if you discern;
Gain heaven, by this discerning!
In such a memory divine,
Nature did form the Muses nine,
And PALLAS, Queen of Learning.

Or is it 'Of her Wisdom' you would learn? ELISABETHA spells it
out.

Eagle-eyed Wisdom! Life's loadstar!
Looking near, on things afar!
Iove's best beloved daughter!
Shews to her spirit all that are!
As Jove himself hath taught her

By this straight rule, She rectifies
Each thought, that in her heart doth rise;
This is her clear true Mirror!
Her Looking Glass, wherein She spies
All forms of Truth and Error.

Right Princely virtue, fit to reign!
Enthronised in her spirit remain,

> Guiding our fortunes ever!
> If we this Star once cease to see;
> No doubt our State will shipwrecked be,
> And torn and sunk for ever.

And crowning all virtues, there is her Justice, through which, in-comparable dominatrix, she embodies a enduring fantasy of the powerful feminine:

> She rules us, with delightful pain,
> And we obey with pleasure!

By her very nature, Astraea is the highest of the virtues, for Justice subsumes all others. (As Dame Justice herself had briskly explained it to Christine de Pizan, 'I could give a rather long account of the duties of my office, but, put briefly, I have a special place among the Virtues, for they are all based on me.') That Elizabeth thus unites all the virtues in her person is a favourite theme. Here, for instance, is the poet Richard Barfield telling, in his *Cynthia*, of a tricky moment for Jove, who is being berated by Juno for Paris's judgement. What is Jove to do, when Venus is his darling, Minerva his dear and Juno his sister and his wife? Fortunately for him, there is one in whom Virtue is so inclined that she unites all the Wisdom, Beauty and Wealth which the goddesses must share be-tween them. So it is to her that he sends 'this Pearle, this Jewell and this Gem'. And 'Thus, sacred Virgin, Muse of chastitie', the poet concludes,

> This difference is betwixt the Moone and thee;
> Shee shines by Night; but thou by Day dost shine:
> Shee Monthly changeth; thou dost nere decline;
> And as the Sunne, to her, doth lend his light,
> So hee, by thee, is onely made so bright;
> Yet neither Sun, nor Moone, thou canst be named.
> Because thy light hath both their beauties shamed:
> Then, since an heauenly Name doth thee befall,
> Thou VIRGO art: (if any Signe at all).

So Elizabeth's light shines brighter than that of either moon or sun, and there can be no contest at all for that apple. The three goddesses in the painting at Hampton Court have clearly got the message and decided to yield to a greater power. In doing so, they have restored a more ancient image than even Paris knew, of the goddess herself, who gave her favours to mortals as she chose, rather than waiting on them [Pl. 29]. This message of supremacy is not given only in classical clothing. In a portrait of the Queen in front of a column on which are shown the three theological and four cardinal virtues, the central position is that of Justice, who seems to be wearing a dress very similar to Elizabeth's own.[2]

The Queen held, of course, an incomparably important place in the theology of her time. Bishop John Jewel, official apologist for the Church of England, calls her its 'only nurse and mother', and other imagery deliberately recalls that other Mother whose cult is now dethroned. The Rose, the Star, the Moon, the Phoenix, the Ermine, the Pearl, all used in the symbolism that surrounds Elizabeth, are all also symbols of the Virgin Mary. Some do not hesitate to give first place to England's own Virgin Queen. In his *Second Book of Airs,* John Dowland urges singers to substitute a *Vivat Eliza!* for an *Ave Maria!* An engraving of the Queen has this legend under her own device of the phoenix: 'This Maiden-Queen Elizabeth came into this world, the Eve of the Nativity of the blessed virgin Mary; and died on the Eve of the Annunciation of the virgin Mary, 1602.' And underneath is a couplet which runs

> She was, She is (what can there more be said?)
> In earth the first, in heaven the second Maid.[3]

What more to say indeed? Except that beyond and below any deliberate political or theological substitution of Elizabeth for Mary, there seems to be another still-flowing current, which continually carries the feminine power of the deity – and insists that it is somehow given recognition.

More immediately, the Queen had her symbolic duties to her

church. In 1563, John Foxe dedicated the first English edition of his *Acts and Monuments* – that lastingly influential Book of Martyrs – to her; he compares the end of the sufferings of the Reformed church in her reign to the end of the persecution of the earliest Christians in the reign of Constantine. The capital 'C' of Constantine encloses a portrait of the Queen, enthroned with the sword of justice in one hand and the orb in the other. The top curve of the 'C' ends in cornucopiae; the bottom curve of the letter, beneath the Queen's feet, is the body of the Pope, holding broken keys. But if the persecution of Protestants was ended, another was beginning, and the Pope was not the only power perceived as working against Christ's true law. As well as the publication of Foxe's tome, 1563 saw the promulgation of an Act of Parliament which was to remain on the statute books for forty years, and heralded the real start of the English persecutions for witchcraft that were to continue until the last quarter of the seventeenth century.[4]

England came relatively late to this cruel madness and it was never to reach the panic proportions of possession there that it did in the mainland of Europe and in Scotland. Yet to the 1,000 or so guessed to have been executed in the English persecution between the first witchcraft act of 1542 and the repeal of the last in 1736, to the countless others harried and beaten and thrown out of their livelihoods by local suspicion if not official trial, that comparison would come as no comfort at all. (And small though the number is by comparison with the estimated 4,400 who died, from a much smaller population base, in the Scottish persecutions, it is still about four times the number of executions of English Catholic martyrs during the period.) This isn't the place to go into comparisons of either the scale or the extent and detailed nature of the persecutions, for that is a different story. But what we can note is that at just the time when the cult of the feminine as repository of all the theological virtues was reaching its height in the fantasized form of Elizabeth, so was constellated the very opposite: the idea of the feminine as carrier of viciousness and evil itself.[5]

This split in the image of the feminine in one part of Europe's offshore island is only a small fissure, of course, compared with the cavernous depths it reached in Europe. Here, the cult of Mary had reached its height between the eleventh and fifteenth centuries; in the century after 1170, over 100 churches and eighty cathedrals were dedicated to her in France alone. And then, in the fifteenth century, and for 300 years, came the witch-hunts, and the depth of negativity towards the feminine that these carried goes, it seems, to a place that Mary's work of redemption cannot reach.

The authors of the *Malleus Maleficarum,* the Hammer of the Witches, emphasized that it was important for preachers to re-member that the whole sin of Eve had been taken away by Mary, and so always to say as much in praise of women as possible. James Sprenger, indeed, held the Virgin in such veneration that he had set up the first lay confraternity for the recitation of the rosary. But for him and his Dominican colleague Heinrich Kramer, em-powered by the Pope to set up a special commission of inquiry into witchcraft and hand over those they held to be guilty to the inquisition, what could rightly be said in praise of women was very little indeed. Their hugely detailed, tightly argued treatise was to become the textbook of European witch-hunters and trial judges for some three centuries, going through thirteen editions in the thirty or so years after its first publication in 1486 and very many more after that. And from its first examination of 'the Three Necessary Concomitants of Witchcraft which are the Devil, a Witch and the Permission of Almighty God' to its last detailing of the proper judicial proceedings in both ecclesiastical and civil courts against witches 'and indeed all heretics', it is testimony to an extraordinary depth of fear and loathing of womankind.

Why it should be women who are particularly susceptible to witchcraft was evident to Kramer and Sprenger from the many writings of the church authorities and their own observations as well. Women know no moderation, so their wickedness plumbs particular depths; they are more feeble than men in mind, body, and memory, liars by nature and governed by their impulses. Their condition is congenital: '[T]here was a defect in the formation of the first woman, since she was formed from a bent rib, that is, rib of the breast, which is bent as it were in a contrary direction to a man. And since through this defect she is an imperfect animal, she always deceives.' She is more bitter than death, because death destroys only the body 'but the sin which arose from woman destroys the soul by depriving it of grace'. She is more bitter than death 'because bodily death is an open and terrible enemy, but woman is a wheedling and secret enemy'.

But above all and especially, 'she is more carnal than a man, as is clear from her many carnal abominations'. It is, finally, the ever-demanding mouth of the womb which leads women to consort even with devils. The conclusion is inescapable: 'All witchcraft comes from carnal lust, which is in women insatiable.' The penalty must be heavier than for any other criminal, because witches are not simply heretics but apostates, who have abjured the true faith which once they knew by offering the devils their bodies and souls. The evils which they perpetrate, say Kramer and Sprenger, exceed all other sins which God has ever permitted to be done, including those of the fallen angels and of Adam himself. 'And blessed be the Highest Who has so far preserved the male sex from so great a crime; for since He was willing to be born and to suffer for us, therefore He has granted to men this privilege.'[6]

The notion of woman's moral weakness found a ready echo in Britain, for the witch-hunts were pursued by Protestants with their own fervour and a common theological justification. In his *Daemonologie*, James VI of Scotland found it easy to explain why this evil should particularly affect women: 'for as that sexe is frailer than men is, as was well proved to be true, by the Serpents deceiving of Eve at the beginning, which makes him the homlier with that sexe ever since'. Twenty years later, in his *Anatomy of Melancholy*, the bachelor Robert Burton confirmed that this 'frailty' was dangerously linked with sexuality: 'Of woman's unnatural, insatiable lust, what county, what village, does not complain?' Yet it took some while for the full continental doctrine to reach Britain; it was only in 1604 that the pact with the Devil was seen as an

essential element in witchcraft at all. So we are left with a paradoxical notion: that this weak creature which is woman nevertheless and of her own nature has extraordinary and fearful powers,
which she can exercise without the diabolical pact. Even in the
Malleus there is some hint of this independence. For 'if we inquire,
we find that nearly all the kingdoms of the world have been
overthrown by women'. Look at the sufferings of the Trojans and
Greeks through Helen, at the misfortune and destruction suffered
by the kingdom of the Jews through the accursed Jezebel and her
daughter Athaliah, at the evil endured by the Romans through
Cleopatra, 'that worst of women'. And so, the authors conclude, it
is no wonder if the world now suffers through the malice of
women. Yet their catalogue of the earlier sufferings of whole
nations makes no mention of the Devil: these women of antiquity
could wreak such havoc, it seemed, all by themselves.

So where did their power come from? Some say that the European witches would gather together by night, and fly on the backs of
animals over great distances, following their leader who was known
as Mistress of the Game, as the Matron, the Teacher, the Greek
Mistress, the Wise Sibilla, the Queen of the Fairies – or as the great
goddess Diana herself, identified by the church authorities as Diana
of the Ephesians, whose cult had supposedly been overthrown so
long ago by the power of the Mother of the new, true God. These
gatherings never became part of British witchcraft, for the Protes-
tant emphasis was ever on individual rather than communal relations with the great powers, both good and evil. But in the charges
held against witches in both Scotland and England, there are also
echoes of that more ancient power, now turned to menace.

In the power of witches to affect the natural world – to flatten
crops and destroy livestock – there were twisted echoes of ancient
earth mysteries. In their exercising of such damage through not
just spells and cursings but 'overlooking', the power of the eye
itself, there is a hint of Athene's own supremacy in the seeing
which is understanding. Like the goddess herself, they will trans-
form into birds. They will take the form of hares, which have ever

been connected with the moon and sacred to the ancient feminine power. To those who perceived such transformations, the time-honoured mysteries of healing turned to destruction. The 'cunning' men and women who used to be respected as the healers in every English town and village had taken their name from the Old English 'cunnan', and the Middle English 'connen', which mean 'to know', and their cunning denoted a knowledge which was practical, skilful, expert, dextrous, and later, wise. But by 1590, a new meaning is recorded, and it is the one we first recognize to this day. Just as the meaning of Athene's own 'craftiness', the skill that gave birth to so many inventions and devices, became soured by suspicion, so did 'cunning' come to mean guileful and sly. And if in England the cunning *men* at least escaped the worst of the witch-hunts, in Scotland the healers were swept up with the cursers in the overall moral panic. And very generally, the women accused were midwives – those priestesses of the basic mystery of birth and regeneration. They were accused of abusing their midwifery skills to kill the babies they would then consume – just as had Lilith, the Lamia, and all those monstrous regiments of feminine spirits turned evil in the world of the fathers.[7]

In those three centuries of madness, countless women paid with their lives for what was perceived as the sin of Eve. The notion of witchcraft arose like a foul miasma from that chasm in perception which had opened between the ideally spiritualized and the earthbound, material feminine, between Mary and Eve. Yet in that darkness too there endured a reconciling image, which continued to carry a more ancient tradition of feminine power. From hidden places in the earth, in cleft rocks or the hollows of trees, the Black Virgin re-emerged into overground consciousness in the twelfth century, and by the middle of the sixteenth, so it's said, there were nearly 200 hundred representations of her image in France alone, and many others all over Europe.

When a modern pilgrim asked the local priest at Lucera in southern Italy why the local Virgin was black, he was told, 'My son, she is black because she is black.' Forty years on, when another visited the miracle-working Virgin of Orcival in France and asked the same question, he was told in a tone that encouraged no further questions at all, 'Because she is.' Fiercely protected by some of their guardians, 'restored' into whiteness by others, ignored or simply accepted by others again, the very many images that have survived down the centuries still carry a *numen* that has nothing at all to do with the effects of candlesmoke or age or any of the sensible arguments that have been advanced to explain it away.

'I am black but I am beautiful,' cries the Shulamite to her lover in the Song of Solomon; as the Queen of Sheba, as we have seen, she brings the ancient feminine Wisdom to unite with Solomon's own. Ean Begg traces the confluence of this and other ancient streams, which together carried the image of the Black Virgin across Europe in the hearts and minds of the Knights Templar and into those of the Cathar Church of Amor which held those values which Roma had suppressed. In the Near-Eastern traditions of Inanna and Lilith, Anath and Neith, in the classical traditions of, among others, Cybele, Mother of the Gods, Artemis or Diana of Ephesus and most especially Isis of Egypt, the image of the Black Virgin took her form, meeting with Celtic deities to embody the ancient power. And that above all was a power which encompassed in an effortless whole both mind and matter, both the spiritual and the material worlds – just as the feminine had done in the old days and for so long.

The Black Virgin is found in the clefts of trees, in rivers. She is of her earth, and when people try to move her images from their place, so it's said, they will become insupportably heavy, or set up an intolerable wailing, or bring disaster, or even death, until they are returned to it. As she is rooted in her earth, so does she govern the mysteries of nature's own cycle. She is a goddess of fertility, and she knows how to ease the pangs of childbirth and to make the milk flow; she is a healer. At the same time, she can turn the established order upside down: she can bring dead babies back to life for long enough for them to be baptized and so escape from limbo to paradise; she will act as midwife to a pregnant abbess and stand in for a nun to allow her to taste undetected the pleasures of sexuality. And at the same time again, she is profoundly associated with matters of the mind, soul and spirit. One of her gifts is to teach children to speak, to bring them the word which is the carrier of consciousness. She is also to be found where schools of initiation and esoteric teaching flourish. Yet she has her shrewdness too, and knows the realities of this rough world: one of the striking aspects of her cult is how often she is evoked as patroness of war and battles. In the many images we still have of her, there is nothing sentimental; these dark faces radiate strength.[8]

In her bringing together of the physical, material world with the realm of mind and spirit, the Black Virgin carries a power which we have seen as Athene's own. In her powers of healing, in her gift of the word, in her presence on the battlefield, the Black Virgin is another epiphany of the goddess. Among other sightings, we glimpse her among local Celtic deities in Rocamadour, where the Black Virgin succeeded Sulevia, Minerva, Iduenna, a triple goddess integrated by Cybele. We know Athene kept classical company with Isis, Cybele, Venus, Proserpina and Jupiter at Vichy, where Viciaco was the personified *mana* of the sacred springs. We can see her qualities and attributes in the many Black Virgins whose speciality is the restoration of sight, and very specifically in the naming of the Cathar castle of Minerva, where 180 followers of the goddess of wisdom were burned to death at the start of the twelfth century. In many places too, the Black Virgin continues the goddess's work of protecting her citadels from attack. The Black Virgin of Aurillac, for instance, helped save her city from the Huguenots towards the end of the sixteenth century by miraculously producing an August snowfall and advancing the hour of dawn. (As in war, so in peace: here is Athene once more manipulating the natural order of things as she had so long ago when she held up the dawn to prolong the bliss of Penelope and Odysseus's reunion.) The victory over the Hugenots came too late to save the original Black Virgin from destruction at their hands. But in the close copy of that original, we can still see the image of Athene as armoured maid [Pl. 23].

As the classical goddesses moved across France, Cybele, Mother of the Gods, became patron of Lyons, and despite the inveighings of its bishop Irenaeus against the Gnostics, the Black Virgin continued here to carry the ancient traditions, praised by Julian the Apostate as 'Wisdom, Providence, the Creator of our souls'. Paris became the principal seat of Isis herself and the many images of Black Virgins in its churches included her own black statue, 'thin, tall, staight, naked or with some flimsy garment', worshipped as the Virgin in St Germain-des-Prés until the sixteenth century. In Marseilles, from her arrival with the Phoenicians at the start of the seventh century, it was the black Artemis of Ephesus who became patroness of the city, to be hailed as 'Virgin of Light'. Athene also had an important temple at Marseilles. But her principal home was in Toulouse, where her own image, dredged from a lake by a Roman consul looking for lost gold, became the Black Virgin, La Daurade. By the sixth century, Toulouse was the home of a Gnostic wisdom school, and many threads of mystery have wound around it since. When Jesus told his disciples that the Queen of the South would arise at the Last Judgement to condemn unbelievers, he was referring to that woman of wisdom, the Queen of Sheba. Queen of the South is also the title of the Countess of Toulouse, and the association of wisdom with this city is insistent. Among the many legends and journeyings of the Queen of Sheba, she becomes Queen Sibylla – ancestress of all Western magicians, and, as we have seen, one of the leaders of the women whom orthodoxy called witches. You can recognize her, they say, by her webbed foot – which associates her in turn to the very ancient Old European bird-goddesses, many of whom appeared as waterfowl. In that footstep we can recognize too La Reine Pedauque, the queen-goddess with the goose-foot, who is buried in La Daurade in Toulouse and who is associated with a magic distaff, one of Athene's own symbols.[9]

So as the ancient figure of Wisdom became corseted by an ever-tighter allegorical armouring, and many of the attributes of the old goddesses passed from the image of Mary into neo–classical abstraction, the old tradition maintained its underground stream. The image of the Black Virgin continued to carry the mysteries and wisdoms of the earth's cycle of life, death and sexuality, to defend the natural energies of land and place, and to unite them with an understanding which stood against the established order's increasing separation of mind and spirit from the material world. The resurgence of these images was far from being simply a left-over of the old beliefs among simple country people. As we know, St Bernard of Clairvaux, who as a boy had received three drops of milk from the breast of the Black Virgin of Châtillon, devoted himself to the study of the Song of Songs which is the recurring refrain of the Black Virgin cult. When he dedicated the first of his Cistercian abbeys, and indeed all subsequent ones to 'Notre Dame', it was not only Mary the mother of Jesus whom he was honouring. Some say that the Black Virgin is the key to the huge surge in the building of church and cathedral dedicated to 'Notre Dame' in the twelfth and thirteenth centuries, and the pre-eminence of her sites among centres of pilgrimage is witness to the enduring force of the ancient feminine power.[10]

Of that power, Athene was one aspect, and she plays an essential part too in another confluence of the underground stream which carried the continuing unity of matter and mind, soul and spirit that orthodoxy insistently endeavoured to separate. The age of Elizabeth, as we have seen, was hailed as the Golden Age come again; to some who apostrophized her virtues, the Queen shone brighter than the sun itself. But Ovid had known that the mining of gold from the bowels of the earth in the Age of Iron had simply contributed to men's wickedness, and it was with the promise of material wealth, it was often claimed, that the devil lured poor women to their pact with evil. When that Roman consul dredged the lake at Toulouse for sunken golden treasure, it was not that fabled wealth with which he came up, but the far greater wealth of wisdom – the image of Athene who became the city's own Black Virgin. The alchemical 'puffers' frantically wielded their bellows in the attempt to trans-form base metals into gold for their own enrichment. But the true alchemists knew that what they sought in the elaborations of their formulae and experiments was not common gold at all, but, *deo concedente*, the 'uncommon gold' whose value was beyond price.

The Western alchemical tradition first emerges in that melting-pot of philosophies and beliefs that was Alexandria, two or three centuries before the birth of Christ, or even earlier than that. Some say it was invented by Isis of Egypt, hailed as foremost among the muses and known too as Justice-Wisdom; she was daughter of the god Thoth, they say, or of Hermes, or perhaps Prometheus. The first texts that survive date from between 300 BC and AD 200, and spread through the Greek-speaking world to form part of the extraordinary wealth of Arab culture. In alchemy's diffusion into the West, Athene was there from the start. The first Christian alchemist, they say, was Gerbert of Aurillac, which as we have seen was one of her cities; it was famous for its fleeces which became golden when left in the river Jordanne to attract particles of that most precious metal. Gerbert became the first French pope too, as Sylvester II, in the year 999 (auspicious inversion of 666, the number of the Great Beast!). He had met during his studies a woman of marvellous beauty, who told him that her name was Meridiana ('lady of the south'), and offered him her body, her wealth and her wisdom if he would trust her. He did, and so, they say, he not only achieved the alchemical great work but introduced Arab numbers to the West, invented the clock, the astrolabe and the hydraulic organ, and had a talking head which seems to have acted like a primitive computer.

Alchemical activity in Europe surged between the twelfth and fourteenth centuries, just when the cult of the Black Virgin was reaching its height, and again after the Sack of Constantinople in 1453, when manuscripts that had been mouldering on dusty shelves flooded into the West. The movement spread, grew and endured. It has been reckoned that more alchemical texts were published in English in the thirty years between 1650 and 1680 than at any other time before or since. The last of the great English alchemists, Sir Isaac Newton, didn't die until 1727.[11]

And what the alchemists sought, and suffered for through hour after hour in their laboratories as they poured over the wealth of arcane imagery in those countless baffling texts, was an understanding of 'the miracles of one thing', that fundamental unity of spirit and matter, and the purification of matter into its highest form which would also be the redemption of the soul. 'Alchemy is not merely an art or science to teach metallic transmutation,' said Pierre-Jean Fabre in his seventeenth-century *Les Secrets Chymiques*, 'so much as a true and solid science that teaches how to know the centre of all things, which in the divine language is called the spirit of life.' In the search for this knowledge, the alchemists carried a tradition which directly opposed the dualistic splits so fundamental to orthodox understandings. This is a mystery of the earth, in whose womb all metals grow from the single seed thrown down by the planets: as the *Emerald Tablet* of Hermes Trismegistus, much prized by alchemists down the centuries, emphasized: 'that what is below is like what is above and that what is above is like what is below, to perpetuate the miracles of one thing'. The very name of the work, *al-khemia*, is taken by some to mean 'black earth' – that prime matter which is not to be despised or transcended, but understood as containing that spirit which is also matter, 'the arcane substance'.

That substance had many names and appeared in many guises, but for many it was the Philosopher's Stone, that pure matter which perfects each imperfect body that it touches (and so also brings eternal life). 'Receive this stone which is not a stone,' says Zosimos in about AD 300, 'a precious thing which has no value, a thing of many shapes which has no shape, this unknown which is known to all.' As to the places where the stone may be found, the legendary Persian philosopher Ostanes tells his disciples, in *The Twelve Chapters,* that these are 'the houses, shops, bazaars, roadways, public stores, mosques, baths, towns, cities. One finds it in the earth and in the sea.' In short, like the whore Wisdom crying in the streets, it is everywhere for those with eyes to see it. The stone, says the sixteenth-century author of *Gloria Mundi*, 'is familiar to all men, both young and old, is found in the country, in the village, in the town, in all things created by God; yet it is despised by all. Rich and poor handle it everyday. It is cast into the street by servant maids. Children play with it. Yet no one prizes it, though, next to the human soul, it is the most beautiful and the most precious thing upon earth and has power to pull down kings and princes. Nevertheless, it is esteemed the vilest and meanest of earthly things.'[12]

In their quest for this all-precious substance, the alchemists could not, finally, rely on any of their texts or treatises. For in working on the transformation of matter, as at least some of them knew, they were working too on the transformation of themselves, and there were no short cuts to that. As the sixteenth-century *Splendor Solis* put it:

> Study what thou art
> Whereof thou art a part
> What thou knowest of this art
> This is really what thou art
> All that is without thee
> Also is within. Amen.

In that study, as alchemy's own fundamental premise asserts, mind and matter, intellectual understanding and hands-on 'doing', spirit and practicality, were of equal importance. 'Pray, read, read, read, read again, work and you will know,' says one of only two 'words' in the *Mutus Liber*, that 'silent book' which communicates its methodology only through pictures. Think, do, do, think – and re-do, re-think, for the alchemical process is one of *circulatio*, fixing the volatile, volatizing the fixed. And in this *ludus puerorum*, this child's play, there must be equal valuing of the feminine and the masculine. As a much-quoted alchemical saw put it: 'The sun needs the moon as the cock the hen.' Sol and Luna, Sun and Moon, Queen and King, Mercury and Sulphur: in its wealth of often sexual imagery, in its constantly sought-for unions and re-unions of opposites, alchemy carries an essential 'contrary' or opposite of its own to the prevailing orthodox denigration of the feminine. Its imagery, indeed, is if anything predominantly feminine: from the finding of the essential prime matter in Mother Earth herself, to the many accounts of gestation in and birth from the sealed womb-like vessels which are the indispensable crucibles of transformation; from the goal of the work expressed as the divine hermaphrodite to the clothing of that image of unity in female dress. (And as above, so below: some of the greatest alchemical teachers were women, from Isis the Egyptian to Maria Prophetissa, inventor of that indispensable culinary aid, the *bain-marie*, and on again.)

So the quest for the uncommon gold leads through an equal if not greater honouring of the feminine to a goal which is an understanding hymned in much the same terms as Wisdom herself, and its essential method is a unity of mind and matter, theory and practice. As the Orphics used to say, 'It would be all over with Athene if she lost her hands!' In the alchemical process which is also individual transformation, Athene's qualities are essential. She *is* Lady Alchemia, dwelling in her castle which is the athanor, the alchemical furnace, with her consort, the Athanor King. In one fifteenth-century illustration, her owl looks on as she carries the sun of consciousness in one hand and her spear and shield with the Gorgon's head in the other. This terrible head is integral to the process, for as the alchemists know, 'there is no generation without corruption', no red gold without first the black putrefaction of which Medusa's head is the emblem [Pl. 30].

This is Athene as queen and crown of the work. But we glimpse her owl-eyes in the darkest images too, as the spark of consciousness in the darkest matter. So, for instance, in an illustration to the fourteenth-century *Aurora Consurgens* — a work thought by some to have been written by St Thomas Aquinas himself — there is an extraordinary and terrifying figure, fishtailed, fur-bodied, one leg made of flaming straw, another skeletal, one arm ending in a black claw, the other in a white hand. It carries a snake and is attacked by a scorpion and a great black bird, in a place that seems both deathly and scarlet with the blood of life. In this place of elemental chaos, of prime matter which is also the gold, perches Athene's owl, standing to the right of the figure, and blowing the trumpet which it holds in its right hand – its very 'rightness' emblem of its clarion call to consciousness. The owl makes less mysterious appearances as well, for instance in the seventeenth-century *Amphitheatre of Eternal Wisdom*, bespectacled and holding two crossed and flaming torches, with candles on either side. 'What good are torches, light or spectacles,' runs the legend, 'to folk who won't see!'[13]

If Athene's gift of consciousness, of the seeing which is understanding, is at the heart of the alchemical process, so too is her most mysterious alliance. The alchemical mysteries, probing as they do into the very womb of earth herself in search of that arcane substance, are intimately bound up with the figure of the smith, who is across times and cultures both feared and revered as the one who transforms the metals which are of earth's own body. We remember the intimacy of Athene and Hephaestus, supreme metal-worker. The Egyptian cosmology offers a variant in which both feminine and masculine powers are united in a single image. The goddess Neith – who as we know was widely identified with Athene – is seen as both feminine and masculine, parthenogenic in the way of the vulture, which is also one of Athene's manifestations. The Egyptian smith-god Ptah, 'He Who Knows the Secrets of the Goldsmiths', was also a creator-deity, the 'sculptor of the earth' who created all beings on the potter's wheel. In this, he is identified with Khnum, 'the father of fathers, the mother of mothers', who in turn is associated with Neith in much the same way as Hephaestus – or Prometheus – is with Athene, when the masculine fashions humans from clay and the goddess herself breathes soul into them. Overarching all these cross-correspondences is the symbol of the parthenogenic vulture, a frequent alchemical image. 'Hear the garrulous vulture, who in no wise deceives you,' is the caption to Emblem 43 in Michael Maier's extraordinary amalgam of image, word and music, *Atalanta Fugiens*. 'The vulture perches on the mountain peak,' runs the accompanying Epigram,

> Ceaselessly crying, 'I am white and black;
> Yellow and red am I, and do not lie',
> The Raven is the same, who wingless flies
> In dark of night and in the light of day,
> For of your art both this and that are chief.

Black and white, yellow and red: these are the colours which symbolize the four stages of the alchemical work itself. So an understanding of the vulture, with its hermaphroditic nature, seems essential.[14]

The career of Count Michael Maier, doctor of philosophy and medicine, imperial court physician and alchemist, spanned the end of the sixteenth and the first quarter of the seventeenth century. In *Atalanta Fugiens*, he takes the story of the beautiful, fleet-footed girl pursued by Hippomenes as metaphor for the alchemical process itself: their final uniting in love, eventually achieved after Atalanta loses pace once too often to pick up the last of the three golden apples of Venus, is the unity not only of masculine and feminine, but of all those other opposites – light and dark, heaven and earth, spirit and matter, consciousness and unconscious – with which the alchemists were so fundamentally concerned. Maier illustrates this pursuit, this process, with fifty Epigrams, Emblems and Fugues for three voices which themselves stand for the three essential elements in the alchemical process: the fluid, quicksilver Mercury, the forceful Sulphur and the Salt which unites them. The whole, as Maier says on his title page, is 'to be looked at, read, meditated, understood, weighed, sung and listened to, not without a certain pleasure'.

To most modern eyes, ears and understandings, bafflement can probably be added to the certain pleasure of contemplation. But what we do know is that in this, as in his very many other alchemical works, Maier drew on a conviction that the ancient mythological tales encoded all the secrets of the alchemical art, known from the beginning of understanding and waiting now to be revealed. Many others held this too – for it was part of the more general belief that all knowledge was an echo of the one original, archetypal truth. The conviction was a lasting one: as late as the mid eighteenth century Pernety's *Dictionary* was to claim that classical mythology had been from the start conceived by the master alchemist Hermes himself expressly to record and conceal the sacred truth of the great doctrines.

So, particularly from the fifteenth century onwards, Saturn, that swallower of the stone, is the blackness of prime matter, 'the lead of the wise'; Jupiter is the natural heat which generates all and rules 'the time of the variety of colours'; Artemis and Apollo are the sister–brother pair. The story of Atalanta is only one of the many which conceal alchemical truth. In the Judgement of Paris can be seen the end of the First Work – the fixing of the volatile – just as the making of the stone and elixir are in the siege of Troy and its fall. 'Make a circle around man and woman,' Maier tells us, 'then a square, now a triangle; make a circle, and you will have the Philosopher's Stone.' For him, the secret was written in the Sphinx's question about what went on four legs, then two then three – the riddle which Oedipus answered as 'man' with such confidence and such disastrous results. In these mythological correspondences, as we have seen, Athene may reign as Lady Alchemia herself in her supreme understanding of the unity of spirit and matter. For Maier, the very birth of Athene is the advent of gold. 'Gold rains down, as Pallas is born on Rhodes, and the Sun lies with Venus' is the heading to this Emblem [Pl. 31]. So we can see that in the union of the masculine and feminine in love that comes about mid-way in this version of the work, what is liberated is the constituent of the work's end which is also a distinctively feminine power.[15]

For Maier, as many others, the type of the alchemist was Athene's own best favourite, Odysseus – 'the artist who errs in divers ways until he reaches the desired goal'. England had her own tradition of the alchemical odyssey, in which Maier was particularly interested, and this was drawn together in the mid seventeenth century by Elias Ashmole – astrologer, antiquary and foundation member of the Royal Society, whose bequest to Oxford University became Britain's first public museum. The philosopher's stone, he says, in the introduction to his *Theatrum Chemicum Britannicum*, 'is not in any wayes Necromanticall, or Devilish, but easy, wondrous easy, Naturall and Honest' – and many others hoped him right. Frances Yates has traced the underground stream which flowed into the work of the Royal Society through its early members. Among these, and most famous of all, was Isaac Newton – whom John Maynard Keynes was to call 'the last of the magicians, the last of the Babylonians and Sumerians, the last great mind which looked out on the visible and intellectual world with the same eyes as those who began to build our intellectual inheritance rather less than 10,000 years ago'.[16]

Newton's contemporaries wrote of his 'elaboratory', in which the fire rarely went out by either night or day, and in which he worked usually until two in the morning and often until five or six. 'His pains, his diligence at those set times made me think,' said his assistant, 'he aimed at something beyond the reach of human art and industry.' Newton himself said that 'they who search after the philosopher's stone by their own rules [are] obliged to a strict and religious life', and the estimated 650,000 words of his al-chemical papers – including extensive notes on Maier's work – attest to the solemnity of his task. In his search to understand the properties of matter, Newton was seeking too a deeper knowing: to discover 'those certain forces by which the particles of bodies . . . are either mutually impelled towards one another . . . or are re-pelled and recede from one another' was for him 'the burden of philosophy'.[17]

By the time Newton died, that essential unity between the physical and philosophical worlds was lost. Already at the start of the eighteenth century, another Fellow of the Royal Society, John Harris, had declared in his *Universal Dictionary of Arts and Sciences* that alchemy was 'an art which begins with lying, is continued with toil and labour and at last ends in beggary'. Within not much more than a decade of Newton's death, the witchcraft for which so many had suffered such terrors – and whose 'demons' he himself had judged to be 'desires of the mind' – was officially at least deemed to be nothing but another vulgar fraud. 'What then has lessen'd in England your stories of sorceries?' asked one early-eighteenth-century commentator. 'Not the growing sect [of free-thinkers], but the growth of Philosophy and Medicine. No thanks to atheists, but to the Royal Society and College of Physicians; to the Boyles and Newtons, the Sydenhams and Ratcliffs.'[18] With the purging of the old beliefs around witchcraft, the Royal Society itself was purged of its mysterious beginnings. In the bright clarity of the dawning Enlightenment, there were to be no darker shadows to bring a depth of dimension and perpective. Lady Alchemia was to be dethroned and replaced by Goddess Reason.

CHAPTER 10

Public Cult and
Private Devotion

At the start of the eighteenth century, Queen Anne went to Bath to sample its curative waters. Her visits sealed its fashionable career, and a Pump Room was built, from which people could agreeably view the baths as they sipped the water and prepared themselves for their own immersion in that steaming, slowly bubbling pool. It was while workmen were digging a sewer under the street near the Pump Room in 1727 that they came upon the head of Minerva, lost and buried for maybe 1,400 years. Some sixty years later, a larger Pump Room was needed to meet the demands of fashion's dedicated followers, and workmen were digging again. This time, they came up with the Gorgon's head and the steps to the Roman temple as well.

So the *beau monde* met Minerva and glimpsed the entrance to her shrine, and that this should have happened just when it did seems entirely fitting. For in the eighteenth century, the classical world became fashionable – and not just fashionable, but passionately admired. More particularly, the admiration was for Greece, for Athene herself rather than her Roman descendant, and this was something entirely new. Ever since Geoffrey of Monmouth's history in the twelfth century, after all, England had known that it, like the other Western European nations, took its descent from Rome. The Romans had in turn, of course, and through Aeneas, come from Troy, so if there were sides to be taken, it would not be the Greeks who were favoured. Many people believed, in fact, that the Turks were also originally Trojans;

so when they conquered Greece, it seemed no more than just revenge for ancient defeat. Nor did Greek culture seem to have much to offer. The alchemists, as we have seen, found their art's origins not in Greece but in Egypt, and they were far from the only ones to trace such lineages; the whole hermetical tradition did the same, and Egypt was indeed generally agreed to have been the cradle of all arts and sciences. When scholars went travelling in search of ancient wisdoms, it was to Egypt, not Greece; it's been estimated, for instance, that no fewer than 250 descriptions of such journeys were published in the 300 years after 1400.[1]

But now it was Greece's turn to become the focus of attention and admiration. People were more interested in its ancient Christian history and the Eastern church. People were also prejudiced: there was a growing perception of dark-skinned races as inferior. People were greedy, too. By the seventeenth century, it had become fashionable for wealthy gentlemen to amass collections of 'ancient marbles', and although the best of these were assumed to have been carried off from Greece by the Romans, competition in Italy was stiff and the search for cheaper sources was keen. 'The Levant', including Greece, was becoming more accessible. Already in 1628 Charles I had benefited from Sir Kenelm Digby's haul of 'Old Greek marble-bases, columns and altars' from the temple of Apollo on Delos, and with the help of the British diplomatic service and British navy, subsequent collectors set to with a will to lift what they could and hack the rest into manageable proportions, making do with legs, arms and heads when torsos were too massive to shift.[2]

Yet beyond all these reasons for the upsurge of interest in Greece was another, less tangible one. The Enlightenment's belief in a continuing march of progress with Reason at its head meant, at its simplest, that later civilizations were superior in knowledge and learning to earlier ones. This approach to human history and development could not, of course, have been further from the time-honoured understanding that once, whether in Eden or in antiquity's Golden Age, human affairs and human beings as well had known a perfection which we must ever yearn and strive to regain. The sense of that perfect time and the longing for it are archetypal; they exercise a pull which can't, it seems, be denied. So certainly the idea that later must mean better because more advanced meant, as Reason saw it, that Greece was superior to Egypt. But still, and paradoxically, there was an abiding sense that because they were nearer the beginning and the source, the Greeks knew things which Reason could not reach.

So, for instance, the Abbé Banier, whose four-volume account of *The Mythology and Fables of the Ancients* was the standard eighteenth-century text, reckoned it happiness 'not to live in one of those Ages, when almost the whole World was plunged in an Abyss of Idolatry'. For him, the reasons for studying mythology are primarily cultural: its themes form so great a part of *belles-lettres*, of poetry, of sculpture, of painting, of the contents of the Cabinets of the Curious, that anyone without a knowledge of them must pass for 'a Man of Narrow Education, deficient in the more essential Branches of polite Learning'. He is not, either, overly impressed with Greece, believing in the old way that its gods and culture had come from Egypt: 'that foolish humour of laying claim to great Antiquity betrays itself in almost every People, but never were any so intoxicated with it as the Greeks'. His approach is the commonsensical one of the reasonable man, his first task to 'clear the Fable of all that appears in it supernatural, all that pompous Apparatus of Fictions, which are glaring and obvious'. So, for instance, in his gloss on the tale of Perseus and Medusa, the three Gorgons are not tusked monsters or savage beasts like wild sheep, nor the parthenogenic and fleet-footed inhabitants of a remote island, nor yet young women renowned for their Prudence, Strength, Foresight and general financial acumen – all of which, he says, have been argued. They are, in fact, three ships of Perseus's voyage, called Medusa, Stheno and Euryale, and Pegasus is a fourth, whose harnessing by Minerva means that Perseus indeed found occasion for a good share of Prudence to manage his ship's sails (Daedalus, the first to understand this art, being not yet born).

As for the turning of people to stone, this is a 'moral fable', which designates the astonishment with which they greeted the great haul of (not the Gorgon's tusks or the Graeae's tooth and eye) but the Elephants' Teeth, Horns of Fishes and Hyenas' Eyes with which Perseus's ships were laden on return from their Libyan expedition.

In Abbé Banier's version, then, the figure of Minerva is solidly allegorical, standing always for Prudence. Elsewhere he rehearses the argument that the story of her birth from her father's head veils 'some of the sublimest Truths in Philosophy and even the Mystery of the Word whereby all Things were created, that is to say, the eternal Ideas in the divine Mind'. He tells his readers of the theories that she was, as goddess of the arts and sciences, 'the Intelligence of her Father', the principle of eternally vigilant Wisdom, that her epithet 'Triton' meant 'brain', that the serpent carried by maidens in her processions was a figure of the very one which had seduced Eve. And 'I can never give in to these Notions,' he declares; 'for how is it to be thought that the Pagans had the most distant idea of these ineffable Mysteries?' For him, the story of Minerva issuing from Jupiter's brain was an etymological reference to her name as meaning Wisdom, and the worship of this goddess was introduced from Sais in Egypt, where she was known as Neith, by the historical King Cecrops.[3]

Yet for all Banier's reasonable modernity, there's an infectious enthusiasm here for the very interpretations he's ostensibly rejecting, and the detail with which he recounts the 'fabulous' and 'superstitious' is both enthralling and enthralled. By the mid eighteenth century, in any case, there were other contemporary roads to Greece. Through Pope's couplets readers could meet Athene as 'Queen of War' in the *Iliad* and as 'Martial Maid', 'Minerva graceful with her azure eyes', in the *Odyssey*. That startling blueness signals, perhaps, her Hellenic superiority over the dark-skinned Levantine. In *Dione*, a mercifully never-performed pastoral tragedy by John Gay, her superiority as the maiden Parthenia, the 'beauteous tyrant of the plains', is positively deathly, for 'whoever sees her loves, who loves her dies'. It isn't long at all before Arcadia is cluttered with corpses, for at least some of whom she must take responsibility, wriggle as she may. ('I never trifled with a shepherd's pain, /Nor with false hopes his passion strove to gain. /'Tis to his rash pursuit he owes his fate, /I was not cruel, he was obstinate.') But when sundry lovers in a confusion of disguises bring death on each other in a succession of misunderstandings, Parthenia can not only claim the high moral ground in teaching lovers to be true, but call down some powerful forces which allude to her true nature as she does so. 'Why stays the thunder in the upper sky?' she demands. 'Gather ye clouds; ye forky lightnings fly. /On thee may all the wrath of heav'n descend, /Whose barb'rous hand hath slain a faithful friend.'[4]

By the turn of the century the upper classes were increasingly turning from other people's interpretations to the chance of their own by reading Homer in the original. By then, too, as well as a wealth of classical ideas and artefacts – soon to include most famously, amazingly, inspiringly and notoriously those amassed by Lord Elgin in Athens – there was an equally compelling idea of the buildings which should properly house them. Half a century earlier, the Society of Dilettanti, a drinking club for rich young men, turned a bit serious under that already numinous light of Greece (and a bit fed up with the *déjà vu* that was Italy), decided to support two highly competent draftsmen in making an exact record of Athenian ruins. The three volumes of Stuart and Revett's *The Antiquities of Athens* came out between 1762 and the end of the century and played an inspirational part in the revolution in style which was the coming craze for the classical. Architectural eyes turned from Rome to Greece, led by Minerva, perfect knowledge, herself. The frontispiece to a 1778 folio of designs by the Adams brothers makes plain, as does their preface, that here is a case where later does *not* mean better. It depicts 'A Student conducted to Minerva, who points to Greece, and Italy, as the Countries from whence he must derive the most perfect Knowledge & Taste in elegant Architecture'. On the map to which the goddess points, Greece is directly below Italy: so perfect knowledge has progressed northward, from Greece, through Italy – and now to Britain.[5]

And before too long, one expression of it at least arrived. By 1807, Lord Elgin's fifty huge crates of 120 tons of marble sculpture had finally been unpacked. When they were opened to exhibition in the shed he'd had built behind his house in Piccadilly, the artistic and fashionable worlds were bowled over. Artists flocked to study and sketch the sculptures; on one occasion a famous prize-fighter was induced to pose naked in various attitudes so that his anatomy could be compared with that of the statues. 'The Greeks were gods, the Greeks were gods,' cried the Swiss painter Henry Fuseli. Mrs Siddons, the celebrated actress, shed tears to see the statues of the Fates. Lord Elgin, declared Benjamin West, president of the Royal Academy, had 'founded a new Athens for the emulation and example of the British student'.

But what had he done to the original?

> Let Aberdeen and Elgin still pursue
> The shade of fame through regions of virtu;
> Waste useless thousands on their Phidian freaks,
> Misshapen monuments and maim'd antiques;
> And make their grand saloons a general mart
> For all the mutilated blocks of art.

Byron was far from being the only critic of Elgin's Marbles; Lord Aberdeen in fact belonged to the Society of Dilettanti, whose official line was that they were inferior in every way to the sculpture from Italy in which its members had such considerable financial investment. But Byron's passionate identification, in *English Bards and Scotch Reviewers*, was not, of course, with such gross concerns, but with Greece itself – that poor broken land, already well established to the poetic sensibility as symbol of liberty most cruelly destroyed.[6]

The decline in her glory had started early. Romans and Goths had stripped Athens of her statues. Early Christians had knocked holes in the Parthenon to install an apse and windows and defaced much of the sculpture. The Turks showed more respect for the buildings: they simply turned the church into a mosque by putting a minaret on top of it and converted the Erechtheum from church to harem for the seraglio of the military governor. But then, in the seventeenth century, when the city was under heavy siege from the Venetians, the Acropolis was destroyed. First the Propylaea, which was being used as a gunpowder store, was struck by lightning (by Jove!) and exploded into ruin. Then the temple of Athene Nike was deliberately torn down to make an artillery position. Finally the Venetians scored a direct cannon hit on the new gunpowder magazine, the Parthenon itself, and it exploded. And then the travellers started to arrive and to offer such sums to a poor and run-down little town for the taking away of bits as were, despite an official ban, irresistible. Even Byron had to admit that Elgin was not the first in a crowded field – though he was certainly 'the last, the worst, dull spoiler'.

> What! shall it e'er be said by British tongue
> Albion was happy in Athena's tears?
> Though in thy name the slave her bosom wrung,
> Tell not the deed to Europe's blushing ears;
> The ocean queen, the free Britannia, bears
> The last poor plunder from a bleeding land . . .

To Byron in *Childe Harold*, Athene appears not simply as her weeping self, but as sign and symbol of Greece – a goddess of place just as is Britannia, whose recent fortunes afford the keenest contrast with Athene's own. Ever since she has reappeared on British coinage at the end of the seventeenth century, Britannia has been celebrated as bringer of fortune to the land which bears her name. Once Athene overcame Poseidon, god of the sea, to rule Athens. Now, from the middle of the eighteenth century on, it is Britannia who will rule the waves – though Dr Arne's anthem doesn't become the national one until the next century. Once it was by sighting the spear of the mighty statue of Athene that sailors returning to Athens would know they were nearly home. If a scheme of 1800 for a 230-foot high statue of Britannia by Divine Providence Triumphant in Greenwich had been fulfilled, the whole world would have known where it was by reference to it: for as the proposer explained, 'as Greenwich Hill is the place from whence the longitude is taken, the Monument would, like the first Mile-Stone in the city of Rome, be the point from which the world would be measured'.[7]

What sadder contrast to such a conceit than the figure which appeared to Byron as he sat in melancholy musing in the ruined Parthenon?

> Yes, 'twas Minerva's self; but, ah! how changed,
> Since o'er the Dardan field in arms she ranged!
> Not such as erst, by her divine command,
> Her form appeared from Phidias' plastic hand:
> Gone were the terrors of her awful brow,
> Her idle Aegis bore no Gorgon now;
> Her helm was dinted, and the broken lance
> Seemed weak and shaftless e'en to mortal glance;
> The Olive Branch, which she still deigned to clasp,
> Shrunk from her touch, and withered in her grasp;
> And, ah! though still the brightest of the sky,
> Celestial tears bedimmed her large blue eye;
> Round the rent casque her owlet circled slow,
> And mourned his mistress with a shriek of woe!

This pathetic figure, however, rallies wondrously to issue a resounding and lengthy curse, first on Elgin – 'loathed in life, nor pardoned in the dust' – and then on Britannia herself, from whom he had learned such despicable behaviour. Britain's perfidious betrayal of allies would leave her hated and alone, her trade would languish, famine break out and government be rendered powerless. As at home, so in imperial realms. 'Look to the East,' cries the goddess,

> where Ganges' swarthy race
> Shall shake your tyrant empire to its base;

> Lo! there Rebellion rears her ghastly head,
> And glares the Nemesis of native dead;
> Till Indus rolls a deep purpureal flood,
> And claims his long arrear of northern blood.
> So may ye perish! – Pallas, when she gave
> Your free-born rights, forbade ye to enslave.[8]

In the righteous wrath of her epiphany to Byron, the goddess reveals an aspect of which we have not heard very much in recent centuries. Far from being the protectress of the established order, the right-hand daughter of paternal rule whom we have come to recognize, she is here its scourge as she defends the very liberty which is in her gift. Established orders, of course, have long annexed that gift to their own use. During the reigns of William III and the first Georges, for instance, Britannia is sometimes accompanied by Liberty in the Phrygian cap whose significance she takes from the hat that denoted the emancipated Roman slave. In one propaganda medal William presents the cap to Scotland, Ireland and England with the slogan 'Veni, Vidi, Libertatem Reddidi' ('I came, I saw, I restored liberty'). George I made much the same sort of point on medals for supporters which showed him being crowned by Britannia accompanied by Liberty.[9] And was not Britannia herself to rule the waves, after all, precisely so that Britons would never, never be slaves?

This aspect of Athene's annexing by ruling regimes has its horrible ironies: during the French revolution, for instance, and in the Place de la Concorde yet, was installed a figure of Minerva as image of both Liberty and the Republic which then presided over the guillotine – and thus over the final severance of mind from body, understanding from matter, which elsewhere she is so keen to keep together.[10] But when the goddess appeared to Byron, the tricky question of when defence of liberty tips into a new tyranny was not at issue: her defence was of the indubitably enslaved – Greeks under Turkey, Indians under the British. When Britannia represents to the eyes of eighteenth-century cartoonists the British constitution, her honour threatened by government, it is this aspect of the goddess as liberty that she embodies. When 'Junius' declares in the 1772 edition of his *Letters* that 'the liberty of the press is the Palladium of all the civil, political and religious rights of an Englishman', that liberty is safeguarded in the goddess's own image. This is the Athene who sides with Prometheus *against* the ruling regime, who sneaks the Titan up the back stairs of Olympus to steal the fire of the gods for the benefit of humankind. And now, 2,000 years and more after Aeschylus has recorded the sufferings of Prometheus bound for his presumption, the Titan is set free!

For Shelley, Prometheus is 'the type of the highest perfection of moral and intellectual nature, impelled by the purest and the truest motives to the best and noblest ends'.

> To suffer woes which Hope thinks infinite;
> To forgive wrongs darker than death or night;
> To defy Power, which seems omnipotent;
> To love, and bear; to hope till Hope creates
> From its own wreck the thing it contemplates;
> Neither to change, nor falter, nor repent;
> This, like thy glory, Titan, is to be
> Good, great and joyous, beautiful and free;
> This is alone Life, Joy, Empire and Victory.

Shelley's *Prometheus Unbound* is freed by the hero Hercules after the arrival of the Spirit of the Hour dethrones the tyrannical Jupiter. Just so was the spirit of the hour to liberate Greece! The identification with her struggle for liberty was irresistible to Romantics in France, in Germany, in Italy – and in the United States too, where solidarity was declared through the rise in the 'Hellenic' college fraternities that take their names from letters of the Greek alphabet. And the identification was not just with Greece's political struggle, but with the gifts of her own Golden Age, recovered at last. Even Lord Elgin can find vindication. 'We are all Greeks,' declared Shelley. 'Our laws, our literature, our religion, our arts all have their roots in Greece. But for Greece . . . we might still have been savages and idolators . . . The human form and the human mind attained to a perfection in Greece which has impressed its images on those faultless productions whose very fragments are the despair of modern art, and has propagated impulses which can never cease, through a thousand channels of manifest or imperceptible operation, to enable and delight mankind until the extinction of the race.'[11]

Law, literature, the arts, the perfection of the human mind itself – all are in Athene's gift and soon the temples to house them begin to appear. The Athenaeum in Boston had been founded in 1807, the year in which Lord Elgin's marbles were first displayed to public view in London, to offer a reading room, library, museum and laboratory in what its first secretary called 'one of the greatest strides toward intellectual advancement that this country has ever witnessed'. The American Academy of Arts and Sciences deposited its own library with it, as did many other learned institutions, and by mid-century it was offering a lending service which was open to (the right sort of) women as well as men.

Those who instituted the Athenaeum in London had no such expansive aims. It was founded in 1824 for 'the association of individuals known for their scientific and literary attainments, artists of eminence in any class of the fine arts and noblement and gentlemen distinguished as liberal patrons of science, literature and the arts'; lest this be thought too inclusive, it was agreed that no one should be admitted to membership unless they had either published a literary or professional work or a paper in the Philosophical Transactions of the Royal Society, or were members of one of the houses of Parliament, 'none of whom can perform their high duties without a competent knowledge of literature'. Women were, of course, excluded on several of these counts. Yet Decimus Burton's classical building in Pall Mall, into which the Athenaeum moved in 1830, is a temple to Athene indeed. Some of the members had wanted an icehouse to complete its amenities. Wilson Crocker, Secretary to the Admiralty and to the club as well, had, however, been much moved by Lord Elgin's marbles; he insisted instead on a replica of the Parthenon frieze to decorate the building's façade, and got his way, as he did on most things. The whole endeavour was crowned by Baily's massive Athene, which inspired the following example of Athenaeum wit:

> All ye who pass by, just stop and behold,
> And say – Don't you think it a sin
> That Minerva herself is left out in the cold,
> While her *owls* are all gorging within?

Henry James, an honorary member, was to judge the Athenaeum 'the last word of a high civilization'. In his privately printed enco-mium at the end of the nineteenth century, the Revd F. G. Waugh praised the high distinctions of its membership and reckoned that 'he was not so far wrong, perhaps, who laughingly declared that there were few mundane problems likely to present themselves which could not be solved *instanter* by some one of the members to be found between four and six o'clock within (its) confines!' Kipling thought that going into the Athenaeum was like entering a cathedral between services. The magazine *Vanity Fair* reckoned it, in 1878, to be the club of the 'unknown and unregarded fogey . . . Superannuated and retired politicians, obsolete authors, dis-banded soldiers, antiquated bores, and the general wreck of past generations dine in its halls or wander painfully up and down its steps like whales that have been left stranded by the falling tide.'[12] Perhaps that is why the Athenaeum's Athene looks so extra-ordinarily bad-tempered [Pl. 34].

When her committee traded the amenity of an icehouse for the finer pleasures of the frieze that honours her birthday, they gallantly pronounced themselves glad to have the opportunity of showing this 'most beautiful specimen of sculpture' restored, as it were, to a degree of perfection never before seen in modern times. Lord Elgin's originals, meanwhile, had caused their owner no end of financial and organizational hassles – the curse Minerva had so wrathfully dictated to Byron seems to have worked. But finally, the collection was sold to the nation and housed in a British Museum which by mid-century had acquired its monumental neo-classical façade.

By then, the craze for classical buildings had reached a peak. 'Very like the Mansion House' is supposed to have been Byron's comment on first viewing the Parthenon, the type of so many more to come. The Lord Mayor's residence had been completed in the mid eighteenth century; the classical craze took off from then. There were classical churches in a spate after the Napoleonic Wars, often in working-class areas; the relative cheapness of the style was one of its attractions, though there is nothing cheap about the extraordinary St Pancras opposite Euston Station, whose sooty Caryatids hold up the porch of the Erechtheum to this day. There were galleries galore – the National Gallery in London, the Royal Scottish Academy and National Gallery of Scotland in Edinburgh were all completed between 1820 and 1860. There were city chambers from St George's Hall in Liverpool to the Town Hall of Todmorden, and entire city centres from Newcastle to Bristol.[13] Even after the enthusiasm was over, it left echoes. A decade into the twentieth century, the supremacy of Greece over Rome was boldly declared with the opening of the Palladium, named for Athene's own image (if more obviously for its Palladian columns) as the largest place of popular entertainment in not just London but Britain – including, most certainly and especially, the Coliseum up the road.

Just about the one thing there wasn't in this craze for the Acropolis, this dignity of temples to Athene's civic virtues, was a reproduction of the Parthenon itself. But if the accursed Elgin had had his way, there would have been that as well. His notion that the National Monument of Scotland to the heroes of the wars should be a full-scale reproduction on Edinburgh's Carlton Hill was agreed, but the funds ran out to leave only columns as a still-standing reminder.[14] What the Athens of the North never achieved, however, the Athens of the South proudly accomplished by the end of the century, and the Parthenon of Nashville, Tennessee, remains the only full-scale replica in the world.

When local dignitaries were casting round for ways in which to celebrate the centennial of Tennessee in the 1890s, and divert public attention from the depression as well, they hit on the idea of a Centennial Exposition on the theme of Nashville as the 'Athens of the South'. The White City was built, with halls in the classical style devoted to History, Machinery and the US Government, an auditorium and Women's Hall in the colonial style, those celebrating Children, Commerce and Mineral-Forestry in the Roman, and the 'Negro building' in the style of the Spanish Renaissance. Besides viewing the many displays in these halls – including the largest exhibition of international art yet seen in the South – and attending lectures, visitors could listen to bands playing by day and night, stroll the 'Streets of Cairo' where there were camel rides and a barber who would shave you from head to foot, ride on real gondolas with real gondoliers on a local lake, watch naughty dances in the 'Cuban village', peer in at a large number of Chinese people in the Chinese one – and much more. And the culmination of this celebration was the most extraordinary feat of all: the construction of the full-scale Parthenon, begun with appropriate Masonic rites in the presence of some 5,000 people in October 1895, and completed some eighteen months later. Every care was taken to make sure the reproduction was faithful to the original; the King of Greece sent drawings, of which the most accurate dated from 1674. And the building endured, to be extensively renovated in the 1920s.[15]

All over Britain, less spectacularly ambitious temples to Athene endured as well. Even when they were new, however, they were not to everyone's taste. The style was as Mrs Jarley described her Wax-Work to Little Nell: not funny at all, but 'calm and – what's that word again? – critical? – no – classical, that's it – calm and classical . . . with a constantly unchanging air of coldness and gentility'. And, as Mr Slum added, as he looked around the exhibit, not only devilish classical but quite Minervan as well. John Ruskin thought that people only pretended to like Grecian buildings because they thought it proper. Everyone, he said, loves Big Ben, no one loves the British Museum: 'it asks for respect, it does not lift the spirits'. To an Edinburgh audience he allowed that the New Town had a certain dignity – 'but I cannot say that it is entertaining'. In fact, he had little opinion of Greek art at all: for him, Sir Joshua Reynolds's study of four cherub heads 'from an English girl' was 'incomparably finer than anything the Greeks ever did'.[16]

But what Ruskin did have was a passionate and idiosyncratic devotion to Athene – in which, for a start, he restored her name to her Greek original in place of the Roman Minerva. What he made of the goddess, however, was entirely his own. In an address to a public audience in Woolwich in 1870, for instance, he took as his text the story of Arachne, and sought thereby to convince his hearers – most of whom worked in the Woolwich Arsenal, and many of whom were women – that it was not what you achieved by education but what deeper use you made of it that truly mattered. At first the tale might, he said, seem to reflect badly on Athene. But then you realized that what Arachne was weaving into her competition piece was not just the ivy leaves of Bacchus – a 'wilful insult to [the goddess's] trim-leaved olive of peace' – but pictures of 'base and abominable things' (by which he meant the sexual dalliances of the Olympians), which would be a 'disgrace to the room of the simplest cottager'. Against this he set the 'special work of honour' of Athene, which was to make her own dresses. And from there he launched into a special lecture to the women of his audience – that their own right and honour should be to provide a decent meal for their man when he came home at night and wear a pretty dress when they did so, as well as a tidy one for their morning's work. For that would mean that they were working at home and not, 'poor simple wretches', agitating for the right to do men's work for them while the men drink until they can't stand, or pick oakum, or go to prison. So, most particularly, women's work had nothing to do with packing cartridges, and they should remember that scarlet was the more delightful when used to make cloaks and petticoats rather than regimentals. And in conclusion, 'all your defences of iron and reserves of cold shot are useless unless Englishmen learn to love and trust each other, in all classes. The only way to be loved is to become loveable and the only way to be trusted is to be honest.'

Just what his audience made of this annexation of the distinctly undomestic Athene to his vision, goodness only knows. Certainly the editors of the Library Edition of his works felt it necessary to attach a summary of his arguments in *The Queen of the Air*, based on lectures at University College London, so 'discursive and difficult' did they reckon it to be. At one level, this is a passionate plea to his readers to engage with the emotional reality of the ancient myths; at another, it is an attempt to relate these to modern scientific discovery. At another again, it is a hitching-post for his hobbyhorses – from the need for institutions for the active employment and so moral reform of the criminal classes, to the necessity for creating *useful* work like road-making, the repair of roads and harbours, dressmaking and education in the arts, to the evils of untrammelled 'freedom'. And through all this can be discerned – just – the image of his Athene, as Queen of the Air, to be found in the Heavens, in the Earth, and in the Heart. For him, just as for so many over so long, she is owl-eyed Prudence; she is Justice, in her contrasting robes of saffron-coloured daybreak, and serpent-fringed indignation; she is Fortitude under her helmet and Temperance in her maidenhood, 'stainless as the air of heaven'. But she is also that air itself, a physical force given shape and name; as *Chalinitis*, the Restrainer, she gives life to animals, vegetative power to the earth, motion to the sea and its essential generation to artificial light as well. In the earth, she is *Keramitis*, 'Fit for Being Made into Pottery'; she is the breath of spirit in matter, 'the queen of all glowing virtue, the unconsuming fire and inner lamp of life', the fire of the heart. And in the heart, she is *Ergane*, the Worker, 'directress of the imagination and will'; 'she does not make men learned, but prudent and subtle; she does not teach them to make their work beautiful, but to make it right'.[17]

Somewhere in there is Ruskin's attempt to reconcile mind and matter, spirit and the clay it must infuse if either is to be transformed; his devotion to Athene is as the force which makes both reconciliation and transformation possible. For William Ewart Gladstone, the 'sublime Minerva' – with her special prerogative of 'War, Policy and Industrial Art' and a 'moral majesty' greater than that of any other Olympian – carried a different, but no less powerful, charge. For nearly the whole of the second half of the nineteenth century, through premiership and public office until his death, he poured out a succession of books and articles on Homer. He knew he lacked the critical faculty, he wrote to a friend; but he was driven by both passion and the belief that he 'might and *should* do good in another way'. The conviction which fuelled him was both deeply his own and entirely traditional: 'The history of the race of Adam before the Advent is the history of a long and varied but incessant preparation for the Advent. It is commonly perceived that Greece contributes a language and an intellectual discipline, Rome a political organization, to the apparatus which was put in readiness to assist the propagation of the Gospel.' For Gladstone, God's truth, there from the start of time, had been known to Adam and Eve. They had passed it down to their descendants, and though it had become corrupted, traces of the original verities had remained. So the Homeric 'trinity' of Jupiter, Neptune and Pluto preserved a distant echo of the true one and Apollo carried aspects of the Redeemer. And as for the birth of Athene, if the Greeks had preserved the tradition of the Logos, the Divine Word, it was 'impossible to clothe it, for the purposes of their system, in a more appropriate form'. We have heard this sort of thing before, in the fourteenth-century *Ovide Moralisé*: the only real difference is that the author of that saw the prefigurement of the true trinity in the form of Triple Diana rather than the Olympian brothers, and Christ in Acteon rather than Apollo.[18]

When Gladstone found himself gripped by the gods, he gave up writing his sermons for Sunday family prayers. Perhaps he thought that with 200 or so in his files he had enough to meet any eventuality; perhaps another daemon had seized his imagination. The

Revd Charles Kingsley, best-selling children's author and muscular Christian, had his own devotion to the ancient myths, and his own sermon to preach through them too. *The Heroes*, his first children's book, was rushed out for the 1855 Christmas trade and much reprinted. It was subtitled 'Greek fairy tales for my children', but these were most certainly fairy tales with purpose. His starting-point incidentally illustrates just how far the Greek revival had by now reached. Although girls might not learn the language as their brothers would, they would be as sure to come across Greek names, words and proverbs. And more: 'you cannot walk through a great town without passing Greek buildings; you cannot go into a well-furnished room without seeing Greek statues and ornaments, even Greek patterns of furniture'. The Greeks besides had given us the beginnings of geometry, geography, astronomy, laws, logic and metaphysics; their language was so beautiful that it had become the common one of educated people the world over, which was why the New Testament was written in it. In short, 'next to the Jews and the Bible which the Jews handed down to us, we owe more to those old Greeks than to any people upon earth'.

But there were other reasons too for learning about the Greek myths. Kingsley believed that the development of peoples was like the development of individuals. So nations that lived long ago and far away were like children, made up of 'men and women with children's hearts; frank and affectionate, and full of trust, and teach-able, and loving to see and learn all the wonders around them; and greedy also, too often, and passionate and silly as children are'. But – and the moral for his young readers doesn't take much seeking – the Greeks were willing to be taught and God rewarded them for it. At first, of course, they had worshipped the one true God; it was only later that they fell into idolatry and then into sin and shame and finally into cowardice and slavery, until they perished out of the beautiful land that God had given them. Fortunately, however, at the time of which Kingsley tells, they still kept the last six of the Ten Commandments and they knew what was right and what wrong. Their stories are about heroes, and we call such [men heroes] in English to this day, and call it a 'heroic' thing to suffer pain and grief, that we may do good to our fellow-men. We may all do that, my children, boys and girls alike; and we ought to do it, for it is easier now than ever, and safer, and the path more clear . . . The stories are not all true, of course, nor half of them; you are not simple enough to fancy that; but the meaning of them is true and true for ever, and that is – 'Do right and God will help you.'[19]

One of Kingsley's favourite heroes was Perseus, tall and skilled in sports as well as brave, truthful, gentle and courteous before he sets out on his mission, unrecognizably transformed when he finally returns after seven years of adventure. 'He had gone out a boy, and he was come home a hero; his eyes shone like an eagle's, and his beard was like a lion's beard, and he stood up like a wild bull in his pride.' In his long poem *Andromeda*, written this time for adults, Kingsley is even less restrained, conjuring Perseus as 'boy in the bloom of his manhood/Golden-haired, ivory-limbed, ambrosial', laughing in the joy of his leaping from billow to billow, 'his breath like a rose-bed', his lips pouring forth 'from their pearl-strung portal' his words of wonder at the sight of the maiden chained to her rock. The union of this pair is ecstatic:

> Beautiful, eager, triumphant, he leapt back again to his treasure;
> Leapt back again, full blest, toward arms spread wide to receive him.
> Brimful of honour he clasped her, and brimful of love she caressed him,
> Answering lip with lip; while above them the queen Aphrodite
> Poured on their foreheads and limbs, unseen, ambrosial odours,
> Givers of longing, and rapture, and chaste content in espousals.

Aphrodite laughingly challenges her chaste sister Athene to hand over her pupil who has turned himself so wholly to love and no longer dreams of honour or danger. But the goddess replies that the marriage of heroes is as dear to her as it is to Aphrodite, 'pure with the pure to beget brave children, the like of their father'. And she decks Andromeda in exquisite jewels fashioned by Hephaestus, a most beautiful veil woven by her own hand and a solemn and lengthy blessing as well before rising 'like a pillar of tall white cloud' to return to Olympus. The Hours and the Graces threw a celebration:

All day long they rejoiced: but Athene still in her chamber
Bent herself over her loom, as the stars rang loud to her singing,
Chanting of order and right, and of foresight, warden of nations;
Chanting of labour and craft, and of wealth in the port and the garner;
Chanting of valour and fame, and the man who can fall with the
    foremost,
Fighting for children and wife, and the field which his father bequeathed
    him.
Sweetly and solemnly sang she, and planned new lessons for mortals;
Happy, who hearing obey her, the wise unsullied Athene.

On this note of praise for Athene's heroic virtues rather than Aphrodite's joys, Kingsley's poem ends. But of course there is a third image of the feminine in the tale of Perseus as well – and that 'beautiful horror' exercises her own fascination. Even in the bowdlerized version of the myth in *The Heroes* – Kingsley glosses over Perseus's conception in the shower of gold and Polydectes's designs on his mother, focusing rather on Athene's commands as his motive force – the description of Medusa has an extraordinary charge. While her two Gorgon sisters are as 'foul as swine', she is so 'fair and sad' that Perseus at first pities her. 'Her plumage was like the rainbow, and her face was like the face of a nymph, only her eyebrows were knit and her lips clenched, with everlasting care and pain; and her long neck gleamed so white in the mirror that Perseus had not the heart to strike.' But as he looked, the vipers' heads appeared with their dry bright eyes and hissed, Medusa threw back her wings and showed her brazen claws – 'and Perseus saw that, for all her beauty, she was as foul and venomous as the rest'.[20]

If it is the virtues of Athene, enshrined in that pride of civic buildings, that gives the nineteenth century its public image of itself, then here is the other side to that bright aspiration. The image of Medusa, of evil concealed by numinously seductive beauty, is a no less abiding expression of the feminine; as Mario Praz has said, 'she was to be the object of the dark loves of the Romantics and the Decadents throughout the whole of the century.' To this day, *être médusé*, to be gripped by Medusa, is a condition many have both longed for and endured. She is the one every man is seeking, the head of Orpheus tells Russell Hoban's hero as he tunes in to *The Medusa Frequency*. 'Behind Medusa lie wisdom and the dark womb hidden like a secret cave behind a waterfall.' She is the one, says the Kraken, who cannot be ignored, intruded upon, possessed or betrayed. 'Love can be lost and beauty, but not this face of darkness made bright. This is the one to whom you can be faithful.'

No image in the Uffizi seized Shelley's imagination with a greater power than hers: for him, as for so many who come after, there is divinity in her bringing together of horror and beauty, of loveliness and 'the agonies of anguish and of death'. Keats calls her *Lamia*, and so places her in that ancient gallery of images of the feminine turned bad. Her beauty is utterly deathly; given the form of 'a lady bright/A full-born beauty new and exquisite', she can only compel her bridegroom's passion and only destroy him once her true serpent nature is revealed. We meet her again in the form of Geraldine, the vampire destroyer of Coleridge's *Christabel*. We see her in the Victorian paintings of sirens luring unwary sailors to their deaths, in Rossetti's portrait of *Lady Lilith*. He knows too that she is also *Astarte Syriaca*, the ancient snake-goddess. And in that she is, of course, also Eve. While Blake has seen in the snake-goddess an image of joyful life, by the end of the nineteenth century Redon's vision brings an extraordinary recapitulation of the final image in Maier's alchemical *Atalanta Fugiens*. But where the mutual destruction of the dragon and the woman is, for Maier, 'the true pathway' of the work of redemption, for Redon there is only the unsurpassed irony of death[21] [Pls. 32, 33, 38].

How on earth are these images of the feminine, the pure and wise and the beautiful and evil, to be reconciled? The question is age-old, and the Victorians must grapple with it in their own way. The reconciliation as we have seen, is precisely Athene's gift; that is why, so very long ago, she sent Perseus to bring her the Gorgon's head. Yet how much place is there for that image of the goddess in those cool halls and monuments, in an era when her principal temple is the gathering place of the most established of the establishment? When the classical sculptor John Gibson suggested that on his own monument to Queen Victoria the Queen should be flanked by representations of Justice and Wisdom, Prince Albert thought rather that Clemency should replace Wisdom – 'since the sovereign is a lady'. And so, of course, it did.[22]

And yet, as if to redress some balance, the old myths are more popular a currency for the Victorians than they have ever been. And the Perseus cycle is the most popular of all, just because, perhaps, it brings those images of the feminine unavoidably together, to be grappled with as Perseus must grapple in the toils of the terrible sea-monster in Burne-Jones's *The Doom Fulfilled*. Not least of the attractions of this scene to so many Victorian painters was no doubt the opportunity to portray Andromeda as nubile female flesh, naked and in bondage. But can we imagine too that somewhere the idea was stirring of a third image of the feminine waiting to be released from the chains forged in the split between 'the good' and 'the evil'? If so, stranded as she still was between the dark imaginal cave of Medusa and the clear classical lines of civic consciousness, she had a while to wait yet. And of that some women, themselves beginning to stir, were painfully becoming aware.

CHAPTER II

The Lamp and the Darkness

When Florence Nightingale was about to set out for the 'great cause' of the Crimean War, they say, she was 'as calm and composed as if she was going for a walk'. Only once did that composure break – when her pet owl Athena, which she had brought home in her pocket from the goddess's own Acropolis, died after being forgotten in an attic. 'Poor little beastie,' she wept when its body was given to her, 'it is odd how much I loved you.'[1]

She became known for that owl. After her illness in the Crimea, the troops gave her another one. On her return from the war, so did her admirer the Duke of Devonshire, this time in silver, together with the offer of a banquet at Chatsworth; she accepted the first and refused the second, as she was to refuse all tributes and honours. That owl Athena was her familiar, its fates were hers. In its first incarnation, it had died because her mother and sister had neglected it, stifled it to death for want of air. In Scutari, she once met it on a cliff path when she was walking home late from the hospital, taking in for the first time, so she wrote home, the great beauty of the view; it came up to her, rose on its tiptoes, and bowed several times before flying away, free. The year after her return from the Crimea, sick and anguished, embattled with officialdom, she wrote to a faithful colleague that she had a vision of 'my poor owl, without her life, without her talons, lying in the cage of your canary and the little villain pecking at her'. This time, she made the connection explicit: 'Now, that's me. I am lying without my head, without my claws, and you all peck at me.'

'It has been your fate,' her mentor Benjamin Jowett once told Florence, 'to become a legend in your lifetime.' Yet without the Crimea, what would have become of her anguished, restless, over-powering energy, which had until then been consistently denied the outlet it needed? On her return from that extraordinary twenty months she made her declaration: 'I stand at the Altar of the murdered men, and while I live I fight their cause.' Without the legend, would as many have listened?[2]

Out of the wards of Scutari, out of that meeting of a private need and a no less urgent public one, there came a lasting shift in collective consciousness. The Crimean War was the first to be reported as it happened; for the first time, people who weren't involved learnt what war meant behind the pride of parading scarlet, what its suffering sounded like when the bands stopped playing. There was a longing for someone, somehow, to do what the army administration had so obviously, horrifically and tragi-cally failed to do: to clean up the indescribable conditions of the hospitals, but more than that, to make a morality out of that awful mess. That Florence Nightingale's letter to her friend Sydney Her-bert at the War Office offering her services crossed in the post with his invitation to her is part of the stuff of her legend. But the statistics which were always her bulwark give shape to the loom on which the legend was woven. At the crudest count: more than half the wounded soldiers who arrived at Scutari hospital at the start of 1855 died in that black filth; a year later, the figure was down to fifteen in every 1,000 and deaths and sickness from 'epi-demics' showed a similarly startling reduction. But more than this, Florence Nightingale's achievement here was already what her many others were to be for the rest of her long life: a work of *moral* dimensions. Whatever else came out of the Crimean War, as the historian G. M. Trevelyan was to say, 'England's gain from it was the life-work of this woman – an immense acquisition of moral territory, if all its secondary consequences and ramifications be followed out.'[3]

That it should be a woman who made these gains was, of

course, the other element in that shift in consciousness. Florence Nightingale's appointment had no precedent. It caused outcry among the establishment; the army commanders in the Crimea made heavy-handed jokes about 'The Bird'; her battles with the military establishment were bitter and never-ending. Yet something was stirring in the collective understanding of 'the feminine'. 'My God,' Florence had written in despair in 1848, after the collapse of her plans to study nursing in Germany, 'what am I to do? Teach me, tell me. I cannot go on any longer waiting till my situation should change, dreaming what the change should be.' Yet in that year too, a deeper change was gathering energy. 'We hold these truths to be self-evident,' declared the women gathered at Seneca Falls in the United States: 'that all men *and women* are created equal . . .' (my italics). And so the American feminist movement was launched. On the other side of the Atlantic, the publication of the Communist Manifesto declared a new vision of the relation of intellect to the material world. Six years after that came the swing to its opposite. Papal declaration underlined the gulf between the spiritual and material worlds already so characterized as 'masculine' and 'feminine': the pronouncement of the Immaculate Conception of Mary not only dogmatized the Virgin's unique preservation from the taint of original sin but by implication separated the nature of divinity further from that of humanity.[4]

In these stirrings, Florence Nightingale carried a meaning that went beyond her own achievement. In the field, she was 'the soldiers' friend'; at Balaclava, they rushed from their tents to cheer her three times three and present her with bunches of wild flowers. The officers told her she would 'spoil the brutes' when she set up her reading and recreation rooms; but the soldiers started coming to class and lecture. When she started banking for them so that they could send pay home, the government was sceptical, for everyone knew the British soldier was 'not a remitting animal'; but when it took over her system, drinking went on going down and £71,000 was sent home within six months. In the wards, she brought still deeper transformation: 'before she came,' said one soldier, 'there was cussing and swearing, but after that it was as 'oly as a church.' She became a symbol of healing itself, and even to see her pass was comfort. 'She would speak to one and nod and smile to as many more,' recalled one veteran. 'But she could not do it all, you know. We lay there by hundreds, but we could kiss her shadow on the walls and lay our heads on the pillow again, content.'[5]

What the soldiers said, the public longed to hear – and not just in England either. That last tribute alone inspired a poem by Longfellow and raised a mighty £10,000 for the Nightingale Fund besides. Songs to 'The Bird' burst into broadsheet – about Angels with Sweet Approving Smiles, The Shadow on the Pillow, The Soldiers' Cheer, The Star of the East. She was the light in darkness, the Lady with the Lamp. A penny biography sold in quantity and universities gave prizes for poems about her as well. Madame Tussaud's waxworks in London presented 'A Grand Exposition of Miss Florence Nightingale administering to the Sick and Wounded' and people flocked to see it. Lifeboats carried her name, paper bags her portrait, mantelpieces her china effigy. The very letters of her name spelt inspiration: Flit On Cheering Angel, urged one popular anagram. And that was before she came home.

And after? The letters, gifts, poems, songs, illuminated addresses and proposals of marriage arrived in hailstorms, the begging letters in shoals. A woman who seemed to resemble her was mobbed in Sheffield by those who wished simply to touch her dress. Yet that was the nearest that any of them got to the real woman, or anyone else besides. 'The buz fuz about my name,' she wrote, 'has done infinite harm,' and she would have nothing at all to do with any of it. Her refusal to carry that surge of longing, that image of the all-powerful, all-healing feminine, was so total that within a couple of years most people thought that she was dead. When she returned from the Crimea, she very nearly was, for her collapse, both physical and emotional, was complete. But within months she was possessed again by the suffering she had seen and the imperative need to ensure that it would never happen again. Over and over she scribbled, on blotter, old envelopes, on any scrap of paper that came to hand, 'I can never forget.'[6]

Nor could she. Her identification with 'her children', the common soldiers, was complete. '"Us" means in my language, the troops and me,' she wrote to Sidney Herbert in 1857 when she thought she was dying, in a letter to be opened after her death. 'I hope you will have no chivalrous ideas about what is "due" to my "memory". The only thing that can be "due" to me is what is good for the troops. I always thought thus while I was alive. And I am not likely to think otherwise now that I am dead.'[7] This time, it was the lengthy and bitter struggle to see established the Royal Commission on the Sanitary State of the Army and to present it with a mountain of evidence, statistics and proposals which had nearly killed her. But she survived again, to extend her concern to the Indian Army and then the Indian people itself. For four years, she got 'a little department all to myself' within the India Office, dealing with civil and military public health. In England, the Nightingale School of Nursing had opened at St Thomas's Hospital in 1860; she tackled the state of midwifery training, of nursing in Poor Law Institutions, of sanitary reform. She wrote annual letters to her probationers and at the age of seventy-six was still making medical reports when one of them died. It is exhausting even to try to tally up the work she did, the causes she pressed. When she died in 1910, in her ninety-first year, she left behind enough written material to fill nearly 200 volumes in the British Museum.

And by then she had been at best a semi-invalid for over fifty years. The woman whose unremitting energy in the Crimea had become part of her legend most usually moved, from the time she was thirty-six years old, only from bed to sofa and back again. She was often fainting and unable to eat, often in terrible pain, unable to move at all. The woman who had moved so fiercely and fearlessly through wards and barracks, who had tackled the army establishment in its bastions, saw no one except by appointment and then only individually; sometimes she wouldn't see them at all, but communicated only by notes sent from her room and back. Diagnoses of what ailed her have not been lacking: her illness has been called 'psychoneurotic', unconsciously 'creative' and even more consciously 'strategic', enabling her to get on with what was important to her unhindered by the demands of the social life she so despised.[8] We could repeat the rumoured sightings of her strolling outdoors and wonder how much deliberation there was in her. We could add that she was compulsive, obsessional; we could discuss the extreme tensions in her family, sibling rivalry and parental complexes; we could note the fact that it would have been a lot handier, financially speaking, if she had been born a boy. And we can imagine the reaction of the woman herself to all that sort of stuff. 'Wondering,' as she once acerbically said of the imaginative faculty, 'is like yawning, and leaves the same sensation behind it and should never be allowed except when people are very much exhausted.'[9] Nevertheless, in the pattern of Florence Nightingale's life, the extraordinary *numen* she carried for so many, and the lasting shifts she catalysed in public affairs, we can see what the ancients would have respected as possession by a god. Now that the gods have, as Jung said, become diseases, we could use his own terminology to talk about identification with an archetype: that depth-charge of psychic energy which takes the shape of Athene and Medusa.

Among that welter of statistical summaries, that plethora of proposals for reform which she left behind her, the innumerable scraps of anguish that cataloguers call the 'private notes' attest to both a driven conviction of rectitude and a terrible and continuing doubt. Was she right to have refused marriage, and if so, why does she so painfully regret her decision? Is she trying to override God's will? The questions recur and recur. 'Oh God,' prays one private note towards the end of that long life, 'lead me. I want to help God. How preposterous, it is He who has to set my work.' And again, 'God is not my private secretary.' What *is* God's will? Over and over, year after year, on torn scraps of paper and the backs of old envelopes, she records the dates on which she knew God to have called her. 'To his service': 7 February 1837. 'To be a Saviour': 7 May 1852. Yet 'I think if I had felt God loved me I could have borne anything', she wrote at the age of forty-five. 'But I never did feel it.' In that year, God called her for the last time. 'To the Cross': 28 July 1865. Over and over, she lists also other significant dates in her life, records and re-records their anniversaries – as if to anchor her physically unmoving self in a psychic reality of time and purpose. Behind the image of that terrible stuckness, that immobilized and isolated figure scribbling and scribbling the lists and questions which bring so little comfort, there is another: that of Medusa in her cave at the entrance to the underworld, the snakes that writhe round her head like ideas which go round and round and have nowhere to go. Florence Nightingale identified herself with that little owl Athena: here is the other pole of that fierce and moving energy. If it was her fate to become a legend in her lifetime, it was no less her fate to live out the split in that once-united power which has been widening for so long – and to do it not just in her own life but for her times.

From the start, there is something of Athene's quality about her. Her very name is that of an ancient city-state. Until her parents hit on the idea of naming her for her birthplace – just as they had called her elder sister Parthenope, the old title of her birthplace Naples – no one had ever thought of such a conceit. And throughout her long years of public concern, it was in the *polis* that she moved and worked. Since her death it is as the inspiration of modern nursing, that especially 'feminine' craft, that she has been valued. It is for her nursing activities too that her political importance has been assessed – as one of those 'heroic pioneers' who led the way in women's emergence from private to public sphere during the latter part of the nineteenth century. But it is doubtful whether this emphasis would have pleased her; it was only when she went 'out of office', her work and influence on army and Indian affairs at an end, that she gave her energy to nursing concerns. And certainly she identified herself with men rather than women. At the limit it was as a man that she described herself – 'a man of action', 'a man of facts'. And a man, too, of sympathy. 'If I were to write a book about my experiences,' she once said, 'I should begin "Women have no sympathy". A woman once told me that my character would be more sympathized with by men than by women. In one sense I don't choose to have that said . . . In another sense I do believe it is true. I do believe I am like a man. But how? *In having sympathy.*'[10]

She was emphatically her father's daughter – and in that a daughter of the patriarchal order as well. In a PS marked PRIVATE in a letter to him from the Crimea, she recounts how Lord Raglan had asked her what her father thought of her being there.

I said with pride my father is not as other men are, he thinks that daughters should serve their country as well as sons – he brought me up to think so – he has no sons – & therefore he has sacrificed me to my country – & told me to come home with my shield or upon it . . . He thinks that God sent women, as well as men, into the world to be something more than 'happy', 'attentive' and 'amusing'. 'Happy and *dull' religion* is said to make us – 'happy and *amusing' social life* is supposed to make us – but my father's religious and social ethics make us strive to be the pioneers of the human race & let 'happiness & amusement' take care of themselves.

This speaks more, perhaps, to Florence's ideal father than the clever, charming, ineffectual and actual one who was so often a disappointment to her. But it was their shared passion for theological and philosophical speculation, based in Unitarianism, which brought Florence to her understanding of God as the perfect being whose laws are discernible through the operation of social and economic conditions and who to each age sends 'Saviours' who help humankind in its progress towards his own perfection. She explored this theme at huge and unwieldy length in the three-volume *Suggestions for Thought to The Searchers After Truth among The Artizans of England*, begun in 1851, and privately published nine years later. By then, she knew herself to be called as one of those Saviours. So all her work was essentially *religious*, as she advanced God's plan for perfection through economic and social reform. For, as she understood it, 'The best preparation for another life must be to rightly value this.' And, as she emphasized, 'God's scheme for us was not that he should give us what we asked for, but that mankind should obtain it for mankind.' This was her Promethean fire, her myth of progress, and her belief in its essentially moral nature never left her. Once, in later years, the Aga Khan came to visit and she reminisced about the many advances she had lived to see in the management of hospitals, drainage, ventilation, sanitation. Did she think, he managed to slip into a pause in the flow, that people were improving? Improving? 'Believing more in God', he said. 'A most interesting man,' she noted after the interview, 'but you could never teach him sanitation.' For her, of course, sanitation was as close to God's heart as to her own.[11]

And she joined battle for it in the very citadels of father–power, armoured like Athene at the right hand of Zeus. Her life after the Crimea was a running metaphor for war; that is where her own fierce warrior energy had found its release and to that place she constantly, as the private notes attest, returned for refuelling. She called God her Commander in Chief – and C in C was what her male colleagues called her. The metaphor was carried into her nursing work: she was Mother Chief to her nurses, and her wards were as barracks to her. In these battlegrounds she was not, finally, a revolutionary: like Athene, she was a daughter of the ruling order. 'I have nothing to do with the making of war or peace', she once said; her work was with war's consequences, not whether it should happen at all. She was never more than a tepid supporter of women's franchise, and got irritated with women's calls for more professional opportunities when her hospitals had more vacancies than suitable applicants. She was as impatient with the 'jargon' about the 'rights' of women, which urged women to do all men do, including the medical and other professions, merely because men do it, as she was with the 'jargon' that said women should do nothing men do: 'you want to do the thing that is good whether it is suitable for a woman or not'.[12]

Yet her reforms were such as to amount to revolution and in her pursuit of 'the thing that is good' she was fearless. Athene works to shift power from Zeus for the progress of humanity in skill and understanding; Florence Nightingale worked ceaselessly against the abuses of authority. The idleness and incompetence of the military hierarchy in the Crimea had sickened her; when her sworn enemy Dr John Hall, Inspector General of the Hospitals, received a KCB for his services, she did not hesitate to dub him 'Knight of the Crimean Burial Grounds'. She was impatient at talk of her 'self-sacrifice' and 'heroism' when the real humiliation and hardship of the Crimea, as she told Sidney Herbert, was 'that we have to do with men who are neither gentlemen, nor men of education, nor even men of business, nor men of feeling, whose only object is to keep themselves out of blame, who will neither make use of others, nor can be made use of'.[13] To her, the Army Medical Board, the army hospitals and the army itself became 'those three sinks of jobbery and official vice'; she could never forgive them for the sufferings of the troops with whom she so passionately identified. She brought a similar hatred of the way in which those in power crush the powerless to her Indian work; she abhorred the way the British there stamped over local customs and was passionate for reforms that would restore land and a means of livelihood to the Indian peasants.

In all this, her approach was always intensely and detailedly practical. There was no use at all, she once said, in angels without hands – just as the Orphics had said that it would be all over with Athene if she lost hers. Her work was very precisely in the goddess's own realm: the transformation of the matter through the work of the mind. At its best, this could touch the quality of Athene herself. When John Stuart Mill died, she characterized that champion of the rights of women as a goddess – the Passion of Reason. 'And he would not at all have considered the gender humiliating. For he was like neither man nor woman – but he was

Wisdom thrilling with emotion to his fingers' ends – impassioned Reason – or reasonable Passion – in the sense that one supposes the Greeks had in their mind when they made Wisdom a woman.' In a sense, of course, she was writing of herself, and at best she could carry an extraordinary authority. 'But it must be done,' she once said, and very quietly, to a doctor who told her that a task was impossible; he did it, of course, and he never forgot the sound of that voice.[14] 'From the first,' said a Poor Law inspector with whom she later worked, 'I had a sort of fixed faith that Florence Nightingale could do anything and the faith is still fresh in me. And so it came to pass that the instant she entered the lists I felt the fight was virtually won and I feel this still.' As for individuals, so lastingly in the popular imagination to which she had long been restored. During the Franco-Prussian war, contributions flowed in to her unsolicited, often from poor people: it was simply assumed she would be in charge of relief.

Yet there is something wrong here. When Athene visited her heroes, she enthused them, enhanced their power. When Florence Nightingale dealt with hers, she all but destroyed them. Certainly she could not have achieved what she did without that fierce and impatient determination. When she returned from the Crimea, Queen Victoria gave her a brooch designed by the Prince Consort which was made up of a St George's Cross, the royal cipher and the inscription 'Blessed are the Merciful'. He was about as far from the mark, of course, as the Staffordshire china people who portrayed her carrying two cups on a small tray and wearing a white flowered skirt, blue bodice with a pink bow and red slippers.[15] But if neither mercy nor cups of tea would have got her very far in the Crimea, there were many who could have wished for more of both in her subsequent campaigns. Her mentor Benjamin Jowett likened her not to Athene, but to the goddess's mirror-image – Eris, the terrible Strife, 'insatiably raging'. She demanded the same driven devotion to the work from her colleagues as she was gripped by herself, and in this she was tyrannical. When the dying Sydney Herbert told her he must resign the

War Office, she refused to either see him or write to him beyond one more blast: 'How perfectly ineffective is a reform unless a reformer remains long enough at the head TO MAKE IT WORK.' Her demands of Arthur Hugh Clough, who died in the same year, were as intolerant. Dr John Sutherland, her faithful secretary until he was all of eighty-eight years old, at least survived, but even he got his wife to excuse him when he was unable to report for duty. 'I am sorry you are ill,' was one response from headquarters. 'But I suppose, as I have not heard again, that you intend me to believe that you are either well or dead. I am so busy that I have not time to die. Here are three things . . .'

They put up with it, because the woman was inspirational. But there was something paralysing, even deathly in her too. Sidney Herbert's last words − 'Poor Florence, poor Florence − our joint work unfinished' − may be the attribution of her own longing. But here is Sir John Lawrence, governor-general of India, fearing that she will find him 'timid and perhaps even time-serving', apologizing for his hesitancy in reform. Here is Colonel Yule, a member of the India Council, assuring her from his deathbed of his great devotion, 'useless as I fear I have been in your great task'. Here is Mr Croft, lecturer in surgery at St Thomas's: 'Alas, that I did so little in nineteen years and left so much undone for such a loveable and adorable leader.' Here, even, is Benjamin Jowett, after seventeen years of friendship: 'I have not been able to do as much as you expected of me.'

This is the sapping, paralysing power of Medusa in her dark cave, and Florence Nightingale knew it. In her private notes of despair, she would accuse herself of being a vampire. 'My work − an idol, a moloch to me,' she noted as late as 1887. But what else had she ever had than that?

'Oh God, what am I?' she had cried in an anguished private note of those dreadful pre-Crimea years when she was struggling still to escape the confines of her family.

The thoughts and feelings that I have now I can remember since I was 6

years old. It was not I that made them. Oh God, how did they come? are
they the natural cross of my father & mother? What are they? A profession, a trade, a necessary occupation, something to fill and employ all my
faculties, I have always felt essential to me, I have always longed for,
consciously or not. My God, what is to become of me? In my 31st year I
see nothing desirable but death.[16]

Her longing had brought her into bitter and lasting conflict
with her mother and her sister, whose devotion to the conventional life of society served only to underline Florence's alienation
from it. She herself dated her illness from her fainting at the culmination of one of those endless passionate rows with her sister, who
had refused to accept some bracelets from her – refused, perhaps,
to be bound thus to Florence's views and aspirations. She was a
bewilderment to her family; her mother told the novelist Mrs
Gaskell, with tears in her eyes, that they were ducks who had
hatched a wild swan. For Mrs Gaskell, she was more than that:

She must be a creature of another race so high and mighty and angelic,
doing things by impulse – or some divine inspiration, and not by effort
and struggle of will. But she sounds almost too holy to be talked about as
a mere wonder . . . I never heard of anyone like her – it makes one feel
the livingness of God more than ever to think how straight He is sending
his spirit down into her, as into the prophets and saints of old. I dare say
all this sounds rather like 'bosh' – but indeed if you had heard all about
her that I have you would feel as I do.

Yet even to Mrs Gaskell, there was something chilling here. She
reported, for instance, the unsparing efforts that Florence made to
comfort the dying son of a village woman; the mother thought of
her as a 'heavenly angel'. But by the time the woman's husband
died, Florence had lost interest in her, 'because her heart and soul
are absorbed by her hospital plans and, as she says, she can only
attend to one thing at once. She is so excessively soft and gentle
that one never feels the unbendableness of her character when one
is near her . . .' Florence once told Mrs Gaskell that if she had her

way, no mother would bring up her own children – they would all be sent to crèches. 'That exactly,' commented the novelist, 'tells of what seems to me to be *the* want – but then this want of love for individuals becomes a gift and a very rare one, if one takes it in conjunction with her intense love for the *race*, her utter unselfishness in serving and ministering.'[17]

The anguish of her long wait to do that as she chose reached a crescendo in *Cassandra*, the coded autobiography that is slipped into the second volume of the sprawling philosophizings of *Suggestions for Thought*. The published version is considerably toned down from the original and the voice has been changed from first person to third. But the lament of the dying Cassandra, the thirty-year-old woman whose gifts never found the expression for which she so longed, is unmistakeably thirty-year-old Florence Nightingale's own. They live under the same curse, and perhaps for the same reasons. It was the fate of Cassandra, princess of Troy, that none of her prophecies – all true – would be believed; this torment was spat into her mouth by Apollo after she had failed to escape his sexual demands by fleeing into the temple of Athene. Was Florence to be equally cursed by her continuing refusal to marry because she felt called to another altar?

'Why have women passion, intellect, moral activity,' her Cassandra cries, 'and a place in society where not one of the three can be exercised?' Because they are entrapped by the conventions and expectations of society – the 'great sacred ceremony' of the day which is dinner, the drives in the carriage, and above all the assumption that any intellectual occupation is 'a merely selfish amusement, which it is their "duty" to give up for every trifle more selfish than themselves'. The answering voice asks, 'Is that all you have to complain of?' And Cassandra replies:

To have no food for our heads, no food for our hearts, no food for our activity, is that nothing? If we have no food for the body, how we do cry out, how all the world hears of it, how all the newspapers talk of it, with a paragraph headed in great capital letters. DEATH FROM STAR-

VATION! But suppose one were to put a paragraph in the 'Times', *Death of Thought from Starvation*, or *Death of Moral Activity from Starvation*, how people would stare, how they would laugh and wonder! One would think we had no heads or hearts, by the total indifference of the public towards them. Our bodies are the only thing of any consequence.

And so Cassandra dies, her physical death only an echo of that death by starvation of intellect and moral activity that has happened years ago. And her dying words are a reproach to her family:

My people were like children playing on the shore of the eighteenth century. I was their hobby-horse, their plaything; and they drove me to and fro, dear souls! never weary of the play themselves, till I, who had grown to woman's estate and to the ideas of the nineteenth century, lay down exhausted, my mind closed to hope, my heart to strength.[18]

Yet if Cassandra's reproach was for 'her people', Florence's was most especially for her mother. Again and again in *Suggestions for Thought* she returns to the selfishness of the mother and maternal expectations that daughters should share their own views of the importance of marriage and the conventional social round. Daughters, she says, are their mothers' slaves, as much as they ever were.

No mother . . . considers her children as anything else but her property. If she would have permitted their 'vocations' and they have none, she says how *she* is disappointed. If, on the other hand, they have 'vocations', and she will not sanction them, she says, what can they want more than she has given them to make them happy? The mother's feeling is, more or less, always a selfish one; she refers everything back to herself. The child is her *thing*.[19]

And yet through all the years of Florence's bitterness – and a refusal even to see her mother that lasted for nine years – there is a longing for acceptance and approval. 'When I feel her disappointment in me,' says a scored-out passage in a private note of about 1851, 'it is as if I was becoming insane.' At about the same time, she told herself that she must expect no help from either mother or sister. 'But I have so long craved for their sympathy that I can hardly reconcile myself to this.' On her return from the Crimea, she was bitter about their reaction to her. 'They like my glory – they like my pretty things. Is there anything else they like in me?' When her mother for the first time ever missed her birthday, she was terrified, more frightened than ever before in her life. She was forty-eight years old.

And yet again, she could not reconcile herself to what the world of the feminine represented to her. 'To be turned back into this petty, stagnant, stifling life,' she scribbled in a tiny hand on the back of an old envelope during a rare visit to her ageing mother. All her life she had fought against the stagnant and the stifling. Her very notions of health and sickness, her very philosophy of nursing, were founded on that battle. Throughout her long life she obdurately refused to countenance the (then new) germ theory of disease. She clung to the old miasmic idea, that disease creates itself progressively out of 'miasmas' or 'influences' that proliferate in conditions of dirt. The notion of infection, or diseases as coming in classes 'like dogs and cats', she found frankly absurd. Had she not, after all, seen in the Crimea how a fever grew in overcrowded conditions first into typhoid and then, as conditions got worse, into typhus? So windows must be thrown open to expel the decaying matter exhaled so prolifically by the lungs; so washing is essential against corruption carried by the skin. The understanding of human nature implied by this doctrine was not lost on Florence. 'To be a good nurse,' she told her probationers, 'one must be a good woman . . . To be a good woman at all, one must be an improving woman, for stagnant matter, sooner or later, and stagnant air, as we know ourselves, always grow corrupt and unfit for use.'[20]

Progress or stagnation, improvement or corruption, work or inertia, the incessant movement of the mind and the painful immobility of the body, the world of affairs and the confines of 'society'. For Florence Nightingale, these were the irreconcilable

worlds of the masculine and the feminine, the opposites between which she was constantly and painfully torn. For her, the
Athene–Medusa connection was broken. The entire realm of
the traditionally feminine was negative – the claims of family, of
true relationship and connectedness. She related to matter by tidy-
ing it up, organizing it, cleansing it. She related to people by prior
appointment. 'Mine has been such a horrible loneliness,' says one
of those private notes. In the citadels of power she felt embattled,
in the drawing-rooms she felt rejected. From her earliest childhood
she had felt that there was something wrong, something monstrous, about her. 'My greatest ambition was not to be remarked,'
she recalled in an autobiographical memoir. 'I was always in
mortal fear of doing something unlike other people . . . I was afraid
of speaking to children because I was sure I should not please
them.'[21] Well, she did do a great deal that was unlike other people.
Could she ever please them by it?

As her long life went on, there was a softening. When she was sixty,
her mother at last died and something in her was at last released. Her
relationships with both men and women lost their voracious intensity and friendships brought comfort. She became plump, more benevolent; there was even some humour. It was Athene's powers that
went first: her eyesight, then, gradually, that keen and restless mind.
The last private note with a date on it in that huge collection is a list of
verses from the Bible which contain the word 'heaven'. It was
written in May 1901 – and May was the month in which God had
called her to be a 'Saviour' so long ago. Five years later, her staff told
the India Office that it wasn't any longer worth sending her papers. In
1907, she received the Order of Merit – the first woman to do so and
one of the very few recipients of that especial sovereign's gift who
was not a member of the Athenaeum Club. So she reached her secure
and honoured place at the height of the Acropolis at last. And it's
doubtful she even knew what was going on as she graciously mur-
mured, 'Too kind, too kind,' to the man from the Palace.

She wanted a burial service with no trappings at the nearest
burial ground, and no memorial at all. In fact, she was buried in

the family plot, carried there by six sergeants of the guards. Her stone is marked simply 'F. N.+ Born 1820. Died 1910.' Many and mostly poorly dressed people came to her funeral. She was a warrior to the very last, for the hymn sung over her grave was the one she had so often quoted to her nurses:

> The son of man goes forth to war
> A kingly crown to gain.
> His blood-red banner streams afar
> Who follows in his train?

The Crimea Memorial in Waterloo Place in London is a massive affair, with its great angel looking over the three guardsmen made from the metal of Russian cannon captured at Sebastopol. As you face it, Sydney Herbert is on the right, his chin sunk in his left hand in the classical posture of mourning. On the left, head slightly turned, is the slight figure of the Lady with the Lamp, the fanciful little oil lamp in her left hand pointing very nearly straight at the Athenaeum Club – and so at the figure of Athene herself, who at some time in the last thirty years of the nineteenth century had, and for the first time, acquired her spear.

The Memorial was unveiled in 1915. There was no ceremony. That, it was felt, would be inappropriate, given the continuing carnage in Europe.

It was Florence Nightingale's personal fate to live with particular intensity in that fragmentation of the feminine which had become the separation of Athene and Medusa. But she carried something for her times as well – which is why her legend endures in quite the way it does. By the last quarter of the nineteenth century, what had been for her a private anguish was increasingly the stuff of public debate and action too. 'It seems,' her Cassandra had said,

as if the female spirit of the world were mourning everlastingly over blessings, *not* lost, but which she has never had, and which, in her discouragement, she feels that she never will have, they are so far off.

By the end of the century, it seemed that Apollo's curse was relenting and Cassandra was being at least tentatively believed. Lytton Strachey was famously to liken Florence Nightingale not to the 'wild swan' which so distressed her mother but to an eagle – that bird of Zeus himself; Constance Maynard, pioneer of higher education for women, had used the same metaphor, feeling that she and her sisters had been shut up like 'eagles in a henhouse'. But now small flights of eagles were beginning to soar. Nursing itself offered increasing opportunities, higher education was becoming more available, that movement which had started in Seneca Falls in 1848 was gathering a determination across Britain as well. Thirty years earlier John Stuart Mill had argued that 'what is now called the nature of women is an eminently artificial thing – the result of forced repression in some directions, unnatural stimulation in others': history seemed to be proving him right.[22]

Yet inevitably there was a reaction. 'The womanly woman,' wrote Eliza Linton at the start of the eighties,

has always been taught that, as there are certain masculine virtues, so are there certain feminine ones . . . She has taken it to heart that patience, self-sacrifice, tenderness, quietness, with some others, of which modesty is one, are the virtues more especially feminine; just as courage, justice, fortitude and the like belong to men. Passionate ambition, virile energy, the love of strong excitement, self-assertion, fierceness, an undisciplined temper, are all qualities which detract from her ideal of womanliness and which make her less beautiful than she was meant to be.

We can only guess what Florence Nightingale would have made of that consignment of the time-honoured feminine allegorical figures of 'justice, fortitude and the like', those echoes of the image of Athene herself.[23]

The following year London audiences could have a good laugh at the very notion of a goddess of wisdom who had anything to say to women at all. When Gilbert and Sullivan's *Princess Ida* sets up her Castle Adamant for the higher education of women, she petitions Minerva as their patron:

Oh goddess wise
That lovest light
Endow their sight
Their unillumined eyes.
At this my call
A fervent few
Have come to woo
The rays that from thee fall
Let fervent words and fervent thoughts be mine,
That I may lead them to thy sacred shrine!

When the young men attack the Castle, however, the eager scholars' resolve to abjure matrimony for learning soon crumbles. Their surgeon, of course, can't stand the sight of blood; their bandswomen can't bring themselves to play martial music; Lady Psyche, the humanities don who has been put in charge of gunpowder, is more in favour of talking things over. It isn't long before Princess Ida gives up her cherished scheme to which 'posterity would bow in gratitude' – especially when the men point out that under that scheme, there would be no posterity to bow. And she joyfully leads her erstwhile students into matrimonial bliss.[24]

This heavy-handed ho-ho reflects a deeper concern. In the same year that John Stuart Mill was pondering the 'artificiality' of what was called 'women's nature', the Professor of Modern History at the University of Oxford was making very clear what it should not be. 'The one thing men do not like,' Montagu Burrows told readers of the *Fortnightly Review*, is the 'man-woman' – of which the 'University-woman' was the exemplar. 'Keep the male and female types essentially distinct. For those young ladies who cannot obtain "a higher education" through their parents, brothers, friends and books at home, or by means of Lectures in cities, let a refuge be provided with the training governesses; but for heaven's sake, do not let us establish the "University-woman" as the modern type.' Within five years, his blunt appeal to men's preferences as the standard for female acceptability had found its justification. Henry Maudsley, eminent psychiatrist and founder of the eponymous London hospital, was warning in the same journal that the intellectual training of young girls could injure not only their brains but their reproductive systems: the expenditure of 'vital energy' needed to establish the menstrual cycle left little to spare and there was only so much to go round. So the woman who studied risked becoming 'something which having ceased to be woman is not yet man'. Too much of this, of course, and the race itself faced if not extinction at least serious impoverishment. This possibility was squarely faced by Dr William Withers Moore in his 1886 presidential address to the British Medical Association: as educated women become 'more or less sexless, the human race will have lost those who should have been her sons. Bacon, for want of a mother, will not be born.' Once an idea becomes a presidential address, and once it becomes a presidential address to the BMA, the doctors' own trade union, then it really has entered into collective consciousness. It could only be a matter of time before someone was talking about racial miscegenation in the search for wives. And sure enough, it was.[25]

As late as 1893, Florence Nightingale was looking back on a lifetime of devotion to her cause and wondering, in one of those still-anguished private notes, about her own nature, her own 'monstrosity'. 'A department – not a man or woman. Mr Jowett was not a Department but a man. Am I a Department?' Two years later, two doctors from Vienna called Breuer and Freud were to make their own contribution to the debate on 'woman's nature' in a work called *Studies in Hysteria*. And the perception of the relationship between Athene and Medusa was poised to take a new turn.

CHAPTER 12

Logos and Psyche

When the sick and aged Sigmund Freud fled his native Vienna in 1938, his friends made sure that one piece in particular out of all his collection of fine antiquities went with him. 'This is my favourite,' he had once told a patient, and held it towards her.

I took it in my hand. It was a little bronze statuette, helmeted, clothed to the foot in carved robe with upper incised chiton or peplum. One hand was extended as if holding a staff or rod. 'She is perfect,' he said, 'only that she has lost her spear.'

Such was Freud's feeling for his little Athene that she stood always on his desk before him as he wrote – and there she still stands to this day in the London house which became his last home and is now his museum [Pl. 40]. His devotion to the goddess was a lasting and intimate one. When in 1912 he gave each of his closest collaborators the antique intaglio worn in a gold ring which signified their membership of the 'Committee', he himself chose one of Athene and her father Zeus. But his honour of the goddess went back further than that. When he'd made his first long-anticipated and long-postponed visit to Rome in 1901, he could, he wrote, 'have worshipped the humble and mutilated remnant of the Temple of Minerva!' The goddess seems to have rewarded his homage, for on his return from that journey he discovered that his zest for life had somewhat grown and for martyrdom correspondingly diminished. So he decided, and despite the disappointing reaction to his monumental inquiry into *The Interpretation of*

Dreams, to push for a professorship. He eventually got it, and a taste for travelling as well. In Athens a couple of years later, he put on his best shirt for the Acropolis. When he got there, he was visited by the oddest sense of disbelief in what he saw before him. Later, he was to explain the feeling as incredulity that the poor student he'd once been should ever achieve such heights. Twenty years on, he still thought those amber-coloured columns the most beautiful sight he had ever seen in his life.[1]

By the start of the twentieth century, there were opportunities enough for Freud to worship the goddess in his home town too. For the government, Athene was sign and symbol of its own faith in liberal rationalism, and they put her on a pillar in full duty dress of helmet, spear and Victory to guard the neo-classical parliament. In the new Museum of Art History, she represented Hellenic culture, posing elegantly in the stairwell in her fashionable high-necked gown with her hair falling in artful ringlets and her spear resting nonchalantly across an arch. The creator of this proper young lady was the artist Gustav Klimt, not yet thirty but already well on his way to becoming one of Vienna's leading artists and architectural decorators. By the time he had finished his own homage to the goddess, however, there was nothing proper in his vision of her at all.[2]

In that extraordinary excitement of the overturn of traditional values in turn-of-the-century Vienna, the Secession movement took as its motto 'To the age its art, to art its freedom' – and Klimt brought the image and energy of Athene to champion that new liberty. His poster for the first Secessionist exhibition in 1897 has Theseus slaying the Minotaur to liberate the youth of Athens; the goddess looks on from the left – the side, so they say, of the unconscious and the feminine – in protective approval. She is highly stylized in her decorative helmet, just as the movement of which she's patron is as yet only an idea, unembodied. But what dominates the entire poster is not Athene herself. It is the disproportionately huge Gorgon's head of a shield that she carries, its fanged grimace and boring eyes both defensive and attacking as it tells us to both 'Keep off!' and 'Watch out!' Medusa's head, reduced in the drawing-room portrait of the art history museum to a neat and tasteful little necklace, here glowers into prominence. Here is the Athene–Medusa energy that takes on the fathers in their citadels, inspiration and fuel for the theft of fire from the ruling order!

In Klimt's extraordinary third portrayal of Athene, that energy is embodied, coiled with all that focus of the lion-about-to-spring hymned by the ancients. No longer neatly ringleted, her reddish hair has both the colour and the touch of a mane, her snakescales gleam on her breast and undulate into the suggestion of serpent and owl behind the left arm that could flex into action at any moment. The head of the goddess and of Medusa on her breast are now about the same size and this balance is reflected in the light that hits the gold of Athene's helmet and Medusa's golden head – a balance of the energies of head and heart which are united by the line of the goddess's golden spear. We can already glimpse what will be born of this union of energies, standing on Athene's right hand: no longer the traditional Nike, winged Victory of the state, but a new image of the feminine, proud and naked as Truth with her flaming red hair [Pl. 37].

How could that extraordinary vision be contained? The ruling order wanted to harness Athene's energy for itself; the Ministry of Culture commissioned Klimt to make three ceiling paintings for the ceremonial hall of the new university, representing Philosophy, Medicine and Jurisprudence. In all of these, of course, the goddess has an ancient and traditional interest, and the overall theme of the 'triumph of light over darkness' was one to whose service she had often been pressed before. But the Ministry reckoned without Medusa.

In 'Philosophy', naked figures – suffering and wondering, adult and child – move through a haze of space dominated by the hint of the Sphinx, spinning in a dreamscape above the head of Knowledge below. In 'Medicine', the now-embodied figure of Hygeia imperiously holds up her snakes before us while behind her naked human forms tangle in bliss and anguish, as the sensuousness of the body meets the skull beneath. The reviewer from the medical journal could only protest that the painter had completely ignored the two main functions of the physician, prevention and cure. But in the image of Hygeia we can see the ancient goddess of life and death. In the final painting, 'Jurisprudence', the triple goddess is illumined in the high distance, her epiphanies as Truth, Justice and Law looking down impassively at the broken, pot-bellied old man bowed in the darkness in the toils of a great octopus whose sinuous shapes are echoed in the coiling of three no less impassive female figures around him. Has Athene abandoned Klimt to critical incomprehension and disdain, withdrawn from earth to leave it once more to the ancient Furies? Is there here a reminder that no one can hope to annex the power even of an Olympian against the threefold force of Fate, the mystic centre which is also the unfolding of creation, imaged in the enfolding octopus? In this last of Klimt's portrayals of Athene as aspect of the once-great triple goddess herself, we can see too perhaps what the other two have already shown us: that the power of the feminine is reduced at man's peril. And that power means that there can be no 'triumph of light over darkness' after all, no glad dawn of the rational and reasonable that does not cast the mysterious shadows of its opposite. There can be no Athene without Medusa if naked Truth is to throw wide her arms to the world.

Freud surely knew that. The dark spanner he threw in the works of prevailing optimism about scientific progress was etched precisely with the warning that there are other forces at work than it dare recognize. He even invoked them at the start of *The Interpretation of Dreams*, taking to himself the terrible cry of Juno as she summons the monstrous snake-haired Allecto, lover of wrath, treachery and war, from Virgil's underworld to bring grief to the heroic Aeneas: 'If I cannot change the will of Heaven, I shall release Hell!' By then, he had intimated something of the power of the feminine from his own clinical work as well. He had seen the hell that women could raise, if not for others then most certainly for themselves, when they came up against the apparently immovable will of the ruling order.

By the time that Breuer and Freud published their own *Studies on Hysteria*, the 'hysterical woman' had already become a favourite and fascinating literary and medical villainess. Thirty years earlier, Jules Falret, a leading French psychiatrist, had warned the Paris medical-psychological society what to expect of them: fantastical and capricious, loving contradiction and argument, obstinate and passively resistant, romantic, lying and often erotic, they would 'stop at nothing, no sacrifice, to achieve their goal'. Medical men in Paris – including the visiting Freud – and the whole of polite society as well, could subsequently see the famous Charcot stopping at very little himself as he stage-managed theatrical displays of hysteria at the Salpetrière hospital. In England, meanwhile, the neurologist Horatio Bryan Donkin recognized that the educational and social constraints under which girls grew up could contribute to their disease. Yet in his essay for the *Dictionary of Psychological Medicine* he didn't hesitate to condemn the hysterical woman's 'exceeding selfishness, delight in annoying others, groundless suspicion and unprovoked quarrelsomeness' and to warn of numerous instances of self-mutilation and 'wondrous filthy habits'. Maudsley made the moral undertow explicit. He denounced the 'moral perversion' of young women who 'believing or pretending that they cannot stand or walk, lie in bed . . . all day . . . when all the while their only paralysis is a paralysis of will'. Nowhere, he thought, was moral insanity better illustrated than among these hysterical women, 'nowhere more perfect examples of the subtlest deceit, the most ingenious lying, the most diabolical cunning, in the service of vicious impulses'.[3]

We have heard that tone, even the words before – in the church fathers' inveighings against Eve, in the witch-hunters' sniffing out of their quarry; we have seen the type of the hysterical woman in age-old images of the feminine gone bad. But Breuer and Freud used to smile when they compared their own patients with the prevailing medical picture. For they knew that 'hysteria of the severest type can exist in conjunction with gifts of the richest and most original kind'. Here, for instance, is Frau Emmy von N., with her unblemished character, well-governed mode of life, moral seriousness, intelligence and energy 'which were no less than a man's', her education, love of truth and many other qualities of a true lady: '[t]o describe such a woman as a "degenerate" would be to distort the meaning of that word out of all recognition'. What Breuer and Freud saw in these women was not the innate psychic weakness posited by so many of their colleagues, but rather an excess of nervous excitation which demanded to be used. And what they also saw, of course, was that it wasn't. Here is the gifted, ambitious, morally sensitive Elisabeth von R., 'greatly discontented with being a girl . . . full of ambitious plans . . . to study or to have a musical training . . . indignant at the idea of having to sacrifice her inclinations and her freedom of judgement by marriage'. Here, most famously, is Anna O., 'markedly intelligent', with her 'powerful intellect' and 'great poetic and imaginative gifts', 'bubbling over with intellectual vitality' – yet leading 'an extremely monotonous existence in her puritanically-minded family'.

These young women were not exceptional. 'Adolescents who are later to become hysterical,' wrote Breuer,

are for the most part lively, gifted and full of intellectual interests before they fall ill. Their energy of will is often remarkable. They include girls who get out of bed at night so as secretly to carry on some study that their parents have forbidden for fear of their overworking . . . The overflowing productivity of their minds has led one of my friends to assert that hysterics are the flower of mankind, as sterile, no doubt, but as beautiful as double flowers.

Was their 'sterility' inevitable? Freud often had to answer his intelligent women patients who wondered how he proposed to help them, if their illness were indeed connected with their circumstances, about which he could do nothing. No doubt, he would reply, fate would be better able than he to relieve them of their illness. 'But you will be able to convince yourself that much will be gained if we succeed in transforming your hysterical misery into common unhappiness. With a mental life that has been restored to health, you will be better armed against that unhappiness.'[4] (Ah, Cassandra, will you never be heard?)

Yet Freud's preferred women were precisely those who had broken through prevailing social conditions and expectations to carve out a life that went far beyond a simple acceptance of 'common unhappiness'. These women, 'of a more intellectual and perhaps masculine cast', in the assessment of his biographer Ernest Jones, 'several times played a part in his life, accessories to his men friends, though of a finer calibre'. He could have instanced Freud's own daughter Anna, who alone of his five children followed her father's trade and made his well-being and 'The Cause' her own considerable life's work. 'Anna Antigone', her father called her. He could well have evoked her as Athene. Among her jewellery is a Roman carnelian, engraved with Jupiter enthroned and crowned by Victory, attended by Minerva. She wore it in a gold clip; it seems likely that it was originally her father's own ring, similar to those he presented to members of 'the Committee', his most trusted colleagues [Pl. 41]. In her defence of his citadel, Anna Freud never faltered. It was under the paternal aegis that she lived and it was under that aegis that she ended her days, her tiny figure pushed in wheelchair outings wrapped up in her father's big wool coat.[5]

But for Freud, it seems, the gulf between personal experience and theoretical understanding was unbridgeable. While he was still a student he had taken on the translation of a volume of John Stuart Mill into German and enjoyed the ideas he found there. There was, however, one crucial exception: he could never take seriously Mill's notion of the equality of women and men. As he was to write to his fiancée, Martha Bernays: 'legislation and custom have to grant to women many rights kept from them, but the position of women cannot be other than what it is: to be an adored sweetheart in youth, and a beloved wife in maturity'. What he believed in the flush of love he essentially believed through to old age. Asked by an American visitor whether it would not be better that both partners in a marriage were equal, he replied that this was a practical impossibility: 'there must be inequality, and the superiority of the man is the lesser of two evils'. It wasn't for lack of thought that he reached such conclusions. In 1915, when he was nearly sixty, he noted that after a century of irresolution and confrontations, the concepts 'masculine' and 'feminine', 'whose meaning seems so unambiguous to popular opinion, belong among the most confused in the sciences'. Nearly twenty years later, and six years before he died, he had still not resolved 'the problem of woman'. The identification of 'masculine' with 'active' and 'feminine' with 'passive', for instance, was too simplistic. At least some of the readers of his *New Introductory Lectures* could share his puzzlement: 'You too will have pondered over this question in so far as you are men.' The rest, of course, and by definition, could not: 'from the women among you that is not to be expected, for you are the riddle yourselves'.[6]

Yet the essential key to that riddle had, for Freud, long been in place. The temple of Minerva in Rome at which he could have worshipped so long ago was a 'humble and mutilated remnant'. His favourite among all his antiquities was his little Athene – 'perfect – but she has lost her spear'. Freud's vision of femalekind is encapsulated in those images of humble remnant, mutilation and loss: how can even a goddess be perfect when she lacks a penis? From this essential lack, and the no less defining sense of inferiority and envy it engenders, all else must follow. Women are incapable of self-reflection; they can have little sense of justice; their 'social interests' are weaker than those of men; their capacity to sublimate their instincts is less. In the very last year of his life, in an unfinished outline of his theories, he was still emphasizing the effects of that all-defining lack. While the boy must overcome his Oedipal attachment to his mother, it did little harm to a girl's development if she persisted in the attachment to her father which she has formed in her longing for a 'penis-child', for '[s] he will in that case choose her husband for his paternal characteristics and be able to recognize his authority'.[7]

There is a coming together of Athene and Medusa in Freud's

vision, no less than there is in Klimt's. But while Klimt invokes that once-mighty feminine power, her fullness hidden for so long, as more than we consciously know, Freud sees only an image of the feminine as intrinsically less than the norm of humankind itself. For him, the 'horrifying decapitated head of Medusa' represents a terrifying image indeed. 'This symbol of horror is worn upon her dress by the virgin goddess Athene. And rightly so, for thus she becomes a woman who is unapproachable and repels all sexual desires – since she displays the terrifying genitals of the Mother.' The man who approaches this image is turned to stone, becomes stiff with terror – which means he has an erection and so is reassured that he at least still has a penis. And if that is the gift of the virgin goddess to men, she has one for women as well. 'People say that women contributed but little to the discoveries and inventions of civilization, but perhaps after all they did discover one technical process, that of plaiting and weaving.' And what was the unconscious motive behind this single discovery, which we know to be the supreme art of the virgin goddess? To achieve more completely, says Freud, what the snakes around Medusa's head and pubic hair on adult female genitals had already suggested: to hide that terrible and irreparable deficiency.[8]

So Freud's little favourite, his spearless Athene, bears Medusa's head to bring reassurance of their potency to men and reminder to women of their intrinsic inferiority. In his belief in that inferiority Freud was, of course, in a very long tradition indeed, adding to centuries of theological and medical teachings his own biological and psychological truth. Nor was he alone in his own time. The year after he published his major work on the interpretation of dreams, for instance, the German psychiatrist Paul Moebius, who had already published his own views on hysteria, brought out *On the Physiological Imbecility of Woman*, in which he argued that woman was physically and mentally midway between child and man. Her nature was more animal than man's, she totally lacked the faculties of criticism and self-control, and if it were not for her fortunate bodily and mental weakness, 'she would be extremely dangerous'. His views may have been extreme. but there was no shortage of people for whom they were essentially true.[9]

As in the lives of individuals so too, for some at least, in the histories of civilizations. In the middle of the nineteenth century, Johann Jakob Bachofen, an eccentric Swiss scholar from Basle, had drawn on Greek and Roman mythology to argue a quite revolutionary notion. These ancient tales, he said, showed clearly that there had been a time in the history of the world when social organization had not been the patriarchy which was now taken for granted as the natural state of affairs, but matriarchy. There had been a time when power lay in the hands of women, not men. His first important work, *An Essay on Ancient Mortuary Symbolism*, came out in the same year as Darwin's *Origin of Species*, and both set out to demonstrate an operation of natural laws which needed no divine intervention. Bachofen discerned a progress from 'crude disorder to increasingly more refined articulation and organization', and in *Mother Right* he detailed the three stages of refinement.

First there had been 'hetairism', when society was characterized by sexual promiscuity, the brutality of men to women. Then came matriarchy, when women, after thousands of years of struggle, founded the family and agriculture and a social system of freedom, equality and peace between citizens whose most defining characteristic was love of the mother and most heinous crime was matricide. And then came patriarchy, which turned all this on its head, favouring instead independence and spiritual values and tending towards social isolation. So intolerable did this new system find the memory of the old, says Bachofen – and using a concept that Freud was later to find so central – that it 'forgot' that matriarchy had ever existed. But the old truths live on – 'in myth, the faithful picture of the oldest era, and nowhere else'.

And in that picture, Athene, 'the motherless daughter of Zeus', plays a crucial part, as the progressive force which guides civilization's unfolding. She is there at the birth of matriarchy, when Aphrodite, who has governed that chthonic realm of the first human era, tries to equal her matchless skill as a weaver and finds that all she can produce are thick unwieldy ropes of plaited willow – 'swampy, earthy, the offspring of the earth' to set against her rival's 'higher, heavenly degree of perfection'. 'Material fecundation and the pangs of childbirth attend Aphrodite's work. Athene brings purely Olympian existence, free from material desire, free from labour pains, and she herself knows only her father, Zeus.' She is there in the movement from matriarchy to patriarchy, from the rule of Demeter to the rule of Apollo.

As long as mankind is immersed in purely material life, woman must rule. Matriarchy is necessary to the education of mankind and particularly of men. Just as the child is first disciplined by his mother, so the races of men are first disciplined by woman. The male must serve before he can govern. It is the woman's vocation to tame man's primordial strength, to guide it into benign channels. Athene alone possesses the secret of attaching bridle and bit to the wild Sycthius, the first horse sprung from the earth at Poseidon's bequest.

It is Athene too who presides over and makes possible the final triumph of Apollo, in the *Oresteia*, that blood-soaked tragedy of patriarchal challenge, matriarchal revenge and patriarchy's final triumph when Orestes is exonerated for the murder of his mother. And there can be no going back. Perseus recognizes the beauty of Medusa, says Bachofen, only when she is wounded, 'breathing out [her] life in the arms of [her] conqueror. Warlike valour destroys all woman's charms. But death puts an end to this depravity. Only now does the queen awaken her adversary's love, never to be fulfilled.'[10]

Bachofen's thesis has probably been embraced more fervently by supporters of the myth of a distant and peaceful matriarchy a century and more after he published it than ever it was in his lifetime. But his myth was also one of progress – from the lower matriarchal stage of civilization to the heights of patriarchy. And that myth of progress was already in the air as he wrote, in the shift in collective consciousness which Athene's energy was stirring. When Florence Nightingale urged her nurses to fling open the windows in the battle against the miasma of disease, it was precisely against Bachofen's ancient chthonic realm of swamp and earth that she was battling, just as she was battling against the rule of the mothers in her own life. When Ruskin hymned Athene as his Queen of the Air, he was letting in that same fresh breeze of progress. The British city which had 'somewhat saucily' styled itself the Modern Athens knew better than any just how fresh that breeze could be (and Athene's 'special tutelage and favour' can still fairly knock you off your feet in Edinburgh's east winds.) For Ruskin, the goddess is first and simply 'the breeze of the mountain and the sea, and wherever she comes, there is purification, health and power'. And you don't have to visit Edinburgh to feel her:

Whenever you throw your window wide open in the morning, you let in Athena, as wisdom and fresh air at the same instant; and whenever you draw a pure, long, full breath of right heaven, you take Athena into your heart, through your blood; and with the blood, into the thoughts of your brain.[11]

Whether that fresh breeze seems to blow us nearer to fulfilment of the human project or dangerously off course depends whether the wind-tossed observer is carried by the myth of human progress or is caught by the gleam of an ancient, golden age. And maybe in the end it isn't a matter of 'either-or' at all, but of trying to keep our understanding of both, of Athene and Medusa as well. At the turn of the twentieth century, another Swiss from Basle, Carl Gustav Jung, embarked on his own odyssey into the human psyche. Right at its end, he was to sum up its purpose, not just for himself but for humankind. 'Man's task', he said,

is . . . to become conscious of the contents that press upwards from the unconscious. Neither should he persist in his unconsciousness, nor remain identical with the unconscious elements of his being, thus evading his destiny, which is to create more and more consciousness. As far as we can discern, the sole purpose of human existence is to kindle a light in the darkness of mere being.[12]

That was his myth of progress. But in its pursuit he was always to emphasize the extraordinary wealth of the deep unconscious, the 'realm of the mothers' which is the fundamental feminine matrix.

The vast and sprawling 'explosion of psychic contents' which is Jung's *Symbols of Transformation* was, he said, 'a landmark, set up on the spot where two ways divided'. The two ways were those of his mentor Freud and his own, and the book laid down his programme of work for decades. It introduces some of his cardinal concepts – psychic energy as the life-force itself rather than purely sexual as it was to Freud, the objective reality of the collective unconscious which underlies the personal unconscious that had so seized Freud's attention. And through the book, Jung traces the journey of the hero, that 'self-representation of the longing of the unconscious, of its unquenched and unquenchable desire for the light of consciousness', which nevertheless must yearn too for 'the healing power of nature, for the deep wells of being and for unconscious communion with life in all its forms'.

'Where leads the way?' asks Goethe's Faust, and Jung, himself both Faust and Mephistopheles, gives Goethe's answer: 'Here, take this key . . . The key will smell the right place from all others:/ Follow it down, it leads you to the Mothers.' For Jung, it is this constant pull to the unconscious as place of not simply regression but resource which is the true and symbolic meaning of incestuous longing, rather than Freud's literalism. From this, the dual nature of the archetypal Mother as both engulfing, to be escaped in the heroic quest for consciousness, and all-giving, to be recontacted as the fundamental nourishment of the deep unconscious. What is 'regression' for heroic youth becomes a bringing together of conscious and unconscious in 'the second half of life' – into which Jung felt himself embarking when he wrote the book. This is no less than the individuation process which is both journey and goal, and the end of it all, it seems, is the realm of the feminine. Underneath the last paragraph of the book, as final punctuation point, is a drawing of an antique cameo. The snake-wreathed staff of Hermes, guide to the underworld, is in the centre, flanked by two serpents and surmounted by a crescent moon and two stars. It is a concentration of feminine symbolism, and it comes from Bachofen's work on mortuary symbolism.[13]

In his own descent into that dark and archetypal realm, Jung met with the personified energies that people the collective unconscious and there began his own love affair with the anima – the feminine aspect of every man who appears in his dreams and fantasies, and who, if he can relate to her as an inner figure rather than simply projecting her on to the women he knows, can become his guide to the wealth of the unconscious. The anima is man's soul-image and has always been there; her energy has taken form through the ages in a myriad of feminine images, both positive and negative, 'now young, now old, now mother, now maiden, now a good fairy, now a witch, now a saint, now a whore'. She is Eve, Helen, and the Virgin Mary. As 'the great illusionist, the seductress', she 'draws [man] into life with her Maya', and as Sophia she 'leads the way to God and assures immortality'. She is the archetype of life itself.[14]

In his time, when the feminine seemed so decisively inferior, Jung's insistence on this essential animating force in man is radical stuff. In a sense too, of course, it is timeless: he is reclaiming an ancient and recurrent perception of the original human as uniting both feminine and masculine – a perception re-echoed in the divine androgyne of alchemy, that art which was for Jung to become such a powerful metaphor for psychic process. Yet he had contemporary biology on his side as well, as he would remind readers when in medical mood. But his valuing of the feminine in man goes far further than a simple acknowledgement of the biological fact that each sex carries a minority of the genes of the other. For him, the anima represents 'all those tendencies and contents hitherto excluded from conscious life'; once past his own mid-life, the man who ignores them risks a loss of vitality, flexibility and human kindness, falling instead into either a crusty and rigid pedantry or a weary resignation, sloppiness and childishness, with a tendency to alchohol.

So a recognition of his own feminine qualities is essential to man's psychic journey and his psychic health. And somewhere in that galaxy of guises which anima assumes there will be both Athene and Medusa – though Jung in fact writes very little about either. But when one of the principal references to the goddess in the whole of his *Collected Works* is as Prometheus's anima, when Medusa is cited in association with other 'terrible' and 'devouring' images of the feminine, we can sense that the old split between 'positive' and 'negative' aspects of this energy is as deep as ever. And through his understanding of 'masculine' and 'feminine' and of the very nature of man and woman, we can trace where that led.[15]

Jung's formulation of the feminine principle as Eros and the masculine as Logos didn't entirely satisfy him; he would have preferred the imaginal resonances of the alchemical Luna and Sol. Nevertheless, the more 'pedestrian' terms seemed to him to pin down certain 'psychological peculiarities', and it's with them that both he – and most of his interpreters – have worked. So his psychic world is governed by two great forces: Eros, the principle of relatedness, 'the great binder and loosener', and Logos, the principle of spirit, judgement, discrimination, of all that can be called 'objective interest'. There is no intrinsic superiority here: 'the function of Eros is to join what Logos has sundered', over and again in the great tidal rhythm of life and within each individual as well. But Jung goes a lot further than this in his formulations, and it's when he equates 'the feminine' with the nature of woman and 'the masculine' with the nature of man that the tide looks to be flowing in another direction altogether.

There's an intrinsic problem here, and Jung knows it: if 'the feminine' is Luna, is woman, is the deep realm of the unconscious, then woman can hardly be said to have any consciousness at all. As she evidently has, there have to be some new elaborations: it is in *man* that the feminine equals the unconscious, while woman has her own *moonlit* consciousness.

An inferior consciousness cannot *eo ipso* be ascribed to women; it is merely different from masculine consciousness. But just as a woman is often clearly conscious of things which a man is still groping for in the dark, so there are naturally fields of experience in a man which, for woman, are still wrapped in the shadows of non-differentiation, chiefly things in which she has little interest. Personal relations are as a rule more important and interesting to her than objective facts and their interconnections. The wide fields of commerce, politics, technology and science, the whole realm of the applied masculine mind, she relegates to the penumbra of consciousness: while, on the other hand, she develops a minute consciousness of personal relationships, the infinite nuances of which usually escape the man entirely.

Ah, Cassandra! That was written first in 1916 and revised in 1934. Is all that women have between-times been wresting from that realm of 'the applied masculine mind', if not in Switzerland then certainly elsewhere, to remain alien to them? For Jung the answer seems to be essentially 'yes'. Feminine consciousness, he will elaborate, 'is of a darker, more nocturnal quality, and because of its lower luminosity can easily overlook differences which to a man's consciousness are self-evident stumbling blocks'. The 'lunatic logic' of woman 'can drive the rational mind to the white heat of frenzy. Fortunately it operates mostly in the dark or clothes itself in the shimmer of innocence.' But if woman is to be faithful to herself, this is what she must accept: 'In women . . . Eros is an expression of their true nature, while their Logos is often only a regrettable accident.'[16]

Where here is Athene to find space for that bright, focused, energy, that consciousness which, in its essential uniting of mind and matter, works its transformations in precisely the realm of the technologies that Jung characterizes as masculine? If Freud's Athene had lost her spear, then Jung gives her little room to wield it; for him, her defining qualities are intrinsically masculine rather than feminine. What sort of a goddess is this then – a god in drag? Jung didn't address the question. But if he had, his answer would presumably have had to do with his notion of woman's animus, her own masculine side.

'The animus,' Jung once said, 'just scares me. It is much more difficult to deal with than anima. The anima is definite and the animus is indefinite.' So little attention did he give this scary entity that it seems really only to figure as a necessary complement to anima, to keep his system in balance. But while Lady Soul, for all her dangers and destructions, for him remains bathed in a glow of life-giving numinosity, his animadversions on the animus are enough to scare anyone. Theory would dictate that a woman who can relate to her animus, as man to his anima, would have access to the qualities of spirit, judgement and discrimination that are wrapped up in the concept of Logos, so transforming it from a 'regrettable accident' to its rightful place as a more complete ex-pression of her own 'true nature'. But back in 1922, Jung was teaching that 'a man must take up a feminine attitude, while a woman must fight her animus, a masculine attitude'. And little that he says subsequently dents that dictum. 'The animus is rather like an assembly of fathers or dignitaries of some kind which lays down incontestable "rational" or *ex cathedra* judgements' – which turn out to be a collective 'compendium of preconceptions', or 'principles which are like a travesty of education'. If the woman happens to be pretty,

these animus opinions have for the man something rather touching and childlike about them, which makes him adopt a benevolent, fatherly, professorial manner. But if . . . competence is expected of her rather than appealing helplessness and stupidity, then her animus opinions irritate the man to death, chiefly because they are based on nothing but opinion for opinion's sake . . . Men can be pretty venomous here, for it is an inescapable fact that the animus always plays up the anima – and *vice versa* of course – so that all further discussion becomes pointless.

And if the woman is intellectual (and so not pretty?) men can have an even harder time of it:

the animus encourages a critical disputatiousness and would-be high-browism, which, however, consists essentially in harping on some ir-relevant weak point and nonsensically making it the main one ... Without knowing it, such women are solely intent on exasperating the man and are, in consequence, the more completely at the mercy of the animus. 'Unfortunately I am always right,' one of these creatures once confessed to me.

What then is a woman to do? There is some little hope: if she can learn to combat her 'animus-possession', to shut animus up and relate to it as an inner figure, then it will be revealed as a 'creative and procreative being' which can bring forth creative seeds that can – make her opinions finally relevant? give her an intellectual *gravitas*? No, those creative seeds will fertilize the feminine side of the man! Just as Jung sees the negative aspects of animus in terms of their effect on men, so he sees its value as enabling women to become men's inspiration. While man's psychic task, in short, is to relate to anima for the sake of his own wholeness, woman's equiva-lent task is to relate to animus for the sake of the wholeness of man. (And Athene, with her presumably well-integrated animus, is for Jung the anima of Prometheus.)

As in theory, so in life. 'No one can get round the fact,' Jung wrote in 1927, 'that by taking up a masculine profession, studying and working like a man, woman is doing something not wholly in accord with, if not directly injurious to, her feminine nature.' Yet he himself was throughout his professional life to attract and rely considerably on women whose own intellectual capacities were often highly developed – and who often, too, put their own 'crea-tive seeds' at the service of his ideas rather than original work of their own. And for him, maybe that was the way it should be. For all his encouragement of his women collaborators, his own con-viction remained unshaken. 'Man's foremost interest should be his work,' he said towards the end of his life. 'But a woman – man is her work and her business.'[17]

His own wife, Emma, however, saw things rather differently.

Her own essay on animus, written in the early thirties, reflects the painful struggle of increasing numbers of contemporary women to understand their own 'true nature' between the claims of home and wider aspirations. But she is very clear that what ails a woman 'possessed' by the animus is *not* a lack of attention to her femininity, but a lack of work for animus to do. '[S]omething masculine in the woman claims attention . . . [T]he feminine element can only get into its right place by a detour that includes coming to terms with the masculine factor.' This for her was one of the demands of the time: 'a certain sum of masculine spirit has ripened in woman's consciousness and must find its place and effectiveness in her personality'. She knew how hard this would be. Women had been conditioned for so long to assume that the masculine was automatically superior that the animus's tyrannical power would take some combating. But what women must learn, and crucially, because it is in the nature of animus to demand it, is to do something for its own sake and *not* for the sake of another human being. There would be opposition from men, many of whom found women's struggle both uncomfortable and unnecessary. But 'what we women have to overcome in our relation to the animus is . . . lack of self-confidence and the resistance of inertia'.[18]

And other resistances too, perhaps. 'Consciousness as such is masculine, even in women,' we read twenty years on, 'just as the unconscious is feminine in men.' This is Erich Neumann, one of Jung's students and one of the most influential figures in the first wave of analytical psychologists as well. For him, this masculinity of consciousness leads to a crucial difference in the structure of male and female. 'Man experiences the "masculine" structure of his conscious as peculiarly his own, whereas woman feels at home in her unconscious and out of her element in consciousness.' She has to be sure a consciousness of her own, but this 'matriarchal' or (following Jung) 'moon-consciousness' is really a phase of unconsciousness itself, waiting passively, with no independent activity of its own, for the spirit-impulse carried towards it by the unconscious. These formulations are of a piece with Neumann's interpretation of the emergence of heroic consciousness from the unconscious realm of the mothers. This is where, with Jung's *Symbols of Transformation*, analytical psychology came in – and Jung himself said that Neumann had placed its concepts on a 'firm evolutionary basis'.

For Neumann, the Perseus cycle is a paradigm of the hero myth, and he unfolds it in a series of tableaux – before our very eyes! In which our hero sets out with the help of Hermes and Athene, 'the tutelary deities of wisdom and consciousness'! In which he slays the Gorgon and the sea monster, thus freeing himself from the Terrible Mother and the Terrible Father at two strokes! In which he gains the treasure by liberating both the captive Andromeda and Pegasus; the spiritual libido of the Gorgon is released and transformed! The final tableau is called The Victory of Athene Over the Great Mother and in it our hero gives the goddess the Gorgon's head as trophy of the struggle. The defeat of the old mother goddess by the 'new, feminine, spiritual principle' is complete.

So Athene and Medusa meet again. But in Neumann's telling, there is no coming together of that long-separated and once great power. It is a story not of uniting, but of conquest, and of Athene as the hero's companion and helper, his 'sister-anima', her warrior aspect rooting for man and consciousness in the battle against the unconscious realm of the Mothers. Athene has become the acceptable face of the feminine to masculine consciousness. Sprung from her father Zeus's head, she is 'profoundly inimical to the chthonic–feminine element in every mother and every woman born of a mother' – as, for him, her judgement for Orestes shows. Something like 2,500 years after Aeschylus's *Oresteia* was first performed, heroic masculine consciousness has claimed Athene as its own.[19]

So where can we go from there?

243

CHAPTER 13

Athene Unarmed

Three thousand years after that golden, whooping, dancing energy burst from the head of Zeus, 3,000 years after that explosive arrival of a new goddess for a new age, where is Athene now?

If you seek her monument, look around – and look up! Never has goddess been so public for so long. All over Europe and well beyond, her latter-day civic temples still stand tribute to that notion of civilized order which was her gift. Her birthday is perpetually commemorated in processions of Parthenon friezes that work their way across countless classical façades. She stands on public buildings in pose after virtuous pose: Justice, Fortitude, Temperance, Prudence and yes, still Wisdom herself. She is elevated on pillars, fully-armed as she steadfastly protects the ruling order. She maintains her ancient alliances: the springs of Sulis still and unchangingly pour their steaming bounty into Bath's healing pools while Minerva presides over the muses atop the city's Victoria Art Gallery and Athene waits for her birthday procession inside. She is sturdy for her own city, her fully-armed statue on its huge pillar outside the Hellenic Academy still to be snapped by passing tourists; they may not always know who she is, but she is surely too important to miss. It is not just in Athens that she is honoured by the establishment's own pillar, either: her statue above the Athenaeum Club in London got its first gilding not short of fifty years ago, and gleams brightly to this day. And at the very start of the last decade of our century came her most extraordinary appearance for well over 2,000 years, in an act of unequalled public

244

devotion. After seven years' work by its sculptor and over fifty volunteers and funds raised from not just civic sources but private ones as well, Alan LeQuire's forty-two-foot-high fibreglass and gypsum reproduction of Phidias's Athena Parthenos was completed to stand in Nashville's own Parthenon as the largest indoor statue in the world [Pls. 35, 36].

Yet wait – there's something wrong here. Where is that golden, whooping, shaft of energy in all this public parade? When Athene was born, the world held its breath: the sun stood still, the ocean was stopped, the earth itself groaned and shuddered. They only got back on course, only refound their rhythm, when that golden girl shook off her armour and relaxed into her own. At the start of this exploration, there was a hypothesis: that in the armouring of Athene we can glimpse not just how a particular feminine energy has defended itself in the era of the sky-gods, but how prevailing consciousness has protected itself against that energy by making sure the armour is bolted well into place. We have seen how the goddess has been armoured since her explosive beginnings, through the images and interpretations that her energy has evoked across the centuries. At the end of the exploration, here's another image again: of Athene contained and constrained by those civic constructions, her own inventions used to bridle her energy and harness it for useful purpose.

That image makes its contemporary appearances. The *Odyssey* is still a ripping enough yarn to be translated into strip cartoon. Athene perches once more in bird-guise in another roof to unite the realms of light and darkness: a decade after the disastrous fire at York Minster, one of the new roof-bosses that illustrate the Benedicite depicts the cockerel and the owl which used to be her creatures [Pls. 42, 43]. In her guise as Britannia, her energy still circulates on our fifty pence piece. These days, though, she's not too confident as she looks towards Europe and a single currency [Pl. 44]. And how much energy is still stored behind those chilly neo-classical façades, inside those stolidly sculpted virtues? The myth of civilized progress doesn't carry the same conviction these days; we know too much about the costs to humans and the planet of that unwavering forward march. Two and a half thousand years on, it's atmospheric pollution rather than human greed that threatens the Parthenon of Athens. A hundred years from its own beginnings, the Parthenon of Nashville needs, it's reckoned, 12 million dollars worth of repair; the structure that contains the only full-scale reproduction in the world of Pheidias's masterwork is crumbling. The metaphor doesn't take much seeking. So can we imagine that energy which is Athene striding free from the structures which have encased her, just as once she leapt from her father's head?

And if she did, what sort of reception would she get? This is a goddess who has always been at the heart of society's concerns for its own nature and ordering, whether high on the citadel or in the exchanges of the market-place. And surely she is right there still, bringing her inventions and resources, ideas and devices, to two of the most heated collective concerns of contemporary Western consciousness. For a start, and at a time when the debate on the 'true nature' of women and men too has seized us as never before, her attributes can at the least make us stop and think about what we mean by 'the feminine'. What on earth (and in the heavens) does it mean that the deity of war and technology should be imaged not as a man but as a woman? The anguish of Florence Nightingale, caught between 'the masculine' world of affairs and the 'feminine' one of hearth and home as her own times understood them, may seem distant to us from today's vantage-points. But maybe it doesn't either. Despite all the strenuous and sometimes pretty strained attempts to distinguish the given from the conditioned in our human make-up, there are women enough today who are wondering about the cost of their place in what used to be called the 'man's world' to indicate that we've still a way to go in this perennial questioning. For some, Jung's exploration of the 'nature of woman' and that inner presence of the opposite sex to our own sound like the antediluvian ravings of a sexist old Swiss who doesn't know his sex from his gender; for others, and by no means

34 and 35. Contemporary temples of Athene: the Athenaeum Club, London, and the Hellenic Academy, Athens.

36. The largest indoor statue in the world: Alan LeQuire's 1990 reproduction of Pheidias's original from the fifth century BC (Nashville, Tennessee).

37. *Pallas Athene* by Gustav Klimt (Historisches Museum der Stadt Wien, Vienna).

38. *Death: 'My Irony Surpasses
All Others'*: Plate 3 from 'A
Gustave Flaubert', lithograph,
1899, by Odilon Redon
(Charles Stickney Collection,
1920, 1651, Art Institute of
Chicago).

39. *Woman with Face Peeled
Like a Fruit*: from the
collection 'Tema e Variazioni',
© Fornasetti.

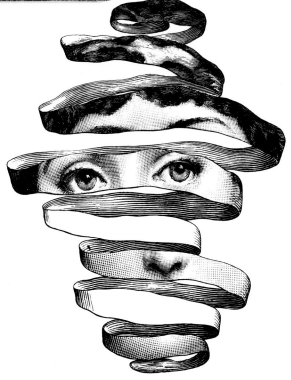

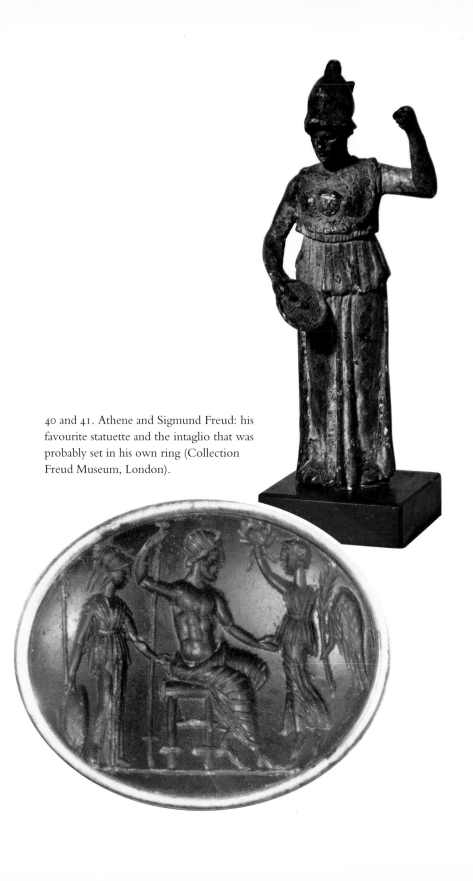

40 and 41. Athene and Sigmund Freud: his favourite statuette and the intaglio that was probably set in his own ring (Collection Freud Museum, London).

42. Athene gingers up Odysseus in *The Comic Strip Odyssey*, retold by Diane Redmond and illustrated by Robin Kingsland (Viking, 1992).

43. Athene's cockerel and owl reappear to signify light and darkness in a contemporary roof boss in York Minster.

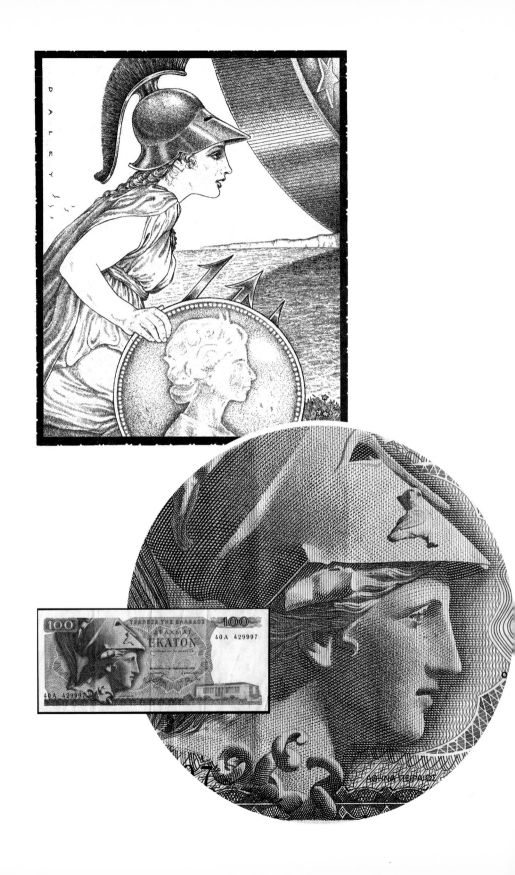

44 and 45. Athene as Britannia contemplates a single European currency in Daley's cartoon (*Independent*, 20 February 1995) and retains some value in her native Greece.

46. Bronze Athene (British Museum).

47. Head of Athene (Museum of Olympia).

only men, he touches on an archetypal truth of lasting value; for others again, it remains important to reconcile his views with a feminist perspective.[1]

The debate is inextricably bound up with another, more urgent and no less ancient. The lasting identification of man and the masculine with superior spirit and woman and the feminine with inferior matter has been one of the running themes of this book; we've seen how the whole story of heroic Western consciousness has been told in terms of spirit's triumph over matter. For Jung, the papal declaration of the dogma of the Assumption of the Virgin in 1950 represented a symbolic union between matter and spirit, a movement towards that ancient understanding expressed in the *I Ching*, where *yin* and *yang* each contain the seeds of the other – an understanding towards which contemporary science is itself striving. Others since, however, have argued that by 'spiritualizing' the 'Body and Soul' of the Virgin, the earthly aspect remains unhonoured. 'Matter,' say Anne Baring and Jules Cashford, 'cannot be recognized or acknowledged from the point of view of its "opposite" – spirit . . . [T]he reinstatement of the feminine principle fails because only part of the feminine principle is acknowledged, and so the split is perpetuated, or perhaps worse, enshrined.'[2]

This is a story that has been played out over millennia, and we know the ills it's bequeathed us. As we begin to realize that for the sake of all our planet-dwellers we need to find ways to cherish rather than exploit our material world, Athene's energy is right there too. One constant thread in the weaving of this book has been the tale of the goddess, Perseus and the Gorgon's head. In the seventeenth century, Francis Bacon found what he needed in it, 100 years later Abbé Banier did too; Charles Kingsley, Bachofen and those Victorian painters made it their own and so did Erich Neumann. The abiding fascination with this story isn't at all surprising, for its pivotal event, Athene's insistence on reclaiming the head of Medusa, is very much to do with trying to hold together spirit and matter, to carry at least a reminder of ancient unions into an era that sees their primary relationship as that of conqueror and conquered. And as we know, the goddess's own *sophia*, her supreme skill in all the technologies she inspires, is very precisely about that crucial understanding of the right and fitting interaction of matter and mind.

So no wonder Athene remains the most public, the most visible of all the Olympians – it's in her nature and her nature is the stuff of our concerns as well. Yet among those to whom it's fallen to dream the myth on, it is often very differently that she's appeared. Many of these contemporary myth-makers take their bearings from the perspectives of Jungian psychology, and in hearing what they have to say about Athene we can get a notion of where we are with the goddess's energy today and maybe where she is leading us.

For a start, there's more than a suspicion that she *isn't a real woman*. 'Athene is a woman, and yet it is as if she were a man' must be one of the comments most often quoted in recent Jungian writings about the goddess and least often given its proper context. Let's have it here: it comes from Walter Otto's beautiful homage to her, and is part of his description of her meeting with her favourite Odysseus as he at last arrives home. In that 'deeply stirring' meeting, says Otto, there is 'not a breath of feminine grace in the lady, not a trace of service to a lady in the man', but rather an expression of love that has to do with advising, helping, encouraging, rejoicing in success, celebrating the union of two clear minds. He is talking, in short, about a way of relating which is not Aphrodite's, nor yet maternal, but nonetheless feminine for that: in fact the rest of his essay is about just how, for him, Athene is indeed a feminine rather than a masculine force.[3]

This small distorted quoting of Otto's intent illustrates a much larger issue: just how difficult it seems to be to reconcile Athene's attributes with understandings of 'the feminine'. The problem is age-old, as Christine de Pizan knew when she was hymning the goddess at the start of the fifteenth century, evoking her attributes in that glorious parade of heroines who would people her City of Ladies. One of those women was Queen Dido of Carthage, 'spoken of only in terms of her outstanding strength, courage and her bold undertaking'. It was because of such virtues, says Dame Reason, that her people changed her name, originally Elissa, and called her Dido, 'which is the equivalent of saying *virago* in Latin, which means "the woman who has the strength and force of a man"'. Her use of the word would have been well recognized. In the Latin Vulgate, *virago* was the name given to Eve by Adam; as Wyclif rendered that moment of Genesis at the end of the four-teenth century, 'And Adam seide . . . This schal be clepid virago, for she is takun of a man.' So at the very start of her independent being, secondary creation though she was, we can still say that Eve partook of the same nature as man. Yet over time that perception could not hold; a virago became a woman who was 'bold and impudent, a termagant, a scold'. And the prudence in government which had been, so Dame Reason told Christine, Queen Dido's particular hallmark became a discretion hardly distinguishable from an obedient silence. In those allegorical statues and interpreta-tions, Prudence became a manifestation of Athene herself, but down in the world of women, Prudence was a good housewife with a padlock on her mouth. 'Everyone look at me because I am a wise woman,' enjoined a sixteenth-century morality: 'A golden padlock I wear on my mouth at all times/so that no villainous words shall escape from my mouth/but I say nothing without deliberation/and a wise woman should always act thus.' Elsewhere, her sister would appear with her finger to her lips to represent her silent obedience.[4] Yet when Harpocrates, the infant sun-god Horus, had made the identical gesture in ancient Egypt, it was not obedience he conveyed, but the mystery of divinity. 'Everything comes from Silence,' said the Gnostics in their turn; for them, Silence was 'the Mother of All', who is also Wisdom.

But even then, as we've seen, orthodoxy was finding it hard to perceive that supreme quality as feminine; by the sixth century, Wisdom had become, in the Western church, an attribute of Christ. Those allegorical representations of Athene as Sapientia still served as reminder of an older way. But as we've seen too, even this was too much for Prince Albert, who had the statue of his wife flanked by a representation not of Wisdom, as suggested by the sculptor, but by Clemency — 'because the sovereign is a lady'. For him, Clemency was clearly safe to be let out among women; it was Florence Nightingale's quality of *mercy* he commemorated in the brooch he designed for her, when unrelenting and driven bloody-mindedness would have been nearer the truth of it, if harder to inscribe. A century on, though, the myth was rehonoured when (and as the 1970s wave of the women's movement swelled) Florence Nightingale became the first woman apart from the monarch and Britannia to appear on a Bank of England note. For nearly two decades she positively radiated light as she faced the wounded soldiers of the Crimea in her abiding guise as the Lady with the Lamp. These days, for our £10, we get Charles Dickens, whose heroines were as wringingly steeped in the moistest of 'feminine' values as his other women were grotesques.

Yet by now, too, the letters of the alphabet which had been one of the gifts of Medusa passed on by Athene were tumbling eagerly across page after successful page to celebrate once more the 'strength and force' that Dame Reason had discerned in Queen Dido so long ago. As the women of the British publishing house Virago said in their celebration of its first twenty years, 'Women may not yet have equal power and influence, but we certainly have the talent'; and so its intentionally many-faceted feminism has shown in novels and poetry, thrillers and cultural critique, literary criticism and biography.[5] Yet if Prince Albert had found it unsuitable to portray Wisdom as feminine, many others since have had the same trouble with such qualities as reflection, assessment, judgement, discrimination, right measure and focused action — all of which are among Athene's own. How on earth can this active, forceful energy be reconciled with those age-old — and still current — lists of the 'feminine' virtues, like softness, gentleness, receptivity, nurturance?

Depth psychology has had its own ideas about that. The classical Jungian scheme of things, as we've seen, offers its own reconciliation, by ascribing the tougher attributes to 'the masculine' but making them accessible to women through a positive relationship with animus. Other schools are more blunt in their evocation of the 'phallic woman'. And you don't have to belong to any school at all to take this a stage further: woman as castrator, as ball-breaker – as invader, attacker, smash-and-grab raider, thieving their masculine essence from men. Yet this is not Athene's way: the heroes who honour her know when she's passed by not because they feel depleted but because they feel enthused, strengthened, taller and straighter than they were before. The cultural historian Camille Paglia offers another notion again: in her own sparky evocation of Athene, she sees her as the first of many representations of the androgyne as 'cultural symbol of mind' – 'a solar androgyne perfect in body, mind and eye' who is the mirror image of Athens itself. For Paglia, Athene 'symbolizes the resourceful, adaptive mind, the ability to invent, plan, conspire, cope and survive. The mind as *techne*, pragmatic design, was hermaphroditic for the ancients, much as the psyche is hermaphroditic for Jung in an era when selfhood expands to include the unconscious.'[6]

Do such formulations work? We have heard Florence Nightingale's anguished self-questioning, towards the end of that long and driven life: 'not a man or woman – Am I a Department?' We have glimpsed the context in which her question arose, the warnings of university professors and medical men against the dreadful 'man-woman' hybrid which would result from women's ambitions to get themselves a decent education. We have heard, too, Jane Harrison's judgement on Athene as 'a sexless thing – neither man nor woman'. In the goddess as androgyne there's for me an echo of this, a suggestion still that Athene's qualities have something of the monstrous and unnatural about them when embodied in a female. The androgyne, as we know, is an abiding image of the first and original wholeness of the human being and as such became one image of the goal of the alchemical *opus*. But for the alchemists, it *was* goal, not process, and in those arcane texts premature hermaphroditic fusions had to suffer the refinements of separation into their male and female constituents before that goal could be reached.

The notion of animus as woman's inner masculine certainly seems to offer access to these troublesome qualities, and a potentially positive one at that. But the way to integration seems fraught with such continuing difficulties that we can at least wonder whether there isn't something askew in the notion itself. Jung's own warnings against 'animus-possession' need to be set in the context of his time and society. But when the warnings re-echo to this day from different Jungian writers, and by no means all of them men, it can sometimes seem that women who seek and find success in job or career risk being pathologized rather than congratulated. Even at best, what the notion of animus doesn't do – any more than does the notion of the 'phallic woman' – is to get beyond the idea that certain qualities of mind and focused, creative assertion remain essentially Other to woman's feminine self rather than intrinsic to it. There's a crucial difference between relating to an aspect of that Other and finding another possible expression of what is as much part of one's 'true nature' as those more 'traditional' qualities. Some people are taking this one on. From her own resolutely feminist viewpoint, for instance, Polly Young-Eisendrath reckons the whole notion of animus as 'inferior objectivity' in women to be stereotype rather than archetype. She still finds that a psychology of gender difference is basically useful, however, and that 'the Jungian concept of a repressed gender complex adds a necessary level of meaning in understanding the experiences of men and women'. Just what that gender difference might be, of course, remains every bit as much the question as ever it was.[7]

Some Jungian writers have dreamt the myth on by suggesting that both animus and anima are at work as inner feminine and masculine within each of us, whether we're women or men. Most dramatically, James Hillman has claimed that 'the *per definitionem* absence of anima in women is a deprivation of a cosmic principle with no less consequence in the practice of analytical psychology than has been the theory of penis deprivation in the practice of psychoanalysis'; he insists that 'to be engaged with anima is to be engaged simultaneously with animus in some way or another' (and presumably vice versa). Verena Kast has also suggested that both anima and animus are at play in both women and men. But still and all, such formulations depend on a notion of what constitutes 'masculine' and 'feminine'. We can't get away from that, and the image of Athene holds us to it as she holds up her shield which is also a mirror for our reflection. 'Perhaps the whole point of Pallas Athene,' says Christine Downing, 'is to help us transcend the facile equation of strength and courage and worldly wisdom with masculinity.'[8]

The whole point? Whether or not, it can seem extraordinarily hard to stay with it, as dangerous to look into that shield which is mirror as ever it was to meet Medusa's eye. At one end of a Jungian spectrum, some would ground archetype in biology: for Anthony Stevens, for instance, to deny the profound significance of the traditional 'masculine' and 'feminine' is 'about as sensible as denying the existence of the penis or the womb'.[9] And those lists of masculine and feminine characteristics which have multiplied in the past two decades do often take their beginnings from biology, drawing their imagery from the *I Ching*, the ancient Chinese book of changes, to give us the masculine as left-brain *yang* – Heaven, the Creative (and from there hot, dry, day, sun, expansion, aggression) – and the feminine as right-brain *yin* – Earth, the Receptive (and from there cold, moist, night, moon, containment, preservation). Yet in those great primal principles that govern all the continuing changes of life, there are also some less expected images. In the Shuo Kua commentary on the *I Ching*, many fragments antedating Confucius, the eldest daughter, the Gentle, is wood, wind, the guideline, work, the principle by which men in the market get threefold value; among other attributes, it is also the sign of vehemence. The Clinging, the second daughter, is fire, sun, lightning; it means coats of mail and helmets, it means lances and weapons; it is the sign of dryness. The third daughter, the

Joyous, the lake, is a sorceress; it means smashing and breaking apart, it means dropping off and bursting open; it is the hard and salty soil.[10] What are we to make of that?

At the other end of that Jungian spectrum, others would move beyond the whole masculine–feminine debate altogether; Andrew Samuels, for instance, would rather we put our energy into examining how women and men relate to the phenomenon of difference.[11] Yet for some people at least, there is value still in trying to discern the depths of those old characterizations. In 1995, a beautiful exhibition in the National Museum in Athene's own home town presented images of the feminine 'From Medea to Sappho'. For the impassioned presenters, the Ariadne's thread that guides women out of the jail of maternity and silence is Action and Reason. For them, in the 'broken mirrors' of the images of the Amazons, Atalanta, Electra, Iphigeneia, Antigone, Ariadne and Sappho, 'women of all periods continually find fragments of their own form'. And the presiding deity of this journey is Wisdom herself, in her form as Gaia, then Metis, Thetis, Demeter, Circe, Medea – 'and of course Athene, the supreme goddess of civilization'.

Holding to the red thread of Ariadne to honour Athene's own principles of Action and Reason is made harder these days by the emphasis on the goddess as pre-eminently and first of all the daughter of her father Zeus – her birth from his head as both his headache and his idea signalling the moment when the old matriarchal order gave way to patriarchy, her judgement at the end of the *Oresteia* setting the seal on the new order, her every action 'all for the father' and his rule. 'We cannot love a goddess who on principle forgets the earth from which she sprung,' says Jane Harrison at the very start of the twentieth century. Over seventy years later, Adrienne Rich, poet and feminist, is urging the privileged women of Smith College in her commencement address to hold to the sense of themselves as 'outsiders' – 'for no woman is really an insider in the institutions fathered by masculine consciousness'; they should guard always against being seduced by 'the myth of the "special" woman, the unmothered Athena sprung from her father's brow'.[12] And many others in between and since have elaborated on this theme.

For Karl Kerenyi, the mythographer who collaborated with Jung on *Science of Mythology*, it is Athene's bondedness to the father which is key to understanding the paradox of the goddess as both mother and virgin in Greek religion; he sees her cult as expression of the dual imperative that she remain virgin ('all for the father') and as mother assure the continuation and strength of the *polis*. His classic study of the goddess has found echo in the perceptions of many others since. Ean Begg, for instance, has compared Athene with the Virgin Mary, also 'promoted to be the statutory female on a patriarchal board essentially hostile to women and nature'. Others have brought the goddess down to earth with a bump. Kerenyi's translator Murray Stein, for instance, finds it hard to keep from seeing her in such American dreams and institutions as the Statue of Liberty, the spirit of enterprise and expansionism, military heroics, Pentagon planning and football. In her highly successful *Goddesses in Everywoman*, Jean Shinoda Bolen looks for her among American women who run the Red Cross, become invaluable executive secretaries for male bosses, oppose the Equal Rights Amendment and dress preppy and well-scrubbed.[13]

Yet this insistence on Athene's bondedness to the father has brought some seriously skewed perceptions. When it's asserted, for instance, that her antagonism to all things feminine means that she and Hera are 'constant enemies', that's a very long way from the glorious account of their ganging-up against Zeus in the *Iliad*; when we learn that this antagonism extended to hiring only priests, never priestesses, in her temples, prejudice sounds stronger than fact. Did the goddess banish the Furies with 'false promises' at the climax of the *Oresteia*? Whatever else her actions may have been about – and we've seen how widely they've been interpreted – it doesn't seem to me that lying was part of it. Is her 'failure' to save Cassandra from Apollo's assault in her temple only to be expected from a goddess so essentially unmaternal? We can at least put in a reminder that Athene, no less than any other Olympian, up to and including Zeus himself, was powerless against the ways of Ate, of Fate.[14]

What this sort of thing illustrates – and curiously, for these authors are as much 'all for the feminine' as ever they perceive Athene as 'all for the father' – is just how 'patriarchal' are the spectacles through which they look. This buying into the image of Athene as nothing but her father's daughter misses, for me, an essential point – which is how she consistently and at every stage endeavours to keep alive in consciousness an awareness of that older, feminine power which is as much of her essence through her mother Metis as is her birth from her father's head. That Athene burst into consciousness at the dawn of the patriarchal order is a given of her nature. That we have been shaped by that order, and still are, is a given of ours. The ways in which that order has received the goddess's *sophia* has been what these pages have been about – and one of the striking things about the exploration has been that those who have dreamed her myths onwards across the centuries have very usually, such are the records of history, been men, and often powerful ones at that. But what this story has also tried to show is how the archetypal energy which is imaged in Athene has consistently held to that red thread of feminine consciousness through all these patriarchal times – and to do it not at home with Hestia, nor in the fields with Demeter, nor yet in the wild and separate places with Artemis, but right there in the hurly-burly of the market-place, right there in the citadels and corridors of power. That is also of her essence, and as we struggle now to move to a new order, a rehonouring of the 'feminine principle', that is also and continually her gift.

'Zeus sees to it' says one recent commentator, 'that Athene passes on his words, deeds, or thoughts, intact and unchanged.'[15] But would Prometheus have seen it like that when the goddess sneaked him up the back stairs of Olympus to steal the fire of the gods? Would Christine de Pizan, or Byron, or Klimt, in their honouring of Athene as guardian of liberty and integrity of individual expression against the ruling order? We have seen

Athene defy her father's wishes and we've seen too just how tena-
cious he is of power. But she keeps at it, carrying in her turn that
push-pull between the old and the new, conservatism and change,
which is an abiding story of our lives. Zeus and his father Saturn
and Saturn and *his* father Uranus had known that in their turn.
But ever since Zeus swallowed Metis, it is between the ruling
masculine energy and a *feminine* one that the tension has been
joined. It is not the birthday tribute of the statesmen or warriors
of Athens which is the most honoured in the Parthenon frieze,
but the gift of women's hands. Athene's care for women at the
great transitions of marriage and childbirth is most often, following Kerenyi, seen as concern for the continuance of the state.
Yet we could imagine too that to come under the protection of
that great aegis would be reassurance indeed for any woman in
that male-dominated world.

So ever since Athene burst from her father's head, there has
been a feminine presence at the heart of that push-pull between
conservatism and change, not just in individual lives but in collective shifts as well. That explosive, awesome birth could hardly be
ignored. But doesn't it re-echo what somehow, somewhere, we've
always known? When Eve and Adam ate that apple, says the
Gnostic text *On the Origins of the World*, 'their mind opened, the
light of knowledge shone for them ... They understood very
much.' Oh happy fault! In that supreme moment of consciousness
awakening, it is Eve who carries what Judith Hubback has nicely
characterized as the scientist in the human psyche, 'going calmly
forward into danger', while Adam takes the as necessary part of
caution. For her, Eve is *natural* woman: she wants what 'any natural
person, unshackled insofar as is possible by prohibitions, inhibi-
tions or conscience, would be likely to want: to find out about the
world in which he or she lives'.[16]

'Hearken O Eve,' says Honnor Morten,

Mother of us all, greatest and grandest of women: you who have been
maligned all down the ages, know at least that one of your daughters

blesses you, and proclaims your choice good. To you, oh Eve, we owe it that we are as gods, and not as children playing in the garden – that we know the good and evil and are not lapt in ignorance and lust. Man had stayed ever in uninquiring peace, but to you was given strength to grasp the apple, to proclaim that woman at least prefers wisdom and the wilderness to idle lasciviousness in Eden.

For the feminist Morten, the end of the nineteenth century was the dawn of a new age of equality between women and men, Eve's courage vindicated at last. A hundred years on, we may not be there yet; but we can see how Athene's own energy has fuelled the movement of women into the very citadels and bastions of the ruling order. 'The political and intellectual emergence of women that has been building for all of this century,' say Roger and Jennifer Woolger, 'may well be this final birth of Athena, so long frustrated, so long a headache to patriarchal Zeus.'[17]

Yet though the birth may have gone well, the development is seen as problematic: beneath her tough exterior, their Athene hides a wounded vulnerability, and the unresolved tension within her apparently whole and androgynous independence leaves her in great insecurity about her 'true feminine identity'. As we move towards the end of another century, their perception is hardly restricted to the pages of psychological journals. 'Now,' said Gloria Steinem at the start of the eighties and in celebration of women's *Outrageous Acts and Everyday Rebellions*, 'we are becoming the men we wanted to marry.' And that, by the start of the nineties, was increasingly seen as precisely the problem. A recent collection of Jungian essays by women and men explores, according to its back-jacket blurb, 'What it means to be a woman in a man's world [!] for those of us who do not wish to stay at home and become "like our mothers" or to strive aggressively and "become like men" . . . Why women are expressing deep disillusionment with the promises of feminism and the reality of career success . . . Why women are leaving careers and rushing to have babies late in life . . .' These are no less the questions that throng the bookstalls in a myriad of popular paperbacks and women's magazines and find their echoes in countless women's minds and hearts.[18]

And in analysts' consulting-rooms, too. June Singer writes of women who come to her suffering from what she can only describe as 'the sadness of the successful woman', who feel – and whether they are married or single, mothers or childless – that they have lost touch with their 'femininity – whatever that is'. For her, this is not simply a problem of and for our times; it is archetypal, because it has to do with the neglect of the universal feminine principle of relatedness in an eagerness to pursue the no less universal masculine one of individual identity.[19]

In such explorations of the current dis-ease of the feminine – and that means of us all, whether women or men – Athene is intimately implicated. That bright and energic image is tarnished by the perception of the goddess as 'all for the father'; just as her femininity is seen to be crushed in her identification with what is still described as a 'man's world', so is the feminine in us seen to be crushed by our over-identification with her. 'If we look at the modern Athenas sprung from their fathers' foreheads,' says Marion Woodman, 'we do not necessarily see liberated women.' Many of them have most certainly proved themselves at least the equal to men in their chosen jobs and careers – but so far from setting them free, that achievement has entrapped them. Very often, she finds, they are chained to some addiction, whether materially, to food or alcohol, or spiritually, to a notion of perfection. Elsewhere, she suggests that a woman's fat body may be the armour of Athene – 'the virgin idealist, sensitive, energetic, a lone leader fighting for a cause . . . aloof, untouchable, undefiled, unawakened to her own sexuality'.[20]

She's not the only one to see Athene's energy implicated in patterns of addiction. As Jan Bauer understands it, 'the vulnerability – or predisposition – of many women alcoholics lies in a strong but unsupported Athenian temperament'. For Bani Shorter, 'it is as a person holding the Gorgon shield that we meet an anorexic woman first of all. Characteristically she appears in maiden form, advancing with tremendous authority and power, like a goddess, hidden behind a formidable defence, ready to attack, always on guard.' This illness belongs, as she says, to a threshold, its onset often coinciding with adolescence. 'Like the appearance of Athene, it manifests itself at the intersection of two epochs in feminine life, two worlds, one characterized by the influence of woman and the other by the influence of man.'[21]

So is it to this that the split between spirit and matter which has so characterized our age has finally brought us – a widespread living out in individual tragedies of the struggle between body and mind? Two themes recur in these writings: the destructive effect of the woman's sacrifice to the paternal spirit and no less destructive lack of relationship with the feminine, the body; and the *fixity* of the condition. Addiction is a terrible stuckness, a continuing and single-visioned feeding of a voracious appetite which is never altered, never appeased – and the very fact that addictions are now so much part of Western experience raises its own question. Is this the suffering not just of individuals but of our time: that while far-sighted, many-counselled Athene seems still to move us onwards, we are also caught in the suffering immobilization of the paralysed and paralysing Medusa in her cave at the edge of the underworld?

In the healing of individuals from that terrible stuckness, these writers would honour Athene. If the story of the woman with anorexia is allowed to unfold naturally, says Bani Shorter for instance, she will fulfil herself primarily within the context of the goddess's image: 'These are women of action, and today especially they are drawn to the forefront of change.'[22] Yet in these accounts, Athene remains the armoured maiden sprung from her father's head, her attributes primarily 'masculine' rather than intrinsic to her feminine energy. If we could imagine ourselves beyond such divisions, could we then imagine Athene getting away from her father's head and idea, free to unbuckle her armour when she chooses and let her energy flow free? Can we imagine an honouring of the goddess that would allow for that? And can we imagine what that whooping, golden, forceful energy might feel like then?

There is nothing dark, moist, interior – to take just some of the attributes of 'the feminine' – about the images of Athene as war-goddess, blazing through the skies, Athene of the Flashing Eyes in the heat of battle. And if by her nature the goddess must bring us to reflect on what we mean by 'the feminine', then this is surely the aspect of it we find hardest to accept of all. Whatever else 'the feminine' may be about, for heaven's sake, it is not about battling and scrapping and exulting in the fight. Is it? However much women may now be trying to move beyond the constrictions of traditional notions of that 'feminine', here's a place where many would not just gladly concede to equally traditional notions of the 'masculine' but insist on them.

Women's understanding of 'the feminine' as the party of peace is long and honourable. It was woven into the very development of the British women's movement: 'Better is Wisdom than the Weapons of War!' cried the banner of the Cambridge women students and graduates in a procession of the National Union of Women's Suffrage Societies in 1908, thus declaring that to give women the vote would itself be a vote for peace. The link between feminism and anti-militarism has been maintained ever since. Indeed, pacifism has been seen as intrinsic to women's psychology. 'Women are mothers,' declared Helene Deutsch, who had been the first leading woman member of Freud's Vienna Society, in her opposition to the Vietnam War. 'They would not allow this killing.' Her premise found a new energy in the writings of eco-feminists during the 1970s and 1980s, which saw women as the particular protectors of life against the destructive forces of masculinist technology – because women *were* life and the natural order in a way that men simply weren't. 'We are woman and nature. And he says he cannot hear us speak but we hear', says Susan Griffin. 'I know I am made from this earth, as my mother's hands were made from this earth, as her dreams came from this earth and all that I know I know in this earth . . .' What made Britain's war over the Falkland Islands particularly painful for many was that it was a *woman* leader, Britannia embodied, who urged it and who cried at the British victory 'Rejoice! Rejoice!'[23]

As below, so above. Into the 1950s, Pope Pius XII was hymning the Virgin Mary as 'Victor in All Battles in the Name of God', enumerating her victories from the defence of Byzantium in 860 through her intervention on behalf of her church in communist China in 1951. Right into the 1980s she would intervene for her people against communist regimes: it was under the banner of the Black Madonna of Czestochowa that Solidarity marched Poland to its liberation. Yet since the second Vatican Council, when liturgies have been given in the vernacular, the great hymning of Mary as goddess of war has disappeared from many invocations. 'Who is this that looks forth like the dawn/ fair as the moon, bright as the sun/ terrible as an army with banners?' the Latin liturgy of the Assumption would hail her, for instance, taking its text from the Song of Songs. 'See the beauty of the Daughter of Jerusalem who ascended to heaven like the rising sun at dawn,' says the English equivalent. When an essay on the Morrigan – the Irish goddess of war and peace, life and death – is published in a collection called *Mad Parts of Sane People in Analysis*, the shift of emphasis is underlined. And as the literature on the myths of the Goddess has grown and increased through the eighties and into the nineties, it is often in the context of a world once peaceful *because matriarchal* that she is invoked.[24]

Did that golden, far-off peaceful time ever exist? Certainly there is little archaeological evidence of fortifications and other war-like buildings from the time when the cult of the Goddess is thought to have reigned. But the imaginal longing to which the mythology speaks needs no such concrete backing. Surely there *was* a time when the image of the feminine was not divided into the opposites expressed by psychological mythologizing as different, yet in this as similar, as Jung and Neumann's Nourishing and Terrible Mothers and Melanie Klein's Good and Bad Breasts! 'She rules us with delightful pain/ and we obey with pleasure,' Sir John Davies had cried of his dominatrix Elizabeth I, and many would see in that a pretty exact evocation of Mrs Thatcher's prime ministerial reign under the second Elizabeth. But in the myth of matriarchy there is another image: of a feminine governance that is all pleasure, no pain. And if that time once was, surely it can come again?

Yet this century has also seen women at war, and it is under Athene's aegis that they have served: it was the goddess's head that appeared on the buttons, collar-tips or other insignia of the Women's Army Corps of both Canada and the United States of America from their creation during the Second World War until their eventual integration into their countries' general armed forces some two decades later. And what can't be escaped is that the yearning for that distant imaginal age of peaceful governance has been expressed at a time when the excoriation by women of men has reached an unparalleled crescendo of violence. The champions of 'the feminine' as the party of peace have waged war on the 'masculine' enemy as never before, and in the battlelines, 'the feminine' has been identified with women and 'the masculine' with men in a way that makes irrelevant all those intellectual efforts to separate sex from gender. Not all women, of course, nor all men neither. But enough for us to recognize that women too carry ferocity and destructive fury and the swingeing weapons of war. Don't we?

Yet to imagine this as an intrinsic part of 'the feminine' seems extraordinarily difficult; there doesn't seem to be a place for these fiercer feelings in the lists of 'feminine' qualities. For women, this has meant either a massive projection of anger and aggression on to 'the masculine' – and that most often means men – or a weight of guilt because 'the feminine' isn't meant to feel like this. Neither way brings us any nearer an understanding of the fullness of 'masculine' and 'feminine', nor of how these universals may be at play in the psyche of individual women and men. Both tend to fix us in old antagonisms, whether expressed in the outer world or in the inner one. Neither way are we brought nearer to the 'true nature' of either women or men.

Ah nature! One of the oddest notions to become entangled in this whole contemporary suffering between women and men has to be the idea that nature is all-giving, nourishing, protective – when anyone who has spent more than an hour in the quietest of countrysides, let alone in desert or jungle, can see and hear that in its beauty and majesty it is also murderous and implacably indifferent to anything but its own continuance. As Camille Paglia succinctly has it, 'Every time we say nature is beautiful, we are saying a prayer, fingering our worrybeads.'[25] The idea of nature as all-bountiful suits a politic that identifies it with women; men and their 'masculine' technologies can then be clearly identified as nothing but nature's despoilers and women's oppressors. But beyond the rhetoric, it's hard to see how this identification can do anything but harm to our attempts to understand the 'true nature' of feminine and masculine, women and men. If women are to identify and be identified with the myth of an all-generous nature, this can only be an enormous and unrealistic burden. Can we allow ourselves to put it down? 'We cannot believe,' says Dorothy Dinnerstein, 'how accidental, unconscious, unconcerned – ie unmotherly – nature really is; and we cannot believe how vulnerable, conscious, autonomously wishful – ie human – the early mother really was. Our over-personification of nature then is inseparable from our under-personification of woman . . . If we could outgrow our feeling that our first parent was semi-human, a force of nature, we might also be able to outgrow the idea that nature is semi-human and our parent.'[26] And that might help to free us all to imagine further what constitutes our true and human natures.

Those goddesses of battle as well as peace – Athene, Inanna, Anat, Sekhmet, Neith, the Morrigan, Brigit – seem to feel the need neither to deny their aggression by projecting it on to the gods nor to turn it inwards in guilt. What their multiple and forceful images suggest is that there is also an aspect of the archetypal energy we call 'feminine' which is engaging, battling, thrusting, kicking, punching, hitting, destroying – and so finally transformative. What the ancient commentary on the *I Ching* reminds us is that the Gentle, the Clinging, the Joyous are also vehemence, fire, sun, lightning, dryness, coats of mail, helmets, lance and weapons. (And who is this who looks forth like the dawn?)

So when Athene leapt out of her father's head brandishing her spear, jangling her golden armour, whooping her war-cry, she was most certainly not alone among goddesses. But watch! Straightway when she sets foot to ground she gives notice that she is bringing something different to the business of warfare. First one step, then the next – the dance she dances they call in Sparta the *pyrriche*, and it's a military drill, to be performed in full armour. Very measured, very controlled – and very unlike any action of that ghastly Strife and her maniac brother Ares, against whom Athene is so constantly pitched in the *Iliad*. Straightway, then, Athene shows us that there is another way to go to war, another way to do battle, than simply charging ahead. Sometimes Ares's way may be what's needed. At other times, it simply doesn't work.

As the women of Athens know well when that war against Sparta seems to drag on and damagingly on. All the men seem to be able to think of doing is more of the same – which has already proved useless. They have no sense at all of fitting the action to the occasion, of what's needed when. When they're home on leave they clump round the market in full armour, carrying their shields with the Gorgon's head on them, all show, all display. And then what do they do? Pick up a few vegetables and a bit of pottery, buy a few minnows and a pancake and carry them home in their helmets as a shopping basket! Then it's off to the front again and no more sex for the wives till they come back. So when Lysistrata has this idea that the women should go on sex-strike and take over the citadel to run the country until the men see sense, it isn't hard to muster her sisters. The men are horrified of course at the very notion of women in power, as well as increasingly frustrated at the way their wives and sweethearts get themselves up in their sexiest gear only to deny them. How can they possibly countenance this double blow to their male pride, the sheer frustration of it? It isn't long before Lysistrata – whose name means 'Army Disbander' –

brings them anguishedly to the negotiating table and after a final hymn to Athene, Protectress of Us All, it's sex and peace all round.

The whole project has in fact been under the goddess's aegis from the start. She looks after the women from the moment she lets them occupy her Acropolis; it's to her that the old ones pray when the men try to attack them there. It doesn't take much seeking to see to whom Lysistrata herself owes her resourceful leadership, her shrewd wisdom, even her impatience with her sexier sisters who're finding all this abstinence a bit more than they'd bargained for. And it's Athene's supreme skill too that Lysistrata draws on to try to make the Magistrate see sense. Are you women such idiots as to think you can resolve the crisis with your spindles and bits of wool? he demands infuriatedly when she starts to explain her analogy. But it might not be such a bad idea to run the City, she says, in the way we women deal with wool.

The first thing you do with wool is wash the grease out of it; you can do the same with the City. Then you stretch out the citizen body on a bench and pick out the burrs – that is, the parasites. After that you prise apart the club-members who form themselves into knots and clots to get into power, and when you've separated them, pick them out one by one. Then you're ready for the carding: they can all go into the basket of Civic Goodwill – including the resident aliens and any foreigners who are your friends – yes, and even those who are in debt to the Treasury! Not only that. Athens has many colonies. At the moment they are lying around all over the place, like stray bits and pieces of the fleece. You should pick them up and bring them here, put them all together, and then out of all this make an enormous great ball of wool – and from that you can make the People a coat.

'Burrs – balls of wool – nonsense!' huffs the Magistrate. And what right have the women to talk of such matters anyway, what have they done for the war effort? Done? yells Lysistrata. Done? They've given the city sons, they've had to see them sent off to war, they're either war widows or unmarried altogether! Don't ask her what the women have done![27]

And by the end of it, they've done the rest. Athene's lesson on another way to go to war got a rare showing in London at the start of the nineties. But by then the stuff of knockabout comedy had also been woven into the warp and woof of a reality which had seized the collective imagination for both inspiration and condemnation to show just how potent that lesson could be.

At the start of the 1970s, 35,000 women marched in New York in declaration of their rights. A decade later, 30,000, then 50,000, encircled and wove their way around the nine-mile perimeter fence of the United States Air Force base at Greenham Common in the south of England in protest against the siting there of cruise missiles. Those two grand gestures were built on countless small ones as the 'Greenham women' who had pitched their camp there made and re-made their primitive shelters against eviction and re-eviction and endured the cold, the wet, the sheer discomfort and the court cases in pursuit of their own conviction. They cooked, they kept house, they pitted the simplicity of traditional 'women's work' against the complexities and might of the defence machine – and they went on doing it. They held festivals and celebrations that emphasized their own freedom and the military's lack of it. They showed just how flimsy was the official notion of security by simply walking into the place and holding a teddy bear's picnic, or weaving a great snake about the place. They used Athene's own imagery against the ruling order, by weaving into that bleak perimeter fence photographs of children, scraps of wool, toys, little mementoes whose value lay in what they expressed of individual hopes and lives; they hung mirrors on the wire so that the military guards were forced to reflect on themselves against the background of their installations.

And the ruling order couldn't stand it. Like Ares, like the army of Athens that Lysistrata took on, they were completely stuck in an escalation of a strategy that evidently didn't work, that could only reinforce the determination of the women to stay and encourage others to join them. At one stage, no fewer than 400 police were sent to evict thirty protesters from the main gate. And terribly, the rage against the women grew with the ruling order's impotence. At first they were dismissed as student feminists, woolly minds in woolly hats. 'Amazon waifs and strays', the local paper called them – thus investing them with warriors' power and defusing it into child-like vulnerability at a stroke. But as time went on, Eris and Ares were let loose in a violent eruption of the shadow side of the forces of law and order. The women were called 'unnatural' – butch, lesbian, filthy, squalid. The local ratepayers' association, fearful of declining property values, took RAGE as its acronym – Ratepayers Against Greenham Encampments. There was something intolerable in the fact that among the runaways, the seekers and the unconventional, there were *ordinary* women – grandmothers, professionals, people like us, or who should have been. The violence against the women escalated. 'If it was up to me,' one American was heard to say, 'I'd pour gasoline over them and burn them.' The imagery of sexual aggression intensified. A bus-load of the military bared buttocks to them as it passed; soldiers exposed themselves; sexual insults were heaped on them; at one stage maggots, excrement and blood were poured on to their shelters and red-hot pokers thrust into them.

In the end, the cruise missiles went because of a Soviet–American treaty rather than anything else; a decade after the Greenham protest was at its height, the world is hardly short of nuclear weaponry. But what that protest showed is that there *is* another way to go to war than that of Ares and his sister. It showed that the warrior energy of Athene can inform the striving for peace – and the building of women's sense of themselves independently of the ruling order. It showed just how great a collective charge the goddess's energy can harness – both in challenge to that order and in holding up her shield which is also mirror to its dark shadow, for all to see and reflect on.[28]

In this adventure, Athene was not, it begins to seem, working alone. 'Amazons' was one of the milder and more predictable epithets slung at the women at Greenham, and that separatist, women-only energy has more to do, perhaps, with the wildness of

Artemis than with either Athene's insistent presence in the citadels of the ruling order or her loving comradeship with men. In the very *ordinariness* of so much of the women's work in those make-shift benders, the cooking and the patient making and remaking of the elements of home, we can even imagine the presence of Hestia, the keeper of the hearth. What seems to emerge from the mythology of Greenham, in fact, is a cooperation among facets of feminine energy which has been rare indeed since they were dif-ferentiated in the reign of Zeus. In his day, they were not only separate but often incompatible. One of the scenes represented on the metopes of the Parthenon, for instance, was the battle between the Greeks and the Amazons – in which Athene was most cer-tainly on the side of the Greeks. To this day, women have known what it is to try to reconcile the different aspects of feminine energy that move through those images of the Olympian god-desses. But what seems to be happening as the goddess gets further from that citadel – further from father Zeus's head, his idea of her – is that her energy can unite in new alliances, in an image of a fuller feminine.

Is this where all our current debates, our attempts to see beyond those traditional lists of 'feminine' qualities, may lead? One of the insistent images throughout this book has been that of Eve, the first woman who is also ancient goddess, Mother of All Living. And just as insistent has been the entangling of her image with that of the serpent which is the ancient symbol of the great round and movement of creation and destruction, life, death and regenera-tion. We have seen this image not just in Eve herself, but in Dea Syria emerging from the maw of the serpent just as an Indian snake-goddess does to this day; we've seen it in Medusa and the mysterious images of the alchemists, in the death-dealing vision of Redon and in Blake's celebration of life's energy. And now here's a contemporary image, one of Fornasetti's variations on the theme. What it represents for the artist is a woman with her face 'peeled like a fruit'. A shocking image? Yet as that peel parts to reveal something of its essence, its coils are serpent too – and so is woman. Eve, the apple, the serpent, the peeling, the biting into that fruit that contains consciousness itself: all brought together in the steadfast gaze of those knowing eyes [Pl. 39].

Athene too is part of that interweaving; she too, as we know, draws on the ancient serpent energy. And another of the themes of this book has been that her particular gift within it is a consciousness that in its transformative interactions of mind and matter is particularly of a feminine sort. The idea of feminine consciousness is not a new one; we've seen its 'dim, nocturnal' quality as understood by Jung and its opposition to prevailing heroic and by definition masculine consciousness as elaborated by Neumann. These perceptions – and the understandings of women's 'true nature' that go with them – have been extraordinarily influential: if there's still a sneaking suspicion that women can't *really* think, any more than men can *really* feel, it's to them that it can in part at least be traced.

Some authors have, however, elaborated from such beginnings. 'Feminine consciousness explores ideas, affects, images and sensations within the inner depths,' says Barbara Stevens Sullivan, for instance; 'they seize the individual's attention, drawing him [*sic*] down into his psyche. Masculine consciousness separates the individual from his dark inner labyrinth: the individual reaches in and pulls something out to be examined in the clear light of day.' Edward Whitmont's identification of a *yang* or masculine consciousness with left brain activity and a *yin* or feminine consciousness with right brain activity is not so far from this: the first strives from centre to periphery, separating, analysing, abstracting; the second draws inward to the centre, to move towards unity, patterns and analogy. Others wonder whether consciousness needs to be 'masculine' or 'feminine' at all. 'Must everything be divided up and differentiated?' asks Verena Kast. 'Perhaps we are dividing something here that is not divisible, and by doing so we are creating artificial conflicts.' In her own scheme of things, 'Consciousness is human potential. The content of our self-awareness, on the other hand, is gender-specific.'[29]

Yet if Athene's bright and focused seeing is little to do with that dim and lunar light, it is not Apollo's either. The sun-god who has been the dominant of Western consciousness shoots his arrows from afar; his realm is that of pure thought, uncluttered by the messy actualities of everyday. When Athene moves, we cry '*I see!*' – and that's the prelude to action that fits thought to the situation, the material to be worked. That is Athene's *techne* and *sophia*. In the realm of Athene Ergane, the Workwoman, the craftworker assesses the material's weight and texture, heat and smell, working out what's needed by way of pressure, liquid, fire. This is Lysistrata unravelling, cleansing, carding the wool – not for the sake of the task itself, not the better to compare the nature of wool with, say, that of chalk or cheese – but so that the people may have a new coat! This is consciousness in and through relationship with the material, the actual. In the realm of Athene Polymetis, Athene of many counsels, we can see how things and situations and people relate and adjust as these relationships change, rather than doggedly following the idea despite what's actually happening.

And in a world where things of the spirit, of intellect, and the realm of matter have for so long been so dangerously divorced, don't we need these skills! When we've had to reinvent a whole new art of 'appropriate technology' because the sort that's dominated has become so unfitted to the matter-at-hand, a rehonouring of Athene's particular gift is surely long overdue. This is a challenge to heroic consciousness. In the days of Zeus, Cassandra, that knowing woman, could not find sanctuary in Athene's temple against the rapacity of Apollo; Fate decreed otherwise. These days, pure science still carries more prestige than the applied sort. Though Athene's energy still has some currency, in her native land at least it's only a tenth of the value of Apollo's [Pl. 45].

But we have hints of what an honouring of feminine consciousness might mean. One example: 'The personal is political!' used to be the rallying cry of the most recent wave of the women's movement – and that insistence on the validity of subjective experience was an extraordinarily powerful basis for both theory and action.

271

Can we hold to that in a world that so values the 'objective' now that Women's Studies are the stuff of PhDs? Another example: Freud was convinced that women had little sense of justice, because of the huge role that envy inevitably played in their penisless lives. Yet what Carol Gilligan found in her study of women's moral decision-making was that their approach had far less to do with abstract notions of 'right' and 'wrong' than with weighing conflicting responsibilities to actual relationships – including their responsibility to themselves.[30] (An example of Whitmont's *yin* consciousness?)

In the coming together of spirit and matter, of mind and material, as the alchemists well knew, it is not just the matter but both which are transformed. When Athene reclaims Medusa's power, both are changed. Where is the container for that transformative energy? Neumann's distinction of the 'transformative' from the 'elementary' or 'matriarchal' feminine rests on what woman experiences 'naturally and unreflectingly' in pregnancy, child-bearing, the growth of her child. But Genia Pauli Haddon gives us a different image. The receptive and nurturing function of the womb is only half of its function: the rest has to do with exerting, pushing forth. 'If we were to define femininity solely in accordance with the womb's birthing power, we would speak of it as the great opener of what has been sealed, the initiator of all going forth, the out-thrusting *yang* power at the heart of being.' For her, *yang* needs to be reclaimed from its association with 'the masculine', women need to reclaim their pushiness. 'It is no longer sufficient for a woman to be assertive solely through the good graces of her animus. She must come to know that sometimes being assertive is feminine.'[31]

The age-old dishonouring of '*yang* femininity' is imaged for Genia Pauli Haddon in the fate of Lilith, so long cast out into the wilderness: 'her deadliness is a perverted, blocked expression of her potential creativity as a bringer of transformation, a pusher-to-birth.' Lilith's banishment, as we've seen, has been shared by many other manifestations of feminine energy unacceptable to dominant consciousness. In his own feminine typology, Edward Whitmont reclaims them, to characterize the Medusa pole as the 'abyss of transformation' to which every woman (and anima) must periodically descend for renewal, and the Athene–Medusa polarity as 'the abysmal strife-and-civilization-generating aspect of the feminine'.[32]

In these reclamations of lost aspects of the feminine, these struggling formulations of what the fuller force might come to mean for the lives of women and men, we need, it seems to me, to call on all Athene's skill as a weaver, all her capacity to weigh and assess the material for its transformation, all that bright and focused vision that leads to the 'Aha!' of understanding. As these pages have tried to show, she has, by the very nature and timing of her birth, had a particular place in the vagaries of developing Western consciousness. As human beings have tried to understand the nature of their world and their own place in it, she has faithfully held up her shield for our protection and as mirror for our reflection. She has insisted that we remember the essential interweaving of mind and the material world in our works of transformation. And she's infused us with a contained and focused energy as we do it. There's one more gift she's given us – and that was at the very start of the whole human adventure. When Prometheus shaped the first human beings, they say, it was Athene who breathed soul into them. As we continue to shape our world and our understandings and to be shaped by them, we could maybe do worse than remember what the potters would call to her as they fired their own clay: 'Come to us, Athene, and hold your hand over our oven!'

Notes

For full details of works cited in these notes, see the bibliography on p. 287.

PROLOGUE: Birth of a Goddess

1. Boer, *The Homeric Hymns*, pp. 137–8; Hesiod, *Theogony*, p. 53; Pindar, *Odes*, 7. 34.
2. Campbell, *The Masks of God: Occidental Mythology*, p. 149.
3. Harrison, *Prolegomena to Greek Religion*, pp. 302–3, 648.
4. Hesiod, *Theogony*, n. 34, p. 153.
5. Jung, *Memories, Dreams, Reflections*, p. 343.
6. Campbell, *The Hero with a Thousand Faces*, p. 3.
7. Pausanias, *Guide to Greece*, IX, 16.4; VIII, 8.3.
8. Calasso, *The Marriage of Cadmus and Harmony*, p. 22.
9. Jung, *Collected Works*, 5, para. 337.
10. ibid., 9i, para. 271.

CHAPTER 1: Under the Aegis

1. Petrakos, *National Museum*, p. 86.
2. Homer, *The Iliad*, pp. 79, 112–13.
3. Hesiod, *Theogony*, p. 53.
4. *Iliad*, p. 377.
5. ibid., p. 243.
6. ibid., p. 451.
7. Boer, p. 69.
8. Graves, *The Greek Myths*, 21. e; Sophocles, *Ajax*, lines 17–18.
9. Sophocles, *Oedipus at Colonus*, lines 688–9.

10. Augustine, *The City of God*, 2, pp. 184–5.

11. Pausanias, I, 26.6.

12. Boer, p. 139.

13. Pausanias, VIII, 36.5.

14. Otto, *The Homeric Gods*, p. 56.

15. Homer, *The Odyssey*, pp. 209–10.

16. *Iliad*, p. 433.

17. Calasso, p. 324.

18. *Odyssey*, pp. 347, 349.

19. *Iliad*, p. 112.

20. Farnell, *The Cults of the Greek States*, I, p. 313.

21. *Odyssey*, pp. 33, 60, 208, 209.

22. *Iliad*, p. 147.

23. ibid., p. 156.

24. ibid., pp. 154, 78–9, 363.

25. Aeschylus, *Prometheus Bound*, lines 34–5.

26. ibid., lines 442–4, 447–54, pp. 33–5.

27. Graves, *Myths*, 75.c, 39.g; Farnell, I, p. 346.

28. Graves, *Myths*, 39.h; 50.f, g.

29. *Odyssey*, pp. 33, 360.

30. *Iliad*, pp. 116, 88–9.

31. ibid., pp. 92, 116, 391, 274.

32. Graves, *Myths*, 75.f, 25.h; Sophocles, *Ajax*, lines 448–9, 1416–20.

33. Jenkins, *The Parthenon Frieze*, p. 11.

CHAPTER 2 : The Maternal Measure

1. Graves, *Myths*, 1.d, 2.1, 9; Farnell, I, p. 284.

2. Hillman, 'Ananke and Athene', in *Facing the Gods*, p. 26; Graves, *Myths*, 11.2; Kerenyi, *Athene*, p. 12.

3. Farnell, I, p. 263.

4. Otto, p. 56.

5. Kerenyi, p. 15.

6. ibid., p. 14; Pausanias, II, 33.1; V, 3.2.

7. Pausanias, IX, n. 197; Kerenyi, p. 31.

8. *Odyssey*, p. 40.

9. Pausanias, I, p. 210n; Royal Horticultural Society, *Dictionary of Gardening*, pp. 1262–3, 1488; Culpeper, *Complete Herbal*, pp. 122–4.

10. Accordingly, I have relied mostly on Ian Jenkins's clear and imaginative account in *The Parthenon Frieze*.

11. Harrison, *Ancient Art and Ritual*, p. 179.

12. Kerenyi, p. 31; Pausanias, VII, 5.4.

13. Kerenyi, pp. 29–59; Graves, *Myths*, 25; Johnson, *Lady of the Beasts*, pp. 156–7.

14. Pausanias, I, 27.4.

15. Hesiod, *Theogony*, p. 42.

16. Hesiod, *Works and Days*, pp. 61–2.

17. Jenkins, pp. 40, 42.

18. Aeschylus, *The Eumenides*, lines 734–41, 658–64.

CHAPTER 3 : The Feminine Heritage

1. Pausanias, I, 14.5; Graves, *Myths*, 8.1; Herodotus quoted ibid.

2. Kerenyi, p. 26.

3. Graves, *Myths*, 8.1; Bernal, *Black Athena*, p. 50; Gimbutas, *The Language of the Goddess*, pp. 68–9; Baring and Cashford, *The Myth of the Goddess*, p. 337.

4. Jung, *CW*, 7, para.109.

5. Harrison, *Themis*, pp. 73, 87–8; Clement, *The Exhortation to the Greeks*, p. 39.

6. Baring and Cashford, pp. 3, 13, 46–54.

7. Gimbutas, *The Goddesses and Gods of Old Europe*, preface.

8. ibid., pp. 112–52.

9. Graves, *Myths*, 72.1.

10. Herodotus quoted in Harrison, *Themis*, p. 267.

11. *Odyssey*, pp. 370–79.

12. Pausanias, I, 5.3; Gimbutas, *Goddesses*, p. 135. Pausanias, VI, 26.3.

13. Ovid, *Metamorphoses*, p. 66.

14. Gimbutas, *Language*, pp. 67, 190, 318; Johnson, p. 47.

15. Johnson, p. 95; *Iliad*, pp. 133, 363; Graves, *Myths*, 39.h; Aeschylus, *Prometheus*, line 488.

16. Gimbutas, *Language*, p. 68–9; Matthews, *Sophia*, p. 213; Nicholson, *The Goddess Re-Awakening*, p. 234; Johnson, pp. 211–13.

17. Begg, *The Cult of the Black Virgin*, p. 43; Johnson, pp. 132, 136; Baring and Cashford, pp. 249, 457–8; Bernal, p. 21; Lurker, *The Gods and Symbols of Ancient Egypt*, p. 106.

18. Perera, 'War, Madness and the Morrigan', in Stein, *Mad Parts of Sane People*, pp. 173–92; Green, *The Gods of the Celts*, p. 120, 170.

19. Shearer, *The Traveller's Key to Northern India*, p. 11.

20. Erndl, *Victory to the Mother*, p. 89.

21. Zimmer, *Myths and Symbols in Indian Art and Civilization*, p. 15.

22. Shearer, pp. 22–4; Zimmer, pp. 212–13; Shri Ramakrishna quoted in Campbell, *The Masks of God: Oriental Mythology*, pp. 164–5.

23. Zimmer, pp. 24–5.

24. ibid., pp. 214–16.
25. Graves, *Myths*, 81.j-n, 159.
26. Euripides, *The Women of Troy*, lines 974–88.
27. Harrison, *Prolegomena*, pp. 292, 298, 297.

CHAPTER 4 : Remembering Medusa

1. Graves, *Myths*, 73; Campbell, *Hero*, pp. 245–6; Campbell, *Occidental Mythology*, pp. 128–9, 155–6.
2. Graves, *Myths*, 33.b, c, 73.t.
3. Gimbutas, *Language*, pp. 132, 207; Johnson, pp. 80, 150.
4. Pausanias, II, 21, 6.
5. Begg, p. 40.
6. Graves, *Myths*, 33.b.
7. Euripides, *Ion*.
8. Graves, *The White Goddess*, pp. 210–11; Shearer, p. 11.
9. *Iliad*, p. 196.
10. Matthews, p. 81.
11. Baring and Cashford, pp. 370–74.
12. ibid., pp. 176, 191; Wolkstein and Kramer, *Inanna Queen of Heaven and Earth*, pp. 53, 37; Perera, *Descent to the Goddess*, p. 17.
13. Wolkstein and Kramer, pp. 12–27, 4–9; Kramer, *From the Poetry of Sumer*, p. 92.
14. Wolkstein and Kramer, p. 9; Baring and Cashford, p. 216.
15. Wolkstein and Kramer, pp. 52–84.

CHAPTER 5 : The Mind of Minerva

1. Graves, *Myths*, 158.3.
2. Grant, *Roman Myths*, pp. 70–71, 107, 109.
3. *New Larousse Enyclopedia of Mythology*, p. 207.
4. Virgil, *The Aeneid*, pp. 27, 28, 51, 200, 213, 214–15, 221–3.
5. ibid., pp. 185–8, 155, 111.
6. ibid., p. 179.
7. Grant, p. 157; *New Larousse*, pp. 207, 202–3.
8. Johnson, p. 140; Baring and Cashford, p. 359.
9. Bailey, *Phases in the Religion of Ancient Rome*, pp. 185–92; Baring and Cashford, p. 405.
10. Seltman, *The Twelve Olympians and Their Guests*, p. 58.
11. Caesar, *The Gallic Wars*, p. 341.

12. Matthews, p. 213.

13. Cunliffe, *The Roman Baths*. You can also read about Bladud from an informative mural while sipping the waters in the Pump Room.

14. Cunliffe, *Baths*; Cunliffe, 'The Sanctuary of Sulis Minerva', in *Pagan Gods and Shrines of the Roman Empire*, pp. 1–14.

15. Matthews, p. 214; Rich and Begg, *On the Trail of Merlin*, pp. 31–2, 176.

16. Green, p. 164; Rich and Begg, p. 46; Johnson, pp. 70–71.

17. Cunliffe, 'Sanctuary', p. 10; Tomlin, 'The Power of the Goddess', in *The Temple of Sulis Minerva at Bath*, pp. 101–5.

18. Cunliffe, *Baths*, pp. 16–18; Cunliffe, 'Sanctuary', pp. 6–9; Toynbee, *Art in Roman Britain*, pp. 161–4.

19. Cunliffe, *Baths*, p. 35; Cunliffe, 'Sanctuary', p. 6.

CHAPTER 6: Fallen Angels and the Daughters of Men

1. Clement, p. 119.

2. James, *The Apocryphal New Testament*, p. 46.

3. Begg, pp. 45–6; Gimbutas, *Language*, pp. 110, 121; Matthews, pp. 213, 219; Ashe, p. 147.

4. Matthews, p. 168; Smith, *Jesus the Magician*, p. 111.

5. Matthews, p. 213; Farmer, *The Oxford Dictionary of Saints*, p. 69.

6. Farmer, pp. 156, 166; Bernal, p. 145; Spencer, *Fair Greece, Sad Relic*, p. 138.

7. Brown, *The Body and Society*, p. 64.

8. Clement, pp. xi–xv, 59, 57, 75, 77, 103, 105, 77–9.

9. ibid., p. 127; Tatian quoted in Pagels, *Adam, Eve and the Serpent*, p. 44, and in Graves, *White Goddess*, p. 47.

10. Justin quoted in Pagels, *Adam*, pp. 42, 43.

11. ibid., p. 42.

12. Brown, *Augustine of Hippo*, pp. 289, 231, 302, 305, 304.

13. Augustine, I, pp. 190, 118–19.

14. ibid., I, pp. 122, 198–9, 120, 50, 65; II, 184; I, 36, 65.

15. Romans 7:14–15, 18, 23–4.

16. See Brown, *Body*.

17. Clement quoted in Pagels, *Adam*, p. 21; Tertullian in Brown, *Body*, pp. 17–19; Brown, *Augustine*, p. 249.

18. Augustine, I, p. 124.

19. Baring and Cashford, pp. 277–88.

20. ibid., p. 280.

21. Chief Seattle quoted in Campbell, *The Way of the Animal Powers*, p. 269.

22. Genesis 1:26–31.

23. Philo quoted in Phillips, *Eve: the history of an idea*, pp. 30, 51.

24. Pagels, *Adam*, pp. 64–5; Aeschylus, *Eumenides*, lines 658–61; Aristotle, *On the Generation of Animals*, p. 111; Aquinas quoted in Phillips, p. 35, and Baring and Cashford, p. 521.

25. Phillips, p. 64.

26. Genesis 3:16–22.

27. Clement and Irenaeus quoted in Pagels, *Adam*, p. 28.

28. Augustine quoted in Pagels, *Adam*, pp. 110–11 and Brown, *Augustine*, pp. 338, 339.

29. Brown, *Augustine*, p. 39; Luther quoted in Phillips, p. 58.

30. Tertullian quoted in Phillips, p. 76.

31. Phillips, pp. 42, 41; Clement, p. 31.

32. Begg, pp. 34–9; Baring and Cashford, pp. 510–12.

33. Tertullian quoted in Phillips, p. 21; John Chrysostom in Phillips, p. 22.

34. 'Adam lay ybounden' in Dearmer et al., *The Oxford Book of Carols*, p. 388.

35. Tertullian quoted in Phillips, p. 134.

CHAPTER 7 : The Seat of Wisdom

1. Baring and Cashford, p. 550; Ashe, pp. 185–6, 192; Seltman, p. 59.

2. Ashe, p. 85; Johnson, p. 132; Lurker, p. 85.

3. Ashe, pp. 202–4.

4. Proverbs 8:22–31.

5. Proverbs 3:19; Wisdom 7:22; Wisdom 8:5; Wisdom 7:25, 26, 29.

6. Wisdom 8:1, 8.

7. Proverbs 3:15–18; Sirach 14:22; Sirach 24:4–5.

8. Proverbs 1:20–22.

9. Wisdom 7:27; Sirach 1:9–10.

10. Wisdom 8:23.

11. Pythagoras quoted in Passmore, *The Perfectibility of Man*, p. 38.

12. Sirach 25:13–21.

13. Sirach 25:23–4.

14. Philo quoted in Engelsman, *The Feminine Dimension of the Divine*, pp. 102, 103.

15. 1 Corinthians 1:20–24.

16. Ashe, p. 214.

17. Robinson (ed.), *The Nag Hammadi Library*, p. 217.

18. Irenaeus quoted in Pagels, *Adam*, p. 69 and *The Gnostic Gospels*, p. 17.

19. Irenaeus quoted in Pagels, *Gnostic Gospels*, p. 48; Pagels, *Gnostic Gospels*, p. 73; Robinson, pp. 101, 99, 467.

20. Robinson, pp. 157–8.

21. ibid., pp. 154, 174, 112.

22. Boethius, *The Consolation of Philosophy*, p. 3.

23. Ashe, pp. 200, 173; Song of Solomon 6: 10.

24. Begg, p. 19; Warner, *Alone of All Her Sex*, p. 304; Matthews, p. 307.

25. Matthews, p. 200.

26. Ashe, p. 209.

27. Proverbs 8: 22; Sirach 24: 9; Ashe, pp. 209–14.

28. Warner, *Monuments and Maidens*, p. 180.

29. Begg, pp. 29–33; Warner, *Alone*, pp. 128–9, 99.

30. Sirach 24: 3, 4.

31. Robinson, pp. 271–7.

CHAPTER 8 : The Armour of Allegory

1. Bacon, *The Wisdom of the Ancients*, pp. 200–201, 216–18; Thomas, *Religion and the Decline of Magic*, pp. 510–11; Yates, *The Rosicrucian Enlightenment*, pp. 156–7.

2. Bacon, pp. 264–5, 238; Bacon quoted in Baring and Cashford, p. 543 and Thomas, *Man and the Natural World*, p. 18.

3. Seznec, *The Survival of the Pagan Gods*, pp. 11–24; Zwingli quoted in Seznec, p. 23.

4. Seznec, p. 24; Thomas, *Religion*, p. 493; Yates, *Astraea*, p. 50.

5. De Pizan, *The Book of the City of Ladies*, pp. 4–5, 6, 16, 10, 11, 254–5.

6. ibid., pp. 69–70, 75–6, 81–2, 203–4, 23.

7. ibid., pp. 14, 9.

8. ibid., pp. 70–73, 75, 74–5.

9. Christine de Pizan quoted in Warner, *Monuments*, p. 204.

10. Scot quoted in Thomas, *Religion*, p. 30; Thomas, *Religion*, p. 746.

11. Yates, *The Art of Memory*, p. 290.

12. Seznec, pp. 84–90, 92–3, 222.

13. Warner, *Monuments*, p. 200; Seznec, pp. 137–8, 94.

14. Seznec, pp. 113, 303; Yates, *Astraea*, pp. 149, 165–6.

15. Alcrati quoted in Seznec, pp. 100–101; Milton, *Comus*, lines 421, 447–52.

16. Proverbs 9:1–6.

17. Warner, *Monuments*, pp. 181, 87, 200–201; Dante, *Paradise*, II, lines 7–9.

18. Camesasca, *The Complete Paintings of Michelangelo*, p. 91; Ashe, p. 29; Phillips, p. 131.

19. Warner, *Monuments*, p. 206.

20. Poe, 'The Raven' in *Complete Stories and Poems*, pp. 754–6.

CHAPTER 9: Virgins, Witches and Uncommon Gold

1. Yates, *Astraea*, pp. 34–5; Ovid, *Metamorphoses*, pp. 32–3; Virgil, *The Eclogues*, IV, lines 4–10.

2. Yates, *Astraea*, pp. 29–87; Davies, 'Hymns of Astraea', in *An English Garner*, pp. 117, 120; de Pizan, p. 14; Barfield, 'Cynthia', in *An English Garner*, pp. 197–8; Yates, *Astraea*, p. 65.

3. Yates, *Astraea*, pp. 78–9.

4. ibid., pp. 42–3; Thomas, *Religion*, p. 525.

5. Information on the English witchhunts from Thomas, *Religion*, and on the Scottish ones from Larner, *Enemies of God*.

6. Baring and Cashford, p. 551; Kramer and Sprenger, *Malleus Maleficarum*, p. 23; Thomas, *Religion*, p. 523; Kramer and Sprenger, pp. 33, 116, 112, 121, 119, 117, 122.

7. James VI quoted in Larner, p. 96; Burton, *The Anatomy of Melancholy*, 3, p. 55; Thomas, *Religion*, p. 525; Kramer and Sprenger, pp. 120–21; Ginzberg, *Ecstacies*, pp. 93, 122; Larner, pp. 207, 4–10; Kramer and Sprenger, p. 121.

8. All this information on the Black Virgin and a whole lot more is in Begg.

9. ibid., pp. 216, 234, 69, 170, 57, 61–6, 53–4, 229, 63, 30, 32; Matthew 12:42.

10. Begg, pp. 25–7; Baring and Cashford, p. 647.

11. Lindsay, *The Origins of Alchemy in Graeco-Roman Egypt*, pp. 197, 389; Begg, p. 113.

12. Fabre and *Emerald Tablet* quoted in Klossow de Rola, *Alchemy*, pp. 8 and 15; Zosimos in Read, *Prelude to Chemistry*, p. 129; Ostanes in Lindsay, p. 144; *Gloria Mundi* in Read, p. 130.

13. *Splendor Solis* quoted in Read, p. 73; Klossow de Rola, pls. 61, 5; von Franz, *Alchemy*, pp. 177–82; Read, p. 81.

14. Lurker, pp. 96–7, 74; Lindsay, p. 216; Maier, *Atalanta Fugiens*, p. 191.

15. Maier, pp. 35, 95; Read, p. 245; Klossow de Rola, pls. 43, 32, 35; Maier, p. 147; Read, pp. 242–3; Maier, p. 151.

16. Read, pp. 161, 125–6; Yates, *Rosicrucian*, pp. 211–48; Keynes, 'Newton the Man' in *Collected Writings*, X, pp. 363–4.

17. Dobbs, pp. 13, 15, 233.

18. Harris, quoted in Thomas, *Religion*, p. 772; ibid., pp. 682–3, 538; Richard Bentley quoted ibid., p. 692.

CHAPTER 10 : Public Cult and Private Devotion

1. Spencer, pp. 9–12; Bernal, p. 157.

2. Spencer, Ch. V; Bernal, pp. 201–4; Spencer, pp. 75–81.

3. Banier, *The Mythology and Fables of the Ancients*, I, pp. v–vi, 27, 29; III, pp. 435–52; II, pp. 295–302.

4. Pope, *Iliad*, IV, line 28, *Odyssey*, I, lines 56, 85; Gay, *Dione, a Pastoral Tragedy*, pp. 152, 158–9, 253–4.

5. Bernal, p. 209; Jenkyns, *The Victorians and Ancient Greece*, pp. 1–6, Adams brothers quoted ibid., pp. 10–11.

6. St Clair, *Lord Elgin and the Marbles*, pp. 150, 166–9; Fuseli quoted ibid., p. 171; West quoted ibid., p. 167; Byron, 'English Bards and Scotch Reviewers', in *The Complete Poetical Works* I, lines 1027–32, p. 261.

7. Byron, 'Childe Harold', in *Works* II, lines 94, 109–114; Warner, *Monuments*, pp. 45–8.

8. Byron, 'The Curse of Minerva', in *Works* I, lines 75–8, 199, 221–8.

9. Warner, *Monuments*, n.27, p. 341.

10. ibid., pls. 11 and 12.

11. Shelley, 'Prometheus Unbound', in *Poetical Works*: 'Preface', p. 205, lines 570–78; 'Preface to *Hellas*', p. 447.

12. Boston Athenaeum, *The Influence and History of the Boston Athenaeum*; Graves, *Leather Armchairs*, p. 45; Cowell, *The Athenaeum*, pp. 10, 18; Henry James quoted ibid., p. 34; Waugh, *The Atheneum Club*, p. 85; *Vanity Fair* quoted in Cowell, p. 45.

13. Byron quoted in Spencer, p. 209; the craze for the classical is delightfully explored in Jenkyns, *Dignity and Decadence*, from which these details are taken.

14. St Clair, p. 265.

15. Creighton, *The Parthenon in Nashville*, tells the story of this extraordinary work.

16. Dickens, *The Old Curiosity Shop*, pp. 271–2, 281, quoted in Jenkyns, *Dignity*, p. 24; Ruskin quoted in Jenkyns, *Dignity*, pp. 61, 162; Ruskin, *The Queen of the Air*, p. 197.

17. Ruskin, *Works*, XX, pp. 371–80; Dixon Hunt, *The Wider Sea*, p. 323; Ruskin, *Queen*, pp. 144–74, 16–17, 69, 117–18.

18. Gladstone, *Juventus Mundus*, pp. 286, 374–5, 269.

19. Magnus, *Gladstone*, p. 123; Kingsley, *The Heroes*, pp. vii–ix, xi, xvii.

20. Kingsley, *Heroes*, pp. 53–4; Kingsley, *Andromeda*, lines 221–2, 239, 251, 394–9, 483–90; Kingsley, *Heroes*, p. 32.

21. Praz, *The Romantic Agony*, pp. 25–7; Hoban, *The Medusa Frequency*, pp. 96, 121; Keats, 'Lamia', in *Poetical Works*, lines 171–2.

22. Warner, *Monuments*, p. 209.

CHAPTER 11 : The Lamp and the Darkness

1. Florence Nightingale quoted in Woodham-Smith, *Florence Nightingale*, p. 105. General biographical material in this chapter is taken from the lives and studies by not just Woodham-Smith but Sir Edward Cook, Elspeth Huxley, A. Matheson, I. B. O'Malley, F. B. Smith, and Lytton Strachey. I have also browsed in the huge deposit of Nightingale papers in the British Museum, particularly the 'private notes'.

2. Vicinus and Nergaard, *Ever Yours*, pp. 110–11; FN quoted in Strachey, *Five Victorians*, p. 327; Jowitt quoted in Cook, *The Life of Florence Nightingale*, I, p. xxiv; FN quoted in Goldie, '*I have done my duty*', p. 268.

3. Trevelyan, *British History in the Nineteenth Century*, p. 307.

4. FN quoted in Woodham-Smith, p. 58; Dorenkamp et al., *Images of Women in American Popular Culture*, p. 414.

5. Woodham-Smith, pp. 176–7; Strachey, pp. 311–14; Woodham-Smith, p. 166.

6. Woodham-Smith, pp. 191, 215–16, 211.

7. FN quoted in Vicinus and Nergaard, pp. 191–2.

8. See for example, Pickering, *Creative Malady*; Showalter, *The Female Malady*.

9. FN quoted in Cook, II, p. 426.

10. Vicinus includes Florence Nightingale among her 'heroic pioneers' in *Independent Women*; Cook, II, pp. 42–4, 4; FN quoted in Woodham-Smith, p. 303.

11. FN quoted in Goldie, p. 172, Strachey, p. 341.

12. FN quoted in Woodham-Smith, p. 272.

13. FN quoted in Goldie, p. 5.

14. FN quoted in Vicinus and Nergaard, p. 343; Strachey, p. 312.

15. Strachey, pp. 316, 342; Woodham-Smith, p. 191.

16. FN quoted in Cook, I, p. 106.

17. Chapple and Pollard, *The Letters of Mrs Gaskell*, pp. 307, 319–20.

18. Nightingale, 'Cassandra' in *Suggestions for Thought to the Searchers After Truth Among the Artizans of England*, II, pp. 374, 386, 394, 410.

19. Nightingale, *Suggestions*, II, pp. 224, 261.

20. Nightingale, *Notes on Nursing*, pp. 19, 8–14, 49–54; Nash, *Florence Nightingale to her Nurses*, p. 5.

21. FN quoted in Cook, I, p. 12.

22. Nightingale, 'Cassandra', p. 404; Maynard quoted in Vicinus, *Independent Women*, p. 14; Mill, *On the Subjection of Women*, p. 238.

23. Linton quoted in Hollis, *Women in Public*, p. 20.

24. Ayre, *The Gilbert and Sullivan Companion*, pp. 307–27.

25. Burrows quoted in Gay, *The Bourgeois Experience*, I, p. 193; Maudsley quoted in Showalter, *Female Malady*, p. 125; Moore quoted in Showalter, *Sexual Anarchy*, p. 40; Showalter, *Female Malady*, p. 126.

CHAPTER 12 : Logos and Psyche

1. Schur, *Freud, Living and Dying*, p. 504; Freud quoted in H. D., *Tribute to Freud*, p. 74; Grosskurth, *The Secret Ring*, p. 57; Freud quoted in Schorske, *Fin de Siècle Vienna*, pp. 202–3; Clark, *Freud*, pp. 320–21; Jones, *Sigmund Freud*, II, p. 27.

2. The information on Klimt and his images of Athene that follows is taken from Schorske, pp. 208–73. He and I, however, see the images very differently.

3. Falret quoted in Micale, *Approaching Hysteria*, p. 229; Donkin quoted in Showalter, *Female Malady*, p. 133; Maudsley quoted ibid., pp. 133–4.

4. Freud and Breuer, *Studies on Hysteria*, pp. 165–6, 207–8, 73–4, 321, 393.

5. Jones, II, p. 469; Young-Bruehl, *Anna Freud*, p. 453.

6. Freud quoted in Clark, pp. 45, 46; Freud, *Three Essays on the Theory of Sexuality*, in *Standard Edition*, VII, p. 219n; Freud, 'The Psychology of Women', in *New Introductory Lectures*, pp. 145–6.

7. ibid., pp. 172–3; Freud, 'An Outline of Psychoanalysis', in *SE*, XXIII, p. 194.

8. Freud, 'Medusa's Head', in *SE*, XVIII, p. 273; Freud, 'The Psychology of Women', p. 170.

9. Moebius quoted in Ellenberger, *The Discovery of the Unconscious*, p. 292.

10. Bachofen, 'An Essay on Mortuary Symbolism', in *Myth, Religion and Mother Right*, p. 58; 'Mother Right', in ibid., pp. 75–6, 144, 110, 174.

11. Ruskin, *Queen*, p. 41.

12. Jung, *Memories*, p. 358.

13. Jung, *CW*, 5, pp. xxiii, xxiv, 205–6, 444.

14. Hillman, in *Anima*, has brought together each and every one of Jung's references with his own critique.

15. Jung, *CW*, 6, paras. 289–95; *CW*, 5, paras. 264–5, 577.

16. *CW*, 14, para. 226; *CW*, 10, para. 275; *CW*, 14, para. 222; *CW*, 7, para. 330; *CW*, 14, paras. 227, 228; *CW*, 9ii, para. 29.

17. Jung, *The Seminars, Volume One: Dream Analysis*, p. 487; McGuire and Hull, *C. G. Jung Speaking*, p. 45; Jung, *CW*, 7, paras. 332, 334, 335; *CW*, 10, para. 243; McGuire and Hull, p. 236; Anthony, *The Valkyries*, gives a picture of Jung's women collaborators.

18. Jung, *Animus and Anima*, pp. 12–13, 5, 23–24, 39, 23.

19. Neumann, *Origins*, pp. 42, 125n; Neumann, 'The Moon and Matriarchal Consciousness', in Hillman et al., *Fathers and Mothers*, pp. 40–63; Neumann, *Origins*, pp. xiv, 213–18, 169.

CHAPTER 13 : Athene Unarmed

1. See, for example, Wehr, *Jung and Feminism*.

2. Jung, *CW*, 9i, paras. 195–7; Baring and Cashford, p. 572.

3. Otto, p. 54.

4. De Pizan, p. 95; Warner, *From the Beast to the Blonde*, pp. 32, 44.

5. *A Virago Keepsake*, p. vi.

6. Paglia, *Sexual Personae*, pp. 84–5.

7. Young-Eisendrath, 'Rethinking Feminism, the Animus and the Feminine', in Zweig, *To Be a Woman*, p. 205.

8. Hillman, *Anima*, pp. 63, 171; Kast, *The Nature of Loving*, pp. 88–94; Downing, *The Goddess*, p. 109.

9. Stevens, *Archetype*, p. 175.

10. Wilhelm, *I Ching or Book of Changes*, pp. 274–9.

11. Samuels, *The Plural Psyche*, pp. 96–100.

12. Harrison, *Prolegomena*, pp. 302–3; Rich, 'Commencement Address at Smith College, 1979', in Dorenkamp et al., p. 121.

13. Kerenyi; Begg, p. 131; Stein, 'Translator's Afterthoughts', in Kerenyi, pp. 75–7; Shinoda Bolen, *Goddesses in Everywoman*, pp. 75–106.

14. Kane, *Recovering from Incest*, pp. 6–7; Layton Schapira, *The Cassandra Complex*, p. 35.

15. Tatham, *The Makings of Maleness*, p. 22.

16. Hubback, 'Eve: Reflections on the psychology of the first disobedient woman', in Ross, *To Speak or be Silent*, pp. 12, 5–6.

17. Morten quoted in Vicinus, p. 1; Woolger and Woolger, 'Athena Today', in *Quadrant*, p. 27.

18. Steinem, *Outrageous Acts and Everyday Rebellions*, p. 149; the jacket blurb is from Zweig.

19. Singer, 'The Sadness of the Successful Woman', in Nicholson, pp. 115–26.

20. Woodman, *Addiction to Perfection*, p. 9; Woodman, *The Pregnant Virgin*, p. 85.

21. Bauer, *Alcoholism and Women*, p. 118; Shorter, 'The Concealed Body Language of Anorexia Nervosa' in Samuels, *The Father*, pp. 172, 175.

22. Shorter, p. 184.

23. Liddington, *The Long Road to Greenham*, traces the women's peace movement in Britain from its early-nineteenth-century beginnings; Deutsch quoted in Sayers, *Mothering Psychoanalysis*, p. 80; Griffin, *Woman and Nature*, prologue, and p. 227. Marina Warner evokes Mrs Thatcher as Britannia in *Monuments and Maidens*; this politician is famously 'all for the father' – to the extent of omitting any reference to her mother in her entry in *Who's Who*, thus declaring herself born of her father alone.

24. Perera, pp. 155–93.

25. Paglia, p. 15.

26. Dinnerstein, *The Rocking of the Cradle and the Ruling of the World*, p. 108.

27. Aristophanes, *Lysistrata*, lines 577–92, p. 204.

28. Details of the Greenham story from Blackwood, *On the Perimeter*, Harford and Hopkins, *Greenham Common*, and Liddington.

29. Stevens Sullivan, *Psychotherapy Grounded in the Feminine Principle*, p. 22; Whitmont, *Return of the Goddess*, p. 142; Kast, pp. 96–7.

30. Gilligan, *In A Different Voice*.

31. Pauli Haddon, 'The Personal and Cultural Emergence of Yang Femininity', in Zweig, pp. 293–5; Pauli Haddon, 'Delivering Yang Femininity', in *Spring*, pp. 133–41.

32. Whitmont, p. 140.

Bibliography

This bibliography lists only those texts of which I've made mention. Editions cited are those I've used.

Aeschylus, *Prometheus Bound*, trs. Phillip Vellacott (Harmondsworth: Penguin Books, 1975).

Aeschylus, *The Eumenides*, in *Oresteia*, trs. Hugh Lloyd-Jones (London: Duckworth, 1982).

Anthony, Maggy, *The Valkyries: the women around Jung* (Shaftesbury: Element Books, 1990).

Arber, E., *An English Garner*, Vol. 8 (London: Archibald Constable & Co., 1903).

Aristophanes, *Lysistrata*, in *Lysistrata and Other Plays*, trs. Alan H. Sommerstein (London: Penguin Books, 1973).

Aristotle, *On the Generation of Animals*, trs. A. L. Peck, Loeb Classical Library. (Cambridge, Mass. and London: Harvard University Press and William Heinemann, 1943).

Ashe, Geoffrey, *The Virgin* (London: Routledge & Kegan Paul, 1976).

Augustine, *The City of God*, trs. John Healey, ed. R. V. G. Tasker, 2 vols., Everyman's Library (London: J. M. Dent & Sons, 1950).

Ayre, Leslie, *The Gilbert and Sullivan Companion* (London: W. H. Allen, 1972).

Bachofen, J. J. *Myth, Religion and Mother Right*, trs. Ralph Manheim (London: Routledge & Kegan Paul, 1967).

Bacon, Francis, *The Wisdom of the Ancients*, in *The Moral and Historical Works of Lord Bacon* (London: Henry G. Bohn, 1852).

Bailey, Cyril, *Phases in the Religion of Ancient Rome* (London: Humphrey Milford, Oxford University Press, 1932).

Banier, Abbé, *The Mythology and Fables of the Ancients*, 4 vols. (London: 1740).

Barfield, Richard, 'Cynthia', in Arber, E., *An English Garner*, Vol. 8 (London: Archibald Constable & Co., 1903).

Baring, Anne, and Cashford, Jules, *The Myth of the Goddess: evolution of an image* (London: Viking Arkana, 1991).

Bauer, Jan, *Alcoholism and Women: the background and the psychology* (Toronto: Inner City Books, 1982).

Begg, Ean, *The Cult of the Black Virgin* (London: Arkana, 1985).

Bernal, Martin, *Black Athena: the Afroasiatic roots of classical civilisation*, Vol. 1 (London: Free Association Books, 1987).

Blackwood, Caroline, *On the Perimeter* (London: Flamingo/Fontana Paperbacks, 1984).

Boer, Charles (trs.), *The Homeric Hymns* (Dallas, Texas: Spring Publications, 1987).

Boethius, *The Consolation of Philosophy*, trs. Philip Ridpath (London: 1785).

Boston Athenaeum, *The Influence and History of the Boston Athenaeum* (Boston: 1907).

Brown, Peter, *Augustine of Hippo* (London: Faber and Faber, 1979).

Brown, Peter, *The Body and Society* (London: Faber and Faber, 1989).

Burton, Robert, *The Anatomy of Melancholy*, 3 vols., Everyman's Library (London: J. M. Dent & Sons, 1932).

Byron, Lord, *The Complete Poetical Works*, ed. Jerome J. McGann (Oxford: Clarendon Press, 1980).

Caesar, *The Gallic Wars*, trs. H. J. Edwards, Loeb Classical Library (Cambridge, Mass. and London: Harvard University Press and William Heinemann, 1963).

Calasso, Roberto, *The Marriage of Cadmus and Harmony*, trs. Tim Parks (London: Vintage, 1994).

Camesasca, Ettore, *The Complete Paintings of Michelangelo* (London: Weidenfeld & Nicolson, 1969).

Campbell, Joseph (ed.), *Myths and Symbols in Indian Art and Civilisation*, by Heinrich Zimmer (Princeton, NJ: Princeton University Press, 1972).

Campbell, Joseph, *The Hero with a Thousand Faces* (Princeton, NJ: Princeton University Press, 1982).

Campbell, Joseph, *The Masks of God: Occidental Mythology* (Harmondsworth: Penguin Books, 1982).

Campbell, Joseph, *The Way of the Animal Powers* (London: Times Books, 1984).

Campbell, Joseph, *The Masks of God: Oriental Mythology* (Harmondsworth: Penguin Books, 1986).

Chapple, J. A. V., and Pollard, Arthur (eds.), *The Letters of Mrs Gaskell* (Manchester: Manchester University Press, 1966).

Clark, Ronald W., *Freud: the man and the cause* (London: Granada Publishing, 1982).

Clement of Alexandria, *The Exhortation to the Greeks*, trs. G. W. Butterworth,

Loeb Classical Library (Cambridge, Mass. and London: Harvard University Press and William Heinemann, 1919).

Cook, Sir Edward, *The Life of Florence Nightingale*, 2 vols. (London: Macmillan, 1914).

Cowell, Frank, *The Athenaeum: club and social life in London 1824–1974* (London: Heinemann, 1975).

Creighton, Wilbur F., *The Parthenon in Nashville* (Brentwood, Tenn.: J. M. Press, 1991).

Culpeper, Nicholas, *Complete Herbal* (Ware, Herts: Omega Books, 1985).

Cunliffe, Barry, 'The Sanctuary of Sulis Minerva at Bath: a brief review', in *Pagan Gods and Shrines of the Roman Empire*, eds. Martin Henig and Anthony King, Monograph 8 (Oxford: Oxford Committee for Archaeology, 1986).

Cunliffe, Barry, *The Roman Baths* (Bath: Bath Archaeological Trust, 1993).

Dante Alighieri, *Paradise*, in *The Comedy of Dante Alighieri the Florentine*, trs. Dorothy L. Sayers and Barbara Reynolds (Harmondsworth: Penguin Books, 1962).

Davies, Sir John, 'Hymns of Astraea', in Arber, E., *An English Garner*, Vol. 8 (London: Archibald Constable & Co., 1903).

Dearmer, Percy F., Vaughan Williams, R., and Shaw, Martin, *The Oxford Book of Carols* (London: Humphrey Milford, 1929).

De Pizan, Christine, *The Book of the City of Ladies*, trs. Earl Jeffrey Richards (London: Picador/Pan Books, 1983).

Dickens, Charles, *The Old Curiosity Shop* (Harmondsworth: Penguin Books, 1985).

Dinnerstein, Dorothy, *The Rocking of the Cradle and the Ruling of the World* (London: Souvenir Press, 1978).

Dixon Hunt, John, *The Wider Sea: a life of John Ruskin* (London: J. M. Dent & Sons, 1982).

Dobbs, Betty Jo, *The Foundations of Newton's Alchemy* (Cambridge: Cambridge University Press, 1975).

Dorenkamp, Angela G., et al. (eds.), *Images of Women in American Popular Culture* (New York: Harcourt Brace Jovanovich, 1985).

Downing, Christine, *The Goddess: mythological images of the feminine* (New York: Crossroad, 1984).

Ellenberger, Henri F., *The Discovery of the Unconscious: the history and evolution of dynamic psychiatry* (New York: Basic Books, 1970).

Engelsman, Joan Chamberlain, *The Feminine Dimension of the Divine: a study of Sophia and feminine images in religion* (Wilmette, Ill.: Chiron Publications, 1994).

Erndl, Kathleen M., *Victory to the Mother: the Hindu goddess of Northwest India in myth, ritual and symbol* (Oxford: Oxford University Press, 1993).

Euripides, *Ion* and *The Women of Troy*, in *The Bacchae and Other Plays*, trs. Philip Vellacott (Harmondsworth: Penguin Books, 1986).

Farmer, David Hugh, *The Oxford Dictionary of Saints* (Oxford: Oxford University Press, 1984).

Farnell, L. R., *The Cults of the Greek States*, 2 vols. (Oxford: Clarendon Press, 1896).

Freud, Sigmund, *New Introductory Lectures on Psychoanalysis* (London: Hogarth Press and Institute of Psychoanalysis, 1993).

Freud, Sigmund, *Complete Psychological Works*, Standard Edition (*SE*), trs. and ed. James Strachey, 24 vols. (London: Hogarth Press and Institute of Psycho-analysis, 1953–74).

Freud, Sigmund, and Breuer, Josef, *Studies on Hysteria*, Penguin Freud Library, Vol. 3, trs. James and Alix Strachey (London: Penguin Books, 1991).

Gay, John, *Dione, a pastoral tragedy*, in *Poems on Several Occasions*, Vol. 2 (London, 1762).

Gay, Peter, *The Bourgeois Experience, Vol I: The Education of the Senses* (Oxford: Oxford University Press, 1984).

Gilligan, Carol, *In a Different Voice: psychological theory and women's development* (Cambridge, Mass.: Harvard University Press, 1982).

Gimbutas, Marija, *The Goddesses and Gods of Old Europe: myths and cult images* (London: Thames & Hudson, 1989).

Gimbutas, Marija, *The Language of the Goddess* (London: Thames & Hudson, 1989).

Ginzberg, Carlo, *Ecstacies*, trs. Raymond Rosenthal (London: Hutchinson Radius, 1990).

Gladstone, William Ewart, *Juventus Mundi: the gods and men of the heroic age* (London: Macmillan, 1869).

Goldie, Sue M. (ed.), *'I have done my duty': Florence Nightingale in the Crimean War 1854–56* (Manchester: Manchester University Press, 1987).

Grant, Michael, *Roman Myths* (London: Weidenfeld & Nicolson, 1971).

Graves, Charles, *Leather Armchairs* (London: Cassell, 1963).

Graves, Robert, *The White Goddess* (London: Faber and Faber, 1948).

Graves, Robert, *The Greek Myths*, 2 vols. (Harmondsworth: Penguin Books, 1985).

Green, Miranda, *The Gods of the Celts* (Gloucester: Alan Sutton, 1986).

Griffin, Susan, *Women and Nature: the roaring inside her* (London: The Women's Press, 1984).

Grosskurth, Phyllis, *The Secret Ring* (London: Jonathan Cape, 1991).

Harford, Barbara, and Hopkins, Sarah (eds.), *Greenham Common: women at the wire* (London: The Women's Press, 1984).

Harrison, Jane E., *Prolegomena to Greek Religion* (Cambridge: Cambridge University Press, 1903).

Harrison, Jane E., *Ancient Art and Ritual* (Cambridge: Cambridge University Press, 1913).

Harrison, Jane E., *Themis* (Cambridge: Cambridge University Press, 1927).

H. D. (Hilda Doolittle), *Tribute to Freud* (Oxford: Carcanet Press, 1971).

Henig, Martin, and King, Anthony (eds.), *Pagan Gods and Shrines of the Roman Empire*, Monograph No. 8 (Oxford: Oxford University Committee for Archaeology, 1986).

Hesiod, *Theogony* and *Works and Days*, in *Hesiod and Theogonis*, trs. Dorothea Wender (London: Penguin Books, 1989).

Hillman, James, *The Myth of Analysis* (New York: Harper & Row, 1978).

Hillman, James, 'On the Necessity of Abnormal Psychology: Ananke and Athene', in James Hillman (ed.), *Facing the Gods* (Irving, Texas: Spring Publications, 1980).

Hillman, James, *Anima: an anatomy of a personified notion* (Dallas, Texas: Spring Publications, 1986).

Hoban, Russell, *The Medusa Frequency* (London: Picador, 1988).

Hollis, Patricia, *Women in Public: the women's movement 1850–1900* (London: George Allen & Unwin, 1979).

The Holy Bible, Revised Standard Version, Catholic Edition, (London: Catholic Truth Society, 1966).

Homer, *The Iliad*, trs. E. V. Rieu (Harmondsworth: Penguin Books, 1975).

Homer, *The Odyssey*, trs. E. V. Rieu (Harmondsworth: Penguin Books, 1981).

Hubback, Judith, 'Eve: Reflections on the psychology of the first disobedient woman', in Lena B. Ross (ed.), *To Speak or be Silent* (Wilmette, Ill.: Chiron Publications, 1993).

Huxley, Elspeth, *Florence Nightingale* (London: Weidenfeld & Nicolson, 1975).

James, M. R., *The Apocryphal New Testament* (Oxford: Clarendon Press, 1924).

Jenkins, Ian, *The Parthenon Frieze* (London: British Museum Press, 1994).

Jenkyns, Richard, *The Victorians and Ancient Greece* (Oxford: Basil Blackwell, 1980).

Jenkyns, Richard, *Dignity and Decadence: Victorian art and the classical inheritance* (London: HarperCollins, 1991).

Johnson, Buffie, *Lady of the Beasts: ancient images of the goddess and her sacred animals* (New York: Harper & Row, 1988).

Jones, Ernest, *Sigmund Freud: Life and Work*, 3 vols. (London: Hogarth Press, 1953, 1955, 1957).

Jung, C. G., *The Collected Works*, eds. Herbert Read, Michael Fordham, and

Gerhard Adler, trs. R. F. C. Hull, 20 vols. (London: Routledge & Kegan Paul, 1957–79).

Jung, C. G. *The Seminars, Volume One: Dream Analysis*, ed. William McGuire (London: Routledge & Kegan Paul, 1984).

Jung, C. G., *Memories, Dreams, Reflections*, trs. Richard and Clara Winston (London: Collins/Fount Paperbacks, n.d.).

Jung, Emma, *Animus and Anima*, trs. Cary F. Baynes and Hildegard Nagel (Dallas, Texas: Spring Books, 1985).

Kane, Evangeline, *Recovering from Incest: imagination and the healing process* (Boston: Sigo Press, 1989).

Kast, Verena, *The Nature of Loving: patterns of human relationship*, trs. Boris Matthews (Wilmette, Ill.: Chiron Publications, 1986).

Keats, John, *The Poetical Works of John Keats*, ed. H. W. Garrod (Oxford: Oxford University Press, 1958).

Kerenyi, Karl, *Athene: virgin and mother in Greek Religion*, trs. Murray Stein (Zurich: Spring Publications, 1978).

Keynes, J. M., 'Newton the Man', in *The Collected Writings of John Maynard Keynes, Vol. X* (London: Macmillan St Martins Press, 1972).

Kingsley, Charles, *Andromeda and other poems* (London: J. W. Parker & Sons, 1858).

Kingsley, Charles, *The Heroes* (London: Macmillan, 1902).

Klossow de Rola, Stanislas, *Alchemy: the secret art* (London: Thames & Hudson, 1973).

Kramer, Heinrich, and Sprenger, James, *Malleus Maleficarum*, trs. Montague Summers (London: Arrow Books, 1971).

Kramer, Samuel Noah, *From the Poetry of Sumer* (Berkeley: University of California Press, 1979).

Larner, Christina, *Enemies of God: the witch hunt in Scotland* (London: Chatto & Windus, 1981).

Layton Schapira, Laurie, *The Cassandra Complex: living with disbelief* (Toronto: Inner City Books, 1988).

Liddington, Jill, *The Long Road to Greenham: feminism and anti-militarism in Britain since 1820* (London: Virago Press, 1989).

Lindsay, Jack, *The Origins of Alchemy in Graeco-Roman Egypt* (London: Frederick Muller, 1970).

Lurker, Manfred, *The Gods and Symbols of Ancient Egypt*, trs. Barbara Cummings (London: Thames & Hudson, 1980).

McGuire, William, and Hull, R. F. C. (eds.), *C. G. Jung Speaking: interviews and encounters* (London: Picador, 1980).

Magnus, Phillip, *Gladstone* (London: John Murray, 1954).

Maier, Michael, *Atalanta Fugiens*, trs. and ed. Joscelyn Godwin (Grand Rapids, MI: Phanes Press, 1989).

Matheson, A., *Florence Nightingale* (London: Nelson, 1913).

Matthews, Caitlin, *Sophia, the Goddess of Wisdom: the divine feminine from Black Goddess to World Soul* (London: Mandala, 1991).

Micale, Mark S., *Approaching Hysteria: disease and its interpretations* (Princeton, NJ: Princeton University Press, 1995).

Mill, John Stuart, *On the Subjection of Women*, Everyman's Library (London: J. M. Dent, 1955).

Milton, John, 'A Mask (Comus)', in *Milton: Poetical Works*, ed. Douglas Bush (London: Oxford University Press, 1966).

Nash, Rosalind (ed.), *Florence Nightingale to her Nurses* (London: Macmillan, 1914).

Neumann, Erich, *The Origins and History of Consciousness*, trs. R. F. C. Hull (London: Routledge & Kegan Paul, 1973).

Neumann, Erich, 'The Moon and Matriarchal Consciousness', trs. Hildegard Nagel, in Hillman, James et al., *Fathers and Mothers* (Zurich: Spring Publications, 1977).

New Larousse Encyclopedia of Mythology (London: Paul Hamlyn, 1968).

Nicholson, Shirley (comp.), *The Goddess Re-Awakening: the feminine principle today* (Wheaton, Ill.: Quest Books, 1989).

Nightingale, Florence, *Notes on Nursing: what it is and what it is not* (London: Harrison, 1860).

Nightingale, Florence, *Suggestions for Thought to the Searchers After Truth Among the Artizans of England*, 3 vols. (London: privately published, 1860).

O'Malley, I. B., *Florence Nightingale, 1820–1856* (London: Thornton Butterworth, 1931).

Otto, Walter F., *The Homeric Gods*, trs. Moses Hadas (London: Thames & Hudson, 1955).

Ovid, *Metamorphoses*, trs. Mary M. Innes (London: Penguin Books, 1955).

Pagels, Elaine, *The Gnostic Gospels* (Harmondsworth: Penguin Books, 1982).

Pagels, Elaine, *Adam, Eve and the Serpent* (London: Penguin Books, 1990).

Paglia, Camille, *Sexual Personae: art and decadence from Nefertiti to Emily Dickinson* (London: Penguin Books, 1992).

Passmore, John, *The Perfectibility of Man* (London: Duckworth, 1972).

Pauli Haddon, Genia, 'Delivering Yang Femininity', in *Spring* (Dallas, Texas: Spring Publications, 1987).

Pauli Haddon, Genia, 'The Personal and Cultural Emergence of Yang Femininity', in *To Be a Woman: the birth of conscious femininity*, ed. Connie Zweig (London: Mandala, 1991).

Pausanias, *Guide to Greece*, trs. Peter Levi, 2 vols. (Harmondsworth: Penguin Books, 1985).

Perera, Sylvia Brinton, *Descent to the Goddess: a way of initiation for women* (Toronto: Inner City Books, 1981).

Perera, Sylvia Brinton, 'War, Madness and the Morrigan, a Celtic Goddess of Life and Death', in *Mad Parts of Sane People in Analysis*, ed. Murray Stein (Wilmette, Ill.: Chiron Publications, 1993).

Petrakos, Basil, *National Museum* (Athens: Clio Editions, 1981).

Phillips, John A., *Eve: the history of an idea* (San Francisco: Harper & Row, 1985).

Pickering, Sir George, *Creative Malady* (London: George Allen & Unwin, 1974).

Pindar, *The Odes*, trs. Sir John Sandys, Loeb Classical Library (Cambridge, Mass., and London: Harvard University Press and William Heinemann, 1968).

Poe, Edgar Allan, *The Complete Stories and Poems of Edgar Allan Poe* (New York: Doubleday, 1966).

Pope, Alexander, *Poems of Alexander Pope*, ed. Maynard Mack (London: Methuen, 1967).

Praz, Mario, *The Romantic Agony*, trs. Angus Davidson (London: Humphrey Milford, Oxford University Press, 1933).

Read, John, *Prelude to Chemistry* (London: G. Bell & Sons, 1936).

Rich, Adrienne, 'Commencement Address at Smith College, 1979', in *Images of Women in Popular American Culture*, ed. Angela G. Dorenkamp, et al. (New York: Harcourt Brace Jovanovich, 1985).

Rich, Deike, and Begg, Ean, *On the Trail of Merlin: a guidebook to the Western mystery tradition* (London: Aquarian Press, 1991).

Robinson, James M. (ed.), *The Nag Hammadi Library* (Leiden: E. J. Brill, 1984).

Ross, Lena B. (ed.), *To Speak or be Silent: the paradox of disobedience in the lives of women* (Wilmette, Ill.: Chiron Publications, 1993).

Royal Horticultural Society, *Dictionary of Gardening*, Vol. 3 (Oxford: Oxford University Press, 1951).

Ruskin, John, *The Queen of the Air* (London: Smith, Elder & Co., 1869).

Ruskin, John, 'The Story of Arachne', in *The Works of John Ruskin*, Vol. XX, ed. E. T. Cook and Alexander Wedderburn (London: Longmans, Green & Co., 1905).

St Clair, William, *Lord Elgin and the Marbles* (London: Oxford University Press, 1967).

Samuels, Andrew, ed., *The Father: contemporary Jungian perspectives* (London: Free Association Books, 1985).

Samuels, Andrew, *The Plural Psyche: personality, morality and the father* (London: Routledge, 1989).

Sayers, Janet, *Mothering Psychoanalysis* (London: Hamish Hamilton, 1991).

Schorske, Carl E., *Fin de Siècle Vienna: politics and culture* (New York: Alfred A. Knopf, 1980).

Schur, Max, *Freud, Living and Dying* (London: Hogarth Press and Institute of Psychoanalysis, 1972).

Seltman, Charles, *The Twelve Olympians and Their Guests* (London: Max Parrish, 1956).

Seznec, Jean, *The Survival of the Pagan Gods*, trs. Barbara F. Sessions (Princeton, NJ: Princeton University Press, 1953).

Shearer, Alistair, *The Traveller's Key to Northern India* (New York: Alfred A. Knopf, 1983).

Shelley, Percy Bysshe, *Poetical Works*, ed. Thomas Hutchinson, (Oxford: Oxford University Press, 1971).

Shinoda Bolen, Jean, *Goddesses in Everywoman: a new psychology of women* (New York: Harper Colophon Books, 1985).

Shorter, Bani, 'The Concealed Body Language of Anorexia Nervosa', in *The Father: contemporary Jungian perspectives*, ed. Andrew Samuels (London: Free Association Books, 1985).

Showalter, Elaine, *The Female Malady: women, madness and English culture, 1830–1980* (London: Virago, 1987).

Showalter, Elaine, *Sexual Anarchy: gender and culture at the fin de siècle* (London: Bloomsbury, 1991).

Singer, June, 'The Sadness of the Successful Woman', in Shirley Nicholson (comp.), *The Goddess Re-Awakening: the feminine principle today* (Wheaton, Ill.: Quest Books, 1989).

Smith, F. B., *Florence Nightingale: reputation and power* (London: Croom Helm, 1982).

Smith, Morton, *Jesus the Magician* (Wellingborough: Aquarian Press, 1985).

Sophocles, *Ajax*, in *Electra and Other Plays*, trs. E. F. Watling (Harmondsworth: Penguin Books, 1976).

Sophocles, *Oedipus at Colonus*, in *The Theban Plays*, trs. E. F. Watling (Harmondsworth: Penguin Books, 1987).

Spencer, Terence, *Fair Greece, Sad Relic: literary philhellenism from Shakespeare to Byron* (London: Weidenfeld & Nicolson, 1954).

Stein, Murray, 'Translator's Afterthoughts', in Kerenyi, *Athene: virgin and mother in Greek religion* (Zurich: Spring Publications, 1978).

Stein, Murray (ed.), *Mad Parts of Sane People in Analysis* (Wilmette, Ill.: Chiron Publications, 1993).

Steinem, Gloria, *Outrageous Acts and Everyday Rebellions* (London: Flamingo, 1984).

Stevens, Anthony, *Archetype: a natural history of the Self* (London: Routledge & Kegan Paul, 1982).

Stevens Sullivan, Barbara, *Psychotherapy Grounded in the Feminine Principle* (Wilmette, Ill.: Chiron Publications, 1989).

Strachey, Lytton, 'Florence Nightingale', in *Five Victorians* (London: Reprint Society, 1942).

Tatham, Peter, *The Makings of Maleness* (London: Karnac Books, 1992).

Thomas, Keith, *Religion and the Decline of Magic: studies in popular beliefs in sixteenth- and seventeenth-century England* (Harmondsworth: Penguin Books, 1982).

Thomas, Keith, *Man and the Natural World: changing attitudes in England 1500–1800* (Harmondsworth: Penguin Books, 1984).

Tomlin, Roger, 'The power of the goddess', in *The Temple of Sulis Minerva at Bath, Vol.2*, ed. Barry Cunliffe (Oxford: Oxford Committee for Archaeology, 1988).

Toynbee, J. M. C, *Art in Roman Britain* (London: Phaidon Press, 1982).

Trevelyan, G. M. *British History in the Nineteenth Century* (London: Longman, Green & Co., 1922).

Vicinus, Martha, *Independent Women: work and community for single women 1850–1920* (London: Virago, 1985).

Vicinus, Martha, and Nergaard, Bea (eds.), *Ever Yours, Florence Nightingale: selected letters* (London: Virago, 1989).

A Virago Keepsake to Celebrate Twenty Years of Publishing (London: Virago, 1993).

Virgil, *The Aeneid*, trs. W. F. Jackson Knight (Harmondsworth: Penguin Books, 1956).

Virgil, *The Eclogues*, trs. Guy Lee (London: Penguin Books, 1984).

Von Franz, Marie-Louise, *Alchemy: an introduction to the symbolism and the psychology* (Toronto: Inner City Books, 1980).

Warner, Marina, *Alone of All Her Sex: the myth and the Cult of the Virgin Mary* (New York: Alfred A. Knopf, 1976).

Warner, Marina, *Monuments and Maidens: the allegory of the female form* (London: Weidenfeld & Nicolson, 1985).

Warner, Marina, *From the Beast to the Blonde: on fairy tales and their tellers* (London: Chatto & Windus, 1994).

Waugh, F. G., *The Athenaeum Club and its Association* (London: privately printed, 1897).

Wehr, Demaris S., *Jung and Feminism: liberating archetypes* (London: Routledge, 1988).

Whitmont, Edward C., *Return of the Goddess: femininity, aggression and the modern Grail quest* (London: Routledge & Kegan Paul, 1983).

Wilhelm, Richard (trs.), *I Ching or Book of Changes*, rendered into English by Cary F. Baynes (London: Routledge & Kegan Paul, 1975).

Wolkstein, Diane, and Kramer, Samuel Noah, *Inanna Queen of Heaven and Earth: her stories and hymns from Sumer* (London: Rider, 1984).

Woodham-Smith, Cecil, *Florence Nightingale 1820–1910* (London: Constable, 1952).

Woodman, Marion, *Addiction to Perfection* (Toronto: Inner City Books, 1982).

Woodman, Marion, *The Pregnant Virgin* (Toronto: Inner City Books, 1985).

Woolger, Roger, and Woolger, Jennifer, 'Athena Today: paradoxes of power and vulnerability', in *Quadrant* (Norwood, NJ: C. G. Jung Foundation for Analytical Psychology of New York, 1987).

Yates, Frances A., *The Rosicrucian Enlightenment* (St Albans, Herts: Paladin, 1975).

Yates, Frances A., *The Art of Memory* (London: Ark Paperbacks, 1984).

Yates, Frances A., *Astraea: the imperial theme in the sixteenth century* (London: Ark Paperbacks, 1985).

Young-Bruehl, Elisabeth, *Anna Freud* (London: Macmillan, 1989).

Young-Eisendrath, Polly, 'Rethinking Feminism, the Animus and the Feminine', in *To Be Woman: the birth of the conscious feminine*, ed. Connie Zweig (London: Mandala, 1991).

Zimmer, Heinrich, *Myths and Symbols in Indian Art and Civilisation*, ed. Joseph Campbell (Princeton, NJ: Princeton University Press, 1972).

Zweig, Connie, ed., *To Be a Woman: the birth of the conscious feminine* (London: Mandala, 1991).

Acknowledgements

The publishers wish to express their thanks to copyright holders for permission to reprint the following extracts:

To Blackwell Publishers Ltd for an extract from *The Victorians and Ancient Greece* (1980) by Richard Jenkyns;

To E. J. Brill N.V. for extracts from *The Nag Hammadi Library* (1984), ed. James M. Robinson;

To Cambridge University Press for extracts from *The Foundations of Newton's Alchemy* (1975) by B. J. Dobbs, and from *Prolegomena to Greek Religion* (1903), *Ancient Art and Ritual* (1913) and *Themis* (1927) by J. E. Harrison;

To Carcanet Press Ltd for extracts from *The White Goddess* (Faber, 1984) and *The Greek Myths* (Penguin, 1985) by Robert Graves, and from *Tribute to Freud* (1971) by Hilda Doolittle;

To Chiron Publications for extracts from *The Feminine Dimension of the Divine: A Study of Sophia and Feminine Images in Religion* (1994) by Joan Chamberlain Engelsman, from 'Eve: Reflections on the psychology of the first disobedient woman' by Judith Hubback, in *To Speak or Be Silent* (1993), ed. Lena B. Ross, from *The Nature of Loving Patterns of Human Relationship* (1986) by Verena Kast, and from *Psychotherapy Grounded in the Feminine Principle* (1989) by Barbara Stevens Sullivan;

To Constable & Co. Ltd for extracts from *Florence Nightingale, 1820–1910* (1952) by Cecil Woodham-Smith;

To Duckworth Publishers Ltd for extracts from *Eschylus: Oresteia* (1982), trans. Hugh Lloyd-Jones, and from *The Perfectibility of Man* (1972) by John Passmore;

To Faber and Faber Ltd and Columbia University Press for extracts from *Augustine of Hippo* (1979) and *Body and Society* (1989) by Peter Brown;

To Harcourt Brace & Company for extracts from *Images of Women in American Popular Culture* (1985) by Angela G. Dorenkamp *et al.*;

To Harvard University Press for extracts from *On the Generation of Animals*

(1943) by Aristotle, trans. A. L. Peck, from *The Gallic Wars* (1963) by Caesar, trans. H. J. Edwards, and from *The Exhortation to the Greeks* (1919) by Clement of Alexandria, trans. G. W. Butterworth;

To David Higham Associates Ltd for an extract from *The Comedy of Dante Alighieri* (Penguin), trans. Dorothy L. Sayers and Barbara Reynolds;

To Inner City Books for extracts from *Alcoholism and Women: The Background and the Psychology* (1982) by Jane Bauer, and from *Addiction to Perfection* (1982) and *The Pregnant Virgin* (1985) by Marion Woodman;

To International Thomson Publishing Services Ltd for extracts from *The Virgin* (1976) by G. Ashe, from *The Collected Works* (1957–79) by C. G. Jung, ed. Herbert Read *et al.* (permission also from Princeton University Press), from *The Seminars: Volume One: Dream Analysis* (1984) by C. G. Jung, ed. William McGuire, from *The Origins and History of Consciousness* (1973) by Erich Neumann, trans. R. F. C. Hull, and from *Astrea: The Imperial Theme in the Sixteenth Century* (1985) by Frances A. Yates;

To Little Brown (UK) Ltd for extracts from *The Female Malady* (1987) by Elaine Showalter, from *Independent Women: Work and Community for Single Women, 1850–1920* (1985) by Martha Vicinus and *Ever Yours Florence Nightingale: Selected Letters* (1989), ed. Martha Vicinus and Bea Nergaard, and from *A Virago Keepsake to Celebrate Twenty-Five Years of Publishing* (1993);

To Macmillan Press Ltd and Cambridge University Press Inc. for an extract from *The Collected Writings of John Maynard Keynes, Volume 10* (1972), ed. J. M. Keynes *et al.*;

To Manchester University Press for extracts from *I Have Done My Duty: Florence Nightingale in the Crimean War, 1854–56* (1987), ed. Sue M. Goldie;

To Orion Publishing Group Ltd for extracts from *The Gnostic Gospels* (Weidenfeld & Nicolson, 1982) and *Adam, Eve and the Serpent* (Weidenfeld & Nicolson, 1990) by Elaine Pagels, and from *Religion and the Decline of Magic* (Weidenfeld & Nicolson, 1982) by Keith Thomas;

To Oxford University Press for extracts from *The Complete Poetical Works* (1980) by Lord Byron, ed. Jerome J. McGann, 'Adam Lay Ybounden' from *Oxford Books of Carols* (1929), ed. Percy F. Dearmer *et al.*, from *The Bourgeois Experience Vol. 1: The Education of the Senses* (1984) by Peter Gay, from *The Apocryphal New Testament* (1924) by M. R. James, from *The Poetical Works of John Keats* (1958), ed. H. W. Garrod, from *Milton: Poetical Works* (1966), ed. Douglas Bush, from *The Romantic Agony* (1933) by Mario Praz, trans. Angus Davidson, and from *Poetical Works* (1971) by Percy Bysshe Shelley, ed. Thomas Hutchinson;

To Penguin Books Ltd for extracts from *Prometheus Bound and Other Plays* (1961) by Aeschylus, trans. Philip Vellacott, © Philip Vellacott, 1961, from *Lysistrata and Other Plays* (1973) by Aristophanes, trans. Alan H. Sommerstein, © Alan H. Sommerstein, 1973, from 'The Women of Troy' in *The Bacchae and Other Plays* (1954; revised edition, 1972) by Euripides, trans. Philip Vellacott, © Philip

Vellacott, 1954, 1972, from *The Odyssey* (1946; revised edition, 1991) by Homer, trans. E. V. Rieu, © 1946 by E. V. Rieu, revised translation © the Estate of the late E. V. Rieu, and D. C. H. Rieu, 1991, from 'Ajax' in *Electra and Other Plays* (1947) by Sophocles, trans. E. F. Watling, © E. F. Watling, 1947, from 'Oedipus at Colonus' in *The Theban Plays* (1947) by Sophocles, trans. E. F. Watling, © E. F. Watling, 1947, from *The Aeneid* (1956; revised edition, 1958) by Virgil, trans. W. F. Jackson Knight, © G. R. Jackson Knight, and from *The Eclogues* (1984; first published by Francis Cairns Ltd) by Virgil, trans. Guy Lee, Introduction, translation, notes and variants in Latin text © Guy Lee, 1980, 1984;

To Persea Books for extracts from *The Book of the City of Ladies* (1982) by Christine de Pizan, trans. Earl Jeffrey Richards, © 1982 by Persea Books;

To Random House UK Ltd, Sigmund Freud Copyrights, the Institute of Psycho-Analysis, and W. W. Norton & Company for extracts from *The Standard Edition of the Complete Psychological Works of Sigmund Freud* (Hogarth Press), trans./ed. James Strachey;

To Random House UK Ltd for extracts from *Sigmund Freud: Life and Works, Volume 2* (Chatto & Windus, 1955) by Ernest Jones, from *Malleus Maleficarum* (Hutchinson, 1971) by Heinrich Kramer and James Sprenger, trans. Montague Summers;

To Rogers, Coleridge & White Ltd, 20 Powis Mews, London W11 1JN and International Thomson Publishing Services Ltd for an extract from *Archetype: A Natural History of the Self* (1982) by Anthony Stevens;

To Spring Publications Inc. for extracts from *The Homeric Hymns* (1987), trans. Charles Boer, from *Anima: An Anatomy of a Personified Notion* (1986) by James Hillman, from *Animus and Anima* (1985) by Emma Jung, trans. Cary F. Baynes and Hildegard Nagel, and from 'Delivering Yang Femininity' (1987) by Genia Pauli Haddon;

To Thames & Hudson Ltd for extracts from *The Goddesses and Gods of Old Europe: Myths and Cult Images* (1989) by Marija Gimbutas, from *Alchemy: The Secret Art* (1973) by Stanislas Klossow de Rola, and from *The Homeric Gods* (1955) by Walter F. Otto, trans. Moses Hadas;

To the Theosophical Publishing House for extracts from *The Goddess Re-Awakening: The Feminine Principle Today* (1989), compiled by Shirley Nicholson;

To University of California Press for an extract from *From the Poetry of Sumer: Creation, Glorification, Adoration* (1979) by Samuel Kramer, © 1979 The Regents of the University of California;

To the University of Chicago Press for an extract from *The Art of Memory* (1984) by Frances A. Yates;

To the Women's Press Ltd, 34 Great Sutton Street, London EC1V ODX for extracts from *Woman and Nature: The Roaring Inside Her* (1984) by Susan Griffin;

To Yale University Press for extracts from *Sexual Personae: Art and Decadence from Nephertiti to Emily Dickinson* (1990) by Camille Paglia;

To the authors for *The Myth of the Goddess* (Viking, 1991) by Anne Baring and Jules Cashford, for *The Cult of the Black Virgin* (Penguin, 1985) by Ean Begg, for *The Making of Maleness* (Karnac Books, 1992) by Peter Tatham, for 'The Concealed Body Language of Anorexia Nervosa' in *The Father: Contemporary Jungian Perspectives* (Free Association Books, 1985) by Bani Shorter, for *The Letters of Mrs Gaskell* (Manchester University Press, 1966), eds. J. A. Chapple and A. Pollard, and for *Inanna Queen of Heaven and Earth: Her Stories and Hymns from Sumer* (Rider, 1984) by Diane Wolkstein and Samuel Noah Kramer.

Every effort has been made to contact all copyright holders. The publishers will be pleased to rectify any omissions at the earliest opportunity

Illustration Acknowledgements

AKG London, 21, 22, 24, 25, 26, 27, 37; The Art Institute of Chicago © 1994, All Rights Reserved, 38; Jennifer Begg, 23; Bibliotecca Apostolica Vaticana, Vatican, 30; British Museum, 3, 7, 10, 14, 46; The Dean and Chapter of York, 43; Deutsches Archäologisches Institut, Athens, 1, 2, 4, 13, 47; Freud Museum, London, 40; Glasgow University Library, Glasgow, 31, 33; Greek Embassy, London, 35; Immaginazione s.r.l., Milan, 39; The *Independent*, 44; Institute of Archaeology, Oxford/Bob Wilkins, 41; Metropolitan Government of Nashville, Tennessee/Gary Layda, 36; Museo Nazionale Romano, Rome, 15; The National Gallery, London, by courtesy of the Trustees, 28; Roman Baths Museum, Bath, 17, 18; The Royal Collection © Her Majesty Queen Elizabeth II, 29; Alistair Shearer, 9, 11, 12, 16, 34; TAP Service, Athens, 5, 6; Victoria and Albert Museum, London, 32; Wiltshire Archaeological and Natural History Society, Devizes, 19.

Index